The
TUSCAN
GIRL

BOOKS BY ANGELA PETCH

The Tuscan Secret

ANGELA PETCH

TUSCAN GIRL

Published by Bookouture in 2020

An imprint of Storyfire Ltd.
Carmelite House
50 Victoria Embankment
London EC4Y 0DZ

www.bookouture.com

ISBN: 978-1-83888-198-6
eBook ISBN: 978-1-83888-197-9

To Giuseppina Micheli and Bruno Vergni,
brave children of the 1920s.
Thanks for the memories.

'Do not be afraid; our fate
Cannot be taken from us; it is a gift.'
Dante Alighieri, *Inferno*

PROLOGUE

Tuscany, 1945

Recently, Lucia's dreams were filled with childhood memories. One hot summer day, when dragonflies skimmed the spangled, shimmering surface of the weir where the children played on Sundays, she'd driven the dozen sheep down to the riverbank and while they chomped on the grass, their teeth tearing at the lush green shoots, Lucia had stripped down to her underwear and blouse. Hanging her long skirt from a willow, she had jumped in by the waterfall, loving the shock of cool on her body, her blouse riding up around her like jellyfish tentacles. She kept her eyes open and floated on the water while watching a frog spring from the rocks. When the boys joined her, she hid for a while beneath the surface, holding her breath until her lungs might burst, wanting to surprise them and nip at their bare toes. Afterwards, she'd rested on the bank under the sun, her long hair draped over the grass behind her head, and when she noticed Massimo staring, she stuck out her tongue and jumped back into the water.

'You look like a mermaid,' he had shouted when she resurfaced, treading water so her budding nipples were concealed.

'Turn around,' she ordered, warning him not to peep. Then she had climbed from the river, picked up her skirt and gone to dry off in the meadow with the sheep.

Her dream tonight was of past Christmas Eves, sitting by her parents and brother, watching flames dance around the yule log that Father had dragged home from the woods. The fire looped and licked at the whorls and twists of the trunk he had chosen, and everyone beat it with their sticks, crying out, '*Cacca, ceppo, give up your gifts…*' The scent of roasting chestnuts, the anticipation of the next day's feast, simple gifts and shrieks of laughter filled her senses.

When she opened her eyes, she realised it was no longer a dream. The shrieks were real terror. Her parents were calling to her to get out quickly, the flames and acrid stench of burning filling her nostrils. Instinctively, she grabbed her brother's coat from the back of the door where it waited for his return that would never come, and slipped her feet into the stout boots under her bed. They had planned what to do if soldiers came. Each one of them had their own escape route. Hers was out through the small window that opened on to the back of the house, then a leap onto the roof tiles of the pigsty carved from the hill, from where the drop to the ground was only one metre. Within a minute she was out of the house and racing through the woods. The sound of her footsteps as she crashed through the undergrowth was drowned by hysterical yelling from villagers as they gathered around the flames. From behind the vast trunk of a beech, she watched their silhouettes as they passed buckets to each other. Hearing gunshots, she ran like a deer up the track.

The noise of her laboured breathing echoed around the cave when she staggered in. It was pitch-black inside, and she felt along the dank stone walls until she was at the furthest point of the cavern. Something soft clung to her forehead as she inched along and she stifled a shriek, before realising it was only a cobweb. She sat on her haunches, leaning against the rock, willing her heart to stop its crazy thumping. The kindling and matches were in a box stowed in a crevice, but she was too afraid to light a fire in case she'd been followed. Eventually she dozed, waking when the thin light of dawn crept through the opening.

Birdsong and the lazy buzzing of a bee filtered into her hiding place like a normal start to the day. From far away she heard a cockerel crow. Normally it would be the signal to roll out of bed, pull on her clothes and start her morning chores. But nothing in her life was routine any more. Tears spilled down her cheeks, splashing onto her brother's coat. She put her head in her hands, the stubbly growth on her scalp bringing back more awful memories. It would have been better if she'd burned in the house fire. She sobbed, rocking back and forth, not caring now if her crying gave her away. There was no point to life.

And then, she felt a fluttering in her belly, like a butterfly grazing its wings against her insides. She placed her hands beneath her clothing and, spreading her fingers over her abdomen as if to protect the butterfly from escaping, she waited. Until she felt it again, and then she stopped crying.

CHAPTER ONE

London, present day

She opened the door to a police constable standing on the landing outside the flat. 'Alba Starnucci?' the woman asked, the expression on her young face troubled. When Alba nodded, she heard the next dreaded question. 'Is there anybody who can be with you? I'm afraid I have bad news.'

*

Alba concentrated on the stained-glass window above the altar where the wicker coffin rested on its stand, white lilies drooping down the sides. If she kept her eyes fixed on the colourful images of trees and mountains and away from what was going on below, she could control her tears.

James's father was standing next to where his dead son lay. His words about James's bright future curtailed at too young an age, his voice breaking with emotion as he described an event from childhood that Alba had never heard before, told of a young man she didn't recognise. Irrationally, she worried that his free spirit would feel claustrophobic inside the woven tomb.

Alba's father squeezed her hand. He and her stepmother, Anna, had come straight from Tuscany as soon as she'd phoned with the tragic news. They sat on each side of her, propping her like bookends. James's parents hadn't acknowledged her once. When she'd arrived at the church, his mother stared over her head at the mourners behind her, waiting to pay their respects, and her husband simply turned away and ignored her. But she didn't blame them. It was her fault James was dead.

The hours that followed were a complete blank. Much later that evening, her parents described how, emerging from the church service to leave for the crematorium, she had turned to them in bewilderment and said, 'Why are we here?'

They'd rushed her to hospital, believing she had suffered a stroke when she continued to make no sense. She plucked at the cotton NHS nightgown, asking the doctor over and over what had happened. Then, four hours later, sitting in the taxi with her parents on the way back to the flat that she and James had shared, she felt the past slowly trickle back. Sitting at home, she scanned the leaflets she'd been given. Transient global amnesia, a benign attack. And the possible causes: sex, immersion in cold water, a blow to the head, alcohol, drugs or stress.

*

The weather had been warm for the beginning of December. In the park where she had walked beside James as he pushed his bike, a couple of gardeners were busy hoeing between shrubs of pruned roses. Two women overtook them on the path, chatting as they jogged. It was an ordinary morning.

'Let's sit outside,' James had said. 'It's warm enough.'

Afterwards, Alba wondered if the sunshine was the real reason or if he'd known what her reaction to his bombshell was going to be and wanted them to be alone, without an audience.

While he was placing their order inside the Pavilion, she'd pulled out brochures for the new warehouse development. She'd wanted to show them to him for a while, but lately there had never seemed to be a suitable moment. She flicked through the glossy pages, imagining how they could arrange a double mattress in the mezzanine area; how it would flood with light from an expanse of glass round the top of the warehouse space. She held the page up to James as he rejoined her.

'Look at this,' she'd said. 'It's described as an urban space. Live-work accommodation…' She broke off as he pulled the brochure from her hands, closed the page and laid it flat between them on the table.

'Alba… I can't,' he said.

'Why can't you? You never want to talk about anything these days.'

He took her hands in his. 'This is so hard…'

She snatched them away. 'What?'

'I can't do this any more…'

'This?' She knew she was repeating everything he said. Maybe it was a way of stopping him from saying more.

'It's over.'

She frowned, shook her head. 'What do you talk about, James? What do you mean?' Her voice was raised, she couldn't think in English properly, suddenly her brain seemed to find it necessary to translate from her native Italian into English and it was coming out wrong. She imagined him telling her any moment now that she was being dramatic, a typical Latin woman, as he often called her in her fiery moments. But that was usually when they were tangled together in bed. Not at ten o'clock in the morning in a park in central London.

'What the fuck are you trying to tell me? Stop talking in clichés,' she'd shouted, pulling the brochure to her chest and standing up. A woman walking her miniature poodle on the path nearby tutted and pulled her pet away.

James had stood up too. 'If you won't listen to me, then what's the point of talking to you?' he shouted back. Before she could reply, he jumped on his bike and cycled off, his sturdy legs pumping up and down in fury.

It was the last time she saw him. The police constable had explained how these accidents happened all too frequently. He must have pedalled up to the traffic lights to turn left, alongside a lorry also turning left. He was crushed; he had died instantly. The young officer had taken hold of her hand and said how sorry she was.

But how could she be sorry? Alba had thought. It was *her* fault. Completely her fault. James had cycled away in a temper and his temper had been caused by her. *She* was the one who was sorry, not the police constable.

*

She was grateful not to return to the flat on her own. Her father and stepmother guided her through the door and took over, insisting she rested while they sorted a meal and tidied up. When she awoke from a dreamless sleep, she heard her parents talking in the next room and, pulling on her dressing gown, she went to join them.

'Darling girl,' Anna said, pulling her stepdaughter into her arms.

'I don't want to cry,' Alba said.

'Cry if you want,' Anna said.

'Come back with us to Tuscany, *tesoro*,' Francesco said.

'How can I?' Alba said. 'What about my job at the gallery?'

'Marcus will understand. We spoke to him and André already at the funeral.'

'I'm not a child, Babbo. I can look after myself.'

She ignored the look that passed between her parents and sat down on the sofa. 'I'll be fine.'

*

After three days, her parents had reluctantly left, and Alba returned to work. Marcus bustled about the art gallery preparing for the new exhibition, trying to be kind to her, rearranging canvases and tweaking flower arrangements. He was counting on huge sales for his latest find: an emerging artist from Cornwall who specialised in seascapes.

'These roses are all wrong, Alba,' he said, lifting the bouquet she'd left on her desk. 'Far too suburban garden. We need something wilder, something to pick up the colours of the sea: eryngium, sea holly, gypsophila maybe. What do you think, darling?'

Alba couldn't think. Her mind was a blank. 'I'll see what I can find in my lunch break,' she said.

He pulled a twenty-pound note from the till. 'Treat yourself to a decent snack, sweetheart. You look peaky.'

It was a relief to be away from his fussing. She was usually on her own in the gallery, but today the press from a couple of national papers was invited, and he wanted everything just so.

She bought half a dozen blue agapanthus from Betty's florist, and when she explained what they were for, she was loaned some spider conch shells to add to the display. 'Not particularly West Country,' Betty said, 'but nobody will know they're from the Pacific.'

Alba badly needed a coffee; her head was pounding. She'd tossed and turned the previous night, the bed seeming twice its usual size without James, the sheets cold. A double shot of espresso might do the trick.

When she returned to the gallery, she realised she'd left the flowers in the coffee shop, and in despair, Marcus went to fetch them himself. 'Go home, Alba. You shouldn't be back at work so soon,' he said as he pulled on his tweed jacket.

On the bus, she cried silently, oblivious to the stares from other passengers. Back in the empty flat, she climbed into bed and willed sleep to come.

She ignored her phone and let the battery run down. Sleep seemed the only way to cope, even if James sometimes appeared cruelly in her dreams, his mat of blond hair blowing in the wind as he smiled and shouted something she couldn't catch, his arms outstretched for a hug. On the third day, she staggered to her fridge. Sour milk, half a shrivelled carrot in the salad drawer. Just as she was trying to face the prospect of going out, there was a pounding at the door. When she opened it, André and Marcus stood there, half hidden behind a large bunch of carnations.

'Oh my God, you two,' she said. 'What are you doing here?'

'Your parents have asked us to sort you out and take you to the airport tomorrow. Your ticket to Italy is booked.'

CHAPTER TWO

Tuscany, present day

'Eat some more of this soup at least, Alba,' Anna said, 'and then you can sleep.'

Alba swallowed half the bowl of chicken broth to please her parents and then climbed the stairs to her room in the converted stable, known as La Stalla. It was much the same as when she'd left home; a couple of dog-eared posters of Italian bands still hung from her wall and her teddy, one eye missing, sat on her pillow. Anna had been using her desk as a sewing table and a colourful patchwork cushion cover lay half-finished by the side of an old treadle sewing machine. Alba's life in London seemed a million miles away, and her heart ached for James. She stared at the view of the mountains dusted with snow. The river beneath her window, where willows waved silvery-green in the afternoon sunshine, was fuller than during the summer months. Normally she would be out there, sitting on the bench by the water or walking up the footpath, breathing in the clean air. But she was exhausted, as if she'd been drugged and, once again, she fell into a deep sleep. It was the only pattern she could live with at the moment.

Downstairs, her father and stepmother talked in half-whispers, although Alba's bedroom was on a mezzanine above the second floor, thick walls in between. 'I wish I could bear her pain,' Francesco said. 'She's so young. It's so cruel.'

'Give her a few days, *tesoro*. She needs time.'

'I'm worried she'll revert to how she reacted when her mother died.'

'She was only eight then.'

'I know… but she refused to speak for six whole months.'

'That was years ago. Come on, let her be for a couple of days and then I'll try and get through to her. Let her settle.'

A couple of mornings later, Alba was staring through the little round window at the first flakes of snow when Anna came into her room, carrying a breakfast tray. 'Freshly baked rolls and coffee. I've brought mine up to eat with you,' she said. 'We have the house to ourselves – Babbo's gone to Bologna until Wednesday.'

'I'm not hungry.'

'Don't believe you. What have you eaten since arriving? Not enough to feed even a lizard.'

'I can't keep anything down.'

'Shall I make you hot water with lemon?'

'Thank you.'

Alba sank back into the pillows, full of love for this woman who'd arrived in her life when she was eight, and going through a difficult period after the death of her birth mother. Anna had been there for her ever since, treating her exactly the same as her younger stepbrother and twin sisters.

When Anna returned, they sat together in silence for a couple of minutes, Alba taking a nibble from a roll, sipping her hot lemon.

'This is good, Anna. Thanks.'

'Look, I know you don't want to talk, but it would do you good, darling.'

Silence.

'Would it help just to let me listen? I know you can't believe anybody can understand what's going on inside you, but... it would help to try and put it into words.'

With a sigh, Alba said, 'I thought we were going to get married.' She started to cry again, wondering where all these tears were coming from. 'I thought everything was good.'

Anna let her talk, without responding. At last, her stepdaughter was starting to open up.

Alba looked at her, speaking in a little voice. 'I'm trying to snap out of it, honestly I am. I feel like a spoiled brat, everybody tiptoeing around me, being so kind. But...' Her tears spilled again. Anna stayed where she was on the side of the bed, not touching her stepdaughter, waiting for Alba to be ready.

'Half my heart is gone. And knowing James was going to break up with me before he died... it's like the five years spent with him mean nothing.' Alba pulled a tissue from the box on her bedside table and blew her nose.

'You think it's been a waste of time at the moment,' Anna said, 'but – and I know you're going to think this is just an old lady spouting wisdom – it will eventually have served its purpose in making you into the person you'll become. You'll learn about yourself from this.'

'Sorry, Anna, but yes – you *are* sounding like you're spouting wisdom.'

'I've never told you much about before I met your lovely dad, have I?' Anna said, ignoring her and pouring Alba more hot lemon.

'I had a few boyfriends. I was no nun. But the man I thought I'd spend the rest of my life with told me, in a note pushed under my door, that he couldn't go through with the huge wedding we'd planned. We were only days away and I had to cancel flowers, guests, venue… it was so humiliating. And at the time, I believed I would never get over it.'

'Oh my God… that's so awful. What a prick.'

'Mm. But best to find that out beforehand.'

Alba fiddled with her sheet, twisting it round her fingers. 'We hadn't got as far as that. I mean, *I* was certain he was going to ask me any day, but he never proposed… and it's my fault he died, Anna. He was fed up with me and went off in a huff. I shouldn't have nagged him.'

'Oh, darling,' Anna said, folding Alba in her arms. 'Of course it's not your fault. All couples argue from time to time. It *wasn't* your fault. It was an accident. A truly dreadful accident.' She kissed the top of the young woman's head, wishing she could bear some of her sadness. 'Now, what I suggest is that you get up for a while. I'll wash your hair for you, and we're going to go for a walk in the snow.'

'I don't feel like it.'

'Tough! I do, and I want you to keep me company. And besides, Davide and the twins will be home in a couple of weeks for Christmas, and I've a million things you can help me with.'

Anna washed Alba's hair at the bathroom sink, massaging conditioner into her scalp. Then she dried her hair thoroughly, gently brushing out her tangles.

'Thanks, Ma,' Alba said, pulling her stepmother down into a hug, and Anna was the one to blink back tears now. She'd never heard Alba call her 'Ma' before, and her heart melted.

Outside, a sprinkling of snow had left a white film on the meadows. Red hips on wild roses were frosted silver, and as they walked along the riverbank, Anna pointed out icicles hanging from willow twigs.

'It's a perfect Christmas scene,' Anna said, snapping away on her mobile phone. 'I might print some of these, instead of buying cards this year.'

'The shops in England have been full of Christmas stuff since October. It's good to get away from it.'

Anna pulled at some strands of old man's beard entwined around a tree. 'I have an idea for this, too. Saw it in a magazine. We'll wind it round a ball of wire and then thread through little Christmas lights.'

Alba wondered if she'd ever have half Anna's flair, imagination and enthusiasm for anything.

'Can we go back now, Anna? I'm cold,' Alba said, gazing at the icicles hanging from the waterfall where holiday guests usually sunbathed.

'Sure. But maybe you can help me bake for the freezer. And I need to make the Christmas cake too.'

'Maybe tomorrow?' Alba knew she was disappointing Anna, who was doing her best with her home-style therapy, but all she wanted to do was sleep. Maybe if she hibernated for a week, she would wake up and everything would feel normal again.

But over the next few days she did make an effort. Her father had been sterner than Anna, coming up to her room and telling her that unless she got up to do something – even a short walk on her own – he would call the doctor. Pulling her into his arms, he'd told her he was missing his daughter, the one with the spirit, who had always been such a great example to her step-siblings, who were coming home in a couple of days. They had both cried, and Alba knew he was being cruel to be kind. As the landscape outside froze over, she began to thaw inside.

Alba walked along the river to a spot near the big waterfall where she used to swim each summer. Ice shapes hung like enormous chandeliers, dripping as they melted a little in the lukewarm midday sun. A birch tree stood stark and still in the frozen air, and Alba's breath created mist like cigarette smoke. She remembered how she'd pretended as a child to puff on twigs; how one year the pool further down the river had iced over and Babbo had arranged an impromptu skating party, and cooked spicy sausages afterwards over a fire for her school friends. She thought of how she'd planned to repeat all these things one day when she and James had babies, even though he hadn't been keen on starting a family. He'd told her the planet was overpopulated and not in a fit state to introduce more children. But she'd been sure she could change his mind. Anyway, he was gone now. It was best to banish such thoughts, she told herself.

She pulled out her sketchbook and spent half an hour drawing the view of the mill, the waterfall in the background, snow-laden clouds in the sky. She blew on her fingers to restore feeling and when she'd finished, she returned to the converted stable where the family lived. Their home stood metres away from the mill, which was now closed up for winter. They only let it out for summer guests.

Inside the house, a pine tree stood in the centre of the living room, waiting to be decorated by the whole family the following day, when her brother and sisters were to come home for the Christmas vacation. The house was full of the aroma of cinnamon and spices from the cake she'd helped Anna bake earlier.

'I think I might go for a longer walk tomorrow morning,' Alba said. 'Before the others get home. I'd like to take a picnic with me and go up to the Mountain of the Moon.'

She chose to ignore the looks of relief that passed between her parents.

'Shall I come with you?' Francesco asked. 'It'll be really cold up there.'

'I'll be fine, Babbo. I'll wrap up warm. I know the way like the back of my hand.'

'And she can take her mobile with her, Francesco,' said Anna.

Alba didn't feel like explaining her need to be alone. How she felt the walk would be good for her, because it would give her space to sort out her thoughts. And once the house was packed with family, with their noise and energy, there would be no more time to think. It would give her a chance to hold a kind of personal wake for James.

Her rucksack was stuffed with a flask of hot soup, sandwiches, fruit, chocolate, thick spare socks and gloves, as well as her sketch pad and pencils. Francesco and Anna had fussed over her, making sure she pointed out the exact route on the map she'd been urged to take, despite her protests about having downloaded a walking map on her phone. They asked her to check, for the umpteenth time, that her mobile was completely charged.

'Anybody would think I was going away for three months on a polar expedition,' she complained.

'Well, you almost are. It's over one thousand metres up there, and you're bound to find snow,' Francesco said. 'Promise me you'll turn back if it's too icy.'

Kissing them goodbye and telling them not to stand on the doorstep too long, as they'd let all the warmth out, she set off, feeling a sense of freedom at being truly alone.

Hoar frost painted every surface with sparkle. The trees were fish bones outlined against the clean light of the sky, and above, a line of pines straggled like a bad haircut along the ridge she was making for. In the distance she heard church bells from the village chime the quarter-hour.

She climbed steadily for thirty minutes, crossing an expanse of meadow that once would have been used for grazing cattle, but was now studded with frosted juniper bushes that bore black berries on their upper branches. They looked like miniature Christmas trees. Anna had in fact cut a couple from the forest to place on either side of the door to the stable, adding festive red bows and baubles. The berries were used for making gin, and her stepmother added them to stews for flavour. Just as Alba was reasoning that the berries were most likely missing from the lower branches because they'd been eaten by wild animals, a pair of roe deer bounded across the path above her, making her jump and drop one of her alpine sticks. She was too slow to take a photo on her phone as the animals disappeared behind rocks, the white around their rear ends seeming like a cruel hunter's target to Alba.

She stopped at midday to drink her soup and eat her rye bread with cheese and rocket leaves, feeling hungry for the first time in days. Anna had included a couple of home-made shortbread biscuits and an orange to her picnic, and she decided to keep those to celebrate her arrival at her destination. Across the valley from where she perched on a moss-covered boulder, beneath which nestled a huge Carlina thistle, known as the poor man's artichoke, she watched the flight of a goshawk, its shadow playing in the sunshine on the sandstone cliffs like a mate. Eventually it disappeared into one of many crannies.

When she was a little girl of nine or so, she had walked these hills with her step-grandfather, Danilo, and been entranced by his stories of wartime. He had fought as a partisan against the Nazis and fascist militia up here during the Second World War. He'd pointed out remnants of the defensive Gothic Line as they passed by, and places where the Germans, the *Tedeschi*, had used caves to store ammunition. He'd shown her trenches on the ridge where they had set machine guns to fire on planes overhead. He'd taken her to a few places where resistance fighters had hidden as they plotted assaults on the invading Germans. They weren't stories, he had corrected her, they were real events. But the way he recounted them to her, a child, had turned them into adventures from a storybook. Since then, she'd done research of her own, reading any documents she could find. And she understood the brutality of what had taken place in this beautiful corner of Tuscany: the massacres, sacrifices and hardships that ordinary people had endured. Babbo had a complete shelf of history books in his study and personal accounts written post-war, and she'd devoured them all. Modern history would have been her second choice after art, if she'd gone to university.

At about two o'clock, Alba reached the ruins of a house, not much more than a pile of stones scattered beneath the ridge of the Mountain of the Moon. A wooden sign had been erected since the last time she had ventured up here. She read the name of the place: SECCARONI.

The silence here was almost noisy. In London, where she'd lived on and off for the last eight years, there was never this sense of quiet and she wasn't used to it. It was normal to hear neighbours arguing, trains rumbling by or sirens from police cars. Here, at over one thousand metres, where the jagged peak of the Mountain of the Moon soared above her, not even a blade of grass moved. She knew the weather could change dramatically. She and Nonno Danilo had been caught out often enough, but her grandfather always knew where there was a hollow, a shepherd's hut or a cave to shelter in while the worst of the storm raged.

The ruins of Seccaroni were almost swallowed by brambles and the strangling vines of old man's beard, their white seed heads like balls of cotton wool. But she could make out the right-angled column of a chimney breast, ready to fall at any moment. There was a gap that once upon a time must have housed a window frame, through which she could see the mountains outlined. She pulled out her sketch pad from her rucksack and, leaning her back against half a remaining wall, she began to draw. Instead of a ruin, her fingers guided her pencil to design what the building might have looked like in the past. She added a couple of metal rings to the outside wall, and a tethered mule. Smoke curled in a wisp from the chimney and she used her fingertip to smudge the effect. A hoe leant against the door, and a pair of worn clogs was discarded to one side, the right clog pointing in towards the left almost as if the person who had been wearing it had walked with a crooked gait. A face peered from an upstairs window, a frown creasing its forehead.

When Alba looked up from her sketch pad, she was startled to see what seemed like a young man through the remnants of the window frame. She wasn't sure if it was shadows playing on the stones, but she thought he beckoned her to follow and she dropped her sketch pad in surprise. She hadn't heard anybody approach the ruin, because she'd been totally absorbed in her work. It had been a long time since she'd enjoyed anything creative.

'Hey!' she called out, and her voice echoed back to her from the steep walls of the mountains. Stepping over the stones, she peered through the frame and from the corner of her eye she caught a glimpse of someone in the distance, standing near a pine tree swaying in the wind at the very edge of the ridge, a long coat flapping around his ankles like a scarecrow. Intrigued, she continued towards him as he disappeared over the edge. These mountains were a lattice of footpaths used by animals and shepherds, but as she approached where he'd stood, she couldn't make out a path or identify where he'd gone. The slope had been swept away by a landfall, the old roots of a turkey oak sticking in the air like ghostly fingers. If she'd advanced four more steps, she'd have hurtled into the ravine below, where a trickle of a stream silvered in the sun.

'Are you all right? Where are you?' she called, but there was no answer. Instead, where it had been still, the silence was replaced by the sounds of a wind getting up, first as a whisper through the trees, and then developing into fierce gusts that whipped her long hair around her face. She shivered, afraid the stranger had come to harm, but there was no sign of him. The pine branches swept back and forth in the storm and Alba told herself that these were what she had seen, mistaking the limbs of a tree for the limbs of a shadowy person. She shivered as thunder clapped and echoed around her and, without warning, it started to rain. Great fat drops at first that quickly changed to curtains of water. Within a couple of minutes, Alba was wet through. She ran to the ruin and crouched against the wall where she'd been sketching, stuffing the pad into her rucksack. She hoped the storm would soon abate. The sky was grey, the sun no longer visible and all she wanted to do now was return to the warmth of her family.

After ten minutes, the rain stopped. But she was soaked. It was hardly worth replacing her wet socks, as her walking boots were sodden. The best solution was to walk back from where she'd come as fast as she could, but the path was muddy now and the going much harder. She kept slipping and was grateful she'd agreed to bring Anna's alpine sticks with her.

As soon as she left the woods and descended to the alpine meadow where she'd seen the Carlina thistles, the sun came out again and as she walked, her clothes started to steam in the warmth. As she looked up behind her from where she'd walked, she realised the peak was no longer visible, a coronet of cloud separating it from the rest of the world, and she hoped the young man had managed to find his way back to wherever he'd come from.

About one kilometre from the stable, she met her father hurrying up the path.

'Thank God, Alba,' he said as he drew near, a look of relief on his face. 'We looked at the peak and could see there must be a dreadful storm up there. When it got to four o'clock, we started to worry in earnest.'

Francesco pulled out his phone to let Anna know all was well, asking her to make sure the immersion heater was switched on and to brew some hot coffee.

'I think I saw somebody else up at Seccaroni, but… I can't be sure,' she told him as they walked down together. 'I hope he's okay. There was a huge storm with masses of thunder and lightning. He went over the ridge towards Fresciano village.'

'I heard there was a group of youngsters squatting up there last summer. But I thought they'd returned to the city by now. Apparently, they were constantly in trouble with the forest guards for making fires in prohibited areas. They wouldn't listen and didn't appreciate the danger. They were off their heads half the time.'

'He looked odd. He was wearing funny clothes – not a typical trekking outfit.'

'There are plenty of abandoned houses up there where he could shelter. I shouldn't worry about him.'

But as they walked the last few metres together, Alba wondered if she really had seen somebody. If she had, she wondered where he'd disappeared. The weather was miserable, and she hoped he'd managed to find shelter somewhere on the mountain.

*

It was good to be in the company of her siblings again. Seventeen-year-old twins Emilia and Rosanna had very different personalities. Rosanna was studying accountancy. She was sturdy and sensible, while her twin floated around in a dream most of the time, her head lost in the stories she so loved to write. Davide, recently turned nineteen, had developed from a gangly, awkward teenager into somebody Alba could now easily spend time with. In his first year at veterinary school in Edinburgh, he loved returning to Rofelle. There'd already been a phone call from the young sheep farmer up the road with a request for him to come up and help with one of his lame ewes.

'So, do you think you'll try and find a job here, or back in Scotland?' Alba asked him at supper that evening.

'Difficult to say. Trouble here is who you know, not what you know.'

After the meal, Alba moved into the living area to help decorate the tree.

'Ma, why do you keep this stuff?' she asked, pulling out a box of tatty paper decorations made from toilet rolls and creased doilies.

'Because they are the first things you all made at primary school,' Anna replied. 'And to me they're more beautiful than the bought stuff.'

The house looked stunning. Garlands of fresh ivy and holly were wound around the beams. Dry twigs painted white, and wooden figures and red bows tied to branches of spruce, festooned the tops of cupboards and window frames. The old Welsh dresser Anna had insisted on shipping out to Italy after she'd married Francesco was decorated with cards, pine cones and an old nativity set from Francesco's childhood. With the stove lit and mulled wine and mince pies handed out, the Christmas spirit was flowing. Alba let herself be swept away with it, pushing thoughts of James to the back of her mind. It wasn't easy, but she was determined not to be a misery.

*

With Anna having been brought up in England, their Christmases were a mixture of Italian and British traditions. The family always dined on traditional salted cod on Christmas Eve. On Christmas Day, there was a typical starter of home-made pasta shapes called *cappelletti*, followed by the English meal of roast turkey and trimmings. A choice of panettone with Prosecco or Christmas pudding was served for afters, and the best Barolo wine accompanied the meal. Anna made her own crackers, filling them with individual presents and jokes, an English custom which always intrigued their Italian guests. Each Christmas, Anna and Francesco invited 'waifs and strays', as they privately described them.

This year they had invited Egidio, the elderly manager of the local tourist office, on his own for his first Christmas after the death of his wife, as well as an even older man called Massimo. He was tiny and hardly said anything throughout the afternoon. Egidio did most of the talking for him, introducing him as one of the oldest residents of the area.

'But I am young at heart,' Massimo announced in a rare chatty moment, a twinkle in his brown eyes. 'Do not underestimate me, my friends,' he said. He enjoyed the turkey and asked for more English stuffing, which was unusual for an Italian.

Presents were opened after the meal. With the stove lit, Anna, a little tipsy and her paper hat now aslant her dark curls streaked with silver, distributed the gifts. The floorboards were soon invisible beneath a sea of wrapping paper and cries of 'Cool', or 'You shouldn't have' and 'How did you know I wanted one of those?' echoed in the large, open-plan sitting room. They all spoke in Italian, although Anna encouraged them to use English when she could.

Alba handed her father an envelope, on which she'd scribbled a design of holly and Christmas trees, and he pulled out a drawing.

'This is stunning,' Francesco said, holding up her sketch of the waterfall and mill. 'Look, Anna. *Bello, no?*'

'*Bellissimo!*' she said. 'It's so good you're drawing again, Alba. You're very talented.'

'I didn't know what else to give you. I'll get it framed as soon as I can.'

Egidio admired it, peering closely at the detail over the top of his glasses. 'If you can sketch me another like this, I would love to use it in the tourist office. Do you have anything else, Alba?'

'Only something I started on the Mountain of the Moon. But it's very scrappy. And it rained, so the lines are smudged. I need to go over it again.'

'I'd love to see.'

She fetched her sketch pad from upstairs and showed it to Egidio while she perched on the arm of his chair. He smiled at her. 'But are you sure you didn't copy this picture from my book in the museum?'

She frowned. 'Absolutely not. I've never seen your book. I imagined this from a ruin I came across. Up at Seccaroni...' She pulled out her phone and scrolled through the images she'd taken on her walk. 'There,' she said, showing him the tumbledown house. 'I've almost convinced myself that I saw a young man up there, too. But if I did, goodness knows where he went. There's no path behind that old house, is there, Egidio?'

'My walking days are over. I wouldn't know. But maybe you saw a hunter. They know the paths like the insides of their pockets. And when they don't have a licence to hunt, they hide themselves very quickly. It happens all the time. People come from Romagna and steal truffles and mushrooms.' He sighed and mumbled something about them being sons of bitches, and Alba smiled at his ripe language.

Egidio peered further at Alba's sketch. 'But this is uncanny. It's almost the same as the picture of the house I mentioned. I'll have a hunt for the book and then you will see what I mean. Your mother is right. You have talent.'

'I'm out of practice, Egidio. Where I work in the gallery in England, there's never any time. I'm always busy selling other people's work.'

'A pity,' he replied. He held up the picture to show Massimo. 'This is the old house up on the ridge at Seccaroni – used by the partisans, wasn't it?' he said. 'You probably know the place.'

The old man shook his head after bringing the sketch close to his eyes to view it better. 'The war was a very long time ago,' he said, struggling to his feet. 'Excuse me, could I use the bathroom?'

As Francesco helped him across the room, Egidio handed the sketch back to Alba. 'Don't leave it too late to do the things you really want to do. If you want to draw, then do so while you can. Life is very short. I know that from personal experience, *cara mia*. Oriana and I… we had many unfinished plans.' He pulled a handkerchief from his pocket and blew his nose loudly.

'I think your glass is almost empty, Egidio,' Anna said, topping up his Amaro *digestivo*.

When Massimo returned, he looked pale and refused a drink. 'I should like to go back to the centre where I live,' he said. 'I'm sorry to break up the party.'

'As soon as I've finished this excellent *digestivo*, we shall leave together,' Egidio said. 'Alba, your sketch would make a wonderful start for my new project. I have an idea to set old photos of buildings next to images of their ruins, before they are swallowed by nature. And your paintings could complement them. It would be good to explain the history of these places before it's too late. What do you say? Can you help me?'

'I'm flattered, Egidio, but I'm going back to England soon. I've lots to sort out.'

'That's a pity. But, if you come back, then the offer is still there.'

The two elderly gentlemen said their goodbyes. It seemed to Alba that Massimo couldn't get away fast enough. Maybe something awful had happened to him during the war and he didn't want to talk about it. It was probably no coincidence that he asked to leave as soon as the subject was brought up.

CHAPTER THREE

On Boxing Day morning, Alba lay on her bed on the mezzanine at the top of the stable. Her eyes traced ice crystals on the edges of the porthole window. The weather was turning colder and she worried about the man she'd seen in the ruins. Was he still out there? She reached for the sketch on her bedside table that she had shown Egidio. It struck her that the young man she'd drawn at the window was very similar to the hippy-type youth she'd imagined disappearing over the ridge… but she'd drawn him before he'd appeared. She ran her finger over the outline of his face. It was weird, too, that the idea for the sketch of the house had come to her from nowhere, and that it should apparently be so similar to the building in Egidio's book; a book she had never seen. *Who are you? What are you trying to tell me?* she asked herself. She couldn't stop thinking about the odd coincidences. Then she told herself to stop being fanciful. Perhaps her mind was playing tricks after all, and the loss of James was fuddling her mind. Flinging back the covers, she jumped out of bed and pulled on jeans, thick socks and a warm fleece. The tourist office was shut today so she couldn't look in Egidio's book, but there was nothing to stop her from walking to the ruins again and checking that she wasn't going mad.

Downstairs, her stepbrother was sitting with his legs over the arm of a squishy leather armchair, reading a paperback.

'Fancy a walk, Davide?' she asked.

'Why not? This book is boring,' he said. 'Give me a sec to put on something warmer.'

Within five minutes they'd started up the hill. The snow hadn't settled after all despite the nip in the air, and the sun shone from a deep blue sky. Alba had forgotten how beautiful these winter days could be in Tuscany. She was pleased it wasn't misty and murky.

'Where are we going?' Davide asked as they walked briskly.

'Towards the Mountain of the Moon. There's somewhere I want to show you. And I'd like your opinion on something that's bugging me.'

'Mysterious. Tell me more.'

'Wait until we get there.'

They kept up a good pace, walking mostly in easy silence. At one stage Davide remarked what a good workout it was, better than being confined in a gym. Stopping to sip water on a ridge in the middle of a meadow, they were amazed when a dozen wild boar rushed across their view.

'Wow!' Davide said as the sound of their hooves pounding over the frosty ground dwindled when they disappeared into a copse. 'That was so sudden, I didn't even get a chance to catch them on my phone. What a sight!'

'We'll preserve it as a memory. Actually, it's been good to leave my phone alone for a while, Davide. I use it all the time at work.'

'What do you want to do with yourself now, Alba? Have you thought about staying here in Tuscany?'

'I've thought of nothing else over the last two days. But I'm not sure whether it's to avoid returning to London and the memories of James… Egidio offered me a kind of job yesterday, researching for the next tourist office project.'

'Give it a go. What have you got to lose?'

'It'd be strange coming to live back home at the ripe old age of twenty-six. I'm not sure.'

'Ma and Babbo would love it. And they'd give you your space.'

After another three quarters of an hour, and a steep climb through a dense beech wood, their boots scrunching over crisp leaves, they reached the ruined house of Seccaroni.

Davide went over to read the sign, which informed passers-by that these ruins of an old house had been uninhabited until a group of partisans used it as their base, from the autumn of 1943 until 1944.

'I had a weird thing happen to me here,' Alba told him. 'I don't want to say anything to Ma and Babbo because they'll think I was hallucinating, or whatever, after me ending up in hospital after James's funeral.'

'Go on, then. Tell *me*.'

'Don't laugh, will you…?'

'You need to tell me first. You're being very enigmatic.'

She hesitated before blurting out, 'I'm beginning to think I might have seen a ghost in these ruins.'

Davide laughed.

'See – you think I'm mad, too,' she said, thumping him. 'I told you not to laugh!'

'Sorry, Alba. I wasn't expecting that. I promise not to laugh again.'

She told him about the young man she'd sketched from her imagination a few days before Christmas, and then the uncanny resemblance to the person she'd seen who seemed to disappear over the crest and into space. 'But weirder still,' she continued, 'Egidio told me about a book he has that shows an old photo of this building as it used to be.' She struck her alpine stick into the ground as she spoke, embarrassed at what she was recounting. 'And he thought a sketch I did from my imagination looks pretty similar.'

He whistled. 'Wow, Alba, kind of paranormal…' He went over to the stones and then walked the few metres to the edge of the ridge. 'And then you say the man you saw disappeared down there? Quite a drop!'

'I know,' she said, approaching him. 'You do think I'm bonkers, don't you?'

'You know me. I'm a scientist. There'll be a logical explanation for this somewhere. You told me it was stormy. Maybe you mistook a shadow for a person in the gloom. And…' He paused. 'Don't get cross with me, but you do have a very vivid imagination. Are you on medication after your amnesia episode?'

'*Porca miseria*, Davide. I'm not taking anything. Babbo suggested it might be a hippy from the city. A group of them was camping up here last summer, apparently.'

Davide had knelt to peer over the edge. 'It looks like there's a gap in the rocks – it could lead to a path.'

She joined him and peered at where he was pointing.

'Now we're here, I'll climb down and investigate,' Davide continued. 'I've a rope and carabiner with me. Always carry them when I'm on walks in the mountains. If you help me from up here, it'll be fine,' he said, pulling the equipment from his rucksack.

'Are you sure you know what you're doing?' Alba asked. 'Shouldn't we wait for somebody else? I don't know the first thing about abseiling.'

'You don't need to. Just be here to phone for rescue if the rope snaps.'

'What?'

'Only kidding, Alba. I know what I'm doing.'

She helped him secure one end of his rope around a tree, and the other end he attached to the carabiner. Then, slowly, he pushed himself out over the edge in a controlled descent. 'There's an opening here, but no path I can see,' he shouted up. 'And if there ever was, it went long ago. There's no evidence of a recent landslide.'

Suddenly, a large bird flew from a ledge in the cliff face, flapping dangerously close to Davide's face so that he stepped back, loose stones falling as his boots scrabbled for purchase again.

'Are you okay?' Alba called.

He regained control, finding a foothold on a protruding rock.

'Just made me jump. Wasn't expecting that. But, wow! I'm pretty sure that was a golden eagle. I really don't want to disturb it any more than I have to.'

'I didn't think there were any in this area. Babbo is always saying how he wants to see them return.'

'I'm ninety per cent sure. In any case, it's definitely a raptor. I'll go a bit further in. Keep a lookout for that beauty for me.'

She watched him disappear into the rock face. The eagle was soaring high in the thermals, and, as long as it kept its distance, Alba stayed quiet.

'I've found something,' she heard her brother call after a couple of minutes. 'Looks like an old box. Can you fasten another length of rope around the tree and drop it down? I'll tie it to the box and we'll haul on it together.'

Alba remembered a couple of knots from her brief venture into Girl Scouts and secured the second rope around the convenient pine. She threw the other end of the rope down the side of the cliff and waited for Davide. The high-pitched whistle of the raptor announced its return and, once again, it swooped down and around him.

'Poor thing,' he said as he reappeared at the top. 'We need to get out of here as soon as possible. I need you to help me pull the box up, Alba. It's quite heavy and riddled with woodworm.'

He secured Alba to the tree before they pulled together on the box so that there was no danger of either of them slipping over the edge. It was hard work, and the box stuck a couple of times on its way up. Davide had to kneel at the edge and loosen the tension on the rope and then pull on it to help the box come free.

'Let's hope it's strong enough with all this banging against the rocks, and we don't lose its contents,' he said.

With a final heave, they pulled the box as it scraped its way over the top. It was made of a dark wood, with metal pieces reinforcing the corners, and was bound with an old rope and locked with a rusty padlock. It reminded Alba of the wooden suitcases she'd seen in old photographs of migrants leaving home to find work abroad.

Davide picked up a stone from the ruined house and hit the padlock a couple of times. It was so rusty that the metal broke apart easily. With his penknife, he cut through the already fraying rope.

'Mind there are no snakes or scorpions inside,' Alba said, as they gingerly opened the lid. The hinges creaked and a spider scuttled from an old sack, covered in a thick layer of cobwebs. As Davide lifted it out, the sack disintegrated, and some metal pieces fell with a clatter back into the box. Alba reached in and picked out an oval plate. There were also a couple of goblets, each one initialled with a looping, scrolled 'B', and Alba gave a low whistle. 'Wow! We've found some real treasure...'

Davide examined the base of the plate and rubbed it with his finger. 'There's a hallmark on this. It could be silver. Goodness, what on earth is this lot doing up here?'

'When the Germans occupied the area, people hid possessions so they wouldn't be plundered,' Alba replied as she took several photos on her phone of the silverware.

'But surely people living up here would have been peasants,' Davide said. 'They wouldn't have had posh stuff like this, would they?'

'Good point! I'd be very surprised. We'll take this lot into the museum and see if they can shed any light. What a find,' Alba said. She sat back on her haunches. 'It still doesn't explain about the young man I saw, though. Where did he disappear to?'

'Perhaps whoever it was took another path.'

'I definitely saw him go down there... where you went,' she insisted.

Her brother gave her a funny look. 'Well, even if you haven't found your ghost,' he said with a smirk, 'you've found treasure instead.' He ducked as she tried to slap him. 'Whoa! You're like a woman possessed... woo-oooh!' he teased, waving his arms about. 'Right, let's go home now. We'll carry this lot between us. The box is too heavy to bother with – we'll hide it in the ruin. It'll be dark soon and I don't want to spend a night on the mountain.'

'You see, *you're* spooked now.'

'Not a bit. I simply prefer the idea of sleeping in my nice cosy bed, after enjoying a Peroni by the stove... and not in the company of a nutter,' he added.

Alba thumped him again and he grinned. 'I'm sure it will all become plain, sooner or later,' he said. 'There are no such things as ghosts.'

She didn't comment, keeping her thoughts to herself, dwelling on the reasons as to why a box of old silver objects should be stashed in a hole near these ruins. Could the find possibly date back to the war and the partisans who used this place?

On the way down, Davide tentatively asked her how she was coping after losing James.

'It's hard,' she said. 'Lonely. All my plans ruined. It's shit, basically. And I know it's selfish, but it's just awful to know that he wanted to break up with me before he died. I hate that... and

I feel his death was my fault. Truth is, we weren't getting on too well for a while, but… I miss him so much.'

'Did he have somebody else?'

'If he did, he was clever. We were living together, remember. I never found lipstick on his collar or a blonde hair on his clothes, the sort of giveaways you read about in novels. There were times when he worked late, but I'm sure I would have known. The scent of somebody else's perfume, or whatever. Him behaving oddly… no, he just told me he didn't feel ready to commit.'

'I'm sorry, Alba. Don't really know what to say. Shit happens.'

'Tell me about it. Anyway, I'm trying to get myself together, but I'm not looking forward to going back to the flat. There's a lot to sort out.'

'I can imagine.'

They continued in silence, their rucksacks heavier now, the treasure within making metallic sounds as they descended. It had turned darker, the sky heavy with snow. Alba could not rid her mind of thoughts of the young man she had seen. If he was one of the hippies who had decided to remain up here on the Mountain of the Moon at summer's end, where was he living now? How could he keep warm? Maybe Davide was right, and she was still not herself after losing James. But she felt pretty sure she hadn't imagined him; he had seemed real. Davide was walking in front of her now along the narrow track. He looked so young. She didn't want him to get hurt like she had been. She felt a sudden rush of sisterly protection.

'Davide, at the risk of sounding cynical, please make sure you get to know your new girlfriend well before you get too involved… don't get carried away by lust.'

'Ha ha! Always straight to the heart of the matter, Alba! Don't worry, I'm not stupid. But I want you to meet her soon. I'm sure you'll like her.'

'I hope so. I'll be a tiger sister if I think she's not right.'

'So very matriarchal and *italiana*...'

'Funny, James was always accusing me of being that. But I *am* Italian. Maybe I should have stood up to him more during our relationship. Then he would have wanted to stay together, and I wouldn't have made him so angry that day... and he'd still be alive.'

'Bad vibes with "should have", Alba. Negative. Think forward, not backward.'

'Yes, signor *Filosofo*. But that's easier said than done. Come on, let's get a move on. I can't wait to show everybody our haul, and I'm hungry. I think Ma is making her famous turkey lasagne.'

CHAPTER FOUR

Tuscany, 1940

'Don't go alone to the river, Lucia,' her mother said. 'Watch out for those Blackshirts. There was a group throwing their weight around this week in the piazza.'

The small platoon of young and eager fascist militia newly posted in Badia had taken to coming down to the river on these hot June days to bathe where the children of Tramarecchia were used to running wild in the meadows and swimming in the weir.

Lucia wondered if her best friend Massimo was doing the same now, all those miles away in Libya, and if he'd found somewhere safe to swim off the African coast. He'd sent a postcard and she'd placed it on the shelf above the fireplace. The corners were beginning to curl and turn yellow. On the front was a coloured photo of a camel in the desert, like a picture from the children's Bible that signor Guelfi had pinned on his classroom wall. Massimo had scrawled a message on the back in his untidy handwriting. *It's too hot here*, it read. The rest of the words had been blacked out and, peer as she might, she couldn't decipher the letters. She was curious to know if he was missing her.

The last time they'd been together had been strange. It had been one of those sultry days at the end of August last year. The morning had started in a blaze of sunshine and her mother had sent her out to the meadows to pick plums for jam. Massimo had followed her down the path, and with his help her pail was full in no time.

'Let's leave it here, under the hedge. Race you to the river,' she'd said. 'We can wash off the plum stains and cool down.'

She'd set off before him, lifting her skirt above her knees to run more freely. And she could run like the wind. It was as if she wanted to recapture the last remnants of childhood. As she ran, scenes from the past filled her mind. She and Massimo had grown up together, but although he was older, she was the ringleader of their little gang of seven friends. When the children's tasks were done – feeding the hens, raking muck from the stables – they would disappear to the river to play. In summer they'd build dams and fish for trout. In winter, if there was snow, they'd play on home-made toboggans, or make skis from lengths of wood. There was never a shortage of games in their children's paradise. Lucia climbed trees higher than some of the boys. Perched fearlessly at the top, she'd jeer down at them to hurry up and join her. She would sing her victory song from the top branches, her beautiful voice ringing out above them. Her clear soprano tone had been picked up by the teacher and he'd urged her parents to send her to choir practices in the main church in Badia at the top of the valley. She had a gift, he said, that should not be wasted.

She was a spirited girl, often getting into trouble. Once, she'd stolen underwear off her neighbour's fence where it was drying and hung it like flags to flutter from the railings on the bridge in Rofelle for any passer-by to see. But now she was growing up. Her blouse was too small for her and she had more flesh on her hips. She was sure Massimo had deliberately slowed his pace as she ran across the grass so that he could view her from behind.

A huge clap of thunder had split the air and it started to rain, sullen clouds covering every centimetre of what had been blue sky. They'd run to shelter in old Pio's house. Two months earlier he had died in his bed and since then, his door had stayed unlocked as if waiting for his return. Lucia bent double inside, hands on her knees, catching her breath from her exertions, and spied Massimo trying not to look at the shape of her through her wet cotton blouse.

'I'm still faster than you,' she'd said, grinning up at him. 'You're an old slowcoach.' She pulled out one of the chairs at the kitchen table. Half a bottle of olive oil sat in the middle of the cloth, and a pile of woodworm dust that had fallen from the beam above.

Her lips were still stained from eating the little red plums, and Massimo had suddenly pulled her clumsily towards him. She'd kept her eyes open, a slight frown puckering her forehead, her mouth stiff against his. And then she'd shoved him away. 'What was all that about?' she said.

'Does it have to be about anything? Didn't you like it?' He'd sat down opposite and watched her.

Wiping her mouth with the back of her hand, she'd replied, 'It's a bit weird, that's all.'

'Wouldn't you like to live with me in a house like this?' He'd pointed towards the vast fireplace where ashes waited to be cleared from beneath a black cooking pot. 'On our own? So that we could pick plums and… kiss on rainy days?'

He'd moved towards her again across the table, but she'd got up to straighten a pair of clogs left abandoned by the fireplace.

'There's more to life than picking fruit and kissing,' she'd said. 'I want more before all that, Massimo.'

She'd leant with her back against the windowsill, a draught from a cracked pane blowing wisps of her curls to frame her pretty face.

'I'm not ready to have babies and be tied to cooking and washing. I want to see more places than old Tramarecchia.' She'd returned to sit in her chair, the table between them a barrier to further kisses. 'I might try and get a job down in one of those big hotels in Rimini. I was talking to Olga, who was back for the feast of *Ferragosto*. She told me about the people she meets – they come from all over Italy, and other countries like France and England. Even America. They give her huge tips. The Americans speak Italian with a funny accent and come back to visit their relatives, and they wear swanky clothes and gold rings on their fingers. And she told me about the market along the seafront where you can buy anything you want…'

'You'd still be cooking and washing, but in a hotel, for somebody else.'

'Well, at least it would be different. Massimo, I'm only fourteen – not ready to pop out babies and work my fingers to the bone on a scrubby piece of land, like our mothers.' She'd looked at him. 'Don't you want more than this place can give you?'

He hadn't replied to that, although his eyes told her more than his silence. If he'd come out with some sentimental statement, she probably would have laughed. As it was, Massimo simply shrugged his shoulders and looked away, fiddling with a rip in the tablecloth.

The rain had stopped, and through the open door she'd watched steam rise from the stone walls that bordered old Pio's vegetable garden. Massimo got up, the sound of his chair scraping against the flagstones breaking the silence.

'Let's get those plums back to your mother before they turn to a soggy mess,' he'd said, ushering her out and pulling the door closed behind him.

Lucia wondered if it was their conversation that afternoon that had caused Massimo to enlist in the army. Whatever his reasons, he was gone within that fortnight and they hadn't seen him since.

The only contact had been the postcard, and that had told her next to nothing.

Everything was now concentrated on the war. In their spare time in the evenings, she and her mother knitted socks and gloves for the soldiers, and slogans appeared everywhere, daubed on the walls: '*Credere, Obbedire, Combattere*', they exhorted, urging everybody to believe and obey *Il Duce* and the Empire and to follow him in the fight.

When Lucia had expressed her wish to find work in Rimini, it was immediately squashed.

'You're to stay here. Who knows what goes on down at the coast,' her father had said. 'The place is swarming with soldiers and militia. It's not safe. You will stay here where we can keep an eye on you. I forbid you to leave.'

And the truth was that even Olga had now returned to the village to be with her family. When Lucia had complained to Olga about how bored she was, when she saw her in the piazza, Olga had told her the city had changed. 'The only way to get tips now, *cara* Lucia, is if you go to bed with the soldiers. And even then they don't always pay… I've heard say,' she added quickly. 'At least here there is plenty to eat. There are chickens and vegetables in our *orti*. There is nothing there. Food is scarcer by the day, and it is requisitioned for the forces. Your father is right to keep you here.'

Lucia sulked and watched as even the village schoolchildren were swept up in the war machine. Each Saturday, they had to march about in the square in Badia Tedalda. Signor Guelfi, their rotund teacher, squeezed himself into shorts and a black shirt and led his straggly band of forty-five youngsters in exercises to become perfect little *fascisti*. The boys, in their black shirts and caps, were known as *Balilla*, the girls, *Piccole italiane* – the fascists of tomorrow. Guelfi was half-hearted and reluctant to push the children too much. But recently he had been inspected by a fascist bigwig from Arezzo and reprimanded in front of everybody. 'These children are too soft, Guelfi,' a slim young man with a chiselled face had bellowed. 'If we are to build up our Empire, we need strong, young warriors. Take it from me, the *Duce* would not be pleased with your efforts. You would be wise to smarten up. He likes to arrive without warning to inspect these manoeuvres.'

Lucia's father had grumbled at supper that night about the stupid propaganda the *fascisti* were stuffing into the minds of schoolchildren.

'At least if they taught them something useful like cooking or outdoor skills, there would be some purpose to it all. Why the Scouts were banned, I do not know. All these children do is parade up and down with wooden guns on their shoulders,' he said, tearing off a hunk of bread to mop up the rest of the tomato sauce on his plate. 'And what does the *Duce* think he is doing? Our army is no match against the allies. How can we possibly win a war against their might? All this talk about "*vinceremo*", we shall win, and the resurrection of the Empire plastered on posters and leaflets. Bah!' He poured himself another tumbler of wine and knocked it back in one.

'Make sure you don't talk like that in the *osteria*, Doriano,' Lucia's mother said, hands on hips, turning away from the sink, 'or somebody will report you and you'll be arrested. Remember, we are all supposed to be loyal *repubblichini*...'

'We might have documents to say so, but my heart tells me otherwise. The high-and-mighty *Duce* might have helped Italy in the past, but I believe power has gone to his head. His stock reply to criticism is "*il Duce ha sempre ragione*". Well, I for one do *not* believe the *Duce* is always right. And I'm not the only one who is disillusioned, I can tell you. All that man wants is rich pickings from the spoils of war. *Porco cane.*' As he swore, he pushed his empty plate away and rubbed his stomach, a grimace on his face.

'Hush, Doriano, walls have ears,' his wife said, her finger against her lips. She turned to Lucia. 'And you be careful not to repeat a word of what your father has said this evening.'

Now, almost two years after Massimo had left, Alba and her family heard on the radio about the defeat of the Italians in the desert in Libya. She remembered her father's words about Italy's weak army and how they were no match for the Allies.

Another postcard for her arrived several months later. This time it was from England.

I've been a prisoner here since 17 July. All danger is over now. I am very well. Sending you good wishes. Do not worry.
Massimo

CHAPTER FIVE

Tuscany, present day

Three months later

'It's good to be back, Anna,' Alba told her stepmother as she drained her coffee. She gazed through the picture window at pots of early fuchsia-pink geraniums decorating the steps on the terrace. 'I'd almost started talking to myself back in London. The flat without James was spooky.'

Anna reached over to squeeze Alba's hand. 'It's good to have you back. I shall enjoy spoiling you.'

She was rewarded with a weak smile. 'I tried so hard to keep going in London,' Alba said. 'Working at the gallery and forcing myself to prepare proper meals for one in the evening and going out with the same old crowd, but… my heart wasn't in it,' Alba said, getting up to pour them both more coffee. 'It didn't feel like home any more. André and Marcus were absolute stars, you know, turning up at the flat with wonderful meals they'd cooked. And… they took charge of clearing out James's stuff for me. I couldn't have done that alone.'

'They are wonderful friends. You needed to go back to London. Babbo and I both understood that. But we did worry.'

'I wouldn't have done anything stupid, Anna,' Alba said, coming over to hug her. 'I cried myself to sleep for nights and nights at the beginning, but' – she shrugged her shoulders – 'he's not coming back. And there's a lot I want to get on and do. I realise now I'd given up on my dreams because of James.'

'Like?'

'My art, for starters. I talked about that a lot with Marcus. And I looked up online about the foundation course at the academy in Florence. I'd love to apply.'

'I'm sure Babbo will be very happy for you.'

'But that's not until October. In the meantime, I've promised to help Egidio out at the tourist office with his ruins project. I might start today, and explore for some inspiration. Plus, I want to see if I can track down more information about the silverware Davide and I found. Egidio hasn't had much luck.'

After breakfast, and with the sunshine beckoning, Alba set off for a walk on the other side of the river towards the village of Fresciano di Sotto. Primroses studded the banks, and orchids were beginning to appear in clumps through the grass like little purple pokers. She noticed other species along her route, which she couldn't identify. Maybe Babbo could take her on a walk with him one day. He was considered a local expert since he'd published his pocket guide to the flora and fauna of the area. As she walked, she thought back to her winter walk up to ruined Seccaroni. She still puzzled over the apparition of the *fantasma*, as her father jokingly described him, but she now put it down to the effects of grief after losing James and her mind playing tricks. Egidio had not been able to tell her much more about the silver, other than it bore the symbol for the old estate of the Boccarini family, but he'd suggested she might find out more at the library down in Sansepolcro. He couldn't find the copy of the book he'd told her about, and he thought she might find one in the city. Both these things were on her to-do list.

She climbed down to the river at a crossing point where there'd once been an old bridge. Now, she had to balance her way across stepping stones. One of them was loose and her foot slipped into the water, wetting her socks and the bottom of her trousers. The water was freezing and she swore loudly. A willow branch trailing in the water quivered on the other bank, and she noticed a figure, stooping to fill an old-fashioned pitcher with water.

A tall, thin woman straightened up and smiled across at Alba. She wore a long sack-like linen dress that came down to her ankles. 'Let me help you dry your feet, signorina,' she said. Her voice was soft and she was well-spoken.

'I'm sorry,' Alba said. 'Excuse my language. I thought I was alone.'

'No matter. Follow me.' The woman turned to climb up a steep path. Crude steps had been dug into the incline lined with large, flat stones secured by wooden pegs. The woman moved at a steady pace, her long grey plait swinging as she moved, whereas Alba was breathless after the steep ascent. At the top, she walked three steps behind the woman, along a narrow avenue lined with beech trees. In a clearing, shaded by tall Mediterranean pines, stood a small stone chapel. Alba had never visited this place before, although she'd heard about a hermitage in the woods.

'Please sit and catch your breath, signorina,' the woman said. 'And allow me to dry your footwear. My bread is almost baked, and the oven is warm. Share with me.'

She indicated a bench in the lee of the church, beside a door to an attached building where Alba noticed the mouth of an oven, closed off with a metal door. A basket containing dried pine cones sat beside a neat woodpile, and one or two items of laundry were drying over a fence.

'You are very welcome,' the woman continued. 'Not many pilgrims pass by at this time of the year.'

'Oh! I'm not a pilgrim,' Alba started, 'I was just walking…'

'It depends how one defines pilgrimage. A journey to a special place is how I like to think of it, signorina.'

'Please call me Alba.'

'Meaning "dawn",' the unusual woman said. 'A new beginning… I am Lodovica, and you must forgive me if I ramble. I'm more used to talking to my thoughts.' Her smile was beautiful, accentuating high cheekbones and eyes so dark they were like night.

She turned to open the oven door and inserted a long-handled metal shovel to withdraw two crusty loaves. Although Alba had eaten a large portion of Anna's tagliatelle *al ragù* at lunchtime, she accepted a warm crust of the fragrant bread.

'Are you thirsty?' Lodovica asked, while she arranged Alba's socks to dry near the embers. 'My drinking water comes from a spring in the woods.' She went inside the building and returned with a glass bottle and two tumblers.

Simple bread and water had never tasted so good to Alba.

'This feels like a religious ceremony,' Alba commented. 'Are you a nun, or something? I'm afraid I'm not religious. I'm not even sure I believe in a God. Sorry,' she added, suddenly feeling awkward that she'd asked personal questions of a woman she had only just met.

'No need to apologise. Yes, I am a nun, but I prefer to be known as Lodovica. I'm a hermit. And, like you, I didn't believe in any type of God when I was younger. And this ceremony, as you describe it, is simply a sharing of refreshments.'

'How long have you lived here?'

'In July it will be ten years.' She rose from the bench. 'Can I leave you for ten minutes, Alba? By then, your footwear should be dry.'

The nun walked to the front of the chapel and pulled open its heavy door and disappeared inside.

Alba was happy to sit beneath the canopy of pines that whooshed back and forth in the breeze, the sound hypnotic like that of waves. She felt oddly at peace in the company of this stranger. An urge to draw hit her and she hunted for charcoal and pad in her bag. Her hand began to fly over the paper as she transferred rough outlines of the stone buildings, mountains in the background, a meadow where a flock of sheep grazed and the huddle of Fresciano's higgledy-piggledy houses in the distance. Pleased with what she'd accomplished, she wandered over to the chapel.

Beside the door was a crude fresco and she read the description beneath. In the sixteenth century, this ruined chapel from 1300 had been restored, because a mule carrying Cardinal Bevilacqua had stumbled and knelt before an apparition of the Madonna.

On a shelf beneath the fresco, Alba noticed a highly polished silver jug containing an arrangement of spring flowers. The style of the jug was reminiscent of the goblets she and Davide had discovered, and as Alba stepped nearer to check, she was shocked to see a swirly initial 'B' engraved on the handle. It seemed such a worldly object compared to the simple earthenware tumbler Lodovica had handed her earlier, and Alba wondered why the woman should have part of this set. She jumped as the nun emerged from the chapel, blinking in the sunlight. Alba felt as though she'd been spying on her and, in her confusion, she blurted out, 'This story – about the mule – do you suppose it really happened?'

Lodovica shrugged her shoulders. 'I wasn't there, of course. But people believe in stranger things.'

'I struggle with dogma,' Alba continued, pulling on the dry socks Lodovica had handed her. 'Those stories of bizarre miracles, of saints with stigmata, outdated rules and regulations of an ancient institution governed mostly by old men.'

Lodovica laughed. 'You sound like me when I was young. Why do you think I've chosen to be a hermit and do my own thing?'

'I haven't the faintest idea. I've never spoken to anybody like you before.'

'Well.' Lodovica smiled. 'Now is your chance.'

Alba paused, drawn to this mysterious woman living so differently. She seemed so content and serene. 'Please don't think me rude, Lodovica. But… living as a hermit. Separating yourself from the real world.'

'Real world?' The nun's voice was almost sharp when she replied.

Alba paused before saying, 'Well, living on your own, far from a village, spending your days like this. Isn't it simply bypassing real life?'

'I believe what I do now *is* real life.'

'What did you do before you came here?'

'I was a fashion model in Milan for one of the famous couture houses.'

Alba gasped, but when she properly examined the woman before her, she could see it. Her striking, unusual looks, her height, the way she walked so gracefully, almost gliding, her shoulders set back. She could imagine her slim body draped in edgy, season-defining fashions. 'Wow,' Alba said, sitting forward on the bench. 'That's so amazing.'

'Why amazing? In the end I found it extremely tedious, and it almost killed me mentally. It certainly was killing me physically.'

Alba's glance was questioning.

'I took drugs to keep my weight down and to cope with men and the stress of it all. Being *here* is real life. I was a zombie in the city. No good to anybody, least of all myself.'

'But… and forgive me, for everybody has a right to live how they want…' Alba started.

'You're going to ask me what I do with my time. What is the point of it all. Right?'

'Right.'

'I'm here for others. I'm not a drain on society. I live self-sufficiently from my vegetable patch and a couple of hens.'

'And who owns these buildings?'

'I bought them from the Curia with the money I earned in Milan. They were ruins when I took them on.'

'So, did you inherit lots of stuff from the Church along with the building?' Alba asked, thinking about the jug. 'Only, I found some silverware with the exact same crest as your vase, the one by the chapel. It was in a box hidden up in the mountains.'

Lodovica stood up, pulling down the rolled-up sleeves of her habit against the freshening wind. 'There were quite a few things left when I took this place on, yes, but... not that piece. I came across that jug in the forest.' She paused, and Alba wondered what she was going to say next, but that seemed to be the end of the matter. 'Would you like to see inside my home?' Lodovica asked. 'It's probably not as primitive as you imagine.'

'I should really be getting back to my family. They'll be worried.'

'Why not spend the night here? I'm sure you have a mobile phone to message them?'

It was an easy decision to make. There was something soothing about this woman's company.

'If you're sure? You probably value your silence. I don't want to be in the way.'

Lodovica cocked her head to one side and looked long at Alba. 'I invited you, Alba.'

The room where Alba was to sleep that night was simple. A tiny window recessed in the thick walls and curtained with a plain cream cotton square looked out over the woods. An enamel candlestick placed on a painted stool and a small wooden box were the only furnishings, apart from a single metal bed and a home-made rug on the floor.

'Where will you sleep?' Alba asked.

'Don't worry, this is for guests. My bedroom is on the other side of the main room.'

The main living space of Lodovica's single-storey home was dominated by a wide fireplace, with wooden trestles placed on either side of the hearth. Ashes glowed in the fire basket and Lodovica blew on a long metal tube to stoke the flames. She unhooked a pot of simmering water from a chain hanging over the fire. 'We'll have tea and you can talk to me. I feel you need to.'

While the shadows lengthened outside, they drank fennel tea from earthenware mugs.

'Tell me what is troubling you, Alba.'

'I'm not troubled… At least, I feel I've now begun to turn a corner.'

There was silence in the room, except for the fire crackling in the grate. Lodovica waited for Alba to speak.

'My boyfriend was killed in a horrific accident not long before Christmas. I thought we would marry, and my dreams were shattered,' Alba said eventually. 'It turned my world upside down.'

'I'm so sorry. That is hard.'

'It happened over three months ago, and I need to move on… I hate to keep talking about it to my parents. They've been so amazing.'

'You can talk to me.'

'You're very kind. I don't know… I've only just met you, but I feel I could tell you anything. And though you're a nun and all that, you wouldn't be shocked.'

'I told you about my life before. Nothing shocks me.'

'If we'd had children, it would have been awful. I desperately wanted James's babies, but he told me he wasn't ready to commit.'

'I lost a baby,' Lodovica said.

'I'm so sorry.'

'The father was married. I believed he would choose me over his wife. But I was wrong.'

Silence fell again between the women, Alba not wanting to pry so soon in this new friendship and Lodovica perhaps not ready to enlighten. Outside, the wind danced up a mini-storm, pine branches tapping against the roof tiles, but inside it was safe and warm.

'Would you like to eat? You could help me prepare, Alba.'

They worked together at a table, beating eggs, chopping parsley, thyme and rosemary to season a frittata that Lodovica fried in a pan over the fire. A side salad of roasted endive and sliced tomatoes completed the simple meal.

'Do you always cook like this?'

'I have a two-ring camping stove for emergencies, but I eat very simply and, as you saw, I have my oven. I fire that up twice a week. You were lucky to happen along today for my fresh bread.'

'I don't know if I could live like this. It's stark.'

'I wasn't sure at first, but it's amazing how little we really need. A bed to sleep on, water, fire and something to eat and drink. Now I relish my time to listen.'

'Listen?'

'I listen to God.'

She pointed to a sampler in a plain wooden frame on the wall with the words 'Let go, let God' embroidered in cross-stitch.

'You said you don't believe in miracles, Alba,' Lodovica said, slicing an apple into quarters. 'I prefer to use the word "sign" rather than "miracle".'

'I don't follow.'

When something amazing happens, then I believe this is a sign. Your turning up here today, for example, was a sign. You needed to talk openly, without fear of upsetting anybody, and you found me here, ready to listen.'

'I would call that coincidence.'

The nun shrugged. 'The terminology is up to you. At any rate, I'm pleased you came along, and I hope you'll feel free to come again.'

They talked for another hour, Alba outlining her project for Egidio at the tourist office.

'Walking helps untangle my thoughts,' Alba said. 'The countryside here is magical – so beautiful but, sadly, dotted with too many ruins.'

'All with their own stories.'

'Exactly.' Alba pulled out the sketch she'd started earlier of the chapel nestled in its surroundings and Lodovica spent a long time examining it.

'That's wonderful. You should nurture this skill.'

'Thank you, Lodovica. I'm planning on applying for an art course that starts in the autumn.' Alba leant back in her chair and decided to tell her new friend about her experience at the ruin of Seccaroni. Now felt like the right time to talk more about the silverware, too. 'You talk of signs. Tell me I'm mad, but I'd value your opinion.'

She described the person she'd seen up on the Mountain of the Moon; how he'd seemed to disappear into thin air. 'I went back with my brother to try to find him again, but he wasn't there and now my family tease me because I think he was some kind of ghost. Actually, now I believe it was grief affecting me.'

Lodovica said nothing, and Alba was pleased she'd made no comment. 'We didn't find anybody up there, but we found treasure inside a box instead – at the point where I'd seen the man disappear.'

'Treasure?' Lodovica asked, getting up to stoke the flames.

'Silver goblets, plates, old and tarnished – in the same style as the vase you've placed beneath the fresco. I told you it has the same markings, and I've found out it represents the Boccarini family crest. Isn't it uncanny that you also have a piece of what seems to be a set?'

The woman turned towards Alba, a frown on her face. 'As I said before, I found that piece, Alba. I felt it needed a good home.' She yawned. 'But it's time for me to sleep,' she said, bringing the conversation to an end. 'I rise very early each morning to pray.' She lit a candle from the fire and accompanied Alba to her room. 'Good night, Alba. Sleep well.'

Alba woke at eight and found a bowl of milk, a couple of slices of yesterday's bread wrapped in a napkin and a pot of home-made blackberry and apple jam on the kitchen table. A note propped against a jam jar of spring flowers told her to enjoy her breakfast and to come again soon. There was no sign of Lodovica. After her breakfast, Alba let herself out of the hermit's house, gently pulling the door to and setting off back to the river path. As she passed the shrine outside the chapel, she noticed that the silver jug had been replaced with a simple pot and she wondered if Lodovica, taking note of what Alba had told her about its origins, had felt the jug too precious to leave outside. The clouds were low this morning, threatening rain, a heavy mist cloaking the tops of the mountains, and she hurried back to the Stalla.

There was nobody in when she arrived home. In a way, she was pleased. She wanted to hug the knowledge of her eccentric new friend to herself for a while, before recounting the events of the last twenty-four hours to others.

Upstairs in her room, she pulled out the unfinished sketch of Lodovica's chapel and worked on it until she was satisfied. This would be her first offering for Egidio, but she decided to complete a further couple before handing them over.

Out of habit, she picked up her phone. It needed recharging after her night away. The screensaver still displayed a photo of herself and James sitting together, beneath a palm tree on Patong beach in Thailand. She wondered when she would feel ready to change it. The pain of losing James was still there, but it was now more of a dull ache. Then she remembered a comment the nun had made to her while they sat by the fire the night before. Something along the lines of being patient with herself; to take a series of small steps to reach another tomorrow.

CHAPTER SIX

'I wondered about going down to Sansepolcro today for a change of scenery,' Alba said at breakfast the next morning.

'To the metropolis?' Anna laughed. 'After London, it will seem really quiet.'

'You know, I won't mind that at all, and the library is good there. Maybe I can dig out more information about the Boccarini estate and the silver. Can I use the Vespa, Babbo?'

'It's due for a service, but I should think you'll be fine. Your helmet is still in the garage somewhere. Oh, and try the tourist office records as well as the library – they have plenty of files on the history of the region.'

The Vespa didn't start immediately but once it sputtered into life, she was off. It would soon be May and the sun was warm on her back through her leather jacket. At the Viamaggio Pass, she stopped to gaze on the view of the reservoir glistening in the valley below. A cluster of ox-eye daisies and yellow rattle caught her eye, and she crouched down to frame a picture on her phone of the wild flowers and the large expanse of water in the background.

Not long after the pass, she braked hard. She had travelled up and down this road for years, but not once had she taken any notice of the ornate gates that caught her attention this morning. Tall, imposing, despite the rust that called out for sandblasting, they were decorated with a large swirling 'B', identical to the crest on the silverware that she and Davide had found. She moved the Vespa to the side of the road and went to peer through the gates. A board announcing that a new boutique hotel would open here was tied to the bars. At the end of a gravelled drive choked with weeds and lined with cypress trees stood an imposing nineteenth-century villa. The house was run-down: a couple of shutters hung lopsided from their hinges and all the woodwork needed repainting. There was nobody about. Alba took several photos of the gates and set off again, certain that she had found the place from where the silverware had originated.

Within another few kilometres, she glimpsed her first sight of the town through the olive groves. The terracotta roof tiles of its old houses were splashes of rust-red through the silvery leaves and contorted trunks. Once again, she pulled in at the side of the road to find her phone for another picture. With the motor switched off, she stood for a few moments enjoying the repetitive song of a chiffchaff. A lizard scuttled across the road and disappeared down a culvert. She hadn't seen one yet up at Rofelle. But it was warmer down here on the plain, and she couldn't wait to go to her favourite bar in the main piazza to linger in the sun over coffee. Sansepolcro was where she used to come each Monday to Saturday for her high school studies, so she knew the town well. When she was a teenager, she'd resented having to return to the quiet of Rofelle, wishing she could live down there and go out with her friends in the evenings. It was such a trek each day up and down on the school bus. But now, having lived in London for eight years, she was loving the tranquillity of the countryside.

She pulled the Vespa off its stand and kick-started it. But it wouldn't go. She waited for a while before trying again, in case she flooded the engine, but – nothing. She decided against leaving it by the road; there were no houses nearby and the Vespa was a valuable vintage 1970s model. She didn't want it stolen. So she freewheeled down the remaining kilometres and then walked it along the flat until she reached a mechanic's workshop her father used. It was at the end of a cobbled alleyway that led to a yard, home to a dozen stray cats and a jumble of rusting motorbikes and classic Fiats. It seemed there was nobody around at first, and she called out, '*C'è nessuno?* Anybody there?'

A man in his fifties appeared from underneath a car. '*Eccomi!*' he said. 'Here I am. How can I help, signorina?'

He wiped his hands on an oily cloth hanging from the back of his dungarees and exclaimed at the beauty of her scooter, running his hands over the bodywork as he asked her where she had found it. After much scratching of his head and fiddling around near the wheels, he pronounced it would be ready in two days' time. He was very sorry, but he needed to order new shock absorbers and as it was Friday, they would arrive Monday at the very earliest, but not to worry, because her little *Vespina* would be perfectly safe in his hands.

'If you like, I could lend you a pushbike,' he said, but Alba explained how far away she lived and thanked him for his kind offer. 'Oh yes,' he said, 'I know the area well. I go truffle-hunting in those woods.'

She left her details and made her way to the bar in the main piazza, snapping images as she went: an old wine barrel planted with lavender and cascades of trailing pink geraniums; sheets hanging from a top-floor window; a cat curled up on the worn front step of a vast door of pitted chestnut wood; a box of vegetables on the pavement outside a greengrocer's that looked like an artist's palette of colour, with shining green peppers, oranges, huge bulbs of fennel and plump lollo lettuces. There was a feast for the eyes everywhere she looked.

The owner of the bar didn't recognise her at first, but when he did, he threw his arms around her as if she were a long-lost daughter and, when he called out to his wife that little Alba

Starnucci was back from *Inghilterra*, there were kisses all round, and her cappuccino was offered on the house, with a cake of her choice thrown in. She lingered over her refreshments, gazing at her compatriots in the piazza. They were beautiful, she decided. At least half a dozen of the girls who walked by could have stepped straight from a fashion magazine, their figures trim, hair raven-black and all with immaculate dress sense, even if it was only jeans and a sweater tied round the waist. They had a way of walking, too, which said, 'I defy you not to look at me', with their shoulders back, bosom forward, a faint wiggle of the hips. And the shoes. Some of the shoes were outlandish, impossible to walk far in, Alba thought, grateful she'd worn her trainers for her unexpected trek with her Vespa. The men pretended not to watch the women as they walked past, but the swivel of the neck was a giveaway. She'd watched an amusing documentary which had joked about Italian men having different sets of muscles in their necks to permit them to watch girls without turning around. She smiled into her coffee at the memory.

Alba decided she would have to catch the bus back home. There was only one a day, and the timing meant she would have to visit the tourist office first to see if they could help her with information about the Boccarini estate. On the way, she popped into the cathedral cloisters to gaze at the faded frescoes. They were mostly country scenes of fishermen along a river, peasants working in fields and a hermit praying in a mountainside cave. It made her think of Lodovica, and she decided to pay her another visit soon. She'd enjoyed her calming company.

After entering the tourist office, Alba explained to the girl behind the counter what she was looking for.

'I'm doing a project on the ruins in the area and I wondered if you had anything about the old Boccarini estate up the road. Or the house called Seccaroni, on the Mountain of the Moon.'

The girl shook her head. 'Let me ask my boss,' she said. '*Un momento.*'

A young man, looking like another Italian god from a magazine, appeared from a back room. He was dressed in jeans and a slim-fitting blue shirt, the sleeves rolled up above his wrists. His hair was well cut, a flop of dark curls on top, fashionably shaved at the sides. He grinned broadly at Alba as, lifting the hinged counter, he came straight over to her and swept her into his arms.

'Alba, *ma come stai?* How long has it been?' He smelled of expensive aftershave, lemony and tangy, and his stubble grazed her cheeks as he planted two hearty kisses on each.

She pushed him away and stepped back. 'Excuse me?' she said. 'Do I know you?'

He roared with laughter. 'You don't recognise me, do you? But you haven't changed at all, Alba.'

And then she twigged, staring in disbelief at this vision in front of her, his deep brown laughing eyes, a broad smile lighting up his handsome face. No way would she have known he was her lovable old schoolmate, Alfiero Paoli. No way. He'd been geeky, with thick-rimmed glasses, baggy clothes, his hair choppy, his curls tamed with so much gel it had looked permanently greasy. They'd been in the same study groups at school and had often done their homework together at each other's houses. Their friends had nicknamed them The Two As because of their initials and the fact that they both always achieved high grades. But he had changed so much; she couldn't believe it.

'Alfi,' she stuttered. 'What a… surprise,' she eventually came out with, rather lamely.

'I thought you'd moved to England,' he said. 'Are you back visiting your parents?'

'I've left London,' she said, not wanting to explain further.

'We must have a drink and catch up immediately.' He turned to the girl behind the counter. 'Marianna, can you hold the fort? I'll take my lunch break now.'

Outside in the piazza, he linked arms with her. 'I have a table booked for one o'clock, but it won't matter if we're early. I want to know everything you've been up to, Alba.'

'*Buongiorno*, signor Alfiero,' the waiter said as they entered a little restaurant nestled within the thick walls of the town. 'Your usual table?' he asked.

'No, Marco, we'll sit outside today. It's plenty warm enough.'

They were led to a table in the corner of the restaurant terrace, ringed by tall terracotta pots containing white oleander. Alba ordered an Aperol Spritz, 'Seeing as I'm getting the bus back to Badia and not driving,' she said, explaining what had happened to her Vespa.

'You mean you still have that old beast? What was it you used to call her?'

'Wanda the Vespa,' she admitted with a giggle. 'Do you remember when you took me down to Pennabilli on your new bike and we crashed on the way home?'

'How could I forget? I have the scar on my leg to remind me. It was when a herd of wild boar ran out in front of us, wasn't it?'

'And you had to wear that plaster for the rest of the summer…'

'How many years ago since we saw each other?' he asked.

'Must be at least eight.'

'Here's to eight years ago, then. *Cin cin!*'

As they leant into each other to clink glasses, a shadow fell across the table.

'What are we celebrating?' The woman who had spoken was stunning. Her hair, shining and luxuriant, was swept up into a bouffant ponytail and large pearl earrings accentuated her tanned face. She wore a high-necked blouse with a stiff ruffle that came up to just below her chiselled cheekbones. And as she leant forward to kiss Alfiero, Alba wondered if her pouting lips might be Botoxed.

Alfiero stood up to welcome her. 'Beatrice, let me introduce you to my old friend, Alba.'

Beatrice looked down at Alba who, in frayed jeans, fleece and sneakers, felt dowdy next to this pair of fashionistas.

'*Salve*, Alba,' she said, before turning to Alfiero to pick a speck of something from the sleeve of his navy cashmere sweater slung over his shoulders. 'I hate you in this colour,' she said. 'So boring.'

'Alba and I haven't seen each other since school,' he continued. 'She's joining us for lunch.'

Beatrice sat down and placed her Gucci handbag on the empty fourth chair. 'I'm really not hungry today, but I'll sit with you,' she said.

Alba chose linguine with a tuna sauce and tucked in, while Alfiero's girlfriend toyed with a salad of mozzarella and tomatoes, leaving half, which Alfiero scooped onto his plate after he'd finished his *bistecca alla Fiorentina*.

There was so much they could have chatted about, but Beatrice seemed to put a dampener on the atmosphere, butting in whenever Alfiero mentioned anything about the past.

As they waited for their espressos, Alba checked her watch. 'I need to leave in five minutes for my bus.'

Alfiero put his hand over hers. 'There is no way you're going on the bus. I will take you myself.'

'But I thought we were meeting later, *caro*,' Beatrice said.

'It was only to go shopping. We can postpone that until tomorrow, surely?'

'Whatever. But I made you an appointment at the tailor. Try not to miss it,' she said, picking up her bag. 'I might see you again, Alba. It's been very interesting meeting somebody from my *fidanzato*'s past.' Then, turning to Alfiero, she added, 'Phone me when you're finished.'

Alba watched her walk away in her tight leather skirt and noted the swivel-head gazes of a couple of men dining at a table further off as she passed by.

Alfiero put the hood down on his black Alfa Romeo, handing Alba a headscarf to keep her long hair tidy. 'It's Beatrice's, but she won't know.'

She noted the designer's name signed across the edge of the scarf and hoped not.

The drive up the hill was smoother and faster than her trip down on her Vespa and she thought she could get used to travelling this way.

'So, do you work at the tourist office?' Alba asked when they'd pulled away from town.

'I manage the Arezzo office, but I commute from Sansepolcro. I have a flat here. You'll have to come and visit.'

'So, what happened to your plans to become an architect?'

He gave her a look. 'It was never *my* plan. It was my parents' dream. I love my job in tourism. Arezzo is the headquarters of the regional tourist board and I get to see a lot of amazing places. Very satisfying. What about you? You were going somewhere with your art, weren't you?'

She pulled a face. 'If I'm honest, Alfi,' she said, using the name she'd always called him by years ago, 'my plans were diverted.' She paused. 'My means-to-an-end job, working in a friend's gallery in London, didn't really end up anywhere. And neither did my relationship…'

'New beginnings, eh?'

'Something like that,' she said, leaving it there. Her grief was still raw, despite the months that had passed. It was easier to bottle it up. She didn't want to cry in front of Alfi.

As they passed the gates to the imposing villa, she asked him to slow down, and told him about the silverware she and Davide had discovered. 'Egidio at the tourist office reckons it was from this old estate. And I realised this morning that everything bears the same family crest that's on these gates. I'd love to find out more. Do you think your office or the library might be able to help? In the excitement of meeting up again, I clean forgot to ask.'

'We do have lots of documents,' he said, accelerating away from the gates and immediately slowing down again to navigate a dangerous bend where flowers had been tied to a fence post in memory of a dead biker. 'I'll see what I can do. Send me an email with the details.'

'Thanks. Come in and have a drink,' she suggested as they drove through the gates of the Stalla. 'Ma and Babbo will be so pleased to see you again.'

He looked at his watch. 'I can't, Alba, I'm meeting Beatrice and I'm already late. Another time.' He leant over to hug her before she climbed out.

She listened to the sound of his car as it navigated the bends back up the hill and went inside the stable to tell Ma and Babbo about her afternoon.

In bed that night, her thoughts drifted back to schooldays and Alfiero. They'd been to the cinema in a hilltop town and sat sharing a beer afterwards, discussing the film. They were due to take their final school exams in a month's time, the *Maturità*, and their talk was all about what they would do afterwards.

Alba was having a gap year in England, but Alfi was bound for Bologna University. They were both excited about the next phase of their lives.

It was late when they'd left on the new motorbike that he'd received for his eighteenth birthday, a more powerful machine than the Lambretta scooter he'd used since he was fourteen. The night air had been cool, her leather jacket thin and she'd held onto him tighter to keep warm. As they drove through the tiny villages, the roar of the bike's motor bounced off the stone houses, echoing through the darkness. She'd wondered if the noise would wake anybody. By now, she was tired and envied them their warm, cosy beds. They passed a tiny bar and she made out a group of men still playing cards at a table by the window.

Just before they'd reached the tall bridge spanning the River Presale, an adult boar had dashed across the road in front of them. Alfiero had swerved to avoid the animal and lost control. Alba had screamed, trying to cling to Alfiero, but fell from the pillion onto the tarmac.

He had passed out, pinned beneath the motorbike, its engine still running. She remembered how she'd tried to lift the bike from his body, but she'd hurt her arm and it was impossible. Her phone had smashed onto the tarmac when they'd crashed and just as she was beginning to despair, frightened a fire might start with the petrol leaking from the upturned bike, a car came along and the driver had helped them.

They'd ended up at the *pronto soccorso* at the hospital. He'd broken his right leg and her wrist was badly sprained. Alfi had to wear a plaster cast for several weeks and her arm was in a sling. Their friends had scrawled vulgar messages on his cast and teased them about what they'd been up to on the bike to have ended up in the road.

But they'd never been a couple. They were simply good friends. She'd never fancied him. After their end-of-school exams, he'd suggested they celebrate on the Mountain of the Moon.

'How about we do a night walk up to the *rifugio*?' he'd suggested.

'Cool!' was her response. She'd thought they'd be in a crowd. As it turned out, it was just the two of them. The walk fourteen hundred metres up the mountain was amazing, the scenery stunning, but when they'd reached the top it had begun to rain, a light drizzle at first which turned rapidly to sheets of water. They were about ten minutes away from the mountain hut where they would shelter that night, but by the time they arrived, they were soaked through. Alfiero's leg was hurting and he'd forgotten to bring his painkillers. He was moody, unusual for him, and she'd tried to lighten him up.

'Maybe the rain will stop soon, then we could light a fire and brew up hot chocolate,' she'd suggested. 'I've brought sachets we can add to hot water.'

'If we can find any dry wood,' he'd snapped.

'I saw a few sticks in that lean-to. Let's get changed first into dry clothes and get organised.'

'What dry clothes?'

'Didn't you bring a change? What are you like?'

'I forgot.'

'Well, wrap your sleeping bag around you or something. Use some imagination.' She remembered thinking how useless boys were.

He'd stormed out, still in his wet clothes, and a few minutes later called to her that he'd got a fire going and she went outside to make hot drinks for them. They ate their supper in the *rifugio* watching the flames from the fire, and he'd calmed down eventually. It had been cosy.

But then it had turned awkward. He'd watched her unroll her bedding onto one of the two sleeping benches and climb in.

'Alba,' he'd said.

'Yeah?' She was sleepy. The walk had been hard and steep, and her eyes were drooping with tiredness.

'This has been so cool. I'm glad we ended up being the only ones in the hut.'

'Mm,' she murmured, 'it would have been a bit of a squeeze with more of us.'

There was silence. She was warm and cosy in her sleeping bag, about to drift off to sleep when he spoke again.

'I really wanted you and me to be alone,' he continued.

She was suddenly wide awake. Embarrassed at this turn of events, she blurted out, 'You're not coming on to me, are you, Alfi? That would be just too weird.'

He'd opened the door to the hut and stormed off again. She'd waited for a while, listening to his footsteps tramping about on the wet leaves. She thought if she were a smoker this would be the obvious stressful moment to light up, but she hated the smell of nicotine, so she'd eaten two of Anna's chocolate brownies instead that she'd brought for breakfast the next morning and thought about what she'd say to Alfi once he came back.

After about a quarter of an hour the door was pushed open.

'Don't say anything,' he said as soon as he came through the door. 'Especially don't tell me I'm like a brother to you and you don't fancy me, because I don't want to hear you say anything corny and I kind of know anyway.'

She'd opened her mouth to protest.

'Don't, Alba!' he said. 'Forget I ever said anything.' He sat down on his bench to pull off his boots.

'You can put the jackets over you to keep warm tonight,' she said. 'They're dry now.'

'It's okay. I haven't really forgotten a change of clothes,' he said, pulling them out of his rucksack.

She threw her walking boot at him when he'd owned up to that and he threw back a wet sock, and then they both burst out laughing and the friendly atmosphere between them was back to normal.

All these years later, Alba had almost forgotten about his overture. Funny how seeing him again had brought back those memories.

Her phone bleeped a message. It was from Alfiero, telling her he'd come across the information she needed and he would drive up to see her in a couple of days.

*

The books and papers Alfiero had brought were spread over the scrubbed pine kitchen table in the Stalla. Wearing faded jeans and a black t-shirt, he looked more like the Alfi she remembered from schooldays.

'Look at this photo,' he said, pointing to a page in one of the books. 'Familiar?' He brought up a photo on his mobile phone that she'd sent late last night, to compare.

Swivelling a book round, he showed her an illustration of a dining room in an old house, the table laid for what must have been a special occasion. 'Look at the silverware,' he said. 'Recognise it?'

Alba read the description below the old photo.

Dinner preparations for Il Duce at the Boccarini estate, 1942

The grainy photo in the book showed a long table laid with fine linen and dishes. The goblets at each place were of highly polished silver, unlike the dented, tarnished silverware that she and Davide had found. But they were of identical design.

'It seems that Mussolini was frequently invited to stay at the Boccarini estate. During the war, it became an unofficial headquarters where fascists and militia of the area met,' Alfiero said, pointing to the lines of a long description beneath the photograph. 'The place was bought from the Boccarini family by a Federico Petrelli, who spent shedloads of money refurbishing the house and garden. The Boccarini family had fallen on hard times, and Petrelli enjoyed showing off his new wealth, holding lavish parties before the war. But he turfed out workers who had been employed on the estate for years. He was not a popular man, by all accounts. He died during the war.'

'This is amazing, Alfi. Thank you so much. And for bringing it all this way.'

'I have some work to do in the area anyway. It's no problem,' he said, 'but I must rush now. I'm late.' He bent to kiss her on each cheek, the Italian way, and she caught the scent of his aftershave. 'I'll catch you some time,' he said, his hand resting on her shoulder.

After he'd gone, Alba continued to read through the documents that described a variety of events in the area from the war years. When she came across a couple of pages about the partisans active in the area, she gasped. Her attention was caught by a sepia photo of a group of youngsters, dressed in an assortment of ragged clothes: work overalls, patched trousers, some wearing caps or felt hats, one muffled by a scarf. Somebody had labelled their names on the photographs in crude handwriting. They were all young; one had tousled curls and the look of an angel, his arm slung around an equally young boy sitting next to him on the ground. Some had gun belts across their chests, and they were all armed in one way or another, with axes, knives or guns. In the middle of the group, leaning on crutches, stood a young man, his appearance very familiar to her. She worked out his name from the caption below: Basilio Gelina. She felt a shiver run down her spine as she read some paragraphs beneath the photo that mentioned the house called Seccaroni. The ruins where she and Davide had unearthed the silverware. It was history coming alive.

In November 1943, a group of young, self-styled partisans acquired a few weapons and grenades from the abandoned concentration camp at Renicci, near Anghiari, as well as from infantry stores in the city. At the beginning of December, they transferred to the desolate location of Seccaroni on the Mountain of the Moon.

The group numbered about thirty, but the members constantly changed. They were joined by Slavs, escaped prisoners and deserters. Occasionally, a German deserter would ask to be included. Many of the Slavs left the group because of the men's inexperience and the location, inhospitable in winter, far from possible sources of food.

She bit her lip as she traced her finger down the rest of the description detailing incursions and capturing of weapons; how the group was supplied occasionally with bread by a local miller and helped by an older man, a former guerrilla in the Spanish Civil War, with the composition and distribution of propaganda.

Almost at the end of the description, a few more lines describing individuals in the group caught her eye and her heart began to race.

Each partisan was given a nickname upon joining the group. Basilio Gelina was known as Zoppo by his family on account of his limp, but as Quinto by the partisans, being the fifth member to enrol. On the night of 14 March 1944, the group burst into the farmhouse of Boccarini.

After ordering supper to be served, they left, taking with them food, clothing, linen, a horse and money.

On 18 March, the group disbanded, several of the members bitter about continued infighting. Quinto and a couple of others left the area to join another partisan group, but were never seen again.

She was on her own in the Stalla; her father and stepmother were in Arezzo for the day. But she needed somebody to tell her to stop being ridiculous, because she was experiencing an eerie feeling about the shadow near the ruins. 'You *are* being ridiculous, Alba Starnucci,' she said aloud to herself. Her words echoed in the empty kitchen and she stepped outside for a while to warm up in the sunshine. Pacing about the terrace, she reasoned with herself. Even if she were to tell somebody, she knew her hunch would be met with disbelief and, most likely, laughter. After a while, she went back into the kitchen. She sorted Alfi's papers into a pile and closed the book. Lodovica had a piece of that Boccarini set, too, Alba was convinced of that. How did it all add up? After pulling on her walking boots and fetching her knapsack and sketch pad, she stepped again into the sunny day. A walk would clear her head and straighten her mind.

CHAPTER SEVEN

Tuscany, early 1944

Kapitän Florian Hofstetter plunged into the river, the sky above him a bruise. Raindrops fell on his face as he turned to float on his back, the water like a blessing. He needed to wash from his mind the brutal images of war. Last week, he'd stopped a group of drunken soldiers from his platoon as they tossed a baby girl from one to the other, like a beach ball. The shrieks of the women had alerted him where he sat in the shade of a pine, reading his pocket guide to butterflies and moths. '*Verdammt noch mal...*' he swore as he jumped up and tore into the band of pink-faced youths. 'What the hell do you think you are doing?' He took the baby from an acne-scarred soldier before she was thrown again.

'*You* should know better, Korporal. Get this group in order and report to me later. And do up the buttons on your jacket.'

Florian handed the baby back to her terrified mother.

'Why bother?' one of the soldiers muttered. 'It's only Italian spawn, after all. One less of the enemy for the future.' He spat on the ground.

Florian would deal with them later, once they were sober, but he doubted his own senior officer, Major Schmalz, would have the same attitude. These men would probably get away with little punishment to speak of.

The following day, he had visited the family to see how the baby was. He was given a hand-carved wooden crucifix by the grateful grandfather, who sat on a chair in the fire recess. The grain resembled the outline of Jesus on the cross. Florian nodded his thanks to the old man, shook his hand and accepted it as a peace offering. He planned to keep it in his breast pocket for the rest of the war.

At home in Bavaria, he'd regularly attended Sunday Mass with his family to keep Mutti quiet. A picture of her ample figure in her embroidered dirndl dress and waistcoat came into his mind, Vater in his best breeches and embroidered socks. He wondered how they were doing. Bavaria was staunchly Catholic. This much he had in common with these Italians, but religion hadn't prevented them from switching sides and joining the Allies. They were now at war with each other.

The sun came out, the sky now a clear blue, and he wanted to stay down by the river, but he had to return to headquarters in Badia Tedalda. Floating on his back, he watched white foam plunging from the waterfall, dancing as it fell on the grey-green river, ripples panning out, lapping against bleached stones. Two black-and-jade dragonflies chased each other over the water, skimming the surface. Later, he would jot these sightings in his notebook bound with black leather, a present from Vater before he left for Italy. He would add *Calopteryx virgo*, Beautiful Demoiselle, and maybe try to sketch the lacy wings later from memory. The heaviness of the water as it plummeted drowned out sounds of battle, but his head was polluted with the sickening sights of war: images of women and children bleeding on the cobbles of a piazza in a mountain village, shot simply because a distant relative was a partisan; killed as a warning to innocent, simple peasants trying to survive in their war-torn country. It sickened him. It sickened him too that he did not have the guts to stand up and object. If he did so, his own parents and young brother back in Bavaria would be punished. His university friend, Walter, a conscientious objector, had paid the price when he learned his parents had been shot because of his refusal to fight. Walter had committed suicide not long afterwards. Florian tussled with the question of what should come first: his principles or the lives of three loved ones? It was easier to keep quiet.

At the edge of the pool, flat, round leaves of gunnera fluttered in the breeze and splashes of bright yellow marsh marigolds shone like brushstrokes in an Impressionist painting. In the meadow behind the priest's house, which had been requisitioned by the army for officers' accommodation, he'd spied the rich blue of a single gentian growing in the bank, like those in his own village back home. There were many other new plants he'd discovered on his brief forays into the meadows, and he'd had to consult his battered field guide to identify them.

Climbing out of the water and treading warily over the sharp stones, he sat to lean against a smooth boulder, an ideal support for his back, sore from sleeping on canvas camp beds and carrying heavy guns. The rain stopped and he closed his eyes, the sounds of the river hypnotic.

Just as he started to drift off, he heard the chatter of women. Two middle-aged females and a girl of about eighteen picked their way down the path, carrying bundles and a basket of clothes. The girl wore a green headscarf, a long plait of coal-black hair hanging down her back. The women stopped at the edge of the water where a couple of flat stones lay out of the shallows, and unloaded the clothes. As the girl bent to beat the clothes, her plait kept falling over her shoulder. '*Uffa!*' he heard her exclaim in frustration as she tore the scarf from her head and used it to tie back her heavy plait.

Florian remained perfectly still. They hadn't noticed him against his rock and willow branches obscured him. The women continued with their work, pounding what he realised was laundry for German soldiers. At one point, the girl held up a large shirt, dipped it in a pot of ash, used as soap, and then, laughing, she spat on the garment. The older women spoke harshly, and she shrugged her shoulders, continuing to beat and rinse the shirt. The girl had spirit, Florian thought. If a German soldier had seen her defiling his uniform, she'd be severely punished – shot even. Civilians had been killed for less.

He watched the girl. As she knelt to wash another item in the river, he saw how beautiful she was: her arms golden-brown and smooth, her face oval and her eyes an intense shade of green. *In another time, another place… Damn the war*, he thought. Watching this group of women doing the laundry was such a normal scene, and for a while he could imagine there was no fighting; that he was on holiday in this region that he had toured and fallen in love with before the war.

The art and history of Florence had captivated him, and he would have stayed longer if he hadn't been called back to enlist for his country. He flicked to the back of his notebook and looked at his sketches of the River Arno seen from the Ponte Vecchio, the face of Botticelli's portrayal of Venus, the view of the city from Piazzale Michelangelo. He sighed, cursing inwardly at the latest tasks he had been ordered to carry out: cataloguing artwork removed from churches and estates in this corner of Tuscany. It went against Florian's better instincts; he considered it a kind of rape. The paintings, altar panels, statues and sundry other minor masterpieces piling up in the temporary storeroom – one of the many requisitioned caverns in Badia hewn from the mountainside by peasants for penning their animals – should stay where they belonged, in his opinion. What right did the Third Reich have to plunder these jewels from ancient churches and palazzi? They were termed spoils of war, he knew that, but his heart was not in it, and he had been thinking for a while of how to play some small part to undermine the pillage.

He closed his notebook gently and snatched another few minutes, watching the women at the river's edge until they piled the wet laundry into their baskets and climbed back up the bank. One of the older women carried her load on her head and started to sing, the other two joining in with the chorus, and he felt as though he was watching a scene from an opera play out before him.

It was three o'clock when they left. If he was to report back for duty in time, he would have to hurry. As he passed the spot where they'd worked, he spotted something at the edge of the water. Half concealed by a fern was the green scarf the girl had worn on her head. He picked it up, folded it carefully and put it in his pocket, hoping he might see her again to return it.

The other officers mostly spent their free time in the little bar in the corner of the piazza, ordering wines and liqueurs, enjoying the company of Maddalena, who flirted with them in exchange for cigars for her father or chocolate for her brothers and sisters. Florian preferred to spend some of his time studying his Italian grammar book. He had reached beyond the level of getting by and was eager to increase his fluency. When the weather was fine, he walked in the meadows near the village. It wasn't wise to stray too far. The range of peaks they called the Mountain of the Moon tantalised him in the distance, but he knew it would be folly to venture up there alone. On an earlier walk, he'd found a cluster of rocks studded with fossils: ammonites and shells from when this area had been under the sea. Near the river, he'd found a fish fossil, *Lampanyctus*, a lantern fish, and one day when he had more time, he planned to hew it out with his chisel to add to his other specimens. Once he returned home, he would buy a cabinet where he could exhibit his Tuscan discoveries.

*

About one week later, three hours of free time stretched before him. The weather for the last couple of days had hovered between brilliant sunshine and grey, metallic skies. The weather in the Tuscan Apennines was unpredictable, but he was used to that from his own home near the mountains and lakes. At the last minute, glancing at the mackerel clouds threatening a storm, he'd slung a woollen scarf around his neck and shoved a pair of mittens knitted by Mutti into his deep pockets, before hiking to a spot that he'd been told was rich with fossils. For a while he watched through his binoculars as a honey buzzard soared above him. As he stood still at the edge of a copse, a black squirrel darted out and scampered up a holm oak. He could hear the tinkling of bells from the meadow he was aiming for and as he rounded the dirt road, he came across a flock of a dozen scrawny sheep. They were guarded by a dirty white Maremmano shepherd dog and a girl. The dog started to bark, approaching him, tail in the air, and the girl called out to him to come to her, '*Vieni qua.*' The animal growled and Florian stood still. These dogs were reputed to be ferocious and he didn't fancy being bitten. The girl walked over warily to grab hold of the dog by the scruff of his neck, pulling him back and shouting something he couldn't understand. His knowledge of Italian didn't extend to dialect.

She was dressed in men's clothing: a darned pair of corduroy trousers held up by string, laced-up boots that were too big for her, a threadbare shirt and a scrap of rag tied in her hair. She looked so unlike the carefree girl he'd seen the other day at the river, but it was her unusual emerald eyes that gave her away.

'*Buonasera*, signorina,' he said.

She gave the slightest nod of her head but stayed where she was, holding onto the dog. He hoped she would continue to keep hold of the growling animal. Having come all the way here, he didn't feel like leaving without his fossil and his hand went into his pocket to pull out his chisel. The girl screamed, maybe expecting him to produce a weapon, and she let go of the dog; the creature hurled himself towards Florian, baring his teeth in a vicious snarl.

'*Platz!*' Florian commanded calmly and authoritatively, holding up one hand. The dog hunkered down on all fours in submission. They had shooting dogs at home; he knew how to control them. Dogs needed to be led and Florian was the dog's new leader. When he was sure the dog was sufficiently subdued, he used one of the recent phrases he had learned by heart: '*Cerco dei fossili*. I'm looking for fossils.'

She pointed to some rocks in the corner of the meadow and he made his way over to where swirls of ammonites were embedded in limestone boulders. Halfway there, he remembered her scarf in his pocket and he turned, holding it out to her. She looked in amazement as he thrust it into her hands. '*Grazie,*' she stammered, looking puzzled.

'*Prego*. I found it at the river. *Al fiume.*'

She was shivering. The air was cool, but it could have been fear too that made her tremble and not simply her thin shirt. He unwound the scarf from his neck and offered it to her.

'*No, no,*' she said, shaking her head.

Florian wondered if she expected to grant him some favour in return, so he simply placed it on the grass at her feet. '*Per voi,* signorina,' he said, using the polite form of 'you'. 'For you.'

Her eyes widened and she giggled before bending to pick it up, fingering the fine wool and then wrapping it round her neck. '*Grazie, grazie!*' she said again.

She stayed near to the rocks, watching him with curiosity as he chiselled out a couple of the fossils. He took care to hammer far enough around the specimens so as not to cause damage. Occasionally she turned to check on the sheep, calling a command to the dog when one of them wandered too far away.

'*Lupi*,' she said to Florian, and when he shrugged his shoulders, she mimed the howling of a wolf, which set the dog off, and she laughed. And he laughed too.

Before they parted, Florian went over to the rock where he had removed the fossils and examined the ground. An idea was forming in his head. He would have to be careful in the way he carried out this idea, but in his heart he knew it was the right thing to do.

*

It was easier than Florian had imagined. At headquarters next day, he measured the small golden door to a tabernacle, removed by order of his commander, Major Schmalz, from the front of a fixed box used for housing consecrated hosts, near the altar of the abbey church. It was almost thirty centimetres square. Choosing the moment carefully and working in the far corner of the cavernous storeroom, his heart pounding in case he was discovered, he pretended to bend to retrieve a rag he'd been using to polish the metal and instead slipped the precious door into his knapsack. Standing up again, hunched over his work to cover what he was doing, he wrapped a block of wood of the same dimensions in a piece of sacking, adding an extra layer of oilcloth before securing the package with cord and labelling it. In his neat handwriting, he wrote the details in the vellum ledger that listed all the purloined artwork. *Item 67: one gold-plated tabernacle door, highly decorative. Purported to be the work of Cellini. Sixteenth century. Location: twelfth-century abbey church of St Michael the Archangel, Badia Tedalda.*

For the rest of his shift, he behaved himself. He wrapped up and listed three rather ugly eighteenth-century oil paintings by an unknown artist, an ornate silver chandelier and a delicate china coffee service taken from the *sindaco*'s house. All the while, as he chatted to the two other soldiers in the storeroom, he assessed the items that he could realistically squirrel out and rescue in the future. He had his eye on a small and charming intricate piece from a larger altar panel that had been plundered from a country church in a mountain village. It was known as a *predella*. The compact images of the Madonna and Child were exquisitely sculpted and fired in glazed ceramic. He thought it probably dated from the early sixteenth century. It felt so wrong to Florian that his countrymen should be stealing pieces of Italian heritage to ship abroad. His quest was to ensure that one day at least some of these works would be returned to where they belonged. Anything he removed would have to fit easily into his knapsack, together with the fossil tools he always carried with him and his butterfly net. This would be his cover, his excuse to escape into the countryside to hide the loot.

*

He wanted to see the girl again. When he returned to the meadow in his free time the following week, he brought a slab of dark chocolate marzipan that Mutti had sent him in her latest parcel, and a couple of bananas from the officers' canteen. She accepted them with a smile and told him she had never tried a banana before and would take the gifts home to share with her family. He had something else in his knapsack, but it would remain there until he was alone.

On that day, the sun was high in the sky and they sat together for a while in the shade of a majestic oak while the sheep grazed, their tinkling bells reminiscent to Florian of the sounds of the flocks on his own Bavarian mountains. He pressed tobacco into his pipe and puffed smoke into the air.

'*Il vostro nome?*' he asked, once again using the formal 'you' to ask her name, and she corrected him, saying he could use *tu* – she was only a shepherdess, a simple girl.

'If I can say *tu* to you,' he said, 'then you must do the same to me.' He was pleased he could communicate successfully. And it was much more agreeable than talking to his textbook. When she smiled, she was truly beautiful. She reminded him of a Renaissance painting by Raphael he'd seen in the Palazzo Pitti. He longed for a time when he could return to visit Florence at leisure, as soon as this war was over.

'My name is Lucia, and yours?'

'Florian.'

She plucked a daisy from the grass next to her and shyly handed it to him. '*Fiore*, flower,' she said. 'Like Florian.'

He had never thought of his name like that, and he liked it. Mutti had christened him after Saint Florian, not a flower.

'And your name means "light",' he said. She nodded and smiled.

The tree was encircled with stinging nettles and she began to gather young, tender ones, using her green headscarf as a kind of glove to protect herself from the stings. He handed her the mittens from his knapsack and she smiled.

'Mamma is making gnocchi tonight. She asked me to pick these to add to them. *Buoni, buoni*,' she said, making a gesture with her index finger held against her cheek. He'd read it was a way of saying something was delicious, but he'd never seen it done before and he copied her.

'Maybe next time Mamma cooks gnocchi, I could save some for my lunch up here, and then you can try them.'

He smiled at the offer and watched her as she continued to collect the nettles, moving gracefully from clump to clump, her long plait swinging as she moved. He wondered what it would be like to free her hair and run his fingers through it. Then she came to sit near him for a few more minutes and he pulled a photo from one of the pockets in his shirt. He felt her breath on his face as she leant in to look. Her eyelashes were long, her skin olive and smooth and he wanted to kiss her. Instead, he pointed out his mother and father standing in front of their summer house in Bavaria. '*Mama und Papa*,' he said. 'Like in Italian. And we also eat gnocchi, but we call them *Knödel*. My favourite is *Schweinbraten mit Knödel*.'

She wrinkled her brow and, giggling, tried to repeat the difficult words and he smiled. '*Schweinbraten* is like your *porchetta*,' and he made a noise like a pig grunting. They were very easy with each other, and the war felt distant as they laughed together. Then she fetched a small basket she had left by the rock and showed him mushrooms that she had collected that morning.

'*Pfifferlinge*,' he said, correctly identifying the chanterelles that also grew in the countryside in his homeland.

Again, she tried to copy the word, stumbling over her efforts. 'We call them *girolle* or *gallinacci*. They are my favourite. *Buoni*,' she said, rubbing her stomach, 'with olive oil and parsley.'

He loved the wholesomeness of her, could have spent all afternoon and evening in her company, but it would soon be time to report for duty. He stood up to go and took her hand in his, bowing his head. '*Auf Wiedersehen*. It is the same meaning as *arrivederci*. Maybe we could meet again?'

He turned to wave before the road curved, but she had already moved on with her flock. Only the dog stared back. When he reached the rock where they had sat together the first time, he looked around to check he was alone. He examined his compass and measured five paces to the south and began to dig a hole with his fossil chisel. It was hard work. He would have to get hold of a small spade for next time. When he was sure the hole was deep enough, from his knapsack he pulled the biscuit tin his mother had sent to him. Making sure the lid was firmly closed on the precious tabernacle door inside, he placed the tin in the bottom of the hole and covered it with earth. There was the usual pile of stones at the corner of the meadow, removed before ploughing, and he used half a dozen of these to cover the fresh patch.

When he was sure he had left no signs of his work, and before he forgot, he wrote 'S5' on an empty page of his notebook. His spirit felt lighter as he hurried back to headquarters, not only because he was enchanted with Lucia, but because he had set a plan in motion to right some of the wrongs done by his fellow countrymen. It was a beginning. That evening, he sketched the rock from memory onto the page of his notebook where he had written S5 and picked up the ammonite to copy, finishing with a signature of Cellini in the corner. If anybody were to pick up his notebook and flick through, they would find sketches of his visit to Florence as well as insects, plants, fossils and landscapes. Portraits of Italy. But for Florian, it was the first clue on his treasure map.

*

The next time Florian and Lucia met, his knapsack contained another gift. Her face lit up when he showed it to her. 'My mother sent me this sweater for winter nights,' he said. 'But I don't need it, Lucia. Will this do?'

He watched her finger the soft cashmere.

'It is *bellissima*. I haven't seen anything so special.'

She smiled at him, hugging the garment to herself before pulling it over her head. 'What do you think?' she asked him as she did a twirl. 'It's too big, and it's obviously a man's, but I could embroider flowers on the cuffs and round the neck, and it will be so warm.'

Then her face fell, and she pulled it off, handing it back. 'I can't possibly wear this. What am I thinking? My parents will ask me how I got it.' She stuffed it back into his hands.

'It is such a shame. I would love to wear something so fine,' she continued, plucking at the shirt she wore. 'Mamma made this for me from one of my brother's. And for the winter months, she adapted a coat from an old blanket. But it's so thick, and it scratches my legs when I walk.'

Florian looked down at her bare legs and the wooden clogs she wore today instead of the ugly men's boots. A strip of material covered the toes, presumably to make them resemble shoes. He noticed she was wearing the green headscarf he'd returned to her.

He held the sweater out. 'Hide it somewhere. It may be useful to you one day, Lucia.'

'No,' she said, throwing it down as if it scalded.

The woollen garment lay between them on the grass, a symbol of the impossibility of their forbidden friendship; a simple thing made difficult.

He picked it up and replaced it in his knapsack.

'How long do you have today?' he asked.

'Longer than usual. My parents have gone to market. Not that they have much to sell.' She looked at him. 'Your people take everything from us to feed themselves. We do the work and you reap the rewards. Not that it was much different before you came. The rich and powerful always take from the poor. If I ruled the world, I'd make sure there was justice. I wanted to study at high school, but my parents made me stay at home. My brother was allowed, but he's dead now. What was the point of all that? I wish I'd been born a man.'

'I'm very glad you're not a man,' Florian said, a shy smile on his lips.

She blushed, but she was still angry.

'The men and boys are all gone now, because of your stupid war,' she continued. 'We women and old men do the haymaking and ploughing now… when we can get to the fields. Nobody ever knows what you *Tedeschi* will order us to do next: "Cut the hay for our horses", "No working in the fields this week", "Clear this area – it is needed for trenches". All these commands mean there's no longer any rhythm to our farming. Crops are strangled by weeds and left to wither in the fields. If we disobey commands and slip out to hoe, we are shot on the spot. The war has changed everything.' She looked at him. 'I don't even know why I am talking to you…'

She got up to go but he pulled at her arm. 'I'm so sorry. *Entschuldigung, mädchen*. Please stay.'

She flopped down again on the grass, plucking at strands. Despite everything, she wanted to spend time with this man who was her enemy. There was silence between them, the sounds of the bells on her sheep filling the space.

'Let me show you one of my special places,' she said eventually. 'It's not far. Let me go first to make sure there is nobody else around. I'll whistle when it's all right for you to follow. The sheep will come too, but that's best – anybody watching will think I'm leading them to the next pasture. Be sure to keep to the edge of the wood and not walk across the open meadow. We don't want to be seen together.'

He sat under a beech tree in the shade and waited for her signal, looking around, all the while scouring for another suitable hiding place. A cannon boomed somewhere further down in the valley towards Rimini. It was like the distant rumble of thunder. Up until now, there had been little exchange of gunfire up here, but he knew it wouldn't stay that way for long. The Allies were making progress, despite Hitler's orders to extend the defensive line across the mountains.

A low whistle interrupted his thoughts, followed by the tinkling of half a dozen bells as the small flock gambolled over the grass towards Lucia. As he passed the edge of the wood, a cock pheasant flew up and he ducked to the grass, his heart pounding. For a while he lay still, his nerves shot. An ant crawled over his nose and he smacked it away. Then another piercing whistle sent him into a spin again. What if the girl had set a trap and summoned partisans to finish him off? After all, he hardly knew her. Could she be trusted? When he lifted his head, there was no volley of guns; just the beautiful vision of Lucia hurrying over, the dog trotting at her heels.

'Are you hurt?' she asked.

He stood up and brushed grass and earth from his trousers. 'I'm fine. Fine. I tripped, that's all.'

'Come on, then. There's nobody around. It's safe.'

She led him to a corner of a field where steam rose into the air like a stage effect he'd seen at the theatre.

He chuckled. 'A hot spring. I didn't know there were any in this part of Tuscany. Near Siena, yes. But not here.'

'Very few know about this place.' She wrinkled her nose. 'I don't like the smell, but in winter it's magical to sit in the water, snow on the ground, and to feel warm. We used to bring Nonna to ease her arthritis. But nobody has ventured here for a long while.'

'Then when this war is over, we can return when it snows, and we will drink wine and dine up here together. How about that? What would you choose to eat, Lucia?'

She laughed. 'I've forgotten what good food tastes like. I even dream about food sometimes.' She closed her eyes and then spoke in a dreamy voice: 'Roast suckling pig with garlic and rosemary, potatoes baked in good olive oil. My nonna's delicious ciabatta. And gelato… We went to the sea at Riccione before the war and I ate my first ice cream there: *pistacchio*… And you? What kind of food do you eat in your country?'

They talked for another half hour. Or at least, Lucia did most of the talking while he listened. He told himself that it was because he wanted to learn more Italian, but he knew he was kidding himself: he wanted to spend more time with this girl. Lucia brought out a tenderness in him that he thought the war had killed. A stone had fallen from his heart. He was late reporting back for duty that afternoon, but he had found hiding place number two for his treasure map.

CHAPTER EIGHT

Tuscany, present day

Alba took a little-used path to Tramarecchia. It was obvious nobody had come this way for a while: a stony track soon changed to an overgrown path, brambles snagging at her fleece, and she was glad she'd brought along secateurs at the last minute, as her father had suggested. The thread from a cobweb brushed her cheek and she snatched it away from her face. She pushed her way through a juniper bush, the straggly thorns catching on her sleeve. And then she realised James hadn't entered her head at all that morning. Instead, her thoughts were full of the partisans' house and the silverware. How life had changed.

James hadn't enjoyed walking. He'd resented her disappearing from his bed to Richmond Park on a Sunday morning, wanting her to stay in, to make love and read the newspaper afterwards. But after a week of travelling on the Tube to work, breathing in the sooty underground odour, crammed up against sometimes sweaty men – the negative side to London – she needed to escape to a park and pretend she was in the countryside. Eventually, she'd given in to him. How many times had she done that? How far had she strayed from being her true self? Part of her felt a pang of guilt for thinking ill of him now he was dead. But his loss had helped her look back with perspective, rather than with rose-tinted spectacles. The unkempt path met with a wider path and a drystone wall, crumbling in parts and overgrown with ferns, lined the sides. Every now and again she heard a dog bark and voices and laughter drift in her direction.

She passed a blue sign indicating the village of Tramarecchia and descended a steep, stony track wide enough for a vehicle. There were fresh tyre marks in the mud. Beneath her she saw a huddle of stone houses built around a small grassy square, and in the middle a series of three traditional rectangular water troughs used in the past by women to do their washing. She wondered how many conversations had been exchanged at these places, how many secrets and sorrows.

The front door and window frames and shutters of the square house were painted bright red, and it was from behind here that the voices were coming. She had believed the hamlet to be uninhabited and, curious, she made her way to the back of the house. A very old man, no taller than five foot, had his back to her as he pruned a fig tree. His companion, a blonde of about forty, steadied his ladder. She spoke Italian with a foreign accent and Alba guessed she was Eastern European, and most likely his carer. So many families needed help nowadays with the elderly. Whereas in the past members of the extended family would take turns to keep an eye on their loved ones, today families were smaller, and scattered. There was little work in the area for youngsters and they moved away.

The woman was urging him to be careful, not to fall or cut himself.

'Oh, Tanya, Tanya, I could do this in my sleep. If you only knew the work that I have done in the past…'

'*Buongiorno*,' Alba said.

They turned to her in suspicion and mumbled an uninterested *buongiorno* in response.

'Is this Tramarecchia?' she asked.

'*Sì*.' They stared at her coldly.

'What do you want?' the old man asked abruptly. And then she recognised the elderly man who had joined them on Christmas Day.

'*Ciao*, signor Massimo. Don't you remember me? You came to our house – I'm Alba. We've already met.'

'*Ah, mi scusi*, signorina. Of course,' he said, slowly climbing down the ladder. 'Without my glasses I can't see far. *Mi scusi, mi scusi*.' He came over and grasped her hand. His grip was surprisingly strong. 'But what are you doing in our little hamlet?'

'I'm helping Egidio at the tourist office. He has a project about ruins in the area and I'm exploring.' She took in a couple of dilapidated houses and the crumbling wall of a house long gone. 'Do you mind if I sit for a while and draw?'

The old man laughed. 'Eeee! Why here? You should go to Sansepolcro and draw the monuments down there.'

The woman said, 'Don't be rude, Massimo. Let her be.'

'But if Egidio has asked you, that's fine. He's a good man. And, you're not a robber,' Massimo said.

'No, I'm definitely not a robber,' Alba said, thinking to herself that there couldn't possibly be anything to steal here.

'Somebody managed to remove a heavy wardrobe from Robertino's old place,' the elderly man told her, pointing to a neighbouring house that was locked up. 'I was going to put bars at my windows, but then I thought it might attract thieves. There is nothing precious in my house.' He paused before adding, 'Except my memories.'

'The ruin over there,' Alba said, pointing to an old tower, 'what is it?'

'An old watchtower.' The old man took her arm and guided her to the edge of his plot, strangled with nettles and couch grass, and pointed to a village on the opposite peak. 'Up there is Montebotolino. That's where you should go and draw your pictures. It has an ancient church and the remains of a castle. The people of Tramarecchia were enemies of Montebotolino, and they built this tower to spy on them.'

'I know Montebotolino well,' Alba said. 'My step-grandfather lived there, and I often slept at his house when he was alive. Did you know Danilo Starnucci? He was also known as Capriolo.'

A smile transformed the old man's face and he grasped Alba's hand, shaking it firmly. 'Danilo's granddaughter, eh! But, why did nobody tell me? He was a good man, a brave *partigiano*, one of the best.' He kissed Alba's hand. 'I am proud to know a relative of Danilo Starnucci.' He turned to the woman at his side. 'Tanya, do we have any of that Vin Santo left in my kitchen? This calls for a celebration.'

'Any excuse,' Tanya laughed, and disappeared through the back entrance of the red house.

To Alba's utter astonishment, Massimo started to speak to her in almost perfect English. 'I remember the story well about your nonno Danilo finding his *inglesina*, his English daughter.'

'You speak English?'

'Yes, I speak English.'

She looked puzzled. 'But why didn't you tell us when you came on Christmas Day?'

'Nobody told me you were Danilo's family. When Tanya returns with the Vin Santo, I shall explain why I know English… if she hasn't drunk it all in the kitchen first.'

Tanya reappeared with three plastic tumblers of sweet fortified wine.

'Any relative of Danilo's is welcome at my house any time,' Massimo said.

'You're speaking *inglese* again, Massimo,' Tanya said. She turned to Alba. 'I don't understand a word. He uses it when he wants to be stubborn or if he's angry and feels like swearing.'

Turning to Massimo, she said, 'I'll leave you with this signorina for ten minutes and go for a walk to the river. Then you can talk in your *inglese*. Behave, now!' She wagged her finger at the old man, and he waved her off with an English 'Goodbye.'

When she was a few metres away, he said, 'She's not a bad girl, and I'm lucky she accompanies me here so I can visit my old house, but she talks too much. I don't want to hear all the details about her family back in Kiev. I prefer silence. In the care centre in Badia there is too much tittle-tattle, too many bells to tell us about mealtimes, times for Mass, time to go to bed. They even tell me when to pee. Bloody hell,' he swore in English, and Alba laughed.

'I think your English is better than mine,' she said. 'My stepmother tries to get us to speak in English as often as possible, but Italian is my first language.'

'Do you mind if I speak in English?'

'Of course not. But why do you speak it so well?'

'I ended up in a prisoner-of-war camp in Suffolk, so of course I speak *inglese*.'

'Really?'

'The British captured us very early in the war, in Libya, in 1941 and imprisoned us in a place called Mersa Matruh, in Egypt. The war took me halfway around the world, you know. That was enough travelling for me for one life.'

'I've never been to Africa, but my father has. He worked there when he was young.'

'Was he in the desert like me?'

'I don't think so.'

'The desert could be beautiful. When the weather was calm, the sand was golden and like a furrowed field. I remember coming across a single desert flower one day, and there was an oasis, shimmering in the sun, and the sky as blue as ours.' He gestured to the sky, clear today. 'But when the storms blew the sand around, it got everywhere. Our tents flapped as if they would fly away, and sand got into our mouths, ears, nostrils and everything tasted of the stuff. *Bah!*'

He paused for a few seconds, as if his mind was back in 1941, and she waited patiently for him to continue. In the distance, from the meadows below Montebotolino, she could hear the bells from Chianina cattle grazing on the new spring grass.

'And all that was without having to contend with the war,' he said after a while. 'I'd gone to Libya on military service in 1939 before Italy joined the war, and it wasn't too bad then. We had food shipped out to us at the beginning: olive oil, pasta, our vegetables, vacuum-packed and dehydrated, because nothing grew in that parched land. They even sent bottled water. Being by the sea, we went swimming in our free time. I was only seventeen. It seemed like a holiday to me, but then the war came.' He stopped.

'Don't talk about it if you don't want to, Massimo,' she said.

'I don't mind, signorina Alba. If you don't mind listening to an old man.'

'I love hearing about the past.'

'When flares lit up the sky at night, I tried to pretend they were fireworks, but of course they weren't. We were on the front line, our artillery always under attack. We learned very quickly that our equipment was inferior to the Allies', and on the second of January 1941, we were taken prisoner.'

'You remember the date so precisely.'

'It was the day after *Capodanno*, but how could we celebrate New Year? We were exhausted, our supplies had stopped coming and we had no water. The only thing we had plenty of was cigars and cigarettes.'

He pulled out a packet of Marlboro and offered one to Alba, which she declined. After he'd lit up and taken his first puff, he said, 'In many ways, I was pleased to be rescued from those conditions. And I know my comrades felt the same. I'm not ashamed to tell you that.'

'Were you treated all right?'

He paused before answering. Alba wondered if he was sifting through bad memories.

'We were walked for two days and two nights to Solum,' he said eventually, 'and then put on a ship for another night until we reached Alexandria. Then Port Said, and eventually Johannesburg. By then, we were five or six thousand. That was the beginning of prison for me for the next few years. I started off in a tent for twenty months in South Africa, after the guards had taken our clothes to burn. We were full of fleas and lice and they dipped us like sheep into disinfectant, and made us stay naked for twenty-four hours. We roasted under the sun and shivered in the freezing night. Then we were issued with clothes patched with bright colours, to show we were prisoners. Each day we were given half a litre of water and a handful of boiled maize. One of the prisoners tried to drink camel urine, he was so thirsty, but I never tried that.'

Massimo paused and stared into the distance.

'I finished my war in Suffolk, where conditions were better. So, you can maybe appreciate why I love to come here to my own place in Tramarecchia. Freedom is precious, Alba.'

'I can't believe what you're telling me, Massimo, in the middle of the Italian countryside, in this tiny hamlet. What a story!'

'I was a very young man when I left here, Alba, but I felt one hundred years old when I returned.'

She looked at his wizened face, thinking back to Christmas Day; how she'd thought he was a frail old man with nothing much to talk about.

'Would you mind if I sketched you sitting in front of your house?'

'Of course not, my darling. Just make me look young and dashing, and give me more teeth,' he said, with a twinkle in his eye. 'Once upon a time, I was handsome.'

It was his hands she concentrated on. Tiny but strong, the fingers blunt, nails cracked and hardened from years of work. While she sketched, he told her how the English had been good to him, despite it being wartime.

'The couple I worked for were elderly. They'd met each other when they were in their late fifties and they had no children, so by the end of my time there, I was like the son they never had. In fact, Mr and Mrs Spink asked me to stay on in Suffolk at the close of the war to work on their farm, but I couldn't.'

She sensed regret in his voice. 'Was that a difficult decision, Massimo?'

She pencilled in details of the fig tree growing up the side of his house and a bucket planted with flat-leaf parsley by the back step.

'I had a girl in Suffolk who was sweet on me. Her name was Molly,' he said, his voice gentle. 'But I had a sweetheart back here, too, called Lucia… and I came back for her.'

'Were you a bit of a ladies' man?' Alba teased.

His mood had changed from the twinkly humour of earlier. 'Perhaps I will tell you all about it another time.'

Massimo looked tired, and she didn't want to put strain on the old man. 'I'd love that.'

'Come and visit me at the care centre in Badia. I'm not often able to come here, unfortunately. It depends how busy Tanya is.'

'Maybe I could bring you myself? If I borrowed Babbo's car.'

His face lit up again. 'Here comes Tanya. Maybe she can sort it for us.'

Before the pair left to go up the track to wait for the *comune* minibus to take them back to the centre, Tanya took Alba's mobile number and promised to get back to her about arrangements.

'You will have to come in and check with the manageress,' Tanya said, 'but I'm sure it will be fine. In fact, it will spare me from coming here, and it will do Massimo good. He's always happier when he's here, aren't you, my love?'

She linked arms with her charge and Massimo reached for Alba's hands to squeeze them. 'See you soon.' He sang the lines from an old English war song: '"We'll meet again, don't know where, don't know when…"' and Alba smiled.

She stayed another quarter of an hour, wandering around the ruined hamlet, drawing details of an old lamp, a step worn from the tread of hundreds of feet, an old door, the green paint flaking off to reveal brown underneath, a rose bush sprouting its first tight, scarlet buds. She tried to imagine the place busy, with children playing in the little square, women singing at the fountain while washing clothes or sprinkling grains of maize for the chickens that scratched around. But the pictures wouldn't come, and the only sound was the wind as it played with the trees, their branches in need of pruning after years of neglect.

Packing up her pencil and pad into her rucksack and zipping up her jacket, she walked home, lines of light from the setting sun glinting through the branches of the coppiced beech on either side of the path.

It had been a good afternoon. The paths she was treading were like arteries leading to the heart of new stories to explore. The ruins along the way hinted at lives once lived, and she was curious to learn more.

*

Ten days later, Alba and Massimo bumped along in her dad's old Fiat Punto down the dirt track to Tramarecchia. As they arrived at the red house the old man drew in a lungful of air. '*Casa mia*,' he said, continuing in a mixture of English and Italian. 'I feel

free here. I have no family left to look after me in my own home
and my doctor won't permit me to live here alone.' He patted
his heart. 'This fellow is not as strong as he used to be. He has
seen too much, maybe.'

He unlocked the door. 'Will you help me open the windows
to air my palace, Alba? I can't reach some of the handles now.
I've shrunk even more.' He laughed. 'My name should really be
Minimo.'

Alba laughed. It had been the first thing she'd thought when
she'd seen him at Christmas. His name, meaning 'biggest', was
not fitting at all; he was short even by Italian standards.

Entering his house was like stepping into the pages of a
children's illustrated storybook. Blackened pots and pans hung
from a dresser in the small kitchen, and an old wood-burning
stove for cooking stood in the corner. A square table and two
chairs took up the centre of the room, and an easy chair sat by
the side of a fireplace that extended across one end of the room,
the hearth sooty from years of smoke.

A room at the back of the house served as a storeroom, with
buckets, baskets and besom brooms, and a modern fridge-
freezer that looked out of place with the rest of the old things.
Upstairs, two bedrooms were furnished with dark chestnut wood
wardrobes and narrow metal beds, the bedheads painted with
flowers and leaves, crucifixes hanging on the walls above. Tucked
in the corner of the bathroom, tiled from floor to ceiling in old-
fashioned 1960s floral patterns, was the tiniest bath she had ever
seen, only slightly bigger than a washbasin. A primitive cylindrical
wood-burning stove for heating water stood in the other corner.
Massimo proudly pointed out the modernisations he'd made to
the house, including the stone staircase and the bathroom lined
with pine boards. 'Before this, we used to water the fields,' he
said. 'Or kept a bucket in the corner of the bedroom.'

'It's all so cute,' Alba said, opening the shutters to a view of the mountains covered in forest. 'Have you always lived here alone?'

'I lived here with my wife until she died. Twenty-four years I've been without her.'

He sighed. 'Let's go out in the open, and I'll tell you some more of my story.'

CHAPTER NINE

For the three hundred Italian prisoners, it was a long, perilous journey from Africa to Liverpool, the danger of torpedoes ever-present. Massimo was violently seasick and was looked after by Salvatore, who came from the island of Sardinia. The pair had struck up an instant friendship on board the packed ship and Salvatore, or Salvo as he preferred to be called, always made sure to find a place next to Massimo.

'Leave it to me,' was Salvo's byword. He was a wheeler-dealer, having traded in donkeys back in his home town of Oristano. He somehow always managed to procure the largest helpings when watery portions of potato soup were slopped onto their metal plates, and one day he proudly produced two tin mugs of real, strong coffee, winking at Massimo when he asked in amazement where he had managed to find it. 'Ask me no questions,' Salvo had said, tapping his nose. 'Just knock it back and pretend you are in a posh bar in *Italia*, watching the pretty signorine walk by.'

One evening, when the sea was calmer and Massimo's stomach felt less queasy, they played a couple of rounds of *briscola* with cards made by a friend of Salvo's from thin cardboard, the images of swords, knaves, feathers and cups skilfully painted by hand.

'I wonder where we will all end up,' Massimo mused.

'At least we know we're going to *Gran Bretagna*, and we'll be on the same continent as *Italia*,' Salvo replied, shuffling the cards and expertly dealing.

'Anywhere has to be better than Africa. I don't think I could look at another potato or endure another sandstorm.'

'Ah, but you and I both know we would eat anything if we had to,' Salvo said, slapping down a trump to win the trick.

Peering under the flapping tarpaulin as their truck bumped over a country road in the middle of the Suffolk countryside, Massimo and Salvo observed the damp green landscape.

'It's not so different from our own mountain weather,' Massimo said. 'But the countryside is so flat.' He gazed over fields of corn waiting to be harvested, a squat, square church tower in the distance, thatched houses huddled nearby. The sky, full of billowing clouds, seemed to bear down on the horizon; there were no peaks of mountains to break up the skyline.

The truck overtook a girl on a bike and there were whistles and catcalls from the prisoners. '*Bella ragazza*,' they shouted, waving as the truck passed her. She wobbled and put one foot down to steady herself, shaking her fist when the wheels splashed puddle water onto her legs.

'At least the women aren't covered from head to toe here, like in Libya,' Salvo said.

'But we'll still be prisoners, remember? Maybe it would be better if they *were* covered up.'

It was all bravado and swagger. Massimo had little experience of women. Having enlisted at barely eighteen, the war curtailed any possible love life. Lucia was the only girl he had tried to kiss. Everybody had expected them to marry when they were older, but the outbreak of war had put an end to that plan.

The men were tipped out of the truck inside a camp holding about fifty huts arranged in rows, encircled by a low perimeter fence, a single soldier guarding the gate. In Johannesburg, the camp where Massimo had been confined temporarily had held six thousand men; there had been two rings of high fencing and an armed guard stationed every fifty metres. But even if the prisoners had wanted to flee, there'd been miles of desert to confront.

The camp was run by Major Strickland, a portly man in his late fifties. He cut a fatherly figure, but he also had an iron will. In passable Italian he gave an introductory speech as the men shuffled into lines on the makeshift football pitch in front of mixed rows of Nissen and army huts.

'Welcome, all of you, to Suffolk. We shall get along just fine if you stick to my rules. I'm looking for men who have laboured on farms to participate in our agricultural war scheme, and anybody willing to learn if they haven't. You'll be taken each day by truck to work on local farms and returned here before nightfall. We have a strict curfew. Anybody who misses the truck and is found to be without their work permit will be punished. We also have a carpentry business on site, making toys and small items of furniture.

'Each prisoner will be issued with one packet of cigarettes a week and paid five pennies a day if he chooses to stay in camp. Those who are chosen to work outside can earn more and will be known as co-operators.

'Nobody is permitted to enter village shops or private houses, and neither are you permitted to receive money or gifts. We have a mobile shop that comes to camp regularly, and so you will be able to buy extra cigarettes or other goods from this facility. Parcels from home can be received via the Red Cross and there are strict limitations on the contents, but your families will be informed of those conditions.

'You may write home twice a month to your families, but you will leave the envelopes unsealed for censorship purposes. Naturally you will pay postage, and you should be aware that it may take months to receive a reply.

'Now get yourselves settled into your huts, and after a warm drink you'll have showers and be issued with prison clothes.' The commandant finished his speech.

The clothes they were wearing were taken from them and burned because of infestation. Their new camp uniform consisted of brown trousers and a shirt with a large red circle sewn on the back. There could be no mistaking them for ordinary civilians once they were outside the camp.

*

Massimo was assigned to a large farm belonging to a couple in their late fifties. Mr and Mrs Spink spoke slowly to Massimo on his first morning and were pleased when he replied in English.

'I learn in Africa,' he explained. 'I use book. *English in Three Months*. Is very difficult but... slowly, slowly.'

In fact, it wasn't hard for Massimo to pick up Mr Spink's instructions. Over the following months, Massimo carried out the same work he'd done as a child in Tuscany with his father and brothers: hedging, ditching, caring for cows and sheep. He knew how to deal with foot rot and eye infections, and saved the farmer a bob or two in vet fees.

Mrs Spink was a good cook and Massimo began to fill out on her rabbit stews and pies filled with plums and apples bottled from her large orchard. There were hens scratching in the yard and occasionally she gave him a dozen eggs to take back to the camp.

'For your breakfasts,' she said, placing them carefully in a brown paper bag. When he took one out there and then and pierced a hole in the top of the shell to suck out the raw egg, she threw up her hands in horror. 'My giddy aunt,' she said, 'how could you?'

'Is very good.' He patted his stomach. 'Good for the stomach. My mother, she always give me when I little.'

'When I *was* little,' Mrs Spink corrected. 'Rather you than me. Oh, my giddy, giddy aunt.'

'Excuse me? Giddy? Aunt?' Massimo asked, and she laughed.

'Just an expression, boy. We don't eat eggs raw in England.'

'One day I make you pasta from your eggs,' he said. 'Very good. Lasagne, tagliatelle, *strozzapreti*.' He brought the tips of his fingers to his mouth and made a kissing noise.

'We'll see,' she said.

It was no holiday camp, but some of the guards were more tolerant than others. On Sundays, when Major Strickland granted permission, the men were sometimes allowed out for a couple of hours. On one of these free days, Massimo introduced the Spinks to Salvo. Together they took over the farm kitchen and prepared home-made tagliatelle with a sauce made from tomatoes and hare.

Mrs Spink sat in the corner of her kitchen, arms crossed over her large bosom, telling them where to find utensils, watching them as they mixed eggs and flour and rolled it out on her scrubbed pine table.

'Oh, my giddy aunt, what are you up to?' she asked as they cut the thin dough into ribbons and hung them to dry on her wooden clothes horse. 'Looks like tapeworms,' she laughed. 'Don't know if we'll get my Arthur to eat that stuff.'

But eat it they both did, mopping up the delicious sauce with hunks of Mrs Spink's home-baked bread. Salvo had produced a bottle of wine from under his shirt to accompany the meal.

'Well, you can come again, young man,' she said, patting her stomach.

'Does he do farm work too?' Arthur Spink asked Massimo, adding, 'That be a pity,' when Massimo told him no.

On the way back to camp, Massimo asked Salvo where he had found the wine.

'Let's just say I haven't been to Mass for years, so I calculated I was owed the Communion wine I'd not taken all that time. And that amounted to a bottle, which I found in a box at the back of the chapel,' Salvo said.

'Let's hope Andreucci doesn't find out it was you. He can be a nasty piece of work.'

The foreman for the chapel construction was a conundrum, showing moments of spite followed by good humour. He still proclaimed that *Il Duce*, as Mussolini was known, reigned supreme and would win the war. He considered anybody working outside the camp for the *inglesi* as a traitor to Italy, on the side of the enemy, and he knew Salvo was friendly with Massimo. They were both classified as co-operators.

'I think Andreucci is sometimes more worried about reprisals on his family in Livorno than being loyal to the *Duce*,' Salvo said. 'His father is high up in the Fascist party and if he got to hear about his son co-operating, there'd be big trouble.'

'Him and most of us, I'd say,' was Massimo's reply. 'Nobody really knows where anybody stands in this war. Best to keep in his good books.'

There were occasional spats in camp when a co-operator would find his clothes shoved into the latrine pit or his food spoiled by urine, but this didn't happen often. The men were tired of war, and life in the British camp was peaceful compared to the ordeals they had been through in the Africa campaign.

At Christmas in the camp, a candelabra made from discarded food tins was lit at Midnight Mass, with candle stubs the men had saved. The chapel was packed with believers and non-believers alike. For an hour they sang and prayed together, feeling a connection with their loved ones back home in Italy worshipping in their own churches, sure that they in turn would be thinking of their missing brothers, husbands and sons.

After the festive period, Massimo was allowed to move permanently from the camp to a room in the stables at the Spinks' farm. He was not the only co-operator allowed to do this. These farm labourers had to report once a week to the camp and there were still strict rules about fraternisation. 'Makes no sense you taking up room in that truck, being fetched and carried each day,' Mr Spink had said. 'Waste of fuel. How about I go and talk to Major Strickland? What about your friend Salvo? Could he be persuaded to muck in, do you think? I could do with extra hands for clearing ditches.'

Salvo didn't need to be asked twice, the lure of relative freedom easy compensation for blisters on the hands and an aching back after a day's unaccustomed work in the open. In addition, the pair earned more. Their allowance went up and they could also earn overtime at one shilling per hour, to rise to one shilling and three pennies. Mr Spink issued them with rubber boots, and they ate three square meals a day.

Mrs Spink set about sorting spare furniture and bedding for their new lodgings in the stables. 'You'll make us some more of that pasta stuff, won't you?' she said, a smile pushing out her plump cheeks as she handed them a box containing an assortment of pans, crockery, cutlery, a kettle and tea for their breaks.

Italian Sundays became a regular feature of the unusual Spink household.

'All we're missing now is two young females to even up this table,' Salvo muttered to Massimo in the Spinks' homely farm kitchen as he served out lasagne the pair had concocted for the elderly couple.

'In your dreams,' Massimo replied. 'Pass the water.'

CHAPTER TEN

England, 1943–46

'I need you to take the cart and horse to South Elmham, Massimo,' Arthur Spink said one sunny morning in late July 1943. 'I need a dozen bales of hay delivered to The Orchards for their horses. Easy enough to find. Big place along the main street. Don't forget your passes when you leave. And take Salvo along with you to help unload.'

It was like a feast day, the freedom of being allowed to drive through the lanes. The sun was buttery-warm on their backs and the pair stripped off their brown shirts, revealing bodies toned and muscular from hard work on the farm.

'We could almost be back home,' Salvo said, relishing the warmth on his bare skin. 'All we need now is a bar for a decent espresso and a girl each on our arm.'

'You never give up, do you? We're not supposed to fraternise.'

'Fraternise? Huh! With the enemy, they say. It doesn't seem like war here. Are your signori Spink the enemy?'

Indeed, the war felt far away to the two Italians, even though Suffolk was peppered with airfields and the men frequently watched Wellingtons fly over, or Spitfires and Mustangs. They shielded their eyes as they looked up from their work, shadows of wings moving across the fields like huge birds of prey.

And then of course there was Major Strickland and his soldiers, who guarded the camp to remind them that they were prisoners, and where Salvo and Massimo now had to report regularly. But the major liked to chat to his inmates in Italian and talk about his holidays in Italy. He liked Italians. Most of his guards were older men, and relaxed. One of the younger ones had once laid down his gun and joined in with their football game, and not one of the POWs had thought to pick up the gun and use it against him.

Privately, Massimo was relieved to be away from battle and the searing conditions of the desert, where sweat had salted his shirt and his feet had been covered in blisters from sand rubbing in his boots. He shuddered to remember the stench of bloated corpses rotting fast in the biting-hot sun, rats feeding on his dead friends and a thirst that could never be slaked. Life here was better, and he blotted out thoughts of how his family might be faring with the German army occupying Tuscany. Occasionally he thought of Lucia, his pretty childhood sweetheart, and wondered how she was doing. But she hadn't replied to his postcards and it was pointless to pine.

At the edge of the village, Salvo and Massimo stopped at a house where the front garden was arranged with a couple of tables laid with checked tablecloths and decorated with jam jars filled with poppies and forget-me-nots. TEA AND HOME-MADE CAKES was scrawled across a board leaning against the gatepost. A young woman wearing a red floral dress, her blonde hair tied up with a matching scarf, hurried out of the front door. She stopped when she saw them, before saying, 'Well, don't sit there gawping all day. You're me first customers. Come on in.'

'We're not supposed to go into shops, remember!' Massimo warned Salvo.

'Let's put our shirts back on and forget about rules,' Salvo replied, reluctant to pierce their dream of a few moments of freedom. The red circles on the backs of their shirts would show the girl instantly that they were POWs. But their dark looks were a giveaway anyway.

The young woman watched them as they buttoned up their shirts. 'You do speak English, I hope?' she said slowly and deliberately.

'Naturally,' Massimo said.

'Enough,' Salvo said.

'Well, I've got Victoria sponge, beetroot, parsnip, rock cakes and tea…'

The men looked at each other, bemused. 'Parsnip?' Massimo said.

'That's right,' the woman said, 'instead of sugar. Parsnips are sweet, so is beetroot.'

Seeing they were still lost, she beckoned them indoors. 'I'll show you.'

The cottage was tiny but cosy, with beams on the ceiling, a huge inglenook fireplace dominating one side of the room and two easy chairs covered in flowery material positioned on either side of the hearth. The simple style was not unlike Massimo's home in Tramarecchia.

The young woman stood at the door while they squeezed past, Massimo brushing against her bosom by accident. His face flushed bright red and, embarrassed, he felt himself stir. She smiled at his discomfort. 'Come in, I won't eat you,' she said and then she laughed. Her head tipped back, her mouth opening wide – it was a joyous sound – and a picture of his sisters, mother and aunt happily sharing gossip around the hearth flickered into his head.

At the back of the room a baby was asleep in a drawer lined with blankets and she put her finger to her lips for them to keep quiet. 'Only just finished feeding him, little terror. Had me up half the night. Can't seem to fill him up.'

She went through to another room and reappeared with a large trug of vegetables.

'I use these to sweeten my cakes. Beetroot, parsnip,' she pointed out.

Salvo and Massimo had never seen these strange vegetables before and they shrugged. 'We try,' Massimo said.

'One slice of each? And two teas? Milk? I use honey instead of sugar because of the stingy rations,' she said.

'You have no coffee?' Salvo asked.

'Sorry. There's a bleeding war on, in case you 'adn't noticed.' She clapped her hand to her mouth. 'Stupid me. Course you know. From the camp, ain't you? I'm Molly.' She held out her hand.

'Salvatore, but Salvo easier,' Massimo's friend said, holding onto her hand as if reluctant to let go of her soft fingers.

Massimo introduced himself and Molly disentangled her hand from Salvo's and placed it in Massimo's. 'I'll have to call you Massi. If 'e's got a nickname, then so must you.'

She spoke quickly and it was difficult for them to follow, but it wouldn't have mattered what she'd said. It was enough to be in the company of pretty young woman after such a long time.

'Make yourselves comfortable at a table outside. You'll make the place look busy. I need to attract more custom. Won't be long,' she said, all but pushing them out of doors and retreating to the back of the cottage.

While they sat waiting for her to bring their order, Massimo cast his eyes around the garden. Along the sunnier side of the cottage was a vegetable garden choked with weeds and a couple of forlorn clumps of parsley going to seed. A roof tile lay on the grass and, looking up, he could see it wouldn't be too difficult to fix. A ladder leant against an outhouse and he went to fetch it, then, picking up the tile, he climbed the ladder carefully. 'Support it for me, Salvo,' he said, while he fitted the tile back onto the roof.

'Lor' love-a-duck!' Molly said, coming out with a laden tray. 'You needn't do that. You're supposed to be customers.'

'Is no problem,' Massimo said, back down from the ladder, wiping moss from his hands onto his trousers.

'Things have got a bit out of hand,' she said, setting cups on saucers and pouring tea onto the milk, 'since hubby went to war.'

Neither of them liked milk with their tea, but it was standard issue in the camp. Tea was always hot and very sweet, usually served with condensed milk.

'I do your garden one day,' Massimo said, pointing to the plot.

'Really?' Molly said. 'Ain't it too late to sow stuff?'

'You can put for winter,' Massimo said. 'I no know names: cabbage? cauliflowers? And… other things. I look dictionary.'

The baby started to cry, and she disappeared into the house.

'You're in there, you are,' Salvo sniggered when she was out of earshot. 'Soon be getting your leg over.' He made an obscene gesture with his arm and Massimo hissed at him to shut his trap.

She reappeared with the baby in her arms. 'Meet Denis. The hungriest baby in the whole of England.'

Salvo stretched out his arms and she passed him over. He positioned the baby against his shoulder and rubbed his back gently until Denis gave a loud belch and they all laughed. 'He no hungry, he have… bad stomach.'

'Wind,' she said, 'we say "wind". Cor, you're a natural. Got kids of your own, have you?'

He shook his head. 'Six brother, one sister.'

'Where are you lot from, then?'

'From *Italia*. I from Tuscany,' Massimo said, 'and my friend, he from *Sardegna*. Is an island.'

'All sounds very exotic, I'm sure. My Ken is somewhere or other like that. On a ship in the middle of some ocean. Merchant seaman. God knows when I'll see him next. 'Asn't even met this little bugger yet.'

They were quiet for a while, lost in their own thoughts.

Massimo stood up. 'We must go. How much?'

'Nothing this time. You mended my roof and you're going to dig my garden for me, ain't you?'

They promised to return soon, and she waved them goodbye. Once they'd dropped the hay off at its destination, they had to hurry, urging the horse on, the cartwheels raising clouds of dust. They didn't stop talking about Molly all the way back, planning how and when they could see her again.

A couple of weeks later at the beginning of September, Massimo and Salvo were sitting on the step of the stable door, drinking coffee that had arrived in somebody else's Red Cross parcel, and which Salvo had managed to barter in exchange for a pair of sturdy second-hand boots. They were making the coffee last. The taste was strong and rich and neither of them could remember the last time they'd enjoyed the real thing. Back home it was made from ground chicory roots, barley or acorns. Real coffee was only drunk in a bar and neither of them were from families who could afford such luxuries. They decided to ration themselves to one coffee every third day, to make the precious beans last.

Arthur Spink came hurrying from the farmhouse, waving his hands.

'Boys,' he called, 'there's been an announcement on the radio.' He stopped, out of breath.

They stood up. 'The war? Is finished?'

'Not yet. But your war with us is over.'

They looked puzzled.

'Eisenhower has been speaking on the BBC. Your country has signed an armistice with the Allies. Mussolini has gone. Marshal Badoglio signed an agreement five days ago. It's Jerry you have to fight now. Not us.' He came over and shook their hands, clapping them both on their backs. 'You're on our side, boys. Mussolini is finished.'

'Mussolini – kaput?' Salvo said, slicing his throat with his hand.

'Not dead, but he's not in control any longer,' Arthur said. 'Come inside and drink a glass of cider with the missus.'

As they walked together to the farmhouse, their boss told them Eisenhower had warned in the broadcast that it wasn't yet time to celebrate. 'But I reckon we can enjoy a glass or two, don't you?'

*

Once news spread round the camp, there were many who thought they would be back in Italy soon, but they were disappointed. Major Strickland called all the prisoners to assemble and explained that it would not be possible to repatriate them for a while; that they were still needed by the British government to work on the land. And this would be the way they would help in the war effort against the Germans, now their enemy.

'You will be considered free men,' Major Strickland explained, 'and you will enjoy increased leisure time. Men who have been living in camp will now be allowed to go outside the perimeter, but all of you will be required to check in with the camp as per usual, even those living on farms. You will serve in units under your own officers and they will report to me. I'm sorry that you will not be returning to your country immediately, but the reports we receive from Italy tell us conditions there are far worse than here. You are better off remaining, I assure you.'

The men wandered off to discuss the turn of events, some angry, most resigned. All around the campground there were clusters of men debating what to do.

'I will stay here,' Massimo said, 'rather than fight in battle. I saw enough bloodshed in Africa.'

'It's fine to talk to me like this, but many will think you are a coward,' Salvo said, his voice low in case they were overheard. 'I agree with you, but I want to see my family again.'

'Don't you think I do too? But we wouldn't be with family. We'd be in a trench somewhere, killing or being killed, or on the run from the militia, fighting with the partisans. I am happy to continue with my war here. Didn't Major Strickland say we were playing our part by working the land for our new allies?'

'I know you're right, Massimo, but keep those thoughts to yourself.'

*

Massimo saw Molly again two weeks later when Arthur Spink asked him to take more bales to The Orchards.

'I need Salvo to help me in the top meadow, so you're to go alone this time. And take these to them while you're at it. A fruit cake and a dozen eggs. They're good friends, and we heard their only son is missing. This bleeding war…' He handed over a basket and Massimo went to fetch the cart and load up the hay.

It was awkward at The Orchards. After unloading, he walked to the back door of the imposing farmhouse and rang the bell. A middle-aged woman came to open the door. He could see she'd been crying. Wiping her hands on her apron, she almost snatched the parcel off Massimo. 'You're one of them Eyeties from up the camp, aren't you? Jimmy's missing in your country. Why aren't you over there fighting instead of him? My mistress is up in her room bawling her eyes out. Bloody disgrace, housing and feeding you lot of skivers.'

Before he could say anything, she slammed the door in his face. He stood there a moment or two, the woman's words ringing in his head. He felt guilty, but what could he do? Even Tenente Montini, the highest-ranked Italian officer in camp, had told them they'd probably have to stay here until the end of the war. Allied transport was needed for soldiers and guns, not for repatriation of prisoners. He wanted to knock on the door and reason with the woman. But his English wasn't good enough, and he could almost touch the grief surrounding the place. The curtains were closed, even though the sun was high in the clean Suffolk sky and at the front door a pot of parched white petunias wilted with neglect. He turned on his heel, climbed back onto the cart and pulled on the reins to command the horse forward.

He could have done with Salvo's company. Despite his friend's carefree ways, he always knew what to say in moments like these. Massimo couldn't help feeling ashamed of his status, but he truly didn't see what purpose it would serve to return to Italy to get himself killed. He willed his mind to blank out memories of Lucia and his family.

'Good afternoon, Massi…' He'd been so sunk within himself that he'd not noticed he was passing Molly's cottage. 'Are you stopping for more cake?'

The clock on the church tower had just chimed three. If he hurried back with the empty cart, he could spare half an hour. He could do with cheering up, and merely looking at her in her buttercup-yellow dress skimming her tanned legs brought a smile to his heart. Her hair hung wet on her shoulders, the damp spreading down to the material straining at her full breasts.

'Just washed my hair while Denis sleeps.' She pulled a towel from the line tied between two apple trees and bent to wrap it, turban-style, around her head. He glimpsed her cleavage while she was bending and once again, he felt desire.

'I'll put the kettle on,' she said, straightening up. 'Fancy a rock cake?'

He frowned and she laughed. 'I'll show you.'

He followed her into a tiny scullery where a pile of dirty plates waited in the sink, as well as a zinc bucket of soiled nappies. She followed his gaze. 'I'll do that lot later. It's too hot to do anything much in the day when it's like this.'

He watched her fill the brown kettle, riddle the small cooking range and add a stick of firewood to strike a blaze. 'This old thing,' she said, 'bane of my life. What I'd do to have one of them new cookers, but here in the sticks, there ain't nothing like that.'

'In the sticks?' he asked, frowning.

'Oh, sorry. I keep forgetting you don't speak English… in the country. My old man dragged me away from the city. Never got used to it, or the funny people round here. They don't like me one little bit…'

Not understanding the idiom, Massimo thought it was a shame she was wasted on an old man.

'I am also from' – he paused – 'the sticks. *La campagna.*'

'Well, I prefer the city. There's nothing to do in this dump. No flicks, no dance hall…' She turned to him from the kitchen drainer where she'd been slicing bread and putting rock cakes on a plate. 'Do you like dancing?'

'*Certo. Naturalmente* I like dancing.'

She took his hand and pulled him into the sitting room. Then she switched on a wireless set, fiddling with the knobs until the squeaks and hisses turned into music. 'This is no good, it's classic rubbish,' she moaned. 'I like 'Arry James and his orchestra.'

She snapped off the radio and hummed a tune. 'This one's a foxtrot,' she said, pulling him into her arms and guiding him over the carpet.

She was slightly taller than him and she kicked off her shoes, so they were at eye level. As she sang, her breath was soft on his face. 'Closer,' she said, 'you can't dance proper like that. Hold me,' she said, pulling him nearer. 'You won't snap me in 'alf.'

She was soft and smelled of soap and apples. How long was it since he'd been held, felt the touch of skin on skin? Her eyes were full of laughter and mischief, and something else.

'Relax, Massi,' she said, guiding his hand to her back. 'Back, back, slide, slow, slow, quick...' She repeated the instructions until they moved together. 'Take them boots off, Massi,' she said, 'it'll be easier.'

As he bent to pull off his rubber boots, his heart hammered in his chest and he wondered if she could hear it, and detect it wasn't from dancing.

She laughed. 'This is fun, but...' She pushed him away and, tucking her dress into her knickers, she said, 'What's more fun is this... the jitterbug.'

He stood back, watching while she moved across the floor, spinning and kicking, laughing like a child, before collapsing into the armchair by the inglenook. She pulled her dress back over her knees.

'I learned that from my GI pal. He was stationed here for a while. Now, *them* lot knew how to dance. But they've moved on. More's the pity.'

The kettle whistled from the kitchen.

'I'm off the idea of tea, Massi. It's too hot. Will water do you?'

Massimo was almost relieved when her baby began to cry and she went to fetch him from upstairs. She returned, clasping him on her hip, and it was like having a tiny chaperone in the room. Not long afterwards, he said goodbye, later than he'd planned.

'Come and see us soon,' she said at the door. 'Come and dance with me again. I'll teach you some more steps.'

He visited again the following Sunday, making his excuses to Salvo and the Spinks. 'Please, Mr Spink, I borrow your bike? I go to church,' he lied, and when Salvo asked him why, Massimo invented a story about it being his mother's birthday and it was something he always did. He ignored Salvo's raised eyebrows and cocky smile, and his comment in Italian about having fun and not doing anything he wouldn't.

Summer drizzle sharpened the colours and scents of the English countryside. The hedgerows were tangled with honeysuckle and cow parsley fringed the lanes. Massimo sped along, the bicycle tyres humming over the flat roads.

Molly was in the garden fetching nappies from the line. 'I'll have to light the fire to dry this blinkin' lot now,' was the first thing she said to Massimo, as if it was the most natural thing in the world to have him turn up again out of the blue.

He leant the bike against the side of the front porch and said, 'I do for you.'

While he laid the fire, she draped damp nappies and tiny clothes over a wooden clothes horse. 'Fancy a fry-up?' she asked. 'I got some eggs and a couple of bangers. Gawd knows what's in 'em, but we can pretend they're meat. Oh, and a couple of tomatoes to throw in the pan. I nicked them from Mrs Toffee Nose's garden next door. Old cow,' she said.

It was hot in the front room with the fire ablaze to dry the washing and they sat eating their late breakfast with the windows wide open. Denis sat in his high chair, chewing on a finger of fried bread. Massimo had brought coffee grains along in a twist of brown paper and he made a cup for Molly.

'Yuck – too strong for me. 'Ow can you drink this muck?' Her hand to her mouth, she went to the kitchen to spit it out in the sink and he laughed.

'*Bene*, more for me.'

'Gimme a brew any day.'

'I dig your garden if it not too wet after.'

'You're a right poppet, ain't you, Massi?' she said, looking him up and down. 'I tell you what, I got some of Ken's old work clothes upstairs. Half a sec.'

She ran up the narrow wooden stairs. The creaking floorboards and drawers being opened was like the familiar sound of home. The huts in the camp were single-storey, as was the stable where he slept at the Spinks' farm. She reappeared with a pair of patched corduroys and a checked shirt over her arm.

'They'll be too long for you. But you can stick his trousers inside your boots and roll up the shirtsleeves.'

As he removed his worn, chocolate-brown shirt, the circle of darker material showing where the red prisoner emblem was removed after 1943, her eyes lingered on his lean, strong body. Then she picked up the baby and went to the kitchen, saying, 'I'll leave you to change yer trousers.'

After the rain stopped, the sun came out, so they moved outside. Molly sat on a blanket under the apple tree playing with Denis, his gurgles and raspberry noises mingling with the sounds of Massimo's spade as he dug over the vegetable plot. 'I bring seeds,' he said, showing her a twist of newspaper, 'cabbage, cauliflowers and *finocchio*. Very good for winter. Fennel. My friend gave me from his parcel from *Italia*.'

Major Strickland had allocated an area for digging at the back of the camp early on for the men to plant whatever they wanted, understanding the Italian need for a plot of earth.

''Aven't the foggiest what fennel is, Massi, but go ahead, feel free.'

She leant against the laden apple tree and unbuttoned her dress to feed her baby. He wanted to avert his eyes but the sight of her made his breath catch in his throat. The homely scene made him long to be back in Tuscany, close to his own family and old friends. Most evenings after a day's work they'd congregate in somebody's house to sit by the fire, or when the weather was warm, under the shade of the walnut tree in the little piazza, exchanging news or advice on how to mend a tool or utensil, how to tend to an elderly relative or sick child, which wild herbs were sprouting in which meadow, where to find the best mushrooms in the woods. And there was invariably a mother feeding her child at the breast. Families were large, there were always babies and toddlers underfoot and they all shared in the caring of them.

She caught his gaze and, misconstruing his thoughts, pulled her cardigan to cover herself. Massimo didn't have enough words in English to explain and continued to dig over the soil, the blade of the spade slicing and turning. He bent to remove roots of weeds and, near him, a robin hopped about at the edge of the bed, waiting for him to unearth worms.

'Time for baby's sleep,' she said, buttoning up her dress. 'I'll make us a sandwich.'

The kitchen was tidier than the other day, with a red gingham cloth on the table and poppies stuck in a milk bottle in the centre. The kettle was boiling, and she poured water into a brown teapot.

'Tea for two?' she laughed, and then she sang the words. He understood the lyrics; they were simple, and when she came to 'Nobody near us, to see us or hear us', she broke off, fiddling with the ring on her finger. 'My Ken used to sing that to me. In fact, he sang it to me when he asked me to marry 'im… he was a soppy old date. I miss 'im.'

'I'm sorry,' Massimo said. 'This war…'

'I miss how he used to be, Massi. He came back on leave and… he was different somehow. Cold and unloving… Not my boy any more. He didn't want to talk and… he didn't want to touch me, neither.'

He could understand why. Naturally he could. He'd heard grown men cry themselves to sleep; brave and blustering in daytime, at night they were on their own to confront the things they'd seen and done in this godawful war. How to explain to this girl here, cocooned in the green English countryside, about the realities of war on the front? He took her hand as she fiddled with the tablecloth and squeezed it hard.

'Fancy a dance?' she said, blowing her nose. 'To cheer me up.'

The half-eaten sandwiches curled in the heat and the tea stewed in the pot while they danced. She sang at first but then their dancing slowed. They stopped, their eyes locked. He pulled her closer, loving the feel of her curves soft against his body. She found his lips and kissed him.

Massimo pulled back and she whispered, 'It's all right. You're all right.'

Then she pulled him to the floor and unbuttoned his shirt, her hands moving to the belt on his trousers, running her fingers over his skin, kissing him again, long and hard, until Massi responded. Instinct took over and he drowned in the sensations, carried away by her touch, the salty, milky taste of her, her tongue like a cat's, the sounds she made, the arching of her body, her nails clawing at his back, dancing with him in another way.

Afterwards, she pulled cushions off the sofa for their heads and fetched a cigarette. They lay on the floor together, passing the cigarette to each other. It was drizzling again, a light breeze blowing at tatty curtains through the open window. Massimo watched as a loose scrap of material snagged against the rough wood on the window ledge. His mother kept a neat house – there would be no loose scraps in her vicinity. They might be poor, but she patched, mended and cleaned in between all her other chores. The other women in the village commented that you could eat off Lorena's floor. She wouldn't approve of this carefree, slapdash girl down here on the floor beside him. And she would definitely not approve of what they had been doing this afternoon. How many times had he received a cuff round the ear for the slightest misdemeanour?

Molly blew smoke rings into the space above them. 'Little 'aloes,' she giggled, turning over to look down on him, her breasts heavy with milk, resting against his chest. 'But I ain't no angel, Massi.'

He didn't contradict her. He was no angel either, sleeping with another man's wife. He wondered if she could tell it had been his first time, and if he'd been good enough for her.

She sat up, bringing her head down to her knees. Massimo, lazy and dreamy, traced the curve of her back along the knobbles of her spine. 'Molly,' he said. 'Forgive me. I so sorry…'

She turned to him. 'Don't be a daft halfpenny bit, Massi. It was just what I needed. It's been a long time. But next time, you wear protection. I don't want another Denis just yet.'

She was so different from the girls back home, who flirted and teased but never let a boy touch them, even through their clothes. And of course, she was married. He felt a pang of guilt as he thought of Lucia back in Tramarecchia, and then dismissed her from his mind almost immediately. She was from another world. Who knew how long this war would go on, and if he would ever see her again? He'd received a couple of brief letters from home, but nothing from Lucia. His young Tuscan sweetheart was most likely married to somebody else by now. Years had passed. He'd confronted death. A man needed to take any type of comfort he could. He pulled Molly down again and kissed her just as Denis started to cry upstairs.

'He needs feeding again,' she said, pulling away from Massimo's arms. 'Lawks, look at the state of me…' She mopped milk leaking from her breasts with her petticoat discarded on the floor. The sight brought back his guilty feelings about sleeping with a married mother.

*

'How was Holy Mass?' Salvo asked when, later that evening, Massimo pushed open the door to their room in the stable. He was lying on his bed, reading a week-old newspaper that Arthur Spink had given him to practise his English. He swung himself up and round, his legs dangling over the side of the bed.

'How many Ave Marias did you recite? And how many Acts of Contrition? You have sex written all over that face of yours, you rascal, *sei birichino*.'

'Don't know what you're talking about. I dug her vegetable garden, that's all,' Massimo muttered. 'I'm tired. We have an early start tomorrow.'

Salvo watched as his friend undressed, not commenting on the scratch marks on his back. 'Your Molly, does she have a friend?'

'Good night, Salvo. We have a field to plough in the morning.' Massimo turned his back. Usually they shared each other's confidences, having grown to be more than brothers. Massimo willed sleep to come so he wouldn't have to talk to Salvo, but his thoughts were full of Molly writhing beneath him on the floor of her sitting room.

*

As he worked the field next morning, Massimo decided he wouldn't visit her again. He wasn't in love with Molly. She was a comfort, that was all. Their affair could only lead to trouble. Her neighbours were bound to notice his coming and going. Her husband would find out. Three lives could be ruined, not to mention the punishment meted out to himself if he was discovered fraternising, because even though he was now considered an ally, there were still rules. Strictly speaking, they were not even allowed to drink alcohol. The conduct of the Italians was always under scrutiny. Two weeks ago, a group of co-operators working on a farm across the valley had gone on strike, demanding better conditions and more pay. Massimo had listened to Mr and Mrs Spink discuss it in their kitchen.

'Old Tom was irate,' Arthur had said, 'he wanted to send them packing. Said his three land girls worked harder than those Italian boys, and he didn't see why he should have to pay them anything. That they were a drain on the country's economy. Thank heavens our two aren't shirkers.'

The Spinks had been good to them. Arthur had even hinted that there would be a job and a cottage on his land when the war was over, if he wanted to stay. Massimo was very fond of them. He'd welled up when Arthur, after a couple of glasses of home-made cider, had grasped hold of his arm and said, 'You're the son we never had. You're part of our little family now, you know. We were too late to have any children of our own. You're a godsend, my lad.'

Massimo wasn't sure what he was going to do with his life if this war ever ended, but he knew, even if he were to choose to make a life in Suffolk, he would have to first pay a visit to Tramarecchia to check on his family. The Allies had been moving steadily northwards up and across the Apennines, but progress was slow, and fighting was bitter along the Gothic Line that ran straight through his area.

Poor Salvo had no idea if his loved ones were still alive in Sardinia. The news from Italy, broadcast on Arthur's old wireless set in the evenings and on *Radio Repubblica* in the camp, was not good. There'd been mention of fierce fighting around Salvo's home town. His parents were illiterate, so he'd never received a letter from them, and he was desperate to return. He talked to Massimo about the island; the sapphire-blue sea he swam in, the taste of prickly pears growing wild at the edge of the cliffs.

However, they both avoided serious talk about fears for their respective families' well-being, as if by unleashing these worries they'd turn into reality.

'*Porca Madonna*, Massimo, you're ploughing a wonky furrow,' Salvo shouted, perching on the side of the tractor. 'Let me take over. Where is your mind?'

Usually, Massimo was precise in his work, but he couldn't stop thinking about Molly, how he wanted to see her again, how he didn't.

'It's nothing, I have a headache, that's all,' Massimo said, climbing out of the seat to let Salvo take over.

'More like ball-ache,' his friend said. 'I think your heart is lovesick.'

'Molly is nothing to me.'

'She doesn't have to mean anything, my friend. If somebody offers you a whole load of lemons, then it is time to make *liquore*—'

'Are we going to plough this field today or not?' Massimo interrupted. Salvo laughed as he turned the ignition and for two hours they worked in silence, concentrating on the task in hand.

'Seriously, Massimo, be careful. *Occhio!*' Salvo said as they walked back to their stable room later that afternoon. 'Women can be trouble. Is Molly really worth it? She's married.'

'I know.'

It was a relief to share his thoughts, and after Massimo had confided in his friend, they returned to their usual, easy patter together.

'If she's all right about it, and you are straightforward with her, then where is the harm? Just ration yourself, that's all,' Salvo reasoned. 'Take comfort from each other. *Porca Madonna*, who knows if we shall be alive tomorrow? A bomb could drop on the camp or on our stable and that would be it. *Finito!*'

That evening, they cooked together over the open fire in the stable using the same method as their mothers back home, turning the meat over hot ashes. Salvo had snared a rabbit a couple of days earlier and they skinned the foraged animal, chopping it into pieces, adding sage, salt and rosemary for seasoning.

'A pity we have no wine to wash this down with,' Salvo said. 'I've been thinking of distilling pears to make a liqueur. I could sell it in camp. What do you reckon?'

'I reckon you could do anything you put your mind to, Salvo,' Massimo laughed. 'But you'd need to get hold of alcohol first. How are you going to do that?'

'Fermented fruit and yeast, my friend. I need to get cosy with a baker's daughter…'

'Or signora Spink. Maybe she would like to taste your liqueurs!'

They chatted for a little while about recipes. Massimo's mother produced peach-leaf liqueur every year, steeping one hundred new leaves in alcohol for one hundred days, adding sugar and shaking the mix once a day. Salvo's favourite was his mother's basil liqueur.

That night Massimo slept straight away, tired from hard work, his mind easy after coming to the decision to only visit Molly from time to time.

*

Despite his best intentions, Molly came to find him the following Sunday. He and Salvo had slept in late and Massimo was shaving in front of a cracked mirror leaning against the pump, his shirt off and foam lathered onto his face.

'I won't come near you with that stuff plastered on you,' she said, plonking herself down on the chair outside the door. 'My feet are killing me. Been all over the place looking for you. I went to the camp first,' she said, pulling Denis out of the pram and onto her lap. She undid her blouse and started to feed him. 'Friendly lot, ain't they? They all wanted to kiss and cuddle the little beggar. I've learned how to say *bel bimbo* and *carino*.'

'*Brava*,' Salvo said. 'You will soon be fluent.' He winked at Massimo.

'They miss their families, don't they?' Molly continued. 'One of your friends showed me a photo of his kiddywinks. Bless 'em.'

'We all miss our families, Molly,' Massimo said, 'of course we do.' He took Denis from her and held him up in the air above his head, so that the baby squealed with delight.

Molly watched him. 'He'll be sick all over you. Hand him over.' He passed the baby back and then she said, 'My family kicked me out when I was fourteen. I don't miss 'em one jot. Been fending for meself ever since.'

The two men looked at each other.

'Well, Molly,' Salvo said. 'I'll leave you to talk alone to Massimo.' Turning to his friend, he frowned a warning, and Massimo held up his hand, indicating for him to stay, but Salvo winked and moved away.

'Why haven't you popped round?' Molly asked, when Salvo was out of earshot.

He paused. 'It's best,' he said.

'Best for you or best for me?' she asked, switching Denis to her other breast.

'Molly, you are married. Your husband…'

'My hubby ain't here and I don't know when or if he's ever coming back.'

'But…' he began.

'Forget about buts. Buts go nowhere.' She looked at him. 'Massi, do you like me?'

'Of course I like you,' he replied. There was nothing not to like about her; she was pretty, fun and brazen – and unlike any of the girls he'd met back home.

'Well, I like you too. In fact, I think you're a bit of all right. So, where's the harm?'

'I no want to hurt you.' He wasn't sure how to tell her he liked her but didn't love her, but she saved him from this.

'There's a war on. I'm lonely. You're lonely. A bit of hanky-panky will do us both good. No strings, Massi.'

'Hanky-panky? Strings?' He frowned. English was so difficult.

She smiled and lowered her voice. 'What we did the other day was hanky-panky. And it doesn't matter, Massi. You don't owe me nuffink… what I mean is, you don't 'ave to marry me 'cos I'm married already, ain't I? And if Ken turns up, so much the better, and then you can bugger off.'

He was once again lost for words with this girl, offering sex to him as if it was something like brushing your teeth or combing your hair. It was lust before love; basic, unromantic. But he wasn't complaining.

She pulled a couple of small tins from her bag with the brand, Peacocks, printed across the lids. 'And in case you're worried – these are for you. I got them from one of the GIs – standard issue for the soldiers, he said.'

He took the contraceptives from her. He wanted to laugh at her sexual appetite. Instead, after she'd tucked Denis back into the pram and told him she'd see him next Sunday, he said, 'See you!'

And without saying another word, she pushed the pram away, turning to wave before setting off down the dusty track behind the stables.

Salvo reappeared almost immediately. 'Just make sure she hasn't got the pox,' he said, adding, 'You're a lucky bastard.'

*

The war dragged on for another year and a half, until 8 May 1945, when Churchill announced VE Day. A big party was arranged in the centre of Bungay a few days later, beneath the Buttermarket and down the length of the high street, everybody contributing what they could: a plate of corned beef sandwiches, cakes or a hoarded bottle of beer to put on the tables.

Salvo and Massimo hadn't technically been classed as prisoners since 1943, but they weren't civilians either. A few people still resented 'the Eyeties' being there, while others were fond of them and welcomed them to the party. Now described as co-belligerents, but indispensable for covering labour shortages, it conveniently took several months for the British authorities to arrange repatriation.

*

Molly was not the only woman on the platform at Diss railway station on a warm day in spring 1946 when Massimo and another hundred or so Italian POWs waited for the train to begin their long journey back to Italy. Dotted about the platform, each couple was entwined like ivy round a tree. Salvo had left two months earlier on compassionate grounds, having received a message from a cousin that his father was on his deathbed and his mother was too old to look after the rest of the family. Massimo had already said his emotional goodbyes to Ma and Pa Spink, as he now fondly called them, with promises to write and maybe return to work on the farm again if life didn't work out back in Tuscany. They'd known about Molly and Massimo for a while, and they'd offered to look after Denis for an hour, so that Molly could accompany Massimo to the station.

Molly was crying. 'Lor' love-a-duck,' she said through her snivels. 'I promised meself I wouldn't blub, but I'm going to miss you so much, Massi.' She clung to him like she would never let go. They'd become almost like a couple, both understanding there were no strings, or at least that was what they'd told each other. But he was fond of her and Denis. The little boy was now a lively toddler, helping or hindering Massimo when he worked on Molly's garden. Massimo had carved him a little train set in his spare time, and learned more words of English through the child. 'Say ta, Denis,' Molly said. And he'd learned how to sing a couple of English songs. Molly might not be a good wife, but she was a good mother. There had still been no word from Ken, and she spoke less and less about when he would come back.

'I will write to you, Molly,' he said, cupping her wet cheeks in his hands. 'And once Ken returns, you'll forget all about me.'

'*If* he returns. And I'll never forget you. Never in a million years. Don't talk rot.' She tucked an envelope into his trouser pocket. 'Here,' she said, 'take this to remind yourself of us. It's a photo I had done.'

But once he set foot on the ferry and crossed the blue-grey sea, it felt like the severing of shackles. He kept the photo in his wallet and glanced at it from time to time. The photo was taken in another world. He wouldn't forget Molly and Denis, but he felt little loyalty to them. He had been a prisoner since 1941, and it was time to start afresh. Selfish as it might have seemed, Massimo's intention to return to his village took first place. He needed to be back with his own family, to help them after their gruelling years under occupation. He needed to start down the road of peace.

CHAPTER ELEVEN

Tuscany, 1946

Each man was handed 10,000 lire as he set foot on Italian soil, and was then left to his own devices. Massimo bought a ticket to travel on a goods train from Rome to Arezzo, and he gazed through the window in horror at the devastation of his homeland. A start had been made on reconstruction and work on new blocks of flats had begun next to charred ruins, some walls half standing like grotesque sculptures, a reminder of the relentless bombing raids. There were piles of rubble and broken masonry in each town the train passed through. Bullet holes had pierced train signs and windows were boarded up where glass had once been. The people waiting on the platforms were mostly thin, shabby shadows. A few fields had been planted with corn, the cobs beginning to sprout. The train chugged past straggling vineyards in need of tending, but he noticed one or two hillsides where vines had been pruned and tied.

He'd forgotten how warm his country could be. His head drooped with fatigue and he dozed as the train rumbled on through the countryside. When he woke, a middle-aged woman passed him a bottle of water.

'Fresh from our spring,' she said, as he swigged, grateful for her kindness. 'Are you hungry, *caro*?'

She mothered him for the rest of the bone-shaking journey, passing him a heel of unsalted, home-made bread, harder than an English loaf, but perfect for soaking up the oil from slices of roasted aubergines and peppers that she shared. Once or twice, she fed a handful of maize to two hens in a woven basket below her wooden seat. 'I'm taking these to my daughter,' she said. 'She's with child and wants me to cook chicken broth.'

There were no questions from the woman about his war, where he had been and where he was going. She shared what she had without prejudice or suspicion. And it was good to be reacquainted with this gregarious side of the Italian character as she chatted about her vegetable garden, how it had done well this year, and the pig they were fattening up for New Year. As he listened to her sing-song voice, he realised how he had missed the easy Italian way of striking up conversation with strangers.

He slept that night on a bench in Arezzo station because he had missed the once-a-day transport to Sansepolcro, the main city nearest his village. Mosquitoes bothered him with their high-pitched whine and when he awoke, the exposed skin on his arms, hands and face was covered in welts.

After a cup of strong coffee and a sugary brioche from a bar, he wandered into the centre. His bus left at three thirty, and he had a few hours to kill. On the walls of the station he made out a faded fascist slogan: 'WE WILL CONQUER', with a painted line crossed through the writing. He wondered about the brave individual responsible for defacing the sign. Maybe a young man or woman – he'd heard talk of many female partisans – had stolen in under cover of darkness to pull down posters of *Il Duce* and leave messages of defiance. His war in the prison camps had been a different experience. He needed to catch up on the happenings in his homeland.

Some of the buildings along the narrow streets were still shells. One of them had been turned into a kind of walled garden where the rusting cab of a British army lorry was converted into a makeshift chicken coop. Along one wall of the bombed building, a vine was trained and an old man, a handkerchief knotted on his head against the sun, hoed a patch of ground where lettuces and tomatoes flourished; a patch of colour and promise amid the fallen masonry, seeds for the future.

The bus for Sansepolcro left from the square outside the station. It was really a converted Lancia truck with benches fixed on the back. Massimo desperately wanted to recognise somebody, to feel a sense of belonging, but despite scrutinising the faces of his fellow passengers, there was nobody he knew. He had to remind himself he'd been away for more than six years; much would have changed. He leant his back against the wooden sides, every now and again turning to peer through the slats at the landscape. As the truck laboured round the bends up into the mountains, the air was cooler and refreshingly welcome. He felt queasy and thirsty, but he guessed it was also apprehension causing his stomach to churn.

He wasn't expecting a welcoming party – he hadn't had time to warn anybody of his homecoming – but he hadn't expected to feel like a foreigner in his own neighbourhood as he picked up the holdall Mrs Spink had given him and jumped down from the truck. 'I shan't be needing it, son,' she'd said, 'I'll not be going away on holiday at my age.'

He looked around. The square at Badia had lost several of its buildings. The little town was like a gaping mouth with missing teeth, but the bar in the corner still stood, where four elderly men played cards at a table under the awning. They looked up as he approached, making his way over the damaged paving stones, and one rose from his seat and hurried over to Massimo. It was his uncle Giulio, thinner, hunched and much older than he remembered.

'Eh, Massimo. *Ben tornato!*' he said, turning to his friends. 'Everybody! This is my nephew. We thought we had lost him for

good to the *inglesi*.' He called to the girl behind the bar to bring
more wine. 'Are you hungry, *ragazzo*? What can you give him,
Elena? *Pane? Formaggio?*'

He pointed to the teenage girl, asking Massimo, 'Do you
remember your little cousin Elena?'

The girl came out with wine and a plate of bread and cheese,
placing it shyly on the table. Massimo remembered his uncle's
young daughter, but not this pretty stranger. He smiled at her
and, blushing, she scurried back behind the bar.

'You'll find Tramarecchia very changed,' Giulio said. 'Why
don't you stop with us tonight? Your parents have moved down
to the *borgo* of Sansepolcro. There's hardly anybody left in the
village now. Stay with us! Your *zia* Rosa will rustle up a supper.
Thank God we have our vegetable garden and a pig and chickens,
for there's still precious little in the shops.'

He spat on the ground. '*Bastardi Tedeschi*,' he swore, and then
made the sign of the cross. '*Grazie a Dio*, the war is over now.'

Massimo thanked him and the pair walked across the square
to his uncle and aunt's house. The town hall was pockmarked
with bullet holes and the mayor's house was gone, as well as a row
of terraced houses that had once lined the street. Uncle Giulio
followed Massimo's gaze. 'Yes, we have seen the war here.' He
pushed open the door and called, 'Rosa, we have a visitor this
evening. Throw some extra pasta in the pan this evening.'

Aunt Rosa cried as Massimo bent to be embraced. 'You've
come back. We all thought we'd never see you again.' She wiped
her eyes on her pinafore. 'Wait until your parents see you. It will
be the tonic they need. Oh, *Massimino*, my little Massimo, how
we have suffered here.'

That first supper was the best of his life. Simple food prepared
with love and natural ingredients. Little slices of home-made
bread toasted over the fire, rubbed with garlic and half of them

topped with chicken livers and sage, half with tomatoes and a hint of chilli pepper. He'd forgotten how good tomatoes grown under a hot sun could taste. That would have been sufficient, but his aunt next served up steaming bowls of home-made *strozzapreti*, known as 'priest stranglers' because they resembled twisted dog collars worn by priests. she had flavoured these with a sauce of courgette flowers. Slices of pecorino cheese drizzled with honey and eaten with quarters of pears followed. 'Pour the boy more Vin Santo,' Giulio declared, his words a little slurred, as he drained his glass.

'That was the most special meal, Zia,' Massimo said, leaning back in his chair, patting his belly. 'I've missed Italian cooking.'

His aunt smiled and started to clear the table. Massimo insisted on helping her, despite her protestations of it being woman's work.

'The women in *Inghilterra* have been doing man's work during the war, Zia,' he told her. 'Driving tractors, taking over men's jobs in the factories, cutting down trees and helping with all kinds of manual labour. And I have been cooking and looking after myself for these past years. I'm sure I am able to help you wash a few pots.'

Afterwards he climbed the ladder to the bedroom on the floor above the kitchen, partitioned off by a thin wooden wall behind which his aunt and uncle slept. The traditional mattress, stuffed with dried corn leaves, rustled as he settled beneath the coarse cotton sheets, and within minutes he was sleeping soundly.

Despite his uncle and aunt begging him to stay longer, next morning he set off early down the hill to his home village of Tramarecchia. He whistled as he walked, breathing in the scents of wild thyme and mint that his boots crushed underfoot. The cicadas were a forgotten sound from the past, and the noise intensified as the morning heat increased. His heart beat a little faster as he rounded the final bend that led down to Tramarecchia, nervous about seeing Lucia after so long, wondering what they would make of each other.

'*Buongiorno*,' he said to three women washing clothes at the village fonts. The youngest pulled her headscarf over her face. The older woman, possibly her mother, stood up to shield her daughters. 'What do you want?' she asked. 'There is nothing here for you.'

He didn't recognise her. 'I am Massimo,' he said, 'Massimo Conti. My home is over there.' He pointed to the far end of the little grassy piazza and noticed, with horror, the burned-out shell of his neighbours' house. 'I'm looking for Lucia,' he said. 'What has happened here?'

'She's gone,' the woman said.

'Good riddance, too,' added the younger one from behind her scarf.

'What do you mean, gone?' Massimo asked, but the women turned their backs on him and resumed their washing without saying another word.

CHAPTER TWELVE

Tuscany, present day

Massimo fell silent and shook his head. Clouds had gathered, covering the sun, and he shivered. Alba gently took his arm. 'Let's get you inside, and after I've tidied these things away, we'll go back up to Badia,' she said.

He didn't seem to register where he was and looked at her, confused.

'Massimo?' Alba repeated gently. 'Are you all right?'

'Lucia and I were childhood sweethearts. There was an understanding between our two families that when she was old enough, we would marry.'

He fell silent again and Alba waited for him to continue. He seemed lost in the past.

'When I returned from *Inghilterra*, I couldn't find her. I hoped that by staying in our village, I would discover what had happened to her.' He pointed to the ruined building and overgrown orchard next to the tower, opposite to where they sat outside his house. 'They burned her house. It's not been lived in since then.'

Alba noticed the blackened, fallen timbers for the first time and pulled out her drawing pad to sketch the ruin.

She looked up at Massimo, his expression replaced by the lined, beaten features of an old man. There were tears in his eyes. She put down her pencil and grasped his hand. 'Are you all right, Massimo? Don't tell me if you don't want to.'

He shook his head. 'Talking to you in English is good. Do you think I'm mad if I say that talking in another language makes those dreadful events seem more removed from me, Alba? Or do you think these are the rantings of an old man?'

She squeezed his hand. 'Not rantings, Massimo, but I don't want you to be upset.'

'It is more upsetting to me to think that she is forgotten. My friends here, you see, they never want me to talk about those times.'

He allowed her to lead him into his little house and she sat him down, covering his knees with a blanket as he was still shivering. In the kitchen, she noticed for the first time the absence of a woman's touch. No embroidered curtain panels at the windows or colourful oven gloves; no pictures on the walls, or bright tablecloth on the kitchen table. The place was sparse and Alba wondered how long ago it was that Massimo had lived there.

She rinsed the glasses and coffee cups quickly, leaving them to drain and then, after padlocking the front door, she helped him into the front seat of the car. As she drove back along the dirt track, she made sure to avoid the holes, feeling the need to make the ride as comfortable as possible for Massimo, who was still silent, staring straight ahead through the windscreen, lost in his own world. She would have liked to ask him more about the war, and to tell him about finding the silver goblets at the partisans' house, but now was not the time.

Walking back to where she'd parked the car, after dropping Massimo back at the care centre, she stopped in front of the town's war monument, a sculpture of a young soldier leaning back in agony as he gazed over the mountains in the distance. Alba had passed by the statue so often and never registered how poignant it was. She stopped to read the inscription, dedicated to the fallen of all wars: 'Make me a tomb where you want,' she read, 'but not in a land where man is a slave.'

She sat down on a bench nearby, deep in thought about Massimo's story. Except it wasn't a story. She considered how today the young think the war has nothing to do with them; that it's something from the past, like the invention of the steam engine or scenes that belong in an old film or a novel. But it was such a defining moment for so many ordinary young people in the 1940s; it changed their lives radically, sending them overseas from remote villages dotted about the country. Wherever you set foot in the world now, there were always reminders within touching distance of wars, like this sculpture of a young man, or a shrine on a mountain path in memory of a partisan – someone who had been a lover, son or husband.

She drove down the hill to the stable, her head full of the Second World War, wondering what had become of Massimo's wife, of Florian and the partisans, and if Massimo would find the energy to tell her the rest of his story.

Over a supper of porcini risotto that evening, Alba recounted details of Massimo's war. Francesco said, 'I read there were over 155,000 Italian prisoners of war detained in England. That's about half the population of Florence.'

'Just imagine all the stories we'll never hear now that their generation is disappearing,' Alba said, helping herself to salad. 'There are so many questions I want to ask him. I wondered if he might know something about the partisans' house up in Seccaroni, and the silver.'

'But if he was a prisoner of war in England, surely he'll not have known much of what went on here,' Anna said.

'But people talk after the event,' Francesco said. 'Somebody may have filled him in when he returned. It's worth asking.'

'If his story is too private, Alba, he might not want to tell you everything,' Anna said, clearing the plates away and setting a bowl of fruit on the table. 'Tread carefully!'

'Of course I will. His carer suggested I visit him next week, to give him time to settle. But I think I'll go and call Alfi now. He'll be fascinated by Massimo's story, and I want to fill him in on what I've found out.' She got up to kiss her parents. 'Night-night. Thanks for everything, you two.'

'She's looking brighter, don't you think?' Anna said after Alba had left the kitchen.

'Thank heavens for this ruins project,' Francesco replied. 'And for Alfi – *and* Massimo.'

*

'*Sì*?' Beatrice's voice answered.

'It's me again, Beatrice. Alba. Is Alfi... Alfiero there?' She thought it strange that Beatrice answered the phone and not Alfi.

'He's in hospital,' came the answer. 'He's had an accident.'

'Oh no! What happened?'

'He fell down the stairs. He has hurt his leg. I must go now. I'm fetching him from hospital.'

'Give him my—'

The phone went dead and Alba ran down the stairs to tell her parents.

'What's up?' Anna asked.

'Alfi is in hospital with a leg injury. I'll go and see him tomorrow, poor chap. His girlfriend sounded stressed.'

'As she would be. I wonder how it happened,' Anna said.

'I have no idea. Apparently he fell down the stairs. I'll find out more tomorrow. I hope it's not the same leg he broke before. Remember the motorbike accident in our last year of school?'

'Oh yes. Poor thing,' Anna said, 'he was in plaster for ages.'

Alba couldn't visit the hospital today, so she decided to pay another visit to Seccaroni. There was something about the place. Her parents decided to accompany her as Francesco wanted to hunt for *funghi*. After the rain of recent days, the air was perfumed, the grass patterned with a mass of purple, yellow and pink flowers. Summer had arrived like a bride. There was field scabious, sainfoin, which was used in the past as a cattle crop, as well as orchids and helleborines. Ruts of freshly churned soil showed where wild boar had recently dug up roots. Bright yellow blossom hung from laburnum trees. The name in Italian, *maggiociondolo*, trinkets of May, was very appropriate, Alba thought. The blossom resembled dangling bracelet charms.

"I'd forgotten how beautiful it is up here,' Alba said to her parents as she gazed up at the Mountain of the Moon. 'It's like being on top of the world.'

'Do you miss London, Alba?' Anna asked. 'It's so quiet here in comparison.'

'No, I don't. It feels like another life,' Alba said, sitting down on a rock to enjoy the view.

'What about the gallery? Your work?' her father asked.

'I'd grown tired of that, too, really. It was a means to an end.'

'To stay with James?' Anna said.

'Yes.' Alba didn't want to talk about him. She wasn't sure how she would react if she started to think about him again. It was better to concentrate on other stuff.

'But I'm loving exploring the ruins,' she continued. 'When I lived here before, I took it all for granted. But they're a kind of gateway to the past. Look what it's thrown up already.'

'Yep, I get that,' her father said. 'Just to think of partisans up here, a war going on, youngsters of your age engaged in a cause. It's hard to conceive of.'

'I think about the young German soldiers, too,' Alba said. 'I expect many of them had never been abroad before. To end up in a place as beautiful as this and not be able to enjoy it. To come here to kill…' She shuddered. 'It's impossible to imagine.'

'Right! Enough about the past,' Anna said, producing a flask from her rucksack. 'Who's for coffee and flapjack?'

'Yay, you're a star,' Alba said. 'I thought you'd never ask.'

Once they'd enjoyed their break, she was content to let them go off and do their own thing.

She watched them start the steep ascent to the spot where Francesco had been successful with mushroom hunts in the past, and then wandered into the ruin. For a while she sat on the box that she and Davide had found at Christmas. It wouldn't take any weight at all for much longer. Like the fabric of this old house, it was crumbling. A lizard scuttled across the remains of a worm-eaten ledge, scattering flakes of plaster. It had a scorpion in its mouth and Alba was amazed it could do that without being stung.

There was nothing much left inside the house to show this was once a place where people had lived. Soon even the bare bones would be swallowed by nature. Finding her sketch pad and coloured chalks, she decided to try and capture some life for this place, some memory. Closing her eyes, she let her mind wander to somewhere in the past. Slowly, the sounds and senses of evening came to her: a fire crackling in the hearth, food stirred in a cauldron resting on a trivet, a metal ladle scraping against the iron pot. Somebody was singing a bawdy song and she heard the laughter of young men, then an older voice urging them to hush. Their voices stilled and then there were murmurs, but she couldn't catch what they were saying. In the firelight, their features were soft and beautiful. She thought she saw a young girl among them, but more likely it was a fresh-faced youth; a couple of the group looked no older than children. An older man, his face dark with stubble, had a fresh scar across his right cheek. It was he who was talking, his half a dozen listeners intent on his words. She thought she caught a likeness to the young man she'd drawn in her earlier sketch, the one she was convinced was called Basilio or Quinto, but the scene was fading from her imagination fast. She opened her eyes and for the next half an hour she concentrated on the images her chalks conjured, choosing bright colours, filling the page with movement, trying to bring warmth to the scene.

On several evenings, in the quiet of her room, she'd googled about war ghosts. There were lots of stories of sightings: phantom Spitfires that haunted the skies above British airfields; ghosts of soldiers hovering in the trenches of Normandy, appearing only to children. The persistent comments about these paranormal happenings were of restless spirits with unsettled business. She watched a film clip made by a group of death seekers, as they called themselves, playing siren sounds in an old pillbox in Cornwall, hoping to conjure up ghosts they felt were somewhere present. Part of her was sceptical about these paranormal investigators, and yet she had pangs of disquiet. Could she too have come upon a tormented spirit in these ruins?

'We're back. Where are you?' Francesco called and Alba jumped, bringing herself back to the present. She stood up and popped her head through what remained of a window and waved. 'I'm in here,' she shouted.

'Looking for more treasure?' Anna called.

'Something like that,' she said, walking over to them as she replaced her book in her rucksack.

Francesco held out his basket and she peered inside. A dozen or so creamy-white mushrooms were nestled there. 'I found treasures of my own. *Prugnoli* for supper!' he announced. 'I told you I would find *funghi* today,' her father said proudly.

*

Later that day, as she rode her repaired scooter down to Sansepolcro, any lingering thoughts about James were dispelled as she enjoyed the scenery unfolding around her. Her mind was more concentrated now on Tuscany, and Massimo's story. As she descended, the landscape changed with each bend. She stopped to take a photo on her phone of a grove of olive trees, splashes of red from poppies in the grass around the twisted trunks like a paint effect, with an old farmhouse in the background. The house looked solid, but it was uninhabited, ivy beginning to smother its shutters. There were so many of these vacant properties dotted about. The human exodus that had started post-war was still going on all these years later, with people giving up work on the land for jobs in the city. You couldn't blame them, she thought, but it was a pity.

A couple of cars with Dutch registration plates overtook her. With the weather warming up, tourists were appearing again. A child waved at her from the car window, and she beeped her horn and smiled at the youngster. The city would be busy today with people visiting the market and sightseers taking photographs in the picturesque backstreets.

She made her way to her favourite bar in the main square and sat at a table while she waited for her cappuccino, watching people clustered around the market stalls, rooting for bargains. She tried three times to phone Alfi. He'd told her about his flat in the centre, but she had no idea where it was, and nobody was answering on his number.

After her coffee break, she dodged her way through the stalls, heading towards the tourist office where he worked, pushing the Vespa, loving the operatic sound of sellers trying to outshout each other, describing their goods, joking, exchanging rude comments. One of the wags held up a huge pair of white frilled knickers and offered to exchange them for Alba's vintage Vespa as she went by. 'That's seen better days, signorina. Like these,' he said, waving the underwear about. 'Let me relieve you of your ancient machine.'

She laughed and replied, 'In your dreams… give those to your nonna.'

She was certain the office would have Alfi's address and she hoped they'd give it to her. Italians were hung up about privacy; they'd even commandeered the English word, but she hoped they'd remember her from last time when she and Alfi had gone to lunch together.

'He lives in Via della Cipolla, number seventy-eight. On the top floor, signorina. Give him our best wishes and tell him to stop skiving,' said the girl called Marianna, who thankfully was on duty again today and greeted Alba with a cheerful smile.

CHAPTER THIRTEEN

Via della Cipolla was a narrow cobbled alleyway. Sheets hung down to dry from a couple of houses and there were boxes and pots planted with fresh herbs on many of the windowsills. Looking at the names of the residents listed at the side of the ornate chestnut door, she found Paoli, Alfiero's surname, and rang his bell a couple of times. Just as she was about to give up, his voice crackled through the intercom. '*Chi è?* Who is it?'

'It's me. Alba. Can I come up?'

'*Ciao*, Alba. Sorry to keep you waiting. I…'

'You've hurt your leg.'

'How did you know?' He yelped in pain and she heard him swear under his breath.

'Just let me in and I'll explain. Where can I leave my Vespa?'

'Bring it inside and park it in the courtyard. I'm on the top floor. Use the lift.'

The door opened with a buzz from the intercom and she pushed the scooter into a central courtyard where a covered well took centre stage, a terracotta vase spilling with white roses and lavender gracing its cover. On the far wall, a stone lion's head spewed water from its mouth into a large marble basin shaped like a shell, the splashing sound echoing around the *cortile*. She whistled under her breath at the upmarket space. Propping the Vespa on its stand in a corner of the courtyard, she pulled aside the two metal concertina doors and took the lift to the third floor.

His keys were on the outside of the door and she let herself in. He was sitting on a black leather settee looking sorry for himself, his bandaged leg propped up on a matching footstool.

'This takes me back a few years,' she said, going over to him to kiss him on each cheek. 'What happened?'

'I fell down the stairs.'

'Take the lift next time,' she suggested. 'Can I get you anything? Poor you.'

'A coffee would be very welcome,' he said, adding apologetically, 'and something to eat? I missed lunch.'

'Didn't Beatrice prepare you anything?' she asked, wishing she could bite back her words. It wasn't her place to criticise, but she was surprised his girlfriend wasn't here to help him. She could at least have left him a tray with a flask of coffee and a plate of sandwiches.

'She had to leave for a meeting in Milan. A fashion fair for work – the highlight of her year.'

'Right, point me in the direction of the kitchen. Cool flat, by the way, very stylish,' she said, taking in the walls bearing abstract paintings and beams painted in a pale lime wash. The look was stark, but it went well with the old building with its high vaulted *cotto* ceilings.

'First on the right down the corridor,' Alfiero said. 'Not sure what's in the cupboard, though.'

The kitchen was a showpiece, its stainless-steel worktops and pristine cooker showing no signs of recent food preparation. A swish espresso machine sat alone on a surface. There were plenty of pods, so she inserted one and placed a cup underneath the nozzle and switched it on. When she opened the fridge, she found six cans of Peroni, a tub of parmesan and a bag of eye creams. There was nothing in the cupboards except for a jar of oregano and a bottle of extra-hot chilli sauce.

'Christ, Alfi, are you on a starvation diet, or what?' she said as she came back into the lounge. His eyes were closed, and he looked pale. 'Did they give you any painkillers at the hospital?' she asked, handing him the espresso.

He opened his eyes and shrugged. 'Beatrice was meant to get some from the *farmacia* but she was running late.' He leant forward to pick up a piece of paper from the coffee table. 'Here's the prescription.'

'Right,' she said. 'Give me some cash and I'll pop out for some bits and bobs. This is ridiculous.' She took the prescription from him. 'Where's the nearest chemist? I'll be as quick as I can.'

One hour later she struggled back to his flat with two laden shopping bags. Eggs, bread, milk, pasta, three jars of ready-made sauce, cheese, ham and a selection of fruit would keep him going. He was asleep and she tiptoed into the kitchen and rustled up a cheese omelette.

'Alfi,' she whispered some minutes later, shaking his shoulder to wake him up.

He winced and brushed her hand from where she had touched him.

'Sorry, Alfi.'

'Badly bruised,' he explained, hauling himself into a sitting position.

She held out a glass of water and the packet of painkillers. 'You're allowed two, four times a day. Here!' she said, handing him a couple. 'And then get this down you.' She placed the tray of food on his lap.

'*Grazie*, Alba. You're very kind.'

She refrained from commenting that it would have been kind of Beatrice to have cancelled her important fashion meeting and stayed to look after him. Instead, she plonked herself down on a leather armchair opposite and watched him devour his eggs.

'That was so good, I can't tell you,' he said, leaning back. 'I can't remember when I last ate.'

'Don't your parents know about your accident?'

He looked at her in surprise. 'Didn't you know? They were killed on a holiday last year. They were on the cruise ship that went down off Lampedusa. They drowned.'

'Oh, fuck. I had no idea. Forgive me.'

'How could you know? We haven't been in touch for years.'

'My parents obviously don't know either, otherwise they'd have told me. I'm so sorry.'

He was quiet for a few moments. She didn't know what to say. He was an only child. An orphan. The word sounded like something from an old book.

'No aunts or uncles?' she asked eventually.

'They live in Sicily.'

'When does Beatrice get back?'

'Two days.'

'Let me stay and look after you.'

He looked at her. 'She'd love that,' he said, with sarcasm.

She wanted to say she didn't care, but she didn't. 'It makes perfect sense,' she said. 'You can't manage on your own. You'd do it for me, wouldn't you, if I was in your position?'

'But you're not. You have a wonderful family, I always thought that. I used to love coming round to your place when we were at school.'

'And I used to envy you being an only child! It was chaotic at times, with the twins and Davide. Like living with a batch of puppies.'

He laughed.

'So, that's settled,' she said. 'I'll let Ma and Babbo know and you can lend me an old t-shirt to sleep in. I'll concoct us a gourmet supper of pasta and ready-made sauce later. If you weren't on painkillers I'd even go as far as running out again for a bottle of wine. But water it will have to be.'

She fetched fruit from the kitchen, which now looked less sterile with the dirty frying pan and utensils heaped in the sink, and they sat side by side, sharing grapes and segments of peaches.

'I wanted to fill you in about those documents you unearthed,' she said. 'Guess what I found out?'

'I haven't a clue. Enlighten me!'

'I'm pretty sure I know the identity of the young man I drew and… you're going to think me crazy…'

'I *know* you're crazy, Alba,' he said, adding, 'in the nicest possible way.'

If he hadn't been so poorly, Alba would have thumped him with a cushion. 'I think I saw him.'

He snorted. 'You're right – I *do* think you're crazy.'

'You can think what you want, Alfi. Nothing like this has ever happened to me. I mean, I'm not religious or anything, or spiritual, but I can't think of any other explanation. I photocopied the page. Look,' she said, coming over to sit next to him. 'That's who I saw.' She pointed to the photograph of the group of partisans. 'Basilio Gelina – otherwise known as Quinto.'

He shook his head. 'I don't know what to say.'

'Neither do I, really. My family think my head's messed up because I've been grieving for James—'

He interrupted her, placing his hand on hers. 'I've been waiting for you to tell me about that, Alba. I'm so sorry. It seems we've both been touched by death recently.'

She looked down at his hand, the dark hairs on the back of his long fingers so different from James's. 'It's getting easier as time goes on,' she said, pulling her hand away. 'And my head is *not* messed, but during my first time up at Seccaroni, I *truly* believed I saw somebody…' She paused before rushing through her next sentence. 'And I wondered if there was some kind of link between the silver I found and… the person I saw.' She looked at Alfi earnestly, as if willing him to believe her theory. 'I told you how there was no pathway down that sheer drop. Unless the person I saw could fly, where did he go? I *saw* him disappear, Alfi. I wasn't hallucinating. I'm not on medication. The only possible explanation for me is that he was some kind of… messenger. He wanted me to find the silverware for some reason.' She produced a second photocopy of the description of the attack on the Boccarini estate, waving it in front of Alfiero's nose. 'Maybe the silver was stolen on this occasion…'

She flopped back against the sofa cushions. 'I'm sounding mad even to myself, but I'm determined to find out more. I'm hoping Massimo might know something about it, since he's lived here all his life.'

'He wasn't in Italy at that time, was he?'

She blew out a huge sigh. 'That's what my parents say. But there's no harm in asking.'

'I suppose there has to be a good reason why that silverware was hidden up near the partisans' house,' Alfiero said, 'although what good would it have done them? They needed guns, food and clothes, not fancy goblets and plates.'

She turned to him. 'Exactly! It's got my head in a spin. Maybe they thought they could sell the stuff and make some money for the cause.'

'Or maybe your ghost was greedy and wanted it for himself?'

She flung her arms around him and he winced with pain as she touched his shoulder again. 'Ouch, Alba. What was that for?'

'For saying it was a ghost,' she said, gently extricating herself. 'Thanks for listening to my crazy ghostly ramblings.'

'*Prego*,' he said with a grin.

*

While he slept that afternoon, she decided to slip out to town, rather than stay in the flat. She borrowed the house keys from his door and took the stairs to the courtyard. A middle-aged woman was deadheading the roses growing on the well, and she turned to look as Alba appeared. '*Buona sera*, signorina. Have you been to visit signor Paoli? How is he?'

It didn't surprise Alba that the woman knew where she'd come from. In a block of flats in Italy it was typical for neighbours to know everything that what went on.

The woman introduced herself. 'My husband is the *portiere*, we take care of things here together.' She leant in closer to Alba. 'I found signor Paoli at the foot of the stairs. I thought he was dead at first, lying there so still and quiet.' She gestured with her secateurs. 'And his girlfriend, shouting and screaming. She wasn't any help at all. My husband is a trained volunteer with the Misericordia – he helps at all the fairs and *feste* in town. He took over and tended to the young signore and called the *ambulanza*. There's always arguing in their place, you know. We've had complaints about the noise.' She tutted.

'He's resting right now, signora,' Alba said. 'He'll live!'

'And you are...?' the woman asked.

'An old school friend, signora. We go back a long way.' She left it at that. 'I'll pass on your good wishes,' she said, even though the woman hadn't asked her to. 'Is it all right to leave my Vespa over there for a couple of days?'

'*Sì, sì*, signorina. I will keep an eye on it.'

Alba was sure she would. Bidding her goodbye, she let herself out of the main door, warm air hitting her as she stepped into the alley from the cool courtyard.

It was siesta time, and most of the shops were closed for the afternoon break, a civilised practice that Alba approved of. It meant there was life in the town in the evenings, shops staying open until eight o'clock, people greeting each other on the streets, lingering at outside bars with their *aperitivi* instead of closeting themselves away in their homes to watch television. She'd learned the expression that an Englishman's home is his castle. But she thought their drawbridges went up too early.

She stopped in the small square of Piazza Garibaldi and sat on a low wall for a while, relishing the late-afternoon sun. She was only a stone's throw from the main square with its popular bars and restaurants, but this place was equally picturesque. Later in summer, it was used for the fair that took place to coincide with the famous crossbow tournament against Gubbio town, enacted in colourful medieval costume, a pageant that made the little town throng with the sounds of drumbeats and bugles summoning all to come and participate. Two cats were stretched out on the warm steps of a house opposite in full sunshine and she pulled out her sketchbook to capture the shape of them. The street lights in this little square were elaborate wrought-iron pieces that would have looked good inside a period house, as would the ornate paving stones on the street, laid in herringbone patterns. Her page was soon filled with images, and when she looked at her watch, it was already half past four, time for Alfi's next dose of painkillers. On the way back to his apartment, she passed Chieli, the best *pasticceria* in town, and selected half a dozen pastries as an afternoon treat. If they couldn't have wine, they could have cake.

'Only me,' she called as she opened the door. She heard water splashing from the bathroom. The door was ajar and as she went past to the kitchen, she saw Alfiero was washing at the sink, his muscular torso and biceps on show. As she went by, he apologised, 'Sorry, Alba, I get used to not shutting the door.'

'No worries, Alfi. That's some dressing you've got on your shoulder. Did you have stitches?'

'It's a bruise,' he said. 'They put something on it to ease the pain.'

It struck her as odd that a bruise should need a dressing, but the hospital doctors obviously knew more than she did.

'I'm brewing more coffee,' she said. 'And it's time for your next dose of painkillers.'

She found a plate to arrange the cakes on and waited until he returned to the living room on his crutches.

'A man could get used to being looked after like this,' he said, easing himself onto the settee.

'Doesn't Beatrice look after you?'

'She doesn't buy cakes. We have to watch our weight.'

'Where did you two meet?' she asked.

'At a fair laid on by our tourist office. "Health and Beauty in Tuscany" was the theme. We invited various organisations in the region. She'd just opened a salon offering natural therapies. It wasn't long after I lost my folks.' He paused. 'I was lonely, she was friendly. We got together quickly.'

'I'd like to get to know her better.'

'She's very jealous, Alba. She's had a hard time and she's… fragile,' he said.

'She didn't seem the fragile type to me.'

'Yes, well, you only met her for about one hour. The more you get to know a person, the more you discover about them.'

'Or, the more differences you discover,' she said, pouring coffee into their cups and offering him the plate of cakes. 'Help yourself, but bags I have this one,' she said, licking her finger and putting it through the middle of a tart filled with fruits of the forest and crème pâtissière.

He laughed and took a small sponge cake, decorated with walnuts and spirals of dark chocolate. 'Very genteel! You haven't changed,' he said.

'But I have. Of course I have,' she said. 'Eight years of being away in England has definitely changed me from the eighteen-year-old you last met.'

'How did you meet James? You don't mind talking about him, do you?'

'As I said, it's getting easier. We met in Cornwall. I'd always wanted to go there. I used to look at photos on the Internet. The secret coves and stormy seas. And there was this programme on British TV that I loved. Starring a hunky actor.' She pretended to fan herself.

'Not *Poldark*,' he groaned. 'It's on Italian TV now. Beatrice loves him, too. I wouldn't be surprised if she made me parade around Sansepolcro in a puffy white shirt, breeches and boots.'

She giggled. 'Well, it's good to know we have something in common. Good girl!'

'I think you're very different, Alba.'

'So, anyway, I went off to Cornwall for a long weekend and I met James when I was walking along a beach off St Agnes, a stunning, romantic coastline, just how I'd imagined. He'd been surfing and he walked out of the sea in his wetsuit and I fell under his magnetic spell.'

Alfiero groaned. 'You women.'

'He smiled at me and invited me into the beach café, and as his hair dried, it was dirty-blond and his eyes were as blue as the sea he loved, and I was hooked.'

'So, it's important to you as well? The looks, the image?'

'Yes and no. It's not everything, obviously. But don't tell me you never eye up a pretty woman? There's always a first attraction, even if it doesn't work out later on…' She paused. 'He was an adventurous guy to be with. He made me feel alive. We travelled a lot. He took me to Thailand, Tanzania, Greece. Always on a shoestring, backpacking and hitching lifts. We stayed in hostels or slept rough on beaches. He showed me a side to countries I'd never have discovered on a normal tourist trail. I loved being with him.'

'I'm sorry if I'm making you sad. Don't talk about him if you don't want to.'

'It helps, Alfi.' She paused. 'If I'm honest, I think I tried too hard to pin him down and he wasn't the type. He wanted to be free, and… I suppose the bottom line was he didn't love me enough. And maybe I was in love with a romantic idea. But I wish we hadn't argued the last time we were together. I wanted us to move into a new flat, I was forever making wedding preparations… I can't rid myself of the guilt, Alfi. He stormed off, and if I hadn't made him so mad, then maybe he would have been concentrating and he wouldn't have died. He cycled all the time in London. He knew about the danger of pulling up on the nearside of a lorry. I must have caused him to be distracted…'

'You shouldn't blame yourself, Alba.'

'I wish I could believe that.'

It was the most she had talked about James since he'd died, and it was a relief.

There was silence before he continued to speak. She was grateful he didn't keep insisting it wasn't her fault. That was something she had to come to terms with for herself.

'I get what you said about having a romantic idea,' he said. 'We're all looking for something, aren't we? Maybe we look too hard sometimes, instead of letting life happen by itself.'

'Now that I've got distance, a perspective, call it what you like, I can see that we really didn't have enough in common. Trailing around the world with James forever wouldn't have been enough for me. One day I want a family, and I couldn't imagine the way of life we had fitting with that dream.'

'I'm not sure Beatrice would want to get pregnant. It would spoil her figure.'

'Do you live together?' When she'd helped Alfi into his bed, she hadn't noticed women's clothes on the chair in his room, or cosmetics on the chest of drawers. The only giveaway was the skincare in the fridge.

'She would like to, but I'm not sure. But she stays over sometimes.'

'Are you hungry after that cake? How about I start to rustle up my killer spaghetti dish?'

'I'm always hungry.'

As she prepped their supper, which wasn't very complicated – opening a jar of sauce and boiling up a pan of water for pasta didn't require much skill – she wondered about Beatrice and why Alfi was with her. He hadn't talked about why he liked her, except to say that he was lonely when they met, having lost his parents so tragically. It was a shame, because he was such a kind guy, ready to help anybody. As she timed the pasta, it occurred to her that maybe that was it. He needed to help Beatrice. He'd said something about her being fragile. To Alba that didn't seem enough reason to be with another person.

They ate their meal together. The food was adequate, that was all.

'Sorry, Alfi! Not the best meal you've ever tasted, I'm sure.'

'When I'm on my feet again, we'll go to the new pizzeria in the square. They bake the most amazing calzoni in a wood-fired oven. I think they're the best I've ever tasted, especially the ones with grilled vegetables.'

They talked for a while about their time at school, wondering what their classmates had ended up doing. Alfi had met up with some of them last year. 'I've taken up a new hobby,' he said. 'I'm a flag-thrower now for Sansepolcro, and Leo and Sergio are part of our team. Remember them? They were both in the football squad. I was never good at sport, but I really enjoy this. I've got some photos on my phone.' He patted the settee and she went across to sit by him, leaning in to look at the images of the Palio as he scrolled through an album.

'I always enjoyed the Palio,' she said. 'It was an annual outing for us kids. A special trip down from the mountains. I hope they never stop putting it on.'

He showed her a video of his group of *sbandieratori*, moving together, criss-crossing each other in figures of eight, throwing their colourful flags up and catching them on the way down.

'Is that you? No way!' she shouted. 'Pause it, pause it,' she said, as they reached a moment when two *sbandieratori* were performing a complex act.

Alfiero looked amazing in his tunic, tights, leather ankle boots and frilly white shirt.

'You're Poldark,' she said, laughing. 'Look at you. Quite handsome, if you don't mind my saying. No wonder Beatrice likes you to dress up!'

He looked at her, caught hold of her hand, his grip strong. 'Don't tease me, Alba.'

'Sorry…' She snatched her hand away and there was an awkward silence while she rubbed her wrist. She stood up, bemused at the change in his mood.

'I'm tired,' she said. 'I think I'll turn in. Can you tell me where to find a t-shirt and a blanket? I'll make up a bed for myself on the settee. Don't forget your next dose of painkillers.'

'You can have my bed and I'll sleep here.'

'No way. You need all the rest you can get. I'll be fine in here.'

'There's a new toothbrush in the bathroom cupboard. Is there anything else you need?'

'Nope. I'm good, thank you.'

They spoke in staccato phrases, the friendly atmosphere gone.

She took a while to get to sleep, thinking again about Alfiero's sharp reaction earlier, hoping they could resume their banter in the morning. She fell asleep after two o'clock and was woken in the early morning by somebody shouting in her ear.

'What the fuck are you doing here?'

Beatrice stood over her, her expression furious, making every effort to wake up all the inhabitants in the block with her shouting.

'I came back from the *Fiera* to look after my boyfriend,' she continued, 'and you're here. I've been gone only a day and you've moved in. Well, you can get up and get out, you piece of shit. *Stronza.*'

Alba, barely awake, wondering at first if this was a nightmare, swivelled round to a sitting position. 'Whoa, Beatrice. Keep your voice down. What are you on about? I came to help Alfi, that's all.'

'His name is Alfiero.'

Beatrice stormed off to the bedroom and her tirade continued. 'I turn my back and you go with another woman,' she yelled at Alfiero. 'I should have stayed in Milan.' She slammed the door to the bedroom and the shouting continued within. Alba heard the splintering of glass as something crashed to the floor, and she decided to make her exit and leave them to it. Pulling on her clothes and grabbing her rucksack, she left the apartment.

Outside in the street, a cleaning truck was clearing the gutters with its brushes. The driver, in bright orange overalls, saluted her as she started her Vespa. The noise of the machine as he passed by muffled her scooter's tinny motor as she accelerated away from Via della Cipolla and through the sleeping town.

The early-morning air was cold, and she was glad of the fleece she'd stuffed into her rucksack. The road up the mountain was empty of traffic and as the sun rose, mist evaporated from the tarmac. In a field to her right, she spotted four deer grazing at the edge of a copse and as she drew nearer, they bounded off into the woods. Her thoughts were full of Alfiero's raging girlfriend and what he could possibly see in her. All she wanted to do now was get back to the calm of her parents' home and fall into bed.

Three quarters of an hour later, she steered the Vespa down the drive, the reassuring view of the mill and stable bathed in early sunshine a welcome contrast to the grim atmosphere she'd left behind. Inside, she made sure she was quiet so as not to wake Ma and Babbo and scribbled a note, leaving it on the kitchen counter, telling them she was back and needed to sleep in late. She fell into bed and almost as soon as her head touched the pillow, she was gone.

CHAPTER FOURTEEN

Tuscany, 1946

Although Massimo was burning to search for Lucia, his first duty was to make his way back down to Sansepolcro and visit his parents. They were sharing a house at the edge of town with another uncle, within walking distance of the Buitoni pasta factory where the two men now worked.

His mother was pegging out clothes when he turned up, unannounced. She shrieked and dropped a pillowcase on the ground. '*Dio mio*, my God, it's my son, *figlio mio…*' and she came rushing over, covering his face with kisses, pinching his cheeks affectionately between her finger and thumb. 'Is it you, Massimino? Is it really you? Wait until your father and Uncle Pippo get back from work,' his mother said, retrieving the pillowcase from the ground and taking it to scrub away the soil in the outside sink. '*Madonna buona*, I never thought I would see this day,' she said, her tears of joy dropping into the water.

That evening, he shared another delicious homecoming meal: his mother's special dish of *ribollita*, the age-old Tuscan peasant's recipe for using up stale bread, adding white beans, black cabbage, celery, garlic, potatoes, the best olive oil – all the staples of a country larder – to make a delicious, substantial soup. He had forgotten how good it was and he ate three helpings, undoing the belt of his trousers at the end and leaning back in his chair.

'I surrender,' he said. '*Basta! Mammina*, enough! You are a magician.'

His father topped up his son's glass with more red wine. 'Your mother is a witch, not a magician,' he said, and everybody laughed when she flicked at him with her kitchen rag.

He sat between his parents on a bench outside the kitchen once everyone had left for their beds. His mother held his hand in hers, leaning back against the building, its huge stones still warm from the day's sun.

'I am so happy, Massimino. To have you home with us is the best kind of dream,' she said.

'Is this home now, then?' he asked. 'What about our house in Tramarecchia?'

'We are better off here,' his father said. 'There is plenty of work. For you too, *figlio mio.*'

'I am never going back to live there,' his mother said, 'not after what happened.'

'What happened?' Massimo asked.

'We don't talk about it,' his mother said abruptly, getting up from the bench. 'I will clear away the plates and make up a bed for you downstairs. It's late, and your father has work in the morning. *Buonanotte*, Massimo.' She bent to kiss her son.

'*Buonanotte*, Mamma.'

His father told him, under cover of the noise of pots and pans being washed in the sink, about the night when soldiers had come to the village and burned down Lucia's house in the square. Her parents didn't escape the flames, but she had run away.

'Some people say she's still out there somewhere. We searched, but nobody could find her. She must be dead by now.'

'But why did the *Tedeschi* only burn that one house?'

'Because they were searching for one of their own men and Lucia's family had been reported to them, because they knew him.'

Massimo shook his head in disbelief at the horrific images that were conjured, almost hearing the cries of Lucia's family trapped inside the burning building, the terror of his special friend as she ran away, maybe badly burned herself. He knew that awful things had happened all the time in his homeland, but the burning of a simple country family in a tiny hamlet was unimaginable to Massimo.

'Why would they do such a thing?'

'Because they were collaborators,' his father said, spitting into the dirt.

'I don't believe you.'

'You weren't here, Massimo. How do you know what went on here during those years? You were in *Inghilterra*.'

There was silence between father and son, and the old feelings of guilt returned to Massimo for having been away from action for so many years. Yes, he had suffered from the war, but he was beginning to realise his sufferings might not begin to compare with what his family had endured.

'Your mother is right to not want to talk about these things,' his father eventually said, rising from the bench. 'Let's not spoil your homecoming with this discussion. *Buonanotte.*' He squeezed Massimo's shoulder and went up to bed.

Massimo stayed outside to smoke another cigarette. Gazing upwards, he watched a shooting star slide its way down the night sky. But he found he had no wishes he wanted to make. All he could think of was his need to get to the bottom of what had happened to Lucia. If nobody was prepared to tell him, then he would have to find out for himself.

The next day, he kissed his mother goodbye and told her he needed to return to Tramarecchia and would live in the family house and work the family meadows. 'Until I know what to do with my life, Mamma. I need time on my own after years of being ordered about. Tell Babbo I don't need a job in a factory. Forgive me.'

Urging him to come down and see them as often as he could, she clung to him for a while and then kissed him before making the sign of the cross. She took her gold chain and medal from her neck and fastened it around his.

'My guardian angel will look after you,' she murmured. 'At least I shall know where you are now, so that will have to be enough for the time being.'

She wrapped a cheese and half a ham into a cotton *saccone* that she had woven for her own larder and waved him off, watching until he disappeared down a side street leading to the bus station.

*

In the first days of being back in his mountain village, Massimo did little more than sleep late and go for long walks during the day, revelling in his freedom and for the first time in seven years doing what he wanted, without permits or curfews. He was warned by his neighbour not to wander too near the peak above Montebotolino.

'The bastard *Tedeschi* have sown mines up there as a leaving present. Agostino lost one of his prize cows last month when she got through the fence, blown into nothing,' Robertino told him. The women who had ignored him at the fountain on that first day when Massimo had returned to Tramarecchia were his wife and daughters. The sisters made a curious pair as they scuttled about the hamlet, casting their eyes down whenever they were in his vicinity. He wondered why they were so afraid of him.

But he preferred to keep to himself anyway. During the war years, he'd always been with others. The greatest gift to him in those first weeks was solitude. When he wasn't rediscovering the mountains that had once been so familiar, he whiled away his time with household tasks: collecting driftwood for his fire from the riverbed; digging the neglected patch of garden, sowing lettuce, tomatoes, courgettes and spinach beet. In the woods, he set snares for pheasants and hares. He had bought a dozen hens and a noisy cockerel in the market square. They soon provided him daily with eggs, and he took what he couldn't consume back to the little market square in Badia Tedalda, selling them for a few lire. He spent that on sugar, coffee and cigarettes. Robertino was happy to exchange eggs for the occasional bottle of home-brewed wine. Massimo needed little else.

In the evenings, he took to lighting a fire outside his front door and sitting on a bench, smoking his roll-ups and gazing at the stars in the black sky. One evening he heard wolves calling from the opposite peaks. He could identify with their wildness, their freedom to roam, and he felt like howling back.

'Why do you sit outside with your fire?' Robertino asked one evening. 'Why don't you use your hearth, like everybody else?'

'Because I can,' was Massimo's simple reply.

He planted a row of deep purple iris along one side of his vegetable patch and dug up young bushes of bright yellow broom from the wild to fence off his plot, thinking back to Molly's English country garden spilling over with roses, and her tangle of strange-sounding flowers like delphinium and snapdragons that she used to stuff into jars on her windowsills.

'What are you planting that stuff for?' Robertino asked, when they were sharing a bottle of vinegary wine another evening, the women sitting on chairs by their front door, darning cotton bed sheets. 'You can't eat any of it,' Robertino observed.

How to explain that he wanted to surround himself with the beauty of nature that he hadn't been able to freely enjoy for so many years? On his walks, Massimo would stop to observe the shapes of the leaves in the canopies of trees above, or bend to examine the many separate petals on an orchid flower, relishing the ability to do what he wanted in his own time. It was too hard to explain to somebody who hadn't been confined for years and years. Massimo knew that his neighbours had not been without suffering, but his own war had been different. His privations had been of another kind.

Occasionally there was a shot from the woods and he would jump, instinctively wanting to dive for cover. He'd done that once and Robertino had roared with laughter. 'They're hunting for boar,' he said. 'If there are any left. The *Tedeschi* stole our game, too. They stole everything, our crops, wine, cheese... even our women. And there's thieving still going on. Somebody stole my best shirt the other day from where it was drying on the bushes. Pah! This country will never be the same again.'

Massimo wanted to tell him to shut up, to stop being a pessimist, to look around and be thankful for everything that lay before them: for the mountains encircling them, the lush forests producing wild strawberries and blueberries, the birds that woke him each morning with their song instead of a camp alarm call, for the river that gushed below the village and gave them fresh, clear water. But he kept his counsel and shut his mouth. It was pointless trying to reason with somebody who had never been parted from this paradise.

One night, he was kept awake in his single metal bed by continuous rounds of gunfire. Robertino had told him the poachers would be busy because the first-ever rigorous hunting regulations were coming into force. People were trying to fill their larders before game shooting was restricted to number and season.

The next day was his birthday, and he left his bed just after dawn, unable to sleep, curious about the hunting that had gone on all night. Up the steep track that led away from the river on the opposite bank, he noticed blood trails and presumed it would be from the corpse of a boar or deer, dragged away by hunters to collect later. But, rounding a corner, he came across the tiny, shivering body of a small dog, crouching beneath a rock. As Massimo approached to examine the creature, it snarled, baring little white teeth, shrinking further back against its shelter. Massimo hunkered down, speaking softly, trying to soothe the injured animal that was frantically licking blood from its front right paw. It was young, probably no more than a few weeks old. Massimo stood up and searched around to see if there were any more puppies, and a metre away from the path, further into the woods, he found the corpses of a fully grown she-wolf and five cubs, shot and left to rot.

The puppy wasn't a dog, after all. He didn't have a gun on him to dispatch the lone cub, and neither did he have the heart to finish off its misery with a rock. Death had been too present in these last years. So, removing his jacket, he reached for the cub, which yelped and whined as he bent to scoop it up. He quickly wrapped the wriggling bundle to avoid scratches, noticed it was a male and hugged him tightly to his body. He stood, rocking it like a baby for a couple of minutes, trying to calm the terrified animal, thinking fleetingly back to the restless, colicky moments of baby Denis, wondering how Molly was and debating if he might drop her a line one of these days. The animal stilled, warm from Massimo's body, and he set off home.

Once he was back, Massimo placed the little cub in an old crate in the storeroom, where onions and hams used to hang when his mother ran the household, and lined it with a piece of sacking for a makeshift bed. He woke and started to whine. Massimo fetched a bowl of milk and added torn-up pieces from a loaf, hoping this substitute for a mother's milk wouldn't harm the little animal. Placing the bowl on the floor, he watched in amusement as the cub devoured his first human breakfast with greedy laps of his little tongue. When he had finished, the cub crouched to wee on the stone floor and Massimo decided there and then that he would build a kennel and place it by the front door. Scooping him up before he could deposit anything more, he went outside with his new charge.

His little tummy was swollen like a ball and his jaws were wet and white from the milk. Massimo wiped it away with his fingers. As they sat together on the front step, the cub turned on his lap three times before plonking down and curling up close to Massimo's stomach, and closed his eyes.

What the bloody hell have I done? Massimo thought as he observed the rise and fall of the little rounded tummy. *I'll call you Lupino, little wolf, and you and I will probably fall out over lots of things before long, including chasing my chickens. But I couldn't leave you to die. What a birthday present I've given myself!*

He stroked the short, stubby fur on top of Lupino's head and nearly dozed off himself on the step.

Massimo's worries were banished from quite early on. The little wolf cub behaved himself and followed him around as if Massimo were his mother: nipping at his trouser legs if he felt neglected, staying near him while he worked in the vegetable patch. Massimo discovered Lupino liked to eat earthworms, and he would sit patiently, head cocked on one side, waiting like a robin for Massimo's spade to reveal another wriggling brown titbit. At first, when Massimo walked in the forest, he made sure to lead Lupino with a rope, afraid he would run off and get lost. If a wolf from another pack were to come upon him, that would mean certain death. And Massimo was growing fond of the company of his new pet that didn't answer back or expect anything more than food and affection.

Sitting by his front step at the end of the day, they would play together, Massimo teasing the cub with a length of string or chucking him pine cones to fetch and carry. When Lupino had chased one of his chickens, he was sternly reprimanded. He knew the animal had understood when his little tail curled under his back legs and he lay down in submission.

'If that dog comes anywhere near my geese, I'll shoot him,' Robertino had said, observing Lupino's antics. Massimo had lied to his neighbours when they saw the new arrival. 'It's an Alsatian puppy,' Massimo said. 'Meet Lupino. They were giving puppies away at market today.' He wondered for how long they would believe him. And once or twice he wondered himself how things would develop. A cub was one thing. A fully grown male wolf, another. But for the time being, he was enjoying the new member of his family.

A couple of weeks after buying them, his hens started to lay fewer eggs. Most days he could collect at least ten, but they were dwindling to six, and he thought about buying half a dozen more next time he was at market. Maybe he'd been swindled and sold old layers the first time. He resolved to be more prudent next time he bargained with the poultry seller. It occurred to him that the presence of Lupino might be slowing down egg-laying, and so he stopped allowing the cub anywhere near the coop.

Early one morning, before the cock had crowed, he heard Lupino barking and he rolled out of bed to peer through his window. The cub was straining at the long chain that secured him at night to his kennel. Massimo caught a movement near the chicken house and watched as a young boy crept away, holding something to his stomach.

My eggs, Massimo thought, and pushing open his window, he yelled, 'Hey, *ladro*. Come back here, thieving rascal!'

The boy turned, eyes wide with fear in a dirty face. Massimo pulled on his trousers and, ramming his feet into his boots, clattered down the stairs as fast as he could. He ran in pursuit of the boy, but he had disappeared.

CHAPTER FIFTEEN

Tuscany, present day

Over minestrone and home-made bread, Alba and her parents discussed arrangements about a lunch invitation for Massimo.

'I kind of feel it's best to not put things off with him,' Alba said. 'It sounds morbid, but he's really quite frail.'

'Let's see if he can come tomorrow,' Anna suggested.

'I'll pop up to the village later this afternoon and sort it. Is there anything I can do to help before then? I'm treating home like a hotel at the moment.'

'Help me make the beds in the mill for the guests arriving tomorrow. Thanks, Alba.'

Jobs completed, two hours later Alba fetched the Vespa from the stone garage at the side of the house. Her phone pinged and she pulled it out, thinking it might be Alfiero. Despite trying to push thoughts of the night she'd spent in his flat to the back of her mind, she was worried about him. The message was from someone else, but she sent Alfiero a line anyway.

Hope things are okay. Take care. Alba

Almost immediately a message pinged back:

Best you keep away.

Slipping her phone into her rucksack pocket, she was puzzled. They'd been getting on so well. If it was something to do with his awful girlfriend, then he needed to sort himself out. If she was honest, she felt a little hurt. If that was the way he wanted it, then good riddance.

*

Massimo was having an afternoon sleep, Tanya told him.

'Oh dear,' Alba said, looking at her watch. It was only three o'clock. 'Is he ill?'

'No, *cara*. But he didn't have a very good night.'

You and me both, Alba thought.

'So, he's having a little rest.'

'Will it be all right to collect him for lunch at my parents' home tomorrow? They really want to meet him,' Anna asked the carer.

Tanya laughed. 'That sounds like future parents-in-law wanting to make sure he is suitable for you.'

Alba smiled. 'Well, if he was younger, I'd be after him like a shot. Wouldn't you?'

'He is a very nice gentleman, signorina,' Tanya said, 'but I like a man to be... how you say it? *Robusto*.' Her raucous laughter bounced off the walls of the care centre.

'I'll pick him up at half past eleven tomorrow. Phone me if anything changes.'

Alba walked across the square to the tourist office to check in with Egidio.

'Ha! Just the young lady I wanted to see,' he said, greeting her with a friendly smile. 'Alba, I have a proposition. I'd like to make your job official and pay you for the work you're doing for us.'

'Really?' she said. 'That's amazing.'

'I was at a meeting yesterday, Alba, and we discussed how useful you'd be with your knowledge of English when the *turisti* come in…' He lowered his voice. 'Keep this to yourself for the time being, but I'm handing in my notice soon. I'm an old man and it's time to move over for younger blood and fresh ideas. So, it's a good time for you to join. Let's talk about it more over an Aperol in the bar,' he concluded, picking up his leather manbag and coming out from behind the counter. 'We'll lock up now. Nobody ever comes in here at this time of day.'

As they sipped their drinks, Alba looked around the little bar, feeling a part of this community again, noticing a couple of old school friends who waved at her from another table. The conversations with Massimo had helped in her understanding of what this little town had been through during the war years; what had shaped the place. The prospect of working in the tourist office really appealed, and would make it easier to carry out further research. She raised her glass to Egidio. '*Cin cin!*' she said. '*Grazie!*'

*

'Let me take your coat, signor Massimo,' Anna said, as Alba guided her old friend through the door into the Stalla. Despite the warmth of the morning, he was still dressed for winter.

'Don't cast a clout until May be out,' he said in English and continued in Italian, 'That's what my English boss always used to say to me. It's funny what I remember in English. But it was always much colder in *Inghilterra*. That was one of the many things I missed about being away from *Italia*.'

'But it's July,' Alba said with a laugh. 'You can take your thick coat off now. It's plenty warm enough.'

'You wait until you're old, *tesoro*,' he said to Alba. 'The cold lingers in your bones.'

They sat straight down at the table. After twenty years of living in Italy, Anna knew that was the way it was. No lingering, polite conversation before the meal; no peanuts and nibbles to spoil the appetite, but simply getting down to the serious business of eating. Anna had made vegetable soup from home-grown produce to start with, which Massimo seemed to enjoy. As he slurped noisily from his spoon, Francesco winked at Alba.

'What else did you miss of Italy when you were a POW?' he asked the old man.

'My mother especially, and my friends,' he said. 'But there were many simple things I missed. Our *toscano* bread, for example. English bread is soft and salty. And the coffee, even though at home we couldn't afford proper coffee. We used to drink roasted barley or acorns.'

He spoke in Italian today, lapsing into occasional dialect. Anna understood most words, but occasionally she had to ask for a translation as he gained speed.

'But I didn't have such a bad time, really,' he continued. 'If you take away the fact that we weren't ever free – even after the Armistice when we were kept on as labourers – I think I had it a lot easier than my family here in Tuscany.'

He fell silent for a few moments, lost in thought.

Alba noted that the way he talked to her parents was different from when she and Massimo were alone together in Tramarecchia. With them, he was more guarded in what he related. He spoke in general terms, explaining about the type of jobs he had to carry out on the farm in England, the differences in the crops he had to help sow and harvest, saying that even the taste of the apples and pears had been different.

'Don't forget it was wartime,' Francesco said. 'The planting would have been different from normal. It was all done to provide as much food as possible in the quickest, easiest way to the population.'

'My friend' – Massimo leant forward in his chair – 'with respect, I know only too well that it was wartime. I could never forget that. All six years of it.'

'Of course, I didn't mean to offend…'

'No offence taken, young man. But it is a time I lived through and you have only read about in your books.'

Alba had never considered her father to be a young man. He had turned sixty. 'Babbo will love you for calling him a young man,' she said with a laugh.

'Everybody is young to me – except for my friends in the care centre prison.' He winked at her.

He refused the second course of roast rabbit and guinea fowl, but ate a side dish of spinach beet that Anna had prepared with plenty of garlic and good olive oil. 'My appetite is diminished,' he explained. 'But I'll have more of your excellent wine,' he told Francesco, holding up his glass. 'Sangiovese, isn't it?'

The home-made tiramisu went down well too, as did the glasses of Vin Santo and hard *cantuccini* biscuits served afterwards, which he had to soak well in the strong *digestivo*. It seemed he had a sweet tooth.

'Your daughter is a special girl,' he said, slightly slurring his words, holding his tiny liqueur glass up to her in a toast. 'I enjoy her company. I never had a daughter of my own.' He hiccupped and apologised. 'So, after my coffee, I wonder if she could take me back to the prison? I feel weary.' He smiled. 'It's wrong of me to call it the prison, I know. They are very good to me at the centre. I have to accept it is my home now.'

He thanked Francesco and Anna politely after his espresso and Alba drove him back to the village, kissing him on his whiskery cheek after she'd delivered him into Tanya's care. In the car, she'd asked him if he knew anything about the partisan raid of the Boccarini estate. He shook his head and turned his face towards the window.

'I've come across a book that talks about the partisans up on the Mountain of the Moon,' Alba continued. 'And a young man called Quinto. Did you know him? I think he went to school in the village.'

There was silence from Massimo, and she wondered if he had dozed off, but after a few seconds, he turned to her and spoke. 'Many things went on around here during the war, but I was in *Inghilterra*, and when I returned to Tuscany, people wanted to forget the war and get on with life.' He turned up the collar on his coat and leant back against the seat and closed his eyes, preventing further conversation.

'I think he'll sleep well tonight,' Alba whispered to Tanya as he tottered off to the residents' living area. 'I was wondering if it would be possible to let him stay a weekend in Tramarecchia?' she asked Tanya. 'I'd be with him. I think he would love it.'

'What a wonderful idea, signorina. Leave it with me and I'll chat with the manager.'

Alba hoped there would be no objections. Massimo deserved a treat. But she couldn't help thinking that he knew more than he was letting on. She hoped he would share more of his stories with her.

CHAPTER SIXTEEN

Tuscany, 1946

After a few days, Massimo's egg supply dwindled again, and he decided he had to catch his thief. He attached thin wire to the gate latch of the hen run, tying a sheep bell to the other end. The nights were warm, and he made a bed outside from his grandfather's thick old shepherd's cloak and lay down next to Lupino's kennel. The cub curled up beside his master and, watching the fireflies before he fell asleep, Massimo wondered why he hadn't done this before. He drifted off with the sounds of an owl hooting and, in the distance, the river splashing over the weir.

Lupino was aware of something first. He growled, then the bell tinkled and, after unleashing him from his chain, the two of them bounded over to the hens. It was the boy again. In his haste to escape, he had tripped over the wire and fallen to the ground. Massimo scooped him up. The young thief wriggled and struggled in his arms before sinking his teeth into his captor's hand.

'*Bastardino*,' Massimo yelped and gave him a cuff round the ear. Lupino jumped up at the lad's heels, nipping and yelping as he flailed his feet, trying to escape.

'Put me down,' the boy shouted.

'I'll put you down once you stop kicking me,' Massimo said. 'If you don't stop wriggling, I'll wallop you again.'

The thief calmed down and Massimo set him on the ground. He kept tight hold of his ear and led him back to the house.

The boy dug his heels in. 'Where are you taking me?' he yelled, and Massimo yanked him onwards.

'We're going to have a little chat about stealing. And, if you're so hungry, I thought I might find you something to eat.'

The boy hung his head and started to snivel, and Massimo took pity. 'Don't worry, lad, I won't harm you, but if we stay out here arguing, you'll wake the rest of the village and you wouldn't want that. They might not take so kindly to a thief in their midst.'

'There's nobody else here except old Robertino and those mean bitches,' came the reply. Something about the boy's voice made Massimo stop and do a double take. Putting his hand under the boy's chin and turning his face upwards, a moment of shock and recognition coursed through him. 'Lucia,' he gasped. 'Lucia, is it really you?'

Her face was streaked with dirt, her hair a greasy mess, her trousers and shirt were in rags and she was barefoot, but her deep green eyes were unmistakably the eyes of the girl he had grown up with.

She jutted out her chin defiantly. 'And so?' she asked. 'What if I am Lucia? What are you going to do with me now?'

Despite her defiance, her eyes were swimming with unshed tears. He pulled her to him, wrapping his arms around her. She resisted at first, then he felt her body shudder and she started to sob.

'Let's get you inside,' he said, leading her towards the house. She went meekly and he shut the front door, gesturing to her to sit at the table.

He felt her watching him as he fetched bread and cheese from the corner cupboard and cut slices from a ham hanging from a hook in the ceiling. She stuffed the food into her mouth, tearing at the bread with her filthy hands, her nails black with dirt.

She gulped down the glass of milk he placed before her and he wondered when she had last sat at a table to eat a proper meal.

Massimo set a light to the fire laid in the hearth and went to fetch water to heat in the cauldron hanging above the fire to pour into the large zinc bowl in the storeroom. 'You can wash, I'll find you fresh clothes, and then we can talk,' he said.

She stopped chewing and looked at him with horror.

'Don't worry. I will leave you alone to bathe yourself. Lucia, it's your old friend Massimo, you mustn't be afraid of me.'

He went outside and sat with Lupino, stroking the cub's fur and wondering what had happened to reduce his childhood friend to her miserable state. Once upon a time, before the war had come in like a mighty storm and blown all their lives apart, there had been the expectation that they would marry. Maybe by now there would have been a young family to care for. But so much had happened to change these plans; the war had sent them down different roads. 'What am I going to do, Lupino?' he muttered aloud. The animal licked his hand and settled down at his feet, his shaggy tail thumping in the dust by the front step.

When he thought Lucia would be finished attending to herself, he went back into the house. She had gone from the kitchen and he called out, but there was no answer. He climbed the ladder to his bed and she was there, curled up fast asleep, her scarecrow hair wet on his pillow. He tiptoed across the wide oak floorboards and pulled the covers gently over her naked shoulders, then went next door to his parents' bedroom. That night he tossed and turned in the big bed, wondering how best to deal with this girl, so deteriorated and fragile since the last time he had seen her. Soon after six o'clock, when he brought her up a cup of boiled milk and ersatz coffee, he found the bed empty.

Now that he had found her and knew she was still alive, alone out there on the mountain, God knew where, he had to find her again. Massimo gathered a few items from his cupboards: half a loaf, a quarter of a pecorino cheese, a jar of damson jam that Robertino had given him, a handful of dried borlotti beans and a chunk of *Capocollo* sausage and placed them all in a sack. He added a knife and spoon and a bottle of milk. Stopping to assess whether these provisions were enough, he grabbed a half-finished bottle of wine as well as a corner of soap. Then, racing up the ladder to his parents' room, he pulled one of his mother's shawls from the chest at the end of her bed. Even though it was August, the nights could turn cold, and she might be sleeping rough. Finally, he took the filthy rags that Lucia had been wearing and thrust them under the animal's muzzle. The wolf spent some time sniffing the torn shirt and breeches, whining and snuffling. 'You're going to help me find her, aren't you, *amico mio*,' Massimo said, scratching the wolf cub behind his ears and tying a home-made leash around his neck.

Massimo had an idea where she might be. When they were young, the little gang from Tramarecchia used to disappear to a cave they'd discovered off the path that led towards the peak of Montebotolino. His father had warned them that route was known as the *Passo dei Ladri*, the Thieves' Pass, and that if they happened to get in the way of brigands, they'd be in serious danger. This warning was most likely a way of keeping the children safe, for the area was prone to landslides, but the thrill of danger had only made the children want to go to their cave more frequently, and it had become a kind of den or a *rifugio* when they wanted to escape from adults. From their homes, they'd each nicked bits and pieces and made the place into a little house: stubs of candles, matches, chipped plates and cups that had been thrown out on the village dump, an old piece of tarpaulin to lie on. Massimo remembered how the boys had carved items from pieces of wood they'd found in the river: hooks for the cave wall, wooden spoons to eat from. He had a scar on his left hand, between his thumb and forefinger, where his knife had slipped in his clumsy attempts at whittling the wood. He touched it now and smiled at the memory of those innocent days.

Massimo and Lupino crossed the river at the weir. The sun was already climbing high in the sky, and the water looked inviting. He bent down to submerge his face and neck while the wolf cub lapped at the cool water, before they started the climb to the Thieves' Pass.

He was breathing heavily when they reached the rock formation that had always seemed to him like the arches of a giant portal to another world. Huge slabs above him were like the turrets of a castle. On the other side of this archway the path led through a dense beech wood, the shadows under the thick canopy dark and foreboding. As children, they had subconsciously stuck closer together whenever they passed through this section, each probably remembering their parents' talk about brigands. In the evenings, when the families in the village took turns to invite each other to their *veglie*, or gatherings, they were used to listening to stirring recitals of passages from the classics, like Dante or Ariosto. Massimo always thought of the opening lines from the *Inferno*, where Dante spoke of entering a dark and savage wood halfway through his life, at a stage when he was lost and troubled. He always recited those lines whenever they passed through the spooky copse:

> *'Halfway along the journey of our life, I found myself in a dark forest; the way ahead was lost…'*
> *'Nel mezzo del cammin di nostra vita, mi ritrovai per una selva oscura, che la diritta via era smarrita…'*

He had done it to distract himself, as well as the members of his little gang, until they were safely through the gloomy tunnel of leaves and out the other side. Here the treeline ended, and the sun shone down on them as they ran towards their cave.

Today, the shade in the woods was a welcome respite from the morning heat and he slowed his pace to enjoy the cool air, Lupino panting as he followed his master. He called out Lucia's name as they approached the rocky outface that hid the cave's entrance. It wasn't easy to find. Thick creepers hung from the top of the outcrop, concealing a slit of an opening in the rocks. Massimo remembered that the landmark to search for was a majestic oak tree growing ten paces to the east. As children, they had tied a rope from one of its thick branches and swung in turns, daring each other to go higher and higher, listening to the creak of the rope as it rubbed against the branch. He was dismayed to see now that the tree had been struck by lightning, its huge trunk reduced to a metre-high blackened stump.

There was no reply to his calls, but Lupino immediately nosed the air and the ground and he was off on the trail, zigzagging his way towards the entrance of the cave. Massimo followed, calling Lucia's name softly, parting the creepers to look within. It took a few moments for his eyes to adjust to the gloom, but eventually he could see that the cave was being used. Searching for signs to help confirm the occupant, he saw a nightdress hanging from one of the wooden pegs he had made all those years ago. It was filthy, covered in scorch marks and holes. In the far corner, a mound of dry leaves and grass was most likely where she slept. The remnants of a fire and an old pot showed where she cooked. He called again, but either she was hiding, or she was nowhere near, for Lupino would surely have detected her scent.

He left the sack and its contents near her makeshift bedding and cursed himself for not having thought to bring a note. Picking up a stick, he scratched his name in the dirt by her bed. That way she would know who had left the supplies.

'She's not here, Lupino, we'll have to come back. We must be patient, my friend.' The wolf cub wagged his tail and Massimo laughed. 'You have no idea what I am saying, have you?' Lupino wagged his tail more vigorously and cocked his head to one side, looking up at the leader of his small pack.

'Come on, Lupino,' Massimo said, yanking the rope to encourage the cub to follow.

He decided to take a longer route back to Tramarecchia. There was another way that led to the river and the weir, a spot where blackberries and wild raspberries grew. He would harvest a few and maybe uproot a couple of plants for his kitchen garden. The route was longer, but it was easier than the earlier climb and Massimo enjoyed his walk, all the while planning how he was going to approach Lucia, who seemed so terrified.

As he drew near the river, Lupino strained at his leash. A woman was singing. A sad tune, sung in a minor key, in a language Massimo didn't understand. The sound of the waterfall muffled his approach, and he stood for a while, listening, watching Lucia dangling her feet in the water, plucking petals from an ox-eye daisy and casting them one by one into the pool as she sang.

A movement from the wolf cub must have caught her peripheral vision and she stopped abruptly, getting to her feet, fear showing in her face. Massimo stepped forward and shortened the leash, so that Lupino was right next to him. 'Don't worry, Lucia,' he called. 'He's tame. He won't hurt you.'

Her shoulders slumped in relief and she smiled weakly. 'Where did you find him?' she asked, approaching them tentatively, holding out her hand to the cub, who strained towards her, rising on his back legs. She let him nuzzle and lick her hand and the little animal seemed to relax her, because she looked up at Massimo, a real smile on her face. In that moment, he caught a glimpse of the Lucia he remembered.

Massimo sat down by the river's edge and patted the space next to him, but she shook her head and moved away.

'Don't be afraid, Lucia.'

She shook her head again and began to walk back up the mountain. He called after her, 'I left you something. Up there in the den,' he added.

She turned back and stood still, a mixed look of fury and terror on her face. It reminded him of an animal frozen in the glare of lights.

He persisted, while he had her attention. 'I'll bring you more food, if you want.'

Again, she shook her head and with some instinct, he understood that the cave was her haven; he should not violate her space and go there uninvited.

'I won't come again if you don't want me to. But if you need anything, you know where I am,' he said, getting up to leave. He strode away along the river, not wanting her to feel she was being followed, thinking to himself that she would be much harder to tame than Lupino. He wanted to know what had terrorised her so much to turn her so wild. Massimo decided that he would help her. No matter how long it took.

CHAPTER SEVENTEEN

Tuscany, present day

Massimo looked pale and even slighter, bundled up again in his large overcoat, but he broke into a huge grin when Alba walked into the care centre. She bent to kiss him on each cheek.

'You're looking a little under the weather,' she said. 'What's up?'

'Only a cold,' he said. 'They make too much fuss in here. At this time of the year, with changes in temperature, it's normal.'

'He can't wait to go to his house,' Tanya said, 'and it works out perfectly because we are short-staffed. But make sure he wraps up warm, please.' She handed Alba a list of instructions and contact details. Turning to Massimo, she wagged her finger and told him to behave.

The old man winked at Alba. 'But of course. Goodbye, Tanya, my dear.' He stood up and was out of the door, as nimble as a child, so that Alba had to catch up with him.

As soon as he was in the front seat and she'd started the engine, he unbuttoned his coat. 'I only put this on to keep them happy.' He let out a huge sigh and sat back, gazing out at the view of the mountains across the valley. The flat tabletop peaks of the Sasso di Simone and Simoncello dominated the skyline; the meadows were yellow with masses of buttercups. It seemed that summer was on its way at last.

'It's so good to be out of that place,' he muttered.

Alba felt sorry for him, wondering what it must be like for a person to have to accept the loss of liberty. He'd had such an eventful, full life from what he'd told her so far. It must be frustrating to be confined and cared for in an institution at the end of one's life. With the best will in the world, with the best staff and facilities, an institution could never replace one's own home.

Massimo wound down the window and leant out to breathe in the air. They were on the dirt track now, rounding the bend past the *canile*, the local dog pound. 'Stop, stop,' he said.

'What's the matter?'

'Let's go and see the dogs,' he said.

'Don't we have to make an appointment? It's closed to visitors, isn't it?'

'Don't worry about that. I know Gianfranco. He'll let us in.'

She parked up under a row of oaks and went to help Massimo out, but he was already walking up the path to the metal gates. The dogs were barking now, her cries of 'wait for me' drowned by their yelping and howls.

'Eh, Gianfranco,' Massimo called, his voice making the dogs more excited. A couple of them started to bay and then the rest of them joined in, sounding like a pack of wolves. '*Sono io*. It's me. Let me in, *paesano*,' he said, using the affectionate term for a fellow villager.

A scruffy middle-aged man wearing hunter's camouflage trousers came out from a building behind the shelters. He carried a shovel in his hand and a couple of the dogs jumped up at the wire netting as he passed. He made a clicking noise with his mouth and they settled down.

'How is he, Gianfranco?' Massimo asked as he approached.

'He'll be better for seeing you. How the devil are you, Massimo?' Gianfranco said, glancing at Alba. 'Haven't seen you in a while. I began to think you'd popped your clogs. Got yourself a new girlfriend, have you?' His smile was friendly, and he shook both their hands.

Massimo ignored his questions and hurried over to a caged area near a house. A small vegetable plot was already planted with a row of tomatoes and salads, a cat curled up on the mat outside the door.

She watched as Massimo opened the door to the last cage. A dirty white mongrel stood waiting, a hound that resembled a Maremmano shepherd dog and something else she couldn't fathom. His tail wagged frantically like a fast metronome, and his tongue hung out of his mouth as if he was smiling.

'Freddie, Freddie, *amico mio*,' Massimo said, bending to pat the dog, who nuzzled up to him. He took a handful of biscuits from one of the large pockets in his overcoat and threw one of them in the air. Freddie jumped to catch it in his mouth and stayed on his hind paws for a moment longer until Massimo threw him another. 'Still life in you, old friend,' he chuckled as the dog lay on his back, waiting for his tummy to be tickled.

'Here, take him out for his walk,' the dog warden said, handing Massimo a lead. 'But remember not to tell anybody. I'll get the sack.'

'What about taking him in the car with us down to Tramarecchia for the weekend?' Alba asked.

Gianfranco shrugged his shoulders. 'There's nobody there to see and nobody to hear I gave you permission,' he said. 'So, that's fine. Let the pair of them have time together.'

She encouraged Freddie into the back seat of the car, and they continued down the track.

'Your dog?' Alba asked.

'My old friend, yes. A house without a dog is not a home. Both of us are locked up now. The centre wouldn't let me keep him, but he's in good hands with Gianfranco and I know he'd invent all kinds of reasons against his adoption if anybody wanted him.'

Massimo let Freddie off the leash as soon as they arrived at the red house, and Alba watched as the dog seemed to take on a new lease of life as he scurried around the green piazza, nosing the grass, stopping at a tree for a while to scent whatever creature had already passed that way, cocking his leg to claim the territory once again. Massimo had removed his vast coat, and when she asked him if that was wise, he'd said, 'Why do you think I agreed to wear it in the first place? The pockets, Alba, the pockets.' He pulled a small package wrapped in a paper serviette from an inside pocket and called Freddie over before placing a small steak on the ground. 'I sneaked it from my plate at lunch.'

Later on, Massimo and Alba sat down by the river fishing from the weir. With the aid of a stout walking stick he retrieved from the house, which, he told her, he'd made from elm wood years ago, his other hand clasped tightly in hers, they'd managed the steep path that led down from the village. Freddie trailed behind them, dawdling frequently to mark his territory. On the way to the river, Massimo had taken her into a copse of pines and led her to a spot where a couple of porcini mushrooms were growing at the base of one of the trees. 'This will be our starter for our supper feast tonight,' he said. '*Che spettacolo!* I always used to find them here and luck is with us today, too.' His joy was infectious, and they did a high five.

Later, his smile again lit up his features as he organised himself at the river, placing a wicker basket in the shallows and then casting out his line into the pool.

'Eee, what more could we ask for? I am in heaven today,' he said, as he waited for the first nibble.

'Well, I'm hoping you actually catch some trout. That salad we made won't fill us up.'

'Be patient, Alba, "All good things come to those who wait".
Abbi un po' di pazienza!

One of the first things they'd done together after Alba had
opened the shutters was to harvest wild plants and flowers for
a salad that Massimo longed to eat again. As well as young tips
of dandelions, there were leaves of bladderwort, or *silene*, as he
called them, and to Alba's surprise, he plucked one of the roses
growing near the house to add to the salad. 'I planted this for
Lucia. She loved her flowers,' he said, mixing in the petals with
marigold and wild mallow flowers, before sprinkling the floral
mix onto the green leaves.

'How you must miss her,' she said. 'I only knew James for five
years, but it was hard when he died.'

He stopped mixing the salad and gazed through the window.
'Si, *cara mia*. We were together for many years. Almost fifty.'

Alba hugged him and then packed the colourful salad into a
plastic container for their al fresco lunch, adding oil, vinegar and
salt from his store cupboard to season it later.

She made up their beds with sheets and blankets that Anna
had packed into the car. 'Take these, Alba,' Ma had said, 'his bed
linen will need airing. And if you need anything at all, whatever
time of night, phone us. We're only down the river. He's a very
old man.'

Everybody seemed more concerned than she was. He was
frail, but being back in his hamlet seemed to rejuvenate him. All
that mattered to her was that Massimo enjoyed spending time
in his old home.

Alba sketched him as he fished and decided to use it as a
draft for a watercolour she would complete at home. She hadn't
brought her paints along, and to achieve the effect of water, she
needed her masking liquid. She also took photos on her phone
to record other details: how the colours of the water changed,

the way it turned frothy-white as it cascaded over the weir. Three dragonflies flitted from a fallen branch, skimming across the surface, and she hoped to recreate their iridescent sparkle.

'More pictures of me?' he asked.

'I want to paint you, Massimo, and I need to remember the details for later. Do you mind?'

He repeated what he'd said on another occasion, about making him look more handsome in her pictures.

'What about if I recorded you talking, too? For Egidio's exhibition? What do you think of that?'

'So that other people could listen?' he asked, looking away from his float. 'I wouldn't like that, Alba. Not at all. I don't mind talking to *you*, but the details of my life are not for the whole world to know.'

'I understand, Massimo.'

And she did. She was honoured that he felt able to share his story with her. In truth, she wouldn't want her own details recorded for others to listen to and critique. It wasn't as if she'd done anything out of the ordinary: she hadn't climbed the highest mountain or invented a life-saving drug. She was just a young woman stumbling along in life. And most likely Massimo felt the same about himself, although many people wouldn't think that way about his story at all. The war had churned the ordinary into the extraordinary.

Her thoughts were interrupted by Massimo's cry of delight as he plucked his rod from the water. Freddie barked, his tail wagging vigorously as a fish wriggled and silvered in the sunlight. Alba watched as her old friend gently and expertly removed the hook from its mouth and stowed it in the basket that rested in the shallows.

'Two more of these fellows and we'll have our meal,' he pronounced, lighting up a cigarette and blowing smoke into the air.

'Bravo, Massimo!' she said, snapping another photo of him, recording the happiness on his face.

'We should really have a permit to do this,' he said, 'so don't show that photo to everybody. I used to have success when I tickled trout, but the water is too cold for me to stay in the river now. When I think how many hours I have spent, bent over the water, waiting for the right time to put my hands around a trout hiding under a rock, soothing it by gently stroking its belly until it relaxed into my grasp.'

He caught one more and they decided two were enough. Together they collected dry twigs and larger pieces of driftwood to make a fire on the riverbank to cook the fish. She looked away as he dispatched them by banging their heads against a stone and he laughed at her. 'You wouldn't be so squeamish if you'd been hungry. Needs must,' he said. 'Lucia wasn't squeamish like you. Not at all.'

With his pocketknife, he cut two finger-width lengths of willow, stripped off their leaves with one movement and used them to spear the fish. 'To make it easier to turn in the flames,' he explained.

Hunks of *toscano* bread, charred fish, Massimo's special salad, all washed down with a couple of beers that had been cooling in the river, made one of the best picnics Alba had ever eaten.

'Even better than my mother's, and that's saying something,' she said to Massimo as he sat on a flat rock, his faithful Freddie next to him, and she lay back on the grass, soaking up the midday sun.

'And better and cheaper than a restaurant,' he remarked. 'We never had the money, me and Lucia, to eat in those places. And she wouldn't have wanted to anyway. She didn't much like mixing with people. She was happiest when she was in the wild.'

He yawned and she suggested they make their way back to the house. Tanya had told her he would need a short nap after lunch.

They passed two wild fruit trees as they slowly climbed the path, and he stopped to point out tiny pears and apples. 'They'll be ready in October. They're excellent for storing away for winter. I remember my mother used to dry them. They were our sweets as children, and she'd put them at the bottom of our Christmas stockings. Children nowadays wouldn't be satisfied with such simple gifts, but for us, they were a treat.'

When he'd got his breath back, they continued. He grumbled about being an old man, telling her how he used to sprint up and down this path.

'You don't do too badly, Massimo,' she said, squeezing his hand that she held to support him up the slope.

Back at the house, she fetched an old lounger from the storeroom and grabbed a blanket to cover him up. He felt the cold, Tanya had warned.

The sun was at its warmest at this time of day, so she arranged the improvised bed for him in the shade of the walnut tree, tucking him up like a child.

'If I was forty years younger, I'd marry you,' he murmured, before falling asleep almost immediately.

In the house she found a broom and a rag and set to removing as much dust as she could from the furniture and walls. She worked out how to light the old Ariston boiler for hot water and washed up the cups she'd left last time they were here. Every now and again she popped out to check on her charge. He slept for two hours.

'Such dreams I had, *cara*,' he said, when she later took him out a cup of sweet lemon tea. Ma had baked a cake for them to enjoy – a fruit cake this time.

'I remember Mrs Spink used to make this,' he said. 'And scones, and jam made from rosehips which she gathered from the hedgerows. I used to enjoy her cakes very much. And rice pudding. Tell your mother *grazie*, but cut me only a thin slice. I remember it's very rich.'

She sat down on a chair next to him and he said, 'Tonight, we shall light a fire in the hearth and tell stories, like we used to do with friends at *veglie* after work was done. I've been racking my brains about some of the things Lucia told me, and that name you mentioned the other day… it sparked a memory in my old head.'

Alba's ears pricked up.

'That boy you talked about. Basilio Gelina… We used to call him Zoppo, "the lame one", when we were at school,' Massimo said. 'We called him that because he suffered from polio. It was cruel of us really, but children are. His mother died giving birth to him. Nobody knew who his father was, and his grandmother brought him up. She was a tough woman, and she taught him to be tough. None of us liked him much.'

'What happened to him? Did he have a family?'

'He died in the war, apparently. And there was nobody else in the family. The line stopped with him.'

'I don't suppose there's anybody around now that would know more about him?'

Massimo shrugged. 'Lucia told me some things about what went on. But it's such a long time ago, Alba. I need to think.'

She touched his arm. 'I don't want to upset you.'

It was hard to fathom the look on his face and she kept quiet, feeling she was intruding too much, but curious at the same time.

Breaking his silence, Massimo turned to her, his eyes glistening. 'Such a lot happened back then. Lucia confided in me eventually. I haven't talked or thought about it for years and years. But maybe now the time is right. My poor Lucia,' he said, his voice full of emotion. '*Poverina.*'

CHAPTER EIGHTEEN

Tuscany, 1944

Lucia waited anxiously on the following Sunday, hoping that Florian might come along. He'd told her he might have time off on that day, and she wanted to warn him that they must be careful not to be seen together. Her father had beaten her when she'd announced that she had met and talked with a German soldier and shown her parents the scarf he'd given her. He'd stood up from the supper table and removed his belt there and then, walloping her until she had cried for him to stop.

'Go to your room and stay there,' he'd shouted. 'How could a daughter of mine do such a foolish thing? Our friends are being killed every day by these butchers. The whole town of Civitella was slaughtered only a couple of months ago. And round here, old people, young people, babies in arms, women working in the fields, children stepping on mines... they die each day because of these monsters. A group was killed in reprisal only the other day up in Badia Tedalda: Letizia Mastacchi, Erminia, Gino Pandolfi... you know them all. And a daughter of mine wants to fraternise with a German soldier. It beggars belief.'

Her mother did nothing to stop the beating, shaking her head at Lucia and wailing as she wrung her hands. 'What will people think? What will become of us if they find out?' she kept saying.

'But he's different,' Lucia said, fending off her father's blows. 'He's a kind man. He gave me his scarf because I was cold.'

'Stupid girl, *scema*,' her father shouted. 'He gave you his scarf because he wanted your body. Get out of my sight, you tart. *Puttana Eva…*'

She'd sobbed herself to sleep that night, and kept out of her father's way for the next few days. Her mother came up to her room in the morning and applied calendula ointment to the weals on her back and shoulders. 'You've always been high-spirited, Lucia, but this is plain madness.'

'But Mamma, he was kind to me. And a gentleman.'

'You're so young and innocent, my child. He is the enemy.'

Lucia started to cry again. 'I hate this war. I hate having to live like a frightened rabbit all the time.'

'You have to think of others, not only yourself. And one day Massimo will return. This German soldier will go back to his own country. Forget about him.'

'Massimo has been gone for *five years*, Mamma. I shall be an old woman by the time he returns, which he probably won't. Why would he want to after he's been in *Inghilterra* for so long? I want to live *now*, Mamma.'

'Don't let your father hear you talk like this. Or anybody else. People have big ears, and they will report you if they think you're with a German.'

'I'm not *with* a German. I was talking to him. That's *all*.'

Her mother shook her head. 'You have to forget you ever met him. Come down now and help me clean out the hens.'

But Lucia couldn't forget about Florian. She'd enjoyed the hours they'd spent together. For a little while, this kind stranger, so tall and blond and handsome, had lit up her boring life. He was like an ancient warrior she had seen in her schoolbook, his helmet shining like a Greek soldier's. The thought of him filled her days.

She waited for Florian for two hours at the side of the road, but he never came.

*

The next time she saw him was when she was queuing for milk rations. Their remaining cow had been requisitioned by the *Tedeschi*. A long line of people with containers stretched around the piazza, waiting for what they could get from the *latteria*. Lucia was near the back, hoping the milk wouldn't run out before her turn came. Florian passed her on his way to drink coffee at the bar. He stopped, clicked his heels, took the jug from her hands and went to fill it in the shop. Lucia turned as red as a prawn as all eyes fixed on her. Her neighbours whispered to each other behind their hands when Florian handed her the brimming jug, the eyes of Giacinta spiteful enough to curdle the milk. Not even acknowledging him with a smile, Lucia took it and left without saying anything, spilling some of the precious liquid as she hurried away.

Later that afternoon, while she was sitting outside her house in Tramarecchia, helping her mother repair a willow basket, Giacinta and her sister Agata wandered over.

'So, what makes your daughter so special to the *Tedeschi*, Maria Grazia?' Giacinta asked. 'The milk was finished by the time it came to us. Have you any left to share?'

'It was sour already,' Lucia replied. 'Mamma is using it to make a small round of cheese.'

'Next time ask your boyfriend to fill up our jugs too.' Agata smirked. 'Or do we have to do something special to earn it?' She gave an exaggerated wiggle of her hips as she walked on.

'What are they talking about?' Lucia's mother asked. 'What did they mean?'

'They are cats,' Lucia said, 'but I was very embarrassed. That German soldier I told you about... he took my container to the front of the milk queue.'

Maria Grazia put down the basket and shook her head. '*Gesù Cristo*... You need to be careful, foolish girl. Can't you see what it looks like?'

'It wasn't my fault he decided to help. I didn't ask him.'

'And why did you lie about the milk going sour?'

'Mamma, why should we give any to those cats? What have they ever done for us? I've seen them steal figs off our tree so many times. And tomatoes and salad from Babbo's *orto*.'

'Nevertheless, you need to think more about how you behave.'

'Behave? I do *nothing* wrong. Sometimes I wish I did, then life would not be so tedious.'

This comment earned her a slap on the face, and Lucia walked off in a huff down to the river. A light rain began to fall as, knees hunched to her chest, she watched fish dart about in the shallows. She wished she were free like them to swim in and out of the current, without a care in the world. Drops on the willows clung like jewels to the slender branches in the evening sunshine, and she looked for a rainbow to appear. But there was none.

Three mornings later, she found him sitting in the meadow puffing on his pipe when she arrived with the sheep.

'Don't do that to me again,' she said. 'What you did caused trouble. And in front of the whole village.'

'What did I do?' he asked, pulling the pipe from his mouth, looking genuinely puzzled.

'The milk... people wondered why you were doing me a favour.'

'Ach! *Entschuldigung*... I'm so sorry! I never thought.'

She smacked the sheep away and stood near him. 'I am so fed up with everything to do with this war. Everybody is suffering. People die, go missing, there is not enough food. We have to make do and mend with these rags.' She pulled at her patched shirt. 'Nothing is straightforward any more. Everybody is divided, friends and family pitted against each other. We thought the war was over last year when Mussolini went. But everything is worse. It is all hateful.' She picked up a stone from the ground and threw it far away across the grass. 'I feel as if my life is on hold.' She sat down and looked at him. 'Tell me something to cheer me up.'

He took out a *salame* and a slab of dark chocolate from his knapsack. 'Will this make your family happy at least?'

'No. There will be a thousand questions about where I got it, why I got it, who gave it to me. What did I do to get it?' She threw another stone.

He continued to hold out the goods and she eventually took them, wrapping them carefully in the cloth which contained her hunk of dry bread and rind of cheese. 'Thank you, anyway,' she said. 'I will invent a story about finding them along the path. If they believe me, it will be a small miracle. How do you say thank you in your language?'

He taught her a few basic expressions and smiled at her attempts to copy them.

'I think your words are ugly,' she said, imitating the *sch* sounds he was teaching her. 'Italian is softer, don't you think? *Grazie* for *danke* and *prego* for *bitte*.'

'I disagree. Our words are beautiful. We have wonderful poems and we have songs that are known the world over.' He recited a couple of lines of what she presumed was poetry:

'Herr, es ist Zeit. Der Sommer war sehr groß... It's a poem about the end of summer,' he said, quiet for a few moments.

Then he started to sing, and she listened, not understanding, but thrilling to the sound of his voice. When he stopped, she clapped her hands.

'What does the song mean? It's beautiful.'

'It's a lullaby that most German mothers sing to their babies. Shall I teach you?'

'*Sì.*'

His voice was deep, melodic. The sound mixed with the song of a lark soaring above. It was a brief interlude from the war, and it cheered her, the words exotic and exciting in their difference, reminding her that there was another world beyond the misery of the present.

> '*Guten Abend, guten Nacht,*
> *Mit Rosen bedacht,*
> *Mit Näglen besteckt,*
> *Schlupf unter die Deck…*'

She mastered the first two lines, and it was his turn to applaud her.

'I will teach you the rest another time,' he said, getting up from where he was sitting. 'But now I have to go.' He took hold of her hand and bowed before kissing it gently and she felt like a princess in a story.

'By the way,' he said. 'I think you should warn your family and friends that there will be more troops arriving in Badia next week.' He paused. 'And life might turn harder for all of you. They are Stormtroopers from the 16th SS division. Hard fighters… ruthless men.' He picked a daisy from the grass and handed it to her. '*Auf Wiedersehen*, and please be careful, Lucia. And I, for my part, promise not to do you any favours when the whole town is watching.'

He bowed again in an old-fashioned form of respect and she watched as he walked away, his cap of blond hair golden in the sunlight. He was tall, erect and so different from any young man she had ever met. And she wanted to see him again.

CHAPTER NINETEEN

Until now, Florian had seen little action in this corner of Tuscany, but that was about to change. Reports were coming in of the combined Allied forces, together with the Italian Liberation Corps, bent on breaking through the defensive Gothic Line that Hitler had ordered to be constructed in central Italy from coast to coast. The atmosphere was tense in the German camp.

Fifty soldiers, under the command of SS Obersturmführer Gerhard Wolf, were sent to order the evacuation of two small hamlets near Campo Gatti, pursuing a new scorched earth policy, suspecting that inhabitants were harbouring partisans. Half a dozen of the group were fired up with anger and bent on revenge, after one of their comrades had been gravely injured by Italian partisans a week earlier. One, Korporal Hans Weber, famous for finishing off scraps from everybody's plates in the canteen, was among the most vocal.

'At least five of the bastards will have to die to pay for Dieter's wounds,' he kept saying. 'The poor bugger will probably lose his foot. I can't wait to get my hands on the rats.'

Florian ordered him to stay close by his side, separating him from his cronies in an attempt to appease an unruly situation. 'Shut up, Weber, with your comments,' he ordered. 'And keep marching with your mouth shut. You're alerting everybody for kilometres around. We won't catch anybody with your bleating.'

They continued along a mule track that led up to the hamlet. As they rounded a corner, they came across a group of peasants working in a field, scything hay. One of them turned to run and he was shot in the back as he fled. The remainder dropped their tools and raised their hands in the air.

'*Non sparare, non sparare*… don't shoot,' one of them pleaded.

'Arrest these men and take them to the village,' shouted Wolf.

They were marched into the tiny, sleepy piazza in Campo Gatti, bordered by a dozen stone houses. A couple of scrawny chickens scratched in the dust, washing was draped over bushes and bright yellow maize cobs hung from hooks on the walls to dry in the sun. Two children were picking fruit from a persimmon tree. It was an everyday scene about to be transformed. A woman at the fountain stooped to pick up her toddler and ran to a doorway, shouting inside to her other children to hide in the stair cupboard. Florian understood everything she said, and he spoke out in Italian, 'Don't be afraid. Just do what you are told, and everything will be fine.'

'You! Hofstetter,' barked the senior leader, 'you know their language. Translate for me.'

Florian moved over to Wolf's side and awaited instructions.

'You have already been warned.' The words of the tall Obersturmführer rang out across the sun-filled square. 'You are aware that anybody harbouring brigands will be shot. These so-called partisans are nothing but traitors, rapists and deserters. You have failed to report them and now they are wounding and killing my men.'

Florian translated as best he could, omitting certain words and adding his own message, knowing the major spoke no Italian. He told them again not to be afraid and to keep calm.

To his horror, the senior assault leader ordered five of the peasants to be lined up by the village fountain and then, gesturing to one of his men who held a light FG42 machine gun, he gave the order: '*Feuer!*'

Four of the peasants died immediately in a hail of bullets and the fifth wriggled in agony on the ground, his cries of pain mingling with the agonised shrieks of his wife, '*Marito mio, marito mio...* my husband.'

Obersturmführer Wolf walked calmly over and administered the coup de grâce with his pistol.

Water continued to trickle from the washing fountain, hens continued to scratch in the dust, but now the air was filled with the sounds of weeping and dogs barking. A young boy ran from one of the houses and flung himself over the body of one of the dead. 'Babbo, Babbo,' he screamed, shaking the corpse, trying to revive it. Another shot rang out. Florian turned to look in horror into the jeering face of Korporal Weber, his gun still smoking. 'That's saved us from another future bastard brigand.' He laughed and shot at two of the hens.

The senior assault leader strode towards him, his voice shaking with fury. 'Did I order you to do that, Korporal? Did I? You will be on night guard duties and rations for the rest of the month. I will not have indiscipline in my ranks. Hand over your gun immediately.'

The simple houses were ransacked for hidden partisans. Cupboards were opened, pots smashed, beds bayoneted. Florian came upon a soldier urinating into a cauldron of food cooking over the fire. Another soldier dragged an old man into the piazza, his wife holding onto him, weeping and begging for mercy. The young paratrooper held a pistol to his head and Florian intervened. 'Leave him be. He's no danger to anyone, soldier.'

'He spat at me.'

'I said, let him go. That is an order.' Florian's voice was steely.

Their stand-off was interrupted by Obersturmführer Wolf calling to the men to line up and make ready to leave for headquarters. 'Our work is done,' he announced. 'Hofstetter. Warn these peasants that we are not finished here. They should be very careful.'

Florian's translation urged the villagers to be careful. He wanted to say more; to ask for forgiveness for what had been done today, but there was little point in appeasing his conscience in this way. He was sickened to his bones at what he had witnessed, utterly revolted at the violence perpetrated in this tiny hamlet by his fellow men. However, he knew it made little sense to act there and then. But it was a turning point for him; the beginning of the end.

Afterwards he learned that one of the dead men was father to ten children, another to seven, and the boy they'd shot was only twelve years old. War was one thing when it involved combat against armed soldiers, but it was completely unforgivable against men armed with hoes and scythes and a boy anguished at seeing his father shot before his own eyes. If the men had indeed been partisans, there had been no questioning. There was no justice or humanity in this act at all.

On the day after the shooting, Florian could take it no longer. He had been trying to play some small part with his protest by stealing back purloined pieces of art. But that was paltry; like trying to quench a desert with one drop of rain. He had tossed and turned in his narrow bed during the night, trying to rid his mind of the brutal images that kept flashing into his brain. There had to be something of more use that he could do against this cruelty. The desire for victory had warped patriotism into barbarism. He was ashamed. He was a German, not a Nazi, and his conscience would not let him be a part of the pointless violence any longer.

What he planned to do filled him with fear. Already his stomach was churning at the idea of it, his hands were clammy, his mouth dry. He pressed his hands against his beating heart as if to try and calm himself. He would need courage like he'd never had to summon before.

At midday, Florian told his fellow officers he was going for a short walk. He took his haversack, butterfly net and camera, telling them he would be fossil- and insect-hunting for an hour, instead of eating with them in the canteen. He was not hungry; he had a stomach upset and they were not to worry about him, he said. But instead of his chisel and hammer, he packed food, his precious notebook, money, spare socks and underwear. Before making his way out of town, he slipped into Major Schmalz's office in the town hall, where the red, white and black swastika fluttered above a tub of colourful geraniums.

The young guard at the door clicked his heels and saluted Herr Kapitän Hofstetter, who usually worked in the office downstairs, and Florian told him to stand easy.

'I have orders to pick up documents and bring them to Major Schmalz in his residence,' Florian told the soldier. Inside the office he closed the door. Removing his camera from his haversack, he photographed the map on the desk, paying careful attention to the bunker locations along the local stretch of the Gothic Line, now renamed the Green Line by Hitler. Then, from a leather folder next to the map, he scribbled a couple of details from the major's handwritten notes, showing planned troop movements for the next few days in the aftermath of the events at Campo Gatti. Finally, he rolled up the slip of paper and pressed it down into the bowl of his unlit pipe.

Within two minutes, he had left the office, once again saluted by the guard. Slowly he walked down the stone staircase of the town hall. His heart hammered in his ribcage and he was prepared to break into a run, expecting to be stopped at any minute and asked where he had been. He made his way across the piazza, which was bathed in midday sunshine. Once he was sure he was out of sight of the town, he hurried to the meadow where he had met Lucia and concealed himself in a copse, hoping she would turn up with her sheep. If anybody were to see him, away from headquarters, he hoped his butterfly net would explain his movements.

The tinkle of bells from a neighbouring meadow alerted him and he rose, making a pretence of catching a non-existent butterfly, and wandered over towards the animals. The Maremmano sheepdog growled, but when he called to him, the animal came over, wagging his tail. Lucia was sitting on a rock eating an apple and when she saw him, she jumped up, throwing the half-eaten core into the bushes behind her.

'I didn't expect to see you again so soon. Are you here to teach me more songs?'

He shook his head and grasped her arm. 'I need you to take me somewhere safe. I have left the German army. They'll come looking for me as soon as they realise that I haven't reported for duty. Quick, Lucia. Think of somewhere.'

She frowned and then tugged him by the sleeve. 'Take off that jacket. There are *partigiani* everywhere. If they see your uniform, they'll shoot you on the spot. And remove your shirt, so you look as if you're working on the land.'

He removed the light khaki jacket, its external pockets stuffed with his pocketknife, torch, wallet and notebook, and then he took off his shirt and pushed everything into his haversack. She stood back to examine his pale skin and hair and then tutted. 'Still not right,' she said, and she pulled off her green headscarf, told him to bend down and knotted it over his blond hair.

'Come,' she said. 'It's not perfect, but it will have to do. There is somewhere I use from time to time, further up towards the pass.'

She left the dog to guard the sheep and was off through the trees. He could hardly keep up with her and she kept turning round to check on his progress. 'Please hurry. I must get back to my flock. If Babbo discovers I'm not with them, he will beat me again.'

He followed her up a steep track, slithering a couple of times on the stones, and then across another meadow, where wild purple thistles studded the mountainside. In his haste, he trampled over orchids and helleborines that he'd never seen before, but this was not the time to record new specimens. Beauty and war didn't mix. In the lee of a rock formation near the pass, Lucia led him through a narrow crack in the boulders, camouflaged by a curtain of thick creepers.

'This is used by shepherds when the weather is bad,' she explained, and when he looked worried, she tried to calm him. 'All the young men are either helping the *partigiani*, or dead, or in the militia,' she said. 'The old shepherds don't come up here. You'll be safe for a while. When I was a child, I played here with my friends.'

It was cool and gloomy inside, the only light coming from a hole in the ceiling above a place where fires had been lit, within a simple circle of blackened stones.

'There is a stream at the edge of the woods,' Lucia said, 'but you're best staying in here during the day. If anybody sees you, they will know straight away that you are not one of us. And don't trample the grass – keep to the stone track. If they see flattened grass, they will investigate and discover you.'

'I don't want to stay hidden, Lucia. I want you to take me to the *partigiani*. Can you do that for me?'

She stared at him, her lovely green eyes wide with fear, and he thought to himself that maybe war and beauty did go together after all.

CHAPTER TWENTY

Tuscany, present day

Sitting by the fire in the red house, his feet resting on the back of Freddie, who lay in front of him, Massimo nursed a small glass of home-made basil liqueur they had found in the storeroom. He turned to look at his young friend. 'Now, Alba *mia*. I have talked a lot about what happened to me, and poor Lucia, during the war. Maybe it's time for you to share your sadness.'

'Anything I tell you will be plain boring compared with what I've just heard. I hope I'm not bad company, Massimo. Is it that obvious?'

'Of course you're not bad company. But I'm good at spotting when somebody is fretting. I grew used to that with my Lucia.'

There was a silence, save for the occasional crackle and spit of wood in the hearth. Alba had lit the fire for Massimo because he had told her that in the centre he missed staring at the flames. 'Radiators are not the same,' he had said.

'I still worry that James's death was my fault, even though I try to kid myself I'm over it,' she told him. 'It's hard to come to terms with.'

'Did you stick a knife in him? Poison him? Push him off a cliff?'

She smiled. 'No. But we argued, and I go over and over in my head that if he hadn't rushed away on his bike in a temper, then he would still be alive.'

'He could have had the same accident at any time. It was not because of something you said. Was he given to depression?'

'No. The opposite. He was so upbeat, Massimo. He had such an appetite for adventure – he'd been to loads of places around the world.'

'Well, then, I think you have to be strong and say to yourself each morning when you get up: "It was not my fault". You need to convince yourself of this, Alba. Otherwise you will drive yourself crazy. And forgive me, but maybe you need to be… humbler about these feelings of yours. You're not a murderer, we've established that. You are not the being that decided if he was to live or die that day. It was James's destiny, and you did not design that.'

She looked across at him and smiled, biting back a tear. 'Thank you, Massimo. You're so wise.'

He shook his head. '*Magari!* If only! I'm not wise, little Alba. I've just lived longer than you.'

'I don't like to bother my parents about James; they're so patient. I keep a lot bottled up inside me. So… thank you. I feel as if you really understand.'

He nodded. 'Now, pour me another drop of this *liquore* and let's sit here quietly without more prattle. I'm tired now. I've talked too much.'

'Do you want me to take you back to the centre?'

'I'd like to stay here another night. Is that possible?'

'It's fine by me, but I need to let Tanya and my parents know. Give me a couple of minutes and I'll be back.' She bent to kiss Massimo's cheek. 'And thank you again for your wise words.'

He squeezed her hand and brought it to his heart. 'Prego, *tesoro*,' he said.

There was no phone signal within the thick stone walls of Massimo's house, and she left him by the fire and trudged up the incline leading away from the village until she had a couple of bars. She shivered after the warmth of the fire.

Her stepmother answered almost immediately. 'Alba, we've been trying to get in touch with you. Babbo was just about to drive up there and check why you haven't answered our calls. Is everything all right?'

'Sorry, Ma. There's no signal in Tramarecchia.'

'The care centre has called to see how you're getting on. And there was a rather disturbing call from Alfiero, too.'

Alba's phone started to ping as messages began to come in. 'Whoops! They're all coming in now,' she said. 'Ma, Massimo wants to stay another night. Do you think they'll let him?'

'Phone the centre and ask. Do you want me to let Egidio know you won't be in for work tomorrow?'

'It's my day off anyway. If I don't phone again, I'll see you tomorrow evening.'

Tanya answered when Alba called the home. 'As long as you think he is coping, signorina,' she said, 'then until tomorrow at five will be fine. We are still short-staffed here. Give him my love and tell him to behave.'

Next, Alba called Alfiero. He answered almost immediately. 'Alba, did you get my texts? Would it be okay to see you?'

'I'm with Massimo in Tramarecchia. I've only just got your messages. There's no signal here. What's up?'

The call ended abruptly. She waited for a while for him to reconnect and then gave up, not wanting to leave Massimo alone for much longer. If she was honest, she selfishly wanted to devote tomorrow to Massimo. It seemed he only opened up about his past to her, and she wanted to hear more without anybody else intruding. And she was still sure he knew more about the silver goblets.

The old man had stoked the fire by the time she returned to the little red house and he was sitting close to the flames. He looked up when she pushed open the door. 'When you're old, your bones grow cold,' he said.

'You're probably tired, too, Massimo. Let me get you ready for bed. Down here again?' she asked.

'Tonight, I think I would like to climb the stairs and sleep in the big bed,' he said. 'Where I was born.'

After she'd helped him, Alba sat downstairs for a while, her thoughts full of Massimo's accounts of Florian and Lucia and wondering if their friendship blossomed into romance. Love helped the world go round, she thought ruefully, and then she immediately banished gloomy thoughts about James. The room smelled of woodsmoke; the chimney probably needed sweeping, but she liked the timeless smell. She picked up her phone to scroll through the messages that had come in. Alfiero had sent half a dozen. They were all short:

Call me when you can

Are you there?

Can we talk?

I can talk now

Where are you?

Feeling guilty, she slipped out and made her way once again up the incline to where she knew she could get a signal. The trees rustled and swayed in the wind that had blown up just before nightfall, clearing the fog that often descended without warning in the summer months. When she tried to connect with Alfiero, there was no answer and, checking, she saw there were no further messages from him. Soft light beckoned through the little windows of Massimo's house as she returned down the slope, but the other buildings were shapes in the dark. She stood for a while observing the scene. Above her, stars were scattered like diamonds in the ashen light cast by the moon and she caught her breath at its beauty before quickening her pace, anxious to capture the impression of the village at night before she lost inspiration. For the next half hour, while the house creaked itself to sleep, she used pen and ink, trying to recreate the soft tones of the ghostly village, contrasting the mood with bold, skeletal outlines of branches against the night sky. When she felt she could do no more, she stopped, leaving her sketchbook open on the kitchen table to dry.

Creeping upstairs, she peeped in on Massimo. He was snoring gently, his slight frame hardly making any outline beneath the covers. She pulled his door to and prepared herself for bed. She couldn't sleep, her mind full of the story of Lucia and Florian, and Massimo's advice about James, which made perfect sense. Eventually, she went downstairs to make herself a chamomile tea. The cinders still had a glow and she placed a couple of thin logs on top, watching the flames dance into life as she cupped her hands around her drink.

She felt at home in this little house, and imagined what she would do if it were hers. There wasn't really much she would change. The windows were small compared with a modern house, but they served their purpose – making the rooms snug in winter and keeping them cool in high summer. She imagined hand-painted plates on the little dresser, instead of the battered pans, and a deep settee to sink into near the hearth. Moving over to the window, that she would dress with simple linen fabric, she gazed for a while at the crescent moon, like a curl among the stars, and then she noticed headlights from a car strobing the bumpy track leading to the village.

The engine cut out and she wondered who could possibly be out at two in the morning. Poachers, maybe? For a minute or two, her imagination went into overdrive, conjuring up stories of robbery and murder. She'd heard that antiques had been stolen from the village of Montebotolino last year; an old hand-carved fire surround and a wardrobe had been removed overnight from the hilltop village where nobody lived permanently any more. She turned the key in the lock of the old front door, disquiet entering her mind. There was no phone signal here; how could she contact the *carabinieri* if she and Massimo were attacked? Freddie growled and came over to stand at her side.

A light tap on the door almost made her jump out of her skin and she reached for the fire poker.

'Are you still up? Can I come in?' It was Alfiero's voice, but she still went to the side window to check. He was using the torch on his mobile phone, the dull light on his face eerie in the dingy moonlight.

Unlocking the door, she put her finger to her lips. 'Massimo is asleep, be very quiet.' She pulled him in and gestured to a chair by the fire.

His face was a mess; congealed blood from a deep cut crusted one cheek. She gasped. 'What happened? Have you been in an accident?'

She went over and peered at the wound. 'That needs stitching. You should go to the *pronto soccorso* to get that seen to straight away.'

He waved her off. 'I'll go in the morning. Alba, can I stay here tonight? I don't know where else to go.' His hands were shaking, and she poured him a glass of the basil liqueur.

'This is all I've got, but get this down you,' she said. 'Or would you prefer tea?'

He shook his head and knocked back the alcohol.

'What happened, Alfi?'

'Beatrice…' he started to say, and then shook his head.

'Where is she? Was she in the accident too? Where did you leave her?'

'There was no accident,' he said, leaning towards the fire, his elbows on his knees, head bowed. 'She did this on purpose,' he said, in a muffled voice.

'My God, Alfi. What are you saying?'

'She had a knife. She went berserk.'

'Have you told the police?' Alba knelt before him and tipped his face to the light, looking in horror at the deep slash on his cheek. 'She's crazy. For fuck's sake, Alfi. You've got to go to the police.'

He looked so weary and defeated, she realised it was pointless lecturing him. She pointed to the daybed to one side of the hearth. 'Massimo slept there last night. He's upstairs tonight, and I'm in the room next to him. Will you be all right here? Just let me wash that cut for you first and we can talk in the morning.'

He told her not to make a fuss, but she insisted on cutting up a clean towel and dipping it in boiled water to bathe his wound. 'We don't want this to go septic. But you must go to the clinic tomorrow morning. You need stitches – it's deep. And then we'll go to the *carabinieri*.'

'No,' he said, grasping her wrist. 'Not the police… they won't believe me, anyway.'

Again, she felt instinctively that the last thing Alfiero needed tonight was advice from her – especially as she felt out of her depth. While she sorted out bedding for him, she suddenly had a brainwave. Alfi didn't want the *carabinieri* involved for some reason, maybe because he felt ashamed. But she knew just the person to help him.

Massimo and Alfiero were drinking coffee together and sharing the rest of Ma's cake when she came downstairs at eight next morning. They were deep in discussion, and Alba watched as the old man placed his hand on Alfiero's arm, a look of concern on his face.

'Your young friend has been in the wars, Alba. We've introduced ourselves.'

'Massimo, do you mind if we postpone today and I take you back to Badia? I need to go somewhere with Alfiero,' she said, helping herself to the rest of the coffee in the pot.

'Alba, please don't change your plans for me,' Alfiero said.

'Alba and I can see each other another day, young man. I think you've taken over as number one today,' Massimo said. 'As long as you don't steal her away from me forever, then I shan't be too jealous.'

Alfiero smiled weakly. '*Grazie*,' he said.

'Is there anybody we should talk to about your being here, Alfi?' Alba asked.

He jerked his head up in dismay. 'There's no need to tell anybody. Work think I'm on annual leave. Beatrice and I were all set to fly to Sicily this morning, but…' His voice trailed off and then he added, 'I don't want her to know where I am.'

'Don't worry. Only you and I will know where we're going.'

His shoulders relaxed as he slumped back in the chair. '*Grazie, grazie*, Alba.' And, turning to Massimo, he said, 'And you too, signore. I apologise for turning up like this. I didn't know what else to do.'

'I am enjoying being with young people again,' Massimo said. 'My house has finally come alive after a long time of feeling empty.' He stood up, leaning on the table for support. 'We will close the place up until next time you visit. Take me back to the centre, Alba, and then sort out your friend.'

*

One hour later, Alba was on the road again, having deposited Massimo. She drove Alfiero away from Badia into the next valley.

'Where are you taking me?' he asked. 'I don't have the energy to protest, but I'm completely in your hands.'

'To see a special woman who I'm sure will be able to help you. I met her back in May, and she is amazing.'

'Will she mind us turning up out of the blue?'

'I haven't been able to warn her because she rarely switches on her phone. She lives cut off, in her own world… but she is amazingly clued up. Fingers crossed she's not gone away.'

Suor Lodovica was in her small vegetable garden, hoeing the weeds between her salad plants, her habit hitched up above her ankles, an old straw hat pulled down to shade her face.

'*Dio mio*,' Alfiero muttered under his breath. 'You've brought me to a nunnery.'

'Be patient. You asked for somewhere to stay, and I feel in my heart this is the safest place. You could talk to me, if you prefer, but I'm out of my depth here, Alfi. Please trust me.'

He held back and she pulled him forward as the hermit stood up, shielding her eyes to peer at her visitors. Then she leant her hoe against the fence and walked over to them with her steady gait.

'I'm so glad you came back,' she said, clasping Alba's hands in her own. 'I've thought of you often… How are you doing?'

'I'm fine, Lodovica. But my friend needs somewhere peaceful to stay for a few days. Are you able to help?'

Lodovica looked at Alfiero. 'If he is willing to be here, then that is fine by me.'

'I'm not a churchgoer,' he said.

'You don't have to be,' she said, smiling at him. 'The only condition I have is that you let me tend to that wound first.'

She beckoned them to follow her into the cool of her stone house and told them to sit at her table, while she washed her hands thoroughly at the sink.

Alba watched as she fetched a first aid box, then gently bathed Alfiero's face, before applying butterfly clips to the cut. 'We'll see if this holds. The important thing is to keep it really clean.'

Alba had forgotten how calming her presence was and she was pleased to see that Alfiero seemed more relaxed. 'Are you medically trained too?' she asked.

'I told you something of my past in Milan, Alba. I used to self-harm, and this was what the doctors used on me eventually. Here, because of where I live, I have a pretty good first aid kit. I have no neighbours or car, remember.'

When she had finished working on Alfiero and removed her sterile gloves, she pulled back the sleeves of her habit to reveal faint scars. 'When I was on the catwalk, they always gave me garments with long sleeves, or tied silk scarves around my wrists. It wasn't good publicity to display injured models.' She rolled down her sleeves and clasped her hands together. 'I was going to have a simple lunch. Will you both join me?'

She asked Alba to wash the slender tips of vitalba, or old man's beard, that she'd collected that morning and then she blanched them, before adding them to an omelette. 'My girls are laying well and I have to think of different ways to eat their eggs. You are helping me out.'

Next, she grated cheese from a hunk of pecorino on the top of the golden frittata in the frying pan and asked Alba to slice boiled beetroot and cold potatoes to make a salad, sprinkling fresh basil and thyme on top. She then placed an unlabelled bottle on the table. 'I think a glass of this Verdicchio will do us well today. An old friend of mine from Jesi visits me from time to time, and he produces this on his estate. I don't like to drink on my own, so can you do the honours, Alfiero?' She fetched three earthenware tumblers from a corner cupboard. 'I don't have wine glasses, but these are good for white wine. They keep it cool.'

The simple food was as delicious as the first time Alba had shared a meal in this place, and the wine was excellent.

'Thank you, Suor—' Alfiero started.

'Call me Lodovica.'

'Lodovica,' he said. 'It's a beautiful name.'

'It means "fighter". Life can be a battle, but there are peaceful ways to withstand.'

'My life lately is far from peaceful,' he said.

Alba listened quietly to her friend and the hermit talking, like the beginning of a slow musical movement.

'My girlfriend can be wonderful, most of the time, but she's so unpredictable. Worse than fiery,' Alfiero said, touching his face below his wound.

There was silence while they waited for him to continue. Alba felt angry with herself for not understanding the signs – his accident on the stairs, Beatrice's curt remarks on the phone – but the last thing she had expected was a woman attacking a man.

Alfiero poured himself another glass of wine. 'She will be so full of apologies when I see her again. Full of love, but I don't know how to cope with her any longer.'

'*Love is gentle, love is kind… Love never fails,*' Lodovica quoted.

'She is very difficult to love at times,' Alfiero said. 'And if I say I'm going to leave her, she says she'll kill herself.'

Lodovica stood up. 'I think you need a long sleep, Alfiero. Alba, please come back in a week. In the meantime, Alfiero and I will find time to talk.'

Alba hugged them both and climbed into her father's old car. She wound down the windows while she drove, letting the summer air blow her anger away, needing the arms of her parents, who had never shown her anything else but true love.

*

A couple of days later, Massimo and Alba were chatting under the walnut tree in Tramarecchia. There was no wind, and even the birds were quiet in the humid Sunday heat. The stretch of River Marecchia that ran alongside her parents' mill was busy with families up from the even hotter coast, and Alba had been only too pleased to pick up Massimo and spend time in his quiet hamlet.

'What you need for here is a hammock, slung between those two low branches,' she said. 'I might hunt one out for you next time I go down to Sansepolcro. I saw some at the market last time I was there.'

'For me, or for you?' he asked. 'At my age I am not about to clamber into one of those things, fall out the other side and break my back.'

They were quiet for a while. Massimo rolled up his shirtsleeves, leant back in his chair and shut his eyes. 'How is your friend getting on?'

'I don't know. I haven't heard from him. I expect Lodovica made him turn off his phone. I hope she can help.'

'It will take time. He talked to me a little about what has been going on. He feels ashamed and worried about what this girl might do if he leaves her. She's threatened suicide several times. Do you know her?'

'I've met her briefly a couple of times. I didn't take to her.'

'I think he likes you, Alba.'

'I like him too. He's very kind.'

'But you're not in love with him.'

She snorted with laughter. 'No way! He's like a brother. I've known him since I started primary school and anyway, he has his peculiar... girlfriend.'

'The poor boy is suffering,' Massimo said. 'But he will be all right in the end, I'm sure.' He opened his eyes to look at Alba. 'And life will mean more to him after he has suffered. If there's one thing I've learned in all my ninety years, it's that only after we have been through a tragedy can we feel *here*.' He thumped his heart to emphasise what he was saying. 'You can have an easy life, sail on a calm sea, but you won't *feel* life if there are no ups and downs.'

'Are you talking about yourself, Massimo?' she asked.

'Not just me. Lucia suffered too, poor girl. Ah, how she suffered.'

CHAPTER TWENTY-ONE

Tuscany, 1944

Lucia knew that contacting the *partigiani* would not be easy. Her father sometimes talked about the young men who had disappeared. 'They're not all dead,' she had overheard him telling her mother one evening. 'Some of them are busy up on the ridge.'

'They cause more trouble than good,' her mother said. 'All these reprisals are their fault. The *partigiani* blow up a bridge, and what good does that do? As a consequence, the *Tedeschi* and militia punish ordinary people. Those young men are a nuisance. The other day I read a poster in the square, asking mothers, wives, sisters and sweethearts to tell their young men to turn themselves in.'

'Hush your talk, woman. So, you'd prefer to listen to propaganda and be ruled by fascist thugs, like that bastard Petrelli, would you?'

'I bet his life is more than comfortable down there on his fancy Boccarini estate,' she said, making a clatter as she washed pots. 'And I bet he never has to wait in queues for scraps of meat that I wouldn't have fed to a dog before this war. I'd prefer it if life returned to normal.'

'Well, you'll be waiting forever if there is nobody to stand up to our occupiers.' When he realised Lucia was listening, he sent her out to fetch more wood, and when she carried in the basket of logs, her mother was sitting meekly by the fire, darning one of her father's socks. There was no more talk of the *partigiani* on the ridge. Her cousin, Moreno, was one of the 'disappeared'. Her aunt had never seemed unduly upset about his absence. She'd even knitted him a waistcoat, a hat and a pair of thick socks 'for when he returned'. Lucia had an inkling that he might well be up on the ridge, too.

At supper, while nobody was looking, she smuggled a lump of cheese into her skirt pocket and the heel of a *toscano* loaf that her mother had planned to use in tomorrow's bean soup. Later, when she was sure her parents were asleep, she climbed from her bedroom window, jumped onto the pigsty's roof abutting the house and made her way to the cave. The full moon cast a watery light on the footpath. She heard the padding of feet behind her and with her heart drumming, she dropped to the ground and rolled behind a bush. A wet nose found her face and she pushed her Maremmano sheepdog away. 'Oh, Primo, you daft animal,' she whispered, pulling herself upright. 'Well, now you're here, you can be my guard. *Su, andiamo*. Let's go!'

Florian was asleep when, three quarters of an hour later, she pushed her way into the cave, but he woke when Primo knocked over an empty tin can, and then he was up and pointing his gun at Lucia.

'It's me. Put that down,' she said. 'We've brought you something to eat.'

As he wolfed down the food, she told him that she would do her best to contact the *partigiani*. Tomorrow she would take Primo and the sheep further up the mountain towards the ridge. 'But I can't promise anything. I might not find them. If I do, what do I tell them?'

'Let me come too. It's not safe to go alone, and anyway I can relay information directly. They need to know it as soon as possible.'

'No, Florian. First, I must find them and warn them about you. They'll shoot on sight if you simply appear from nowhere, even if I'm with you. I'm not sure who is in that band – they might not even know me. There are all kinds of people in our hills from all over the place: evacuees from the cities, deserters from both sides. They could shoot me, too. I'll pass by the cave again as soon as I know something. Be ready to join me when you hear the tinkle of the ram's bell. And make your body darker. Rub in some dirt. You look too pale and clean.'

She got up to leave.

'Do you have to go already? It's lonely up here. Talk to me for a while,' Florian said, grabbing her arm.

'I can't. If my parents discover me gone, there'll be hell to pay.'

He squeezed her hand. '*Danke schön. Entschuldigung.* I'm sorry. I'm selfish. You are already doing too much for me. *A presto*,' he said. 'See you soon.'

She was glad to have Primo by her side as they made their way home. She let him guide her, her mind full of the feel of Florian's hand touching hers, rather than the path ahead.

'I'm taking the sheep higher up the mountain today, Babbo,' Lucia told her father early the next morning. 'The meadow is full of milk thistle, and I noticed them eating fallen acorns yesterday.'

It was all right for pigs to eat acorns, but it gave sheep diarrhoea. 'So, can you pack me extra food today, Mamma? It's a fair way, and I'll be back just before dark.'

'Maybe I should come with you to check,' her father suggested.

'No,' she said, too quickly, before changing her reply in case he suspected something. 'I thought you had to repair fences today… But if you really think I can't manage, come too.' She mentally crossed her fingers, hoping he wouldn't thwart her plans.

'No, you're right. I'll leave it to you. I've plenty to do here.'

Her plan was to take the sheep higher towards the ridge and see if she found anyone. She was very nervous about the outcome, but she wanted to help Florian, and if she could be of help to the *partigiani*, then so much the better. She decided to make as much noise as possible as she approached the area that people were warned to avoid. Her father had been told the track was mined, but one evening, well in his cups, she'd overheard him tell Mamma that it was a way of keeping nosy villagers away from the *partigiani* camp. She hoped he was right, but she still decided to keep to the fields with her sheep instead of using the stony paths. The only trouble was that her sheep kept stopping to graze on the new pastures; at this rate they wouldn't reach the ridge before nightfall. She shouted at Primo to drive them on.

'*Avanti! Cammina!*' she kept calling at the top of her voice. And Primo barked at his charges, nipping at their cloven hooves, so that they kept bleating, their bells around their necks clanging as they moved in a noisy huddle up the slopes.

She stopped in a meadow just below the treeline of Monte dei Frati. Ordinarily, she would have enjoyed the chance to rest and sit in the shade to eat her pack of food. But she was keeping this for Florian, and her nerves drove hunger away today. Despite the noise she and her flock made, nobody appeared. There was not a single trace of anybody up here. She tried singing a couple of songs. There was one that Primo liked. When he was a puppy, she'd sung it over and over because it made him howl and that made her laugh. She tried it today to attract attention to herself, rather than to raise a laugh. Still nothing. After a couple of hours, she led her charges away from the ridge and back towards the cave.

*

Alone, sitting in the half-light, Florian had had plenty of time to agonise about his actions. He worried he'd been impetuous; what would happen now to his family? When would his senior officer, Major Schmalz, send out men to search for him? Would the *partigiani* believe he wanted to help them? Most of all he was tortured by the thought of sweet Lucia reaping consequences stirred by what he had done in a moment of despair. He seriously considered putting his pistol to his head, but then the creepers parted and Lucia was next to him. All thoughts of death disappeared.

'Try to save as much of this as you can, Florian,' she said, handing him the cloth containing bread, cheese and slices of *trippa* that her mother had prepared. 'I don't know when I can manage to come up to see you again.'

'But what happened with the *partigiani*?'

'Nothing. I made enough noise to wake the whole of Tuscany, but nobody showed themselves. I'm sure they are up there somewhere, though.'

'Lucia, while you've been away, I've done nothing but think. I've come up with a plan.' He picked up a jagged stone from the ground and handed it to her. 'I need you to hit me hard on the leg. And I mean hard.'

She pulled a face. 'What are you talking about? Are you mad?'

He outlined an idea he'd considered during the night. It might not work, but if it did, it would solve many issues. 'I'm putting you in danger, and that weighs heavily, Lucia,' he said, reaching out to take her hand. 'I intend to limp back today to headquarters and tell them that I fell badly while looking for fossils. I passed out and that is why I didn't return last night.'

'So, you've changed your mind? Today was all a waste of time for me? I don't understand.'

'I haven't changed my mind at all. My plan is to spy *for* the *partigiani*. I can get information to them if I return to my platoon. In that way I will be useful. But first, I need to let the *partigiani* know.'

'It's too dangerous. What if nobody believes you? You could be shot by either side.'

'Maybe that's the best solution anyway. What else can I do? I can't go on as before.' He rubbed his hands over his face and she moved nearer, pulling them away.

'I don't want you to be shot, Florian.'

He held onto her, and then his mouth found hers.

It was the first time she'd been kissed in a way that melted her insides and stirred sensations that rippled up and down her body. She wanted more. Florian pulled her closer, nuzzling her neck, whispering her name over and over and she pressed into him, sinking into the moment.

He pulled away. 'Lucia, I want to make love to you, but…' He cupped her face in his hands and looked deep into her eyes. 'You are very beautiful, and you are very young, and… who knows what will happen to us? It's too soon.'

There was so much she wanted to say to him in that moment: how it didn't matter to her if it was too soon – that if they were to die tomorrow, then there was all the more reason why they should make love while they could. But she didn't know how to tell him. She was overcome with shyness.

Lucia stepped away. 'I'm going to talk to my father about the *partigiani*. I feel he knows more than he likes to let on. Something that you said reminded me of an angry remark he made to Mamma about standing up to the enemy. I will try my best, Florian. If I'm wrong, God knows how he will react, but I don't know what else to do.' She was silent for a while, thinking of the beating her father had given her. But she would prefer to die than not see Florian again. She had no choice.

'We need to have a way of leaving messages for each other. Can you manage to come to the cave in any free time you have?' She showed him a niche in the wall at the back of the cave. 'We can leave messages here.' She found a stone to conceal the hole.

'All free time has been cancelled. The Allies are getting closer… But I will see what I can do,' he said. 'Even if it means stealing up here at night.'

'I will bring the sheep to graze in these meadows, but not every day. I need to be careful not to arouse suspicion.'

Florian handed her the sharp stone. 'And now you have to hit me hard.'

'I can't,' she said, shrinking back. 'Don't ask me to do that to you.'

'Then find me a stout stick outside that I can lean on. At least do that for me.'

Peeping through the creepers to make sure there was nobody about, she left to go and search at the edge of the wood near the cave. Primo rose from where he had been watching the flock and shook his shaggy coat. '*Bravo*, Primo,' she said as he padded over to her, his tail wagging.

When she entered the cave again, blood was flowing from Florian's right leg and his face was drawn with pain. '*Crucifix*,' he swore in German. 'It hurts like hell.'

She made to tear a strip from her shirt to bind his leg and staunch the bleeding, but he told her to stop. 'Remember, I hurt myself when I was out alone. There would be nobody to tend to my wound. My story has to ring true.' He grimaced and she saw that he had gouged a large lump of flesh below his knee.

She cried silently as she helped him to his feet and handed him the stout stick that she'd found beneath the trees, and then she couldn't help herself. She clung to him, her hot tears soaking into the army shirt he had retrieved from his haversack. He pulled away, staring into her eyes with unspoken words, and as she watched him hobble down the track, she wondered if they would ever see each other again.

*

Back at headquarters, Florian was sent straight to the dispensary. The military doctor stitched up his leg and gave him a tetanus injection, suggesting he forget about hiking alone in the Tuscan countryside. 'We are at war, my friend,' he said, 'not on an entomologists' jamboree. Come back and see me in one week and be sure to keep that wound clean. You are lucky I am not going to report you to Schmalz.' After he had finished his official reprimand, he picked up a board from the shelf above his desk, onto which three swallowtail butterflies had been pinned, and he smiled at his patient. 'But I understand why you are so eager, Hofstetter. I too have found some very fine specimens in this region.'

Florian had overcome the first hurdle. Nobody suspected him of anything covert. It was strange to be back. He felt as if he had 'TRAITOR' emblazoned across his forehead for all to see; that any minute he would be arrested and questioned about the true origins of his injury. That night, images of dead partisans and grieving wives loomed in and out of his feverish dreams. He awoke before dawn, his pillow drenched with sweat.

If he could pull off his double life, then it would have to be done with subtlety and stealth. He hoped his nerves would stand up to it. As daylight filtered through the shutters of his billet, he thought about the best way to proceed. The way into the next stage of his plan to help the partisans was through a weak link. And for Florian, this was the miserable apology for a man, Hans Weber, who had thought nothing of shooting a child in front of his mother on that awful day in Campo Gatti. Bile came into Florian's mouth as the blood-filled scene once again flickered in his mind like a horror movie. He rushed to the toilet to be violently sick. For a while he sat on the edge of his hard bed, before pulling out his pipe, from where he had removed the slip of paper with details of troop movements. He packed the bowl with tobacco and lit the aromatic flakes, the familiar actions soothing his nerves. His plan of action would start tomorrow.

On the following evening, Florian shivered as he let himself out into the cool Apennine air. Weber was on night duties, and Florian wandered to his post outside the munitions store, a large opening in the rock face. Previously it had been used as a stable by its rightful owner. Now it was a space requisitioned for the storage of weapons and ammunition, fortified by a new, sturdy door. As Florian approached, Weber straightened from his slouch against the wall. 'Who's there?' he shouted at the sound of footsteps.

'At ease, Korporal. I couldn't sleep. I needed company.' Florian lit up his pipe. As the tobacco entered his lungs, it calmed his queasy stomach. 'Feel free to smoke,' he told the guard.

Weber pulled a cigarette from a packet. 'You should try one of these instead of that pipe, Herr Kapitän,' he said. 'Turkish tobacco. Sulima. Made in Dresden, my home city. Our Führer tells us we should not smoke, that it will give us lung cancer, but I need not follow everything he says.'

'I visited your city before the war. Beautiful. I remember dining in a restaurant on the River Elbe.'

'I'm from a poor family. No restaurants for us, but we used to picnic on the banks.'

Florian lit Weber's cigarette with his match. As nicotine and pipe tobacco mingled in the Tuscan air, Florian leant with one foot against the wall. 'It was a good exercise at Campo Gatti,' he said. 'You did well.'

'Not what Wolf thought. Now I'm on night shift for a whole month. And it's fucking freezing. When will they issue us with our winter coats, do you think?'

'Have a mouthful of this,' Florian said, removing a hip flask from his pocket. 'It's local grappa. Not bad. Not as good as our Schnapps, but it does the trick.'

'Nothing is as good as our own food and drink, Herr Kapitän. *Danke*,' Weber said, swigging a generous amount of the fiery liquid. He spluttered and then laughed. 'It's warming parts that have been cold for too long,' he said, handing back the flask.

'If I can't sleep, I'll bring you more tomorrow. Good night, soldier. I hope the morning comes soon for you.'

Weber clicked his heels as he returned Florian's greetings. '*Heil Hitler!*' he said, his arm outstretched in salute.

Florian had begun his seduction of Weber. He was careful not to visit him on his watch every night, to avoid suspicion. During the next few days, he rose from his bed on alternate nights to exchange small talk with the corporal. By now they were on Christian name terms, despite Florian's senior rank. They talked about the might of Germany, and Florian listened to Hans' account of his time with the *Hitlerjugend*; how he had been singled out for his prowess with a gun. 'I shot rabbits on my uncle's farm from the age of six,' he said proudly. 'So I have no difficulty in that field.' He patted his fat stomach and chuckled. 'My problem is this. If I had to run after a rabbit, then I would fail.'

Florian sweetened him up with extra rations, bringing him half a tablet of chocolate one night, a box of *Rumkugeln* that his mother had sent him in a parcel on another occasion. Weber ate the gifts with gusto, his piggy eyes lighting up every time a gift was proffered.

It rained hard towards the end of the week and Weber, instead of standing at his post, was sheltering in the doorway to the munitions store.

'Why don't we sit in comfort inside?' Florian suggested. 'There'll be nobody about on such a filthy night.'

Weber unlocked the heavy padlock with a key concealed in a niche above the door arch and the two men entered the store. Perched on a couple of boxes of ammunition, they passed several minutes in chit-chat.

'I intend to get back for Christmas to my folks,' Weber said. 'If I bring down a plane, I'll enjoy ten days' leave. All it takes is one lucky bullet to the pilot's brain.' He picked out a rifle from a crate and aimed it towards the rough roof of the cavern, making a shooting noise as he pretended to pull the trigger. 'Ten days at Christmas with good food and beer, and I can see my sweetheart again,' he said. 'I might even propose.' Replacing the rifle, he pulled a photo from his shirt pocket and showed it to Florian. A buxom girl with blonde hair waved from her perch on a bridge, the spires of the Catholic *Hofkirche* cathedral soaring in the background.

'*Hübsch*,' Florian said, handing it back. 'She's pretty. I have no girl back home. It makes life simpler,' he said.

'I need a piss,' Weber said. 'Keep watch for me.'

He handed his gun to Florian. The man was stupid and sloppy, Florian thought, glancing round at the stash of ammunition, assessing the stock of rifles, cartridges and light machine guns. Without thinking twice, he picked half a dozen hand grenades from an open box and placed them in the knapsack he'd used to carry his mother's cakes. These would help oil the next stage of his plan. He hoped it would work. But he would have to act fast. There was bound to be a tally kept of the contents of this store.

Just before dawn, the rain stopped and Florian bid Weber good night.

'Maybe you should get some sleeping tablets for your problem,' Weber said as he locked the door to the munitions store. 'You must be dead on your feet from lack of sleep.'

Florian *was* tired; his spirit was tired, but now he had renewed purpose to his life.

CHAPTER TWENTY-TWO

Lucia plucked up courage and went to talk to her father in the stable, where he was mucking out their one remaining goat. 'Babbo, can I talk?'

'You can help and talk at the same time. Shovel this soiled hay out of the door so we can spread it on the vegetable garden.

'I'm worried about Bellarosa,' he continued, smacking the goat on her rump. I think she has mastitis and I don't know how I'm going to get hold of the vet. He's always helping the *Tedeschi* with their horses.'

'*Their* horses? You mean the horses they have stolen. Have you tried warm compresses with rosemary, comfrey and dandelion?'

'Of course,' he said shortly.

Lucia realised she could wait forever for the best moment to talk to her father, but there was never going be a best moment. She blurted out, 'Babbo, I need to get in touch with Cousin Moreno and the *partigiani*.'

Her father stood stock-still, his back to her, and she waited for him to whirl around and deliver a blow. Instead, when he turned, his face was full of concern.

'What are you asking of me?'

'You heard me.'

'Why do you think *I* can help?'

'I think you know why.'

He put down his pitchfork and walked over, grabbing her arm. 'Come with me. We can't talk here. Even the stone walls have ears in this village.'

She followed him at a trot out of the farmyard and up the path to their meadow.

'Sit down,' he ordered, pointing to the flat rocks they'd used as makeshift tables for spreading out harvest lunches before the war. 'Talk!'

'I told you about the *Tedesco* I met.'

Her father bristled; she watched his fists clench, but she continued. 'He wants to help us. He hates the Nazis.'

'How do you know he is sincere?'

She hung her head and shrugged her shoulders. 'I just know.'

'Where is he now?'

'I need to know first if you will help me.' Her heart was pounding; she had to get this right. 'If I tell you, how do I know you will not turn him over to the *partigiani*? The other day you said we need to stand up to our enemy. Babbo, this could be so important.'

'Who else knows about this?'

'Nobody.'

Her father was quiet for a couple of moments. Eventually, he sighed and, turning to his daughter, he chucked her gently under her chin. 'You have always been my wild, green-eyed girl, haven't you? I have kept you in the dark on purpose. It was enough to lose your brother to this war and my heart is heavy at the thought of putting your life in danger too.'

She waited, not knowing what to say, half expecting him to use his fists. Instead, he said, 'You can come with me tomorrow. We leave at dawn, but not a word to anyone else. Not even your mother.'

She'd been right about the *partigiani* being somewhere near the ridge. She followed her father up the same path she'd driven the sheep, but as the sun began to rise in the salmon-pink sky, her father pulled a cloth from his pocket.

'Lucia, from here on, I will blindfold you,' he said. 'It's best for your sake that you don't know exactly where I'm taking you. Don't worry, you won't fall. I'll hold onto you all the way.'

She stumbled a couple of times, whether on roots or stones she couldn't tell, but her father righted her each time and after about ten minutes they stopped. He told her to wait. 'Alessio here will be guarding you until I return, so don't be tempted to peek.'

She hadn't heard anybody approach and was surprised when a young man told her curtly not to move, that he was armed and would shoot.

'She's my daughter and the cousin of Moreno,' she heard her father say. 'Relax! But don't let her out of your sight. She's spirited, this one.'

Waiting for her father to return, five minutes became more like fifty. But eventually she felt him back at her side, saying, 'Come!'

She was still blindfolded and disorientated. Once again, she stumbled and once again her father helped her up as they walked another few metres. 'You can take it off now,' he said when they stopped.

She rubbed her eyes and focused on the scene before her. She was in a stone hut. A small window let in a splinter of light and two men sat at a table on upturned barrels. In one corner she noticed a pile of blankets where a younger man was resting. He sat up when they entered. His hair was long and matted, his clothes ragged.

'Sit here!' one of the men ordered, vacating his seat. 'Your father tells us you have information.'

She'd never seen this man before; his accent was strange. A jagged scar pulled his mouth out of shape and his eyes were blue and cold. She wondered if he was even Italian.

'I have a German friend,' she said.

The second man spat on the floor. 'Friend?' he said with sarcasm.

'He wants to desert, Stancko,' Lucia's father said. 'He told my daughter he would spy for us.'

'How do we know he is not a spy for them?' the man called Stancko with the scarred face and foreign accent asked. 'Only last January we unmasked a German claiming he was a defector. He was one of their spies. We shot him there and then.'

'My friend has a map for you,' Lucia said.

'Where is he?' the foreign man asked.

She didn't answer. Her legs trembled and her heart threatened to burst from her ribcage, but she stayed silent.

'Well, how can we meet this friend?' the foreign man, who seemed to be the leader, asked again.

'I can help with that, Stancko,' her father answered. 'I will bring him to you myself.'

'No, not here. Bring him halfway. You know where we mean, Gori. At the cross. He does not need to know about this place. First, we need to be sure we can trust this *friend*,' the leader said with a sneer.

Lucia was beginning to wish she had not become involved in this cloak-and-dagger meeting. The only consolation was the knowledge that her father was obviously involved with these *partigiani*. They knew his surname and seemed to respect him. He would surely look after her, but would he look after Florian, too?

'He returned to his headquarters at Badia,' Lucia said, explaining about the injury he had feigned. 'I'm not sure when he can get away to leave me a message again. We set up a system. As soon as I can, I will let my father know.'

The young man rose from the blankets in the corner and limped over to peer into Lucia's face. 'I know you,' he said. 'Lucia, isn't it? We were at school together. Well, well, well…'

His breath was stale, his teeth yellow, and she racked her brains to remember who he might be.

'Huh,' he said. 'Pretending to forget, are we? Nothing changes… I'm used to being ignored.'

And then she remembered. Basilio – an unusual name. But back then he'd been fat and worn a heavy caliper on his right leg and they'd teased him for his limp. The man before him was as skinny as a string bean and dragged his right leg, but the whinge-ing voice was the same. As children they'd tried to include him in their games, but he'd thrown their kindness back in their faces: 'You're only being friendly because I'm a cripple,' he'd say, 'I don't need your kindness.' He was arrogant and unpleasant, teasing the younger children, tripping them up with his calipered leg; it was easier to ignore him than include him. They'd nicknamed him Lo Zoppo, the lame one. Their unkindness had been a form of self defence against his bullying. 'You're pretty, aren't you?' he continued 'Quite the ugly duckling transformed.'

Her father took hold of her arm, standing between her and the lame young man. 'We need to leave, Quinto,' he said. 'Excuse us.' He led Lucia to the door, and as he replaced the blindfold he murmured, 'He can be a nuisance, that one… it's a shame he recognised you.'

Outside, she said, 'But you called him Quinto. That's not the name I remember.'

'It's safer to use different names in this business. Come, we must hurry.'

She was blindfolded again for the first part of the trek back down the hill. Her father was brusquer as he tied the cloth round her eyes, and then somebody else came so close to Lucia that she could hear breathing. 'Let me make it more secure,' the person said. The voice was deep and assured, and unmistakably a woman's.

Lucia was surprised. She'd imagined partisans to be in groups consisting solely of men, and she wanted to engage this mystery woman in conversation. 'That's better,' the female partisan said after she had adjusted the blindfold, and Lucia felt a hand push something into her pocket. 'Take her away, Gori.'

Her father gripped her arm as they descended, and when they were at a safe distance he removed the scarf from her eyes and spoke in anger. 'So, you have been seeing this German again, even though I warned you not to. I should beat you.'

'If you do, then I will not help your *partigiani*. Because they *are* your band, are they not? You can beat me to death, Babbo, but then you could lose a way of standing up to our enemy.' Something told her that if she didn't speak up for herself in the next few moments, then her life would never be worth living.

The look on his face was half anger, half admiration as she continued, 'You too are not the person we think you are. The war is making us all walk different paths, Babbo. I shall keep your secret, if you respect mine.'

He pulled her to him and kissed the top of her head. 'I am proud of you, my little Lucia. But I fear for you, too. This isn't a game we are playing.'

She looked up at him. 'I know that, Babbo. But we need to trust each other. This German is a good man. I know it.'

That night, in the quiet of her bedroom, she pulled a scrap of paper from the pocket of her skirt hanging over her chair.

> *I want to talk to you. We need more women to join the fight. I will come to you. Destroy this note.*

There was no name. Lucia held the note above the candle, her heart fluttering with a mixture of fear and excitement. She brushed the ashes into a heap with her hands and when they were completely cool, she opened the window and threw them out, watching the pieces drift away on the slight breeze. It took her ages to fall asleep, her mind a whirl from the day's happenings.

*

The autumn rains started and fell for ten days solid. In ordinary times, the farmers would have danced for joy, but no new crops had been planted at the start of the season and last year's wheat rotted further in the storm. On the eleventh day there was a lull. The sun came out and Lucia told her mother she was going to pick early blackberries so they could make jam.

'It will be sour jam,' her mother said. 'I have no sugar.'

'We can bottle the fruit with apples instead,' Lucia said, 'and add honey from our hive.' She escaped with her basket and called Primo to heel before her mother could stop her.

There was no need to search for a message. Florian happened to be in the cave. 'I can't stay long, Lucia,' he whispered. 'I am meant to be having stitches removed from my wound. Tell me what happened with your *partigiani*. When I didn't hear from you, I began to worry.'

'The *partigiani* said they will meet you. When can you get away again?'

'I'm not sure. How can we communicate?'

Lucia thought for a moment. 'You can see our house from Badia. Use your binoculars. I'll hang a sheet from my bedroom window in the morning as a signal for you to come to the cave that night. Mamma will think I am airing my bedding.'

'That should be possible. I've earned a reputation as an insomniac who wanders around the camp at night.'

On her way home, she pulled at blackberries, scratching herself in her haste to gather some for the promised jam, yelping at the pain. She sucked the blood from the back of her hand and almost dropped her basket when a woman behind her said, 'Wipe it with this.'

Lucia spun round. A girl with a red scarf tied round her head and dressed in baggy trousers, held at the waist with a thick leather belt, offered her a none-too-clean handkerchief.

'*Dio buono*, where did you spring from? I thought I was alone,' Lucia said.

'You crash about enough to alert the whole of Tuscany,' the girl said with a grin. 'You've a lot to learn.' She dabbed at the blood on Lucia's hand.

She was vaguely familiar to Lucia. And then it clicked. 'Are you Chiara? Chiara from that awful choir we were forced to join when we were younger?'

'Chiara dell'Acqua is my *old* name. But wipe that from your mind. My name now is Rossa.' She held out her hand and Lucia took it, her fingers almost crushed by Rossa's firm grip.

'You were so bad,' Lucia said. 'Pretending you were tone-deaf when you had a beautiful voice… and what about the time you let free your pet rat in the middle of the Christmas concert in church? There was pandemonium.'

'But what a way to get out of future practices.' Rossa winked at Lucia. 'Now, to business. Did you destroy my note?'

Lucia's eyes widened. 'It was you…' she said. 'I didn't recognise your voice.'

'I'm a woman of many disguises,' Rossa said. 'I can change my voice, my looks, my identity if necessary. And we women are useful to the cause. There are many things we can get away with, and we need more recruits.' She popped a couple of blackberries into her mouth, pulled a face and then turned to grasp Lucia's arm, her eyes steely as she spoke. 'There is something specific I need your help with, Lucia. I need you to listen carefully.'

She picked up the basket of fruit and they set off down the mountain. As they walked, Rossa outlined the first mission that Lucia was to take part in with the resistance. Just before the hamlet, Rossa kissed her goodbye on both cheeks. 'This is as far as I go. Talk to nobody about what I've told you. If this is to work, the fewer people who know beforehand, the better,' she said. 'We need it to be a huge surprise.'

'I promise. And… *grazie*. I am proud to be involved.'

Later that week, Lucia was one of the many resistance supporters recruited to carry wood up to the highest peak above Tramarecchia. She had slipped out of the house not long after supper, telling her mother dozing by the fire that she was going to check on the chickens. 'I saw a fox lurking near the run this morning,' she lied. 'I won't be long.'

Outside, she moved with speed, retrieving the faggots of firewood she and her father had stealthily added to over the last few days. Rossa had warned her that they would not be the only ones making their way up the mountain and, true enough, soon they were joined by a dozen or so men and women, including her own father, who had said he was going out to drink wine at the *osteria*. Everyone climbed in silence up the mule track. One old man pulled a *treggia*, a wooden work sledge, piled high with kindling and sticks. There was no conversation exchanged; a nod of the head was sufficient as, one by one, they reached the point on the mountain where two men, hats pulled low over their brows, took the fuel to add to a stack that was already more than one metre high. Just as quickly as they had come, they all departed, and Lucia and Doriano were back home within the hour, staggering their arrivals as arranged.

At nine o'clock exactly, she peered through the small kitchen window above the stone sink. A hunter's moon hung high above the Apennines and she called out to her parents, pointing at the flames that blazed in a necklace of fire against the night sky.

'It's worked,' she shouted, startling her mother, who had nodded off. Her father followed her as she rushed outside to join other villagers gazing up at the peaks.

'Unusual forest fires,' someone murmured, 'to be at such regular intervals. Never seen anything like it.'

Lucia and her father exchanged glances and smiled. It would not do any good to reveal that they had been involved, when fascists lived cheek by jowl with communists and rebel sympathisers. On the following morning, when leaflets were picked up in the whole of the Arezzo region explaining the reason behind these fires, Lucia and her father kept their feelings to themselves, but Lucia's heart was filled with pride and a deeper sense of commitment as she read the words Rossa and other fellow resistance fighters had printed and scattered during the night.

> 'We, the partisans of the Arezzo region, have lit fires to show that resistance against the nazifascisti repubblicchini is strong; to prove to anybody who has any doubts that this mountain area is widely controlled by the partigiani; that we are well-equipped with arms and ammunition supplied by the Allies, who frequently drop supplies, and that we will never surrender. Join us in the fight for freedom.'

In retaliation, leaflets were distributed by the militia, describing partisans as brigands who raped women and stole from ordinary people. Many of the brigands, their propaganda stated, were young people who had no pride in their country and who had joined bands of murdering Slavs, English, Russians and Americans who were using them as slaves.

Lucia read aloud to her mother as they stood in the queue outside the butcher's shop. Somebody had said there was tripe available, and already a long queue was forming. Tripe with beans and fresh herbs would make a change. Maria Grazia was illiterate, and she listened carefully as her daughter read from the poster pinned to a tree in the piazza:

'Mothers, Wives, Sisters and Fiancées, denounce your young men to the nearest military command and you will help rid our country of these brigands.'

'That again… who would report their own child to the authorities?' Maria Grazia said with a snort of derision. 'Setting family against family. That is pure evil.'

Over the next couple of weeks, whenever a message filtered through, Lucia joined Rossa and other young women at night, their faces blackened with charcoal, wearing dark clothes to merge with the shadows, to cover government posters with their own. But they had to be careful. *Il Duce's* pseudo-government of Salò had broadcast that being part of the revolutionary resistance would result in death by firing squad. The corpses of three young partisans had hung recently from trees in the piazza for three days as a warning. But rather than deter the resistance fighters, it increased their fervour, making them more resolute than ever to fight for liberation.

CHAPTER TWENTY-THREE

It was three weeks before Lucia could introduce Babbo to Florian. With all the recent activity, it had been hard for Lucia to leave her message. When the two men eventually met, it was awkward. The sky was black as Lucia led her father to the cave. Florian was sitting near the back, and Lucia rushed to greet him.

'Leave him be,' Doriano said, holding her back. 'I will deal with him directly.' He approached Florian. 'My daughter tells me you want to defect and meet the *partigiani*. How do I know you are telling me the truth?'

'Why do you think I have risked coming here in the middle of the night to meet you?' Florian answered.

'It could be because your leaders have sent you. How do you think you can help us?'

'By revealing to you the latest troop movements, new positions, our plans for attack. I have a roll of film with details of maps I've copied. With the English moving further north, there are many changes afoot. You would be wise to trust in what I have to tell you.'

'Trust!' her father said with scorn. 'Trust is an impossible word in time of war.'

Lucia listened to the two men who meant so much to her dancing around each other's comments in the cave. They were both tense. So much depended on the outcome of this meeting. She longed for her father to be gone so she could sit and talk quietly with Florian, but she knew it was impossible; her father would never leave them alone.

'Lucia, you will stay here while I take signor Florian up to the *partigiani*.'

'Let me come with you, Babbo.'

'You will stay here.'

It was useless to protest. As the two men moved to leave the cave, Florian's fingers brushed against her hands in the lightest of touches, and she wanted to grab hold of him and never let go.

'We have to walk for three kilometres. Can you do it with your injury?' Doriano asked. 'My daughter told me how you feigned a walking accident.'

'I am fine.'

'I am armed, so if you make one false move, then I won't think twice about using this,' Dorian said, pulling his hunting rifle round from where it was slung across his back.

Lucia gasped. 'Babbo!'

'This is a matter of life and death,' he said, his gaze fixed on Florian.

'I have as much to lose as you, if not more, signor Gori,' Florian said. 'You need to trust me.'

'We'll see about that. Keep abreast of me and say nothing while we walk. Come! They are waiting for us.'

Lucia made to follow, but Doriano stopped her. 'No. You stay here.'

'But…'

'No buts. Stancko is expecting two people. If three arrive, he will shoot.'

Florian lifted his knapsack onto his back and Doriano ordered him to reveal the contents before they left.

'It is for your partisans,' Florian said. 'Hand grenades. I can procure more, with help.' He handed the bag to Doriano. 'Here, look for yourself. There is no trick, signore. As I said, you need to trust me.'

*

As the two men walked away from the cave, Florian willed himself
not to panic. If his idea was to succeed, he would need to keep a
very cool head. He had to believe the partisans would accept him.
There was no going back. He concentrated on putting one foot
in front of the other, pushing away anxiety behind the physical
act of simply keeping up with Lucia's father. His leg was still sore,
and the scar pulled where the stitches had been, but the pain
was bearable. Not a single word was exchanged between the two
men as they walked. It was a windy night, the branches striking
against each other in the thick woods lining the mountain path.
No torch was used, though the moon threw scant light, and only
when they emerged from the forest into a meadow was visibility
slightly clearer. Against the night sky, the eerie outline of a huge
cross loomed over them.

As they drew nearer, what he'd thought were rocks at the foot
of the cross moved, and half a dozen men stood up in the gloom.
Florian heard the unmistakable sound of a gun's safety lever being
pulled back to firing position and then Dorian called, 'Hold your
fire! It's me. Gori. I have the *Tedesco* with me.'

The man known as Stancko walked over to the pair and briefly
flashed torchlight into their faces, lingering longer on Florian's.

'Come,' he ordered.

Florian and Gori followed the partisan leader to a shelter of
stones near the cross, a shepherd's hut, and the three men bent
double to enter a low doorway. The other men remained on
guard outside.

Stancko pulled a piece of sacking across the entrance and lit
a stub of candle that rested on a niche coated with wax.

'I'm told you want to defect,' Stancko said.

'Yes. I want to help you.'

'How do I know you're not a spy for the *Tedeschi*? What use are you to me? I have enough men to feed as it is.'

'I believe I can be useful.'

'Prove it.'

'I have photos of a map that I copied, and I can get you plenty of guns and ammunition.' He handed over the film and his knapsack. 'This is just for starters. There's plenty more where these came from.'

'A few grenades? An undeveloped roll of photographs?' The Slav looked at him with distaste. 'We need more than this. In fact, we already have more than this.'

'We know that you receive supplies from the British,' Florian said. 'That you are expecting another drop soon.'

Stancko muttered, 'The fact that the Germans know that airdrops occur is not a useful piece of information to me.' He shook his head. 'You're wasting my time.'

'They know about your wireless,' Florian continued. 'They located the source by switching off the electricity in the Badia area hamlet by hamlet until your last broadcast was cut off… they're in the process of working out your code. They also know about the planned airdrop on Mount Simoncello.' He produced a rough sketch of the map he had photographed. 'I stole into my commander's office to get this. Look, these crosses mark the spot where they expect the plane to land.'

'*Dio cane*,' Doriano swore as he scrutinised the copy. 'We need to warn them to abort—'

'No,' interrupted Florian. 'You should let it go ahead and arrange a counter-attack. That way, you kill two birds with one stone. Eliminate the men who come to the drop to catch you – and there will be many – and stage a simultaneous attack on the munitions store in Badia while most of the German forces are deployed elsewhere. I have made a careful reconnaissance of this store.'

Florian sat back, his heart thumping, hoping that his idea had struck home.

Stancko was quiet for a few seconds.

'I still do not know whether I should believe you. You need to tell me why you are doing this.'

Florian sighed. 'I am sick of this war,' he said. 'My heart is stone cold at what I've witnessed my own people do.' He paused as images from the most recent massacre replayed in his head.

'I was at Campo Gatti a few weeks back,' he resumed, his voice low. 'I witnessed how innocent people were shot, even a child. This is not the first time this has happened, and I feel revulsion in my bones, in my whole being...' He clamped his hands over his mouth as bile rose and he made for the doorway. But he didn't make it; vomit splashed over his shoes and against the stone wall of the refuge.

'If that was an act, Stancko, I should say it was a very good one,' Doriano said.

Stancko shouted in Italian to one of the men outside to keep guard on the German, as he was coming outside to breathe in fresh air.

'And when you have composed yourself, you will outline what you have discovered. We must make plans.'

Lucia had almost dozed off in the cave when a couple of hours later she heard footsteps. Her father was alone, and she feared the worst. 'What have they done to him?' she asked, clutching her father's jacket.

'He made his own way back. He needed to return before dawn.'

'And did they believe him?'

'We will see what happens. Now, hush. We need to hurry before your mother realises you are gone. I told her I was poaching for tomorrow's supper, but there is no excuse for *you* not being in your bed.'

Back in the house, Lucia tiptoed up the stairs to her room, under cover of the noises her father was making through the thin walls. She heard him throw his boots onto the floorboards and grumble to his wife that there was not even a hare leaping about the Tuscan meadows at the moment, and that he might just as well have stayed at home in his bed. 'I caught nothing except most likely a cold,' he complained.

Alba listened to the sounds of her parents' mattress rustling with its stuffing of dried corn leaves, and her mother telling him to settle down and stop his noise. She willed herself to sleep for the remaining couple of hours, but all she could think of were the risks Florian was taking. 'Please keep him out of danger, dear Lord,' she prayed. 'He's a good man. You know he's a good man.'

CHAPTER TWENTY-FOUR

Tuscany, present day

The following Sunday, Alba took herself up towards the Mountain of the Moon to the partisans' house once again. She needed time to herself after the stress of the last few days with Alfiero. Massimo and the other residents of the care centre had been taken on a coach trip down to the Maremma coast, and she hoped the change of scenery would lift her old friend's spirits after all his talk of war, and the courageous acts of Florian and Lucia. Today, she intended to walk and paint. The carpet of wild flowers that she'd seen on her last walk here had withered in the heatwave, the scent of scorched herbs culinary, and she walked slower with the extra weight of her watercolours and supplies on her shoulders. But with each step she felt her mind straighten out. Massimo's simple advice had helped, and slowly but surely her guilty feelings over James were diminishing.

She worked for an hour, sitting in the shade of a large pine. A lizard kept her company, scuttling up and down the bark hunting for insects, and she included an image of the little creature, transposing it to the broken stone wall in front of the partisans' house. If only she could apply artistic licence to real life, she thought to herself, and sort out arrangements to let Massimo live in his own place, where he was happiest, with his memories.

It was the small shapes in front of her that she captured: an empty snail shell next to a pine cone, a rusting cooking pot housing an old sage plant, the withered petals of the rose that had bloomed so luxuriantly the last time she was up here. As she painted the shape of the partisans' house, she wondered if this was the place where Lucia had been brought blindfolded. How frightened she must have felt; how brave she was; how in love she must have been to have taken the enormous risk of approaching her father with her request to be taken to the *partigiani*. Alba wondered how she would have reacted had she been there during the war years. Her generation had never been tested in such a situation.

When the water in her jar was empty, she walked down the path and bent to refill it from an old iron bath. Despite the drought, the water still gushed from the spring-fed spout, drowning out other sounds, so that when her eyes were covered by somebody's hands, she screamed and kicked out.

'*Porca miseria*, Alba. That bloody hurt.'

It was Alfiero. He removed his hands almost immediately from her eyes and rubbed his knee.

'Don't *ever* creep up on me like that again, you idiot,' she yelled. 'You frightened the life out of me.'

He held up his hands in apology. 'Sorry, I didn't mean to scare you.'

'What are you doing up here anyway?'

'Nice welcome! Hey, Alfi, how great to see you. How's it going?' he said sarcastically.

Her heart had stopped its crazy thumping and she relented, despite the invasion of her much-needed solitude.

'Sorry, I thought you were a mad axeman,' she said. 'What *are* you doing up here?'

They walked to where Alba had been working and she sat down, indicating a large stone opposite for him. He looked so much better than when she had left him at Lodovica's a week ago, his face tanned, the scar on his cheek beginning to heal.

'I've been let off for the afternoon for good behaviour. So I thought I'd walk up the mountain. I didn't know you'd be here too.'

'How are you finding living with Lodovica?'

'She's a slave driver! She had me digging in chicken manure all yesterday afternoon. Seriously, Alba, she's amazing. I was sceptical when you left me with her. But we've talked and talked. I feel like a new man.'

'That's great,' she said, dipping her brush into the jar to wet a fresh square of paper. 'And what are you going to do about Beatrice?'

'Change the locks, warn her I will take out an injunction if she pesters me again…'

'Wow!' Alba stopped, brush in mid-air. 'Alfi, I can't believe the change in attitude.'

'This week's given me perspective. I hadn't realised how out of hand it had all become, how much I was putting the blame for her behaviour on myself.'

'You and me both. Massimo has helped me realise James's death is not my fault. Why can't we work these things out for ourselves?'

'We lose sight of what's real when life turns dramatic… something like that.' He shrugged his shoulders.

She changed her brush to a sable, mixed two greens and pressed the brush down firmly, one eye on the line of trees on the ridge above them. 'Do you think you'll be able to stick to your plans?'

His pause was momentary, but it showed he knew it wouldn't be easy. 'Lodovica has promised to stand by and be my mentor. I shall try my best. Incidentally, she wants to see you. Something about a silver jug. What does she mean?'

Alba paused, her brush hovering over her work. 'It's weird, Alfi. She has a piece of silverware with a crest identical to the one on those Davide and I found up here. She told me she'd found it in the forest.'

'Really? I didn't see it this week. She uses earthenware pottery. Silver doesn't seem her style.'

'Exactly. I wondered why she had it. Interesting. Maybe I should try and phone her.'

'She hardly ever has her phone switched on, remember. You'll be lucky.'

'Then I'll have to pay her a visit.'

She continued to paint the line of trees and Alfiero watched her, noticing how, as she concentrated, she endearingly rested her tongue on her bottom lip. He moved over to look at her work. 'Love it, Alba.'

'Thanks... I have so many ideas for this project.'

She abandoned the watercolour, not being able to fully lose herself in it with Alfiero present, and searched for the bread rolls she'd made up that morning.

'Want to share lunch?'

'Let's pool what we've got. Lodovica fired up her oven yesterday and made rosemary focaccia.' He pulled a brown paper bag from his rucksack. 'And I have plums from her tree. Do you know, I was worried about her vegetarian diet, but I really haven't missed not eating meat,' he said, patting his stomach.

'Tell me that again when you have a plate of garlic sausages and a T-bone steak and chips in front of you,' she said.

He smiled. 'Yep, you're right. It's easy not to be tempted if it's not in front of you.'

'I feel that way about Lodovica's escapist way of life,' Alba said, biting into her ham roll, 'but each to their own. She's doing no harm.'

'She's done me a load of good. In fact, she's recommended I take time out of work and try to get away to sort myself out and distance myself from Beatrice.'

'Out of sight, out of mind?'

'Yeah! But the idea appeals, anyway. I can't remember the last time I had a break.'

The words were out of Alba's mouth before she could think them through properly. 'How about escaping to Tramarecchia and helping me keep an eye on Massimo? He's so desperate to live in his own little house.'

'I'm not so sure I'd make a good carer. I wouldn't have to wipe his bum, would I?'

'Honestly, Alfi. He's frail, that's all.'

'It would certainly give me space from Beatrice. She would never find me there. She's a city girl, through and through.'

'Have a think about it. It'd only be for one or two days a week while I'm at work. The rest of the time, I can take over. We could work out a shift system. I'll talk to him.'

*

'This is a wonderful idea,' Tanya said when Alba broached the subject the following morning. 'He's in the garden. Go and tell him your plan.'

Massimo was seated on his own on a bench by the centre's vegetable patch. His eyes were closed but they opened when he heard Alba approach down the shingle path, and he beamed her a smile.

'Come and sit down next to me, *cara mia*. What are you up to today?'

She hesitated before grasping one of his hands. 'What would you think about letting me and Alfiero come to live in your house with you?'

He frowned. 'But I thought you two were not…'

She shook her head. 'No, no… I'm not explaining myself well.' She started again. 'I know how much you prefer being in your own home in Tramarecchia to living here.'

'I was dreaming about such a thing.' He pointed at the centre's vegetable garden laid out like a parterre. 'This is ornamental – it needs a good digging over and plenty of sheep *letame* adding. And look at those,' he said, pointing to a line of trees with colourful, crocheted scarves wrapped around the trunks. 'Can you explain to me what purpose those serve? They'd be far more use around our old necks...' His laughter came out like a wheeze.

'Let your dream come true,' Alba continued. 'Alfi and I can take turns to live in the house. That way, we'll be there if you need us. To tell you the truth, Massimo, I love it there too.' She squeezed his hand gently. 'What do you say?'

His eyes were watery when he replied. 'You would be my new family.'

Alba had to blink back her own tears. She stood up and pulled him to his feet. 'Let's go and talk to your prison governor,' she whispered, and the old man grinned.

*

Ma and Babbo teased her about living with two men, but they fully backed her plan, once it was all agreed with the centre. Tanya had told her she'd never thought Massimo should be there anyway, surrounded by patients with dementia. 'There's nothing wrong with his head, he's just elderly and needs a little extra help. He likes being with you, Alba,' she said. 'And he can come to us for the occasional weekend. That way you will have a break. We'll see about arranging a phone line for you, too. There is a grant available for that.'

Alba was relieved she wouldn't have to disappear halfway up the mountain for a signal on her mobile phone if ever there was an emergency. Lodovica had endorsed the idea for Alfiero, too. 'She says it will take me out of my own problems,' Alfiero had said when he'd phoned to confirm a day later. 'And I like the old man. We'll all be old one day. Hopefully somebody will look after me when I'm in need.'

A system was devised so that Alfiero covered for Alba from Tuesday through to Friday morning. Massimo moved back into the main bedroom he had occupied with Lucia, and Alba and Alfi would use the little single room in turn.

When they both helped him move in, he could not thank them enough. 'I don't know how to repay you.'

'You can start by not saying thank you all the time, signor Massimo,' Alfiero said. 'It's our pleasure, is it not, Alba?'

'Of course! Now, what shall we eat tonight?' Alba asked.

'Tonight, we will have a party and cook steaks on the *brace*, with charcoal,' Massimo said. 'They always give me thin vegetable soup at the centre. I dream about T-bones, even if I can't get my teeth into them.'

'Alfiero is vegetarian,' Alba said. 'Just *insalata* for him.'

'No way,' came Alfi's vehement reply.

'That didn't last long,' Alba said, laughing.

As darkness fell, they sat outside the front door with Massimo wrapped up warm in the cooler evening air, and between them they finished a bottle of red.

'Lucia liked her glass of wine,' Massimo said, raising his glass to the stars, '*Cin cin, tesoro mio!*' he said. 'It was always a good way to finish off a day of work. And that is when she used to talk to me about the past. Later, when she was ill, she tended to repeat her stories and I would listen. It did her good, even if I had heard them all before.' He turned to his young friends. 'And now I am old, and Alba is very patient when she listens to me.'

'Massimo, it's not a question of patience. I love your stories, and I'm honoured to be a listener,' Alba said. 'Now, it's late.

We'll get you up the stairs and I'll leave you with Alfiero for the next few days.'

*

'Alfiero is a good man,' Massimo said when he and Alba were eating a late breakfast on the Friday, after Alfiero had left in his Alfa. 'He's had a hard time with that girl, and no family to help him through it.'

'Don't worry, I'll keep an eye on him. Now, what do you want to do today?'

'Can you help me clear Lucia's things? They've remained in the wardrobe since she died nearly twenty-five years ago.' He sighed. 'It's the right time now, with you as my guide.'

'Are you sure?'

'I don't want strangers rifling through her things when I am gone and commenting on her eccentricities,' Massimo said. 'And today it will rain, so no gallivanting to the river with your paintbrushes.'

She laughed. 'How did you guess what I wanted to do?'

'I'm getting to know my new family,' he said with a twinkle.

Alba swallowed the lump in her throat and, after clearing away the dishes, she helped him upstairs.

'You sit on the bed and I'll put things next to you and you can tell me how you want me to sort them.'

She started with the wardrobe. There were very few clothes, mostly patched, typical wrap-around country pinafore dresses. 'I think these are too far gone to be of use to anybody,' Alba said, starting a pile for the bin.

She pulled out a cotton summer dress with puffed sleeves, printed with tiny poppies. 'This is lovely, really vintage.' She held the dress against her body. 'We can't throw this away. There are boutiques in Arezzo that we could sell this to. And this,' she said, producing a white broderie anglaise blouse with pretty mother-of-pearl buttons. 'It's lovely.'

'Those came in a parcel from Molly, a few months after I'd left England. I'd written, telling her how my life was working out in Italy and she sent a few things: two pairs of tweed trousers for me and half a dozen cotton shirts. And a couple of dresses for Lucia. Do you know, Lucia never wore that dress.'

'Maybe she was jealous.'

'She had no reason to be. In fact, Molly remarried later. Her husband, Ken, never came back and Molly's American GI came all the way to England to fetch her after the war. We kept in touch for years, sent Christmas cards, but our correspondence petered out in the end. She was a nice girl. Wait, I have a photo of her somewhere.'

He pulled open the drawer in the bottom of the wardrobe and lifted the lining paper to produce a bundle of cards and letters tied in a ribbon. 'Take a look through these. There should be a couple of photographs, including one of young Denis when he graduated from university. He was a mechanical engineer.'

Alba sorted through the airmail envelopes, peering at the old stamps and straggly handwriting until she found a handful of black and white photos. A pretty blonde with a snub nose and sausage curls grinned at her. She was sitting in a swing chair on the porch of a house, a little boy with a crew cut on her knee. There was another taken at a future date, with Molly, her waist a little thicker, her hair styled in a bob, arm in arm with a stocky man. Massimo peered at the photo. 'That is Chuck, her husband.'

Most of the contents of Lucia's wardrobe was fit only for the ragbag, but Alba tactfully told Massimo she would recycle as much as she could. It seemed sad that a lifetime's possessions should end up as rubbish.

'That dress and blouse,' Massimo said. 'Would you like them?'

'I'd love them,' she replied, although the dress needed to be seriously altered. The waist was tiny. '*Grazie*. I'll treasure them.'

'She was very thin,' Massimo said. 'She never really returned to the Lucia I knew when we were younger. But none of us was the same after the war.'

CHAPTER TWENTY-FIVE

Tuscany, 1944

Florian was on edge all day. Tonight was the night. It would either blow up in his face or mark the start of the rest of his war. It was hard to act normally. As he listened to Major Schmalz detailing the final elements of the planned attack on the Simoncello airdrop, he hoped that Stancko had been successful in organising cooperation from the other two partisan groups in the zone. Three quarters of the Germans at the Badia headquarters were being deployed to thwart this operation at Simoncello, and Stancko's small band would be no match. His insides were churning. He glanced at his watch. Only three more hours until it would all kick off.

On his latest visit to Stancko and the partisans, they had huddled round a portable wireless in the house up on the Mountain of the Moon, listening to General Alexander, Supreme Allied Commander, entreating the Italian resistance to double its efforts.

'*L'Italia Combatte*' – Italy fights back – was the title of the message, relaying to covert radio stations all over Italy that the Gothic Line would probably be the last line of German resistance against the Allies and northern Italy.

'Those of you in German-occupied territories,' the General had said in so many words, 'do as much as possible to destroy transportation of German arms in whatever way you can. The work you are doing is good. This is the right time to act. The German soldiers are discouraged and tired and have diminishing means of transport. Do not blow up bridges or damage roads, but attack troops and hinder their transport. Observe carefully where they lay mines and which direction their cannons are pointing. Find out where their munitions and fuel stores are. Gather the information and send it to us and, if you can, destroy these stores…'

'The timing is perfect,' Stancko said to his group as the announcement came to an end. He ordered the wireless to be moved immediately to another location. 'We all know what we have to do, and we will do it well,' he told the group. For the first time, he shook hands with Florian, his grip firm. When he spoke Florian's name and thanked him in German, his accent was perfect, and Florian realised he had been accepted by a fellow defector.

Back in Badia Tedalda, Florian was making progress with his part in the combined plan. He had jumped down from the truck where he was nervously waiting with twenty other soldiers.

'Don't wait for me, I'll hitch a ride on another truck,' he said to the driver. He clutched his stomach and swore. 'That shitty sausage I ate yesterday. It's rotting my guts. I need to crap again.'

There was nervous laughter from the men, and he heard one of them comment that he too was scared. Florian let the comment go. The least fuss at this stage of the game, the better. He raced towards the toilet block, and when he was out of sight of the trucks, he ran up the stairs to a toilet on the second floor of the empty barracks where he had concealed a Sten gun with a noise suppressor. He had no intention of jumping onto any vehicle any time soon.

From the window, he watched the movements in the square outside the former town hall where the swastika flag fluttered gently in the breeze. A military Mercedes had drawn up outside the main entrance and an officer, new to Florian, emerged from the passenger seat. He noted the insignia on the man's field uniform and raised his eyebrows as he recognised the high rank of general. Major Schmalz came down the steps to greet him and both men saluted the Reich and entered the building. Florian hoped there were no last-minute changes being made.

Fifteen minutes later, four trucks crammed with soldiers left the square along the main route in the direction of Simoncello. Florian waited until the piazza was empty, slipped down the stairs and made his way along the shadows of the buildings towards the munitions store.

Korporal Weber was on guard again, as expected, but Florian observed another soldier with him. His heart sank, cold fear filling his chest. It would be harder to deal with two men on his own. He checked with his fingers for the knife in his boot. Adrenaline kicked in, his heartbeat pulsating in his ears. Hidden in the shadows of the doorway to the closed butcher's shop, Florian watched the two men patrol back and forth in front of the entrance to the munitions store. He waited until the second guard was at some distance and then emerged from his hiding place.

When Weber smiled at him in welcome, he returned the greeting, drawing closer as if to shake the man's hand. Instead, he stuck his knife in deep just below Weber's ribs, angling it to his heart. There was a muffled scream as Florian tugged the knife out and stuck it in again from the side. As the dead man slumped to the floor, the second guard turned and quickened his pace, his rifle extended. But Florian was ready. The silencer on his gun sounded a dull thud in the night. It was followed by a second thud as the dying guard followed Weber to the dirt.

Moving quickly, Florian used his knife for a second time as the guard's face registered horror in a silent scream. With a last gurgle, he was gone too. Florian refused to think of these men as individuals. Instead he focused on the image of the dead boy cradling his father's body and the way Weber had boasted of the killing in the canteen later, while stuffing food into his mouth. Florian felt a strange satisfaction that a wrong had been righted.

With shaking hands, he fumbled for the key to the munitions store and dragged both bodies inside, out of sight. Then he emerged, checking there was no movement outside, willing his fingers to stop trembling. He flashed his torch twice in the direction of the woods above the store. On-off, on-off. Within seconds, Stancko and six of the band were inside the store and loading up sacks with everything they could manage. Florian urged them to hurry and then concentrated on positioning the Torpex sticks towards the boxes in the centre of the store. He unwrapped the wire from around his waist and, after attaching it to the dynamite, moved backward as slowly and steadily as his thumping heart would allow. He swore softly as he almost tripped over the dead bodies of the German guards. Then, with a nod from Stancko, he bent to light the fuse and the men stepped out of the door, pulling it to.

In ten minutes the men were up the hill, moving with stealth through the woods away from Badia with their loads. After fifteen minutes, there was a huge explosion and the sky lit up like celebration fireworks. The men punched the air and then dispersed, carrying their spoils through the dark forest.

Florian made his way up to the cave where he had arranged to meet Lucia. Seccaroni would be his new billet from now on, but first he wanted time to be alone with his Tuscan girl. There was extra weight to his load as he hurried up the path, his rucksack pulling on his shoulders with the special gift he had secreted from the art store. God only knew if there would be another chance to hand it over.

She was standing at the back of the cave when he pulled aside the creepers and she moved forward with a cry. 'You're safe, you're safe! I've been out of my mind.' She threw herself into his outstretched arms and he hugged her close, his body trembling now not with fear but desire.

'I heard the explosion,' she said. 'The sky lit up and I was so afraid you wouldn't come back.'

'It went well,' he told her, sparing the details of the two guards he had killed. 'Let's hope the same is true of the next mission. The guns and ammunition we acquired tonight should help, and Schmalz will have to halt movements while he waits for more men and supplies to arrive.'

'Florian, I'm afraid…'

He stopped her words with feverish kisses, and she clung tighter, returning his passion with her own. Then, she pushed him away and started to unbutton her shirt.

'Are you sure?' he whispered, gazing at her breasts.

'I've never been so sure in all my life.'

Afterwards, she lay in his arms while he slept. In repose, the worry lines on his brow were gone. His body was well toned, lean and strong but his skin was pale, compared with the countrymen she'd seen working in the fields, and washing at the fountain afterwards, their mahogany-brown torsos glistening with sweat and water in the sun.

What she had done with Florian this evening might seem wrong. It went against everything she had been taught by the priest and her mother. You never made love to your husband before marriage – not before a ceremony conducted in church when vows were officially exchanged. But she didn't care a lira. Florian had made her feel alive, and none of what he had done to her felt wrong. Her whole body sang with passion; the pain that throbbed inside her was a gift from him and she wanted more. She blew softly on his face to wake him, giggling as he shook his head as if to ward off an insect. She moved even closer to leave a butterfly kiss on his cheek with her eyelashes. This time he woke, and caught hold of her arms, threatening to tickle her if she didn't behave. They gazed deep into each other's eyes and kissed again.

'I think I love you,' he whispered to her as he nibbled her ear.

'You only think?'

'All right, I love you, and if I had the powers to magic away the war, then I would see you every day. We would slowly discover one another, you would introduce me to your parents, and then…'

She waited for him to continue but he lay back, his arms behind his head.

'And then?' she asked.

'I don't have those magic powers.'

'But we can make our own magic,' she said, sitting astride him, pinning him with her body.

'Those eyes, those green eyes,' he said. 'They've put a spell on me.'

'My lovely old nonno used to say I must be descended from a Saracen pirate because of my eyes. My family travelled down to the coast each winter with their animals on the *transumanza*, and he joked that it must have happened then. He was always teasing my nonna about running off with the pirates instead of planting artichokes, while he was tending the sheep. But it was only a joke. They loved each other very much. Would you object if I had pirate blood?' She leant forward to kiss him again, but with much self-control, he stopped her.

'Seriously, Lucia,' he said, lifting her off and reaching for their clothes scattered about on the dirt floor of the cave. 'Next time we have to use protection. What if you get pregnant?'

'Then you will marry me, and we will wait for this baby to come, and after a few months we will make more together and live happily ever after, with a squabble or two that we would solve by doing this.' She was naked, her long hair covering her breasts; she wound her curls up in her hands and pulled them on top of her head, revealing herself to him, and he imprinted the image on his brain. It was an image that would have to sustain him through the difficult times he knew were coming. He picked up her shirt and helped feed her arms into the sleeves. 'Put this on before you completely bewitch me,' he said.

He kissed her again before pulling a rectangular parcel wrapped in oilcloth from his haversack. 'I took this from the art store. It was stolen from somewhere near here and it deserves to remain in Tuscany. I hope it's still in one piece after this evening.' He smiled shyly. 'I think it is exquisite, and each time I looked at it, I thought of you.'

She gazed at him. Nobody had ever said such sweet words to her. She unwrapped the cloth with care and gasped at the small plaque, its bright blue, yellow and white ceramic glaze shining in the gloom of the cave. The figures were of a Madonna holding a plump baby wearing a coronet of flowers.

'This is too beautiful for me,' she said.

'Keep it safe, and each time you look at it, think of us and the family we will have one day. When the time comes, when this damned war is over, we shall return it to its rightful place. For now, you should have it. It is special, like you, *meine Liebe*. And you are Italian. It should stay in the church where it came from, so that all your people can enjoy it. Keep it safe.' He leant to kiss her. 'But now, I have to leave for the Mountain of the Moon.'

He slung the rucksack on his back and before he left, she clung to him, wishing she could go too. He kissed her long and deep and then pulled away. 'I have to go, *mein Schatz. Pfiat Di,*' he whispered, 'may God protect you.'

When he was gone, she sat with the image of the mother and baby in her lap, running her fingers over the intricate artwork and then, after wrapping it again in the cloth, she dug at the very back of the cave with an old spoon and gently placed the plaque in the hole she'd made. She was careful to remove signs of her digging and, so that she would remember where she had hidden it, she scratched a tiny cross one metre above in the rock face. It was safer here than back home where her mother would no doubt come across it, no matter how carefully she concealed it.

CHAPTER TWENTY-SIX

Tuscany, present day

On the following Saturday morning, after Alba had helped Ma with the changeover for the guests in the mill, she sat in the garden, drawing with her pastel crayons. A fading rose, rust fringing the edges of the petals, matched her mood as she worked. While she rubbed brown with her finger into the velvety red on the page, her head was full of Massimo's stories. When she'd recounted the events to her parents at breakfast, they were visibly moved.

'I bet there are many stories like his, Alba,' her father said. 'Swallowed by time, taken to the grave.'

'I know that after the war, people were keen to make a fresh start, wipe the slate clean, if you like. There will have been resentments – I believe there still are today… In fact, when we bought the mill, the vendor confided to us that somebody else had been interested in purchasing it, but that he didn't agree with his politics and past, so he wanted us to have it, even though the other man had offered a higher price.'

'It's so strange he will only talk to *me* about it,' Alba said, pouring herself more coffee. 'Alfi tells me he has never opened up to him about the past. And he only uses English with me. He says it's easier not to speak in Italian when he talks about the war.'

'A psychologist would have a field day,' Anna said. 'It must be a kind of therapy for him, I should imagine. He feels removed from it by not using his mother tongue, and yet it's a way of getting it out of his head by sharing. He's clearly very fond of you.'

'I feel so… privileged,' Alba said, searching for the correct word. 'But responsible, too. He doesn't want me to record him talking, so he doesn't want the whole world to know his story, but something of it needs to be told.'

'Maybe you can tell it through your paintings, Alba,' Francesco said. 'Art is up for interpretation, isn't it? You'll find a way, I'm sure.'

She was sketching a sprig of rosemary growing within a circle of river rocks when Alfiero called. 'Come up to the *rifugio* at Monte dei Frati today. For old times' sake,' he said.

'Do you know, Alfi, that would be just great. I need a change. I can't stop thinking about Massimo, and I feel my head will burst. How did you find him last week?'

'Quiet. But he still had me doing more tidying up in the garden. What with him and Lodovica, I'll be an expert soon. What I don't know about the different varieties of manure, and which farmer has the best, is nobody's business.' He laughed. Alba realised she hadn't heard his laughter in a while.

'I'm setting off now. What time shall I pick you up?' Alfiero asked.

'Tell you what, I'll make my own way and see you up there later this afternoon. And I want to drop in on Lodovica first. What can I bring?'

'Nothing – just yourself! I've got it all under control, even the food.' He paused. 'Maybe bring your sleeping bag, because I thought we'd stay overnight in the *rifugio*. If I leave now, I'm hoping to get there before anybody else has the same idea.'

There was an unwritten agreement about these walkers' huts that it was first come, first served; you couldn't book them, and they were free of charge. This *rifugio* only had capacity for two, so it was best to arrive early.

*

The sky was a moody blue after lunch as she set off, and she packed a light waterproof in her rucksack. Ma had given her a container of roasted vegetables marinated in olive oil, a jar of preserved courgettes with chilli peppers as well as slices of her famous English fruit cake to add to whatever Alfiero would provide.

Stopping by at Lodovica's involved a slight detour, but she was curious to see her. Alba was careful not to slip off the stepping stones as she crossed the gurgling stream. There would be no time today to dry her footwear, if she was to get to Alfiero before dark.

Unusually, Lodovica was resting on the bench outside the chapel when Alba arrived at the hermitage.

'*Salve*,' Lodovica said in greeting, patting the seat next to her.

Alba bent to kiss both her cool cheeks. 'I'm on my way to a night on the mountain with Alfiero. He gave me your message. Thank you for looking after him.'

'It was a pleasure,' she said. 'He's a pleasant young man. On the way to recovery, I hope. Now… the silver jug,' Lodovica began. 'He told me you'd mentioned it.'

'Yes, it's been puzzling me why you should have such a thing.'

'I know. And I wanted to explain.' Lodovica sighed. 'I had an uncle who died in the war.' She paused. 'His name was Basilio – Basilio Gelina.'

Alba's eyes rounded. 'Quinto,' she said, her voice breathy as she recalled Massimo's story about the young boy from his school who had become a partisan.

'When you told me that you thought you had seen somebody up on the Mountain of the Moon, I knew immediately what you were talking about. You're not the only one with a sixth sense.'

Alba turned to her. 'Sixth sense? I don't know… I'm not convinced now if I really did see anything.'

She felt the nun's hand gently on top of hers. 'Don't be scared, Alba. He has appeared to me in dreams since I was a child. And he led me to the silver jug in the forest. I never knew him, but I do know that he was very disturbed, and suffered from a hard life.'

'So… you think your uncle owned this silver? I'm not sure if I can believe all this, to be honest,' Alba murmured.

'There is a lot we don't understand about life… and the shadow of death. I know you've been worried, maybe thinking you were going a little mad. I wanted to allay your fears.'

'How can I not be frightened? It's… spooky. I prefer to push it out of my mind and not to believe it.'

'I think Basilio is trying to tell us something.'

Alba shivered and got up to leave. 'I have to go – it'll be dark soon. I don't really know what to say.'

'There's no need to say anything, Alba. The first time you came here, I talked to you about there being a reason for us to have met. Hold that in your thoughts. Maybe you and I should pay a visit to these ruins together quite soon.'

The first part of Alba's walk was steep, and she set herself goals to reach the top, her mind going over Lodovica's words, which had given her a lot to think about. But up in the fresher air, the birds singing and the breeze playing on her face, she felt anything but spooked and she concentrated on the here and now.

Every five hundred paces she allowed herself a breather, thankful it wasn't as hot as the past days. When she reached the meadows at the top, she sat for a while on a boulder painted with the red and white waymark sign. There was a three-hundred-and-sixty-five-degree view of the countryside, the plains on one side extending as far as the sea down to the Rimini coast. *A study in blue*, she thought, committing the image to her phone, planning how she would try out an abstract painting when she was home. The mountains stretching away on the other side were hazy purple and grey, the occasional rusty, terracotta red of an isolated farmhouse punctuating the scene, the roads twisting around the valleys and heights like grey snakes. It wasn't difficult to conclude why these peaks had been fought over for the vantage point they offered. From here to the *rifugio*, it was another three quarters of an hour. She would arrive just before six.

The final stretch was through an area known as the forest of ghosts and once again Quinto, or Basilio, dropped into her thoughts. Was what she'd seen really Lodovica's uncle? She half expected him to appear again in the shadows cast by the trees. The beeches were twisted by the elements so that they looked like figures about to break into a macabre dance. Giving herself a shake, she told herself sternly that there was no such thing as ghosts, just welcome shade after her hard walk, and the rustling whisper of leaves in the gentlest of breezes.

*

Alfiero had been pleased to find the *rifugio* empty when he arrived at midday, and he had immediately deposited his large rucksack inside the wooden hut by way of proving it was his for the night. It was rarely used, but the way his luck had been lately, he thought, somebody else might have got there first. He mentally ticked off the first hurdle from his list. His next task was to collect firewood to cook the meal he had planned. At the base of a huge fir, where he'd gathered handfuls of cones to use as firelighters, he'd been lucky to find half a dozen *Boletus edulis*, Alba's favourite king porcini. Things were going well, and he felt a long-forgotten tingle of optimism.

With only a few things left to do, he pulled his book from his rucksack and sat in the shade to read. He couldn't remember the last time he had held a book in his hands and felt so relaxed. Beatrice had always wanted to be out and about in the city. He should have said no to her so many times, he realised that now, but the relationship had tied him up in such knots that in the end he couldn't think straight. Lodovica had been a lifesaver. She'd persuaded him to talk and had given him perspective again, and he was slowly claiming back his identity. And Massimo had a quiet strength that had worked wonders. The old man didn't talk much, but when he did, he seemed to know the right thing to say.

The way Alba had appeared back in his life seemed like perfect timing, too. Maybe it was destiny; he didn't quite know how to define it, but he knew it felt right when he was with her. He'd talked about his feelings to Lodovica, and she'd advised him not to be in too much of a hurry; to show Alba just enough affection. Lodovica had said that if love was going to blossom and it was meant to be, it would happen in its own time. At last everything was falling into place in his life. The letters began to blur on the page and his thriller dropped into his lap as he fell asleep under the trees. When he woke two hours later, it was a scrabble to add the finishing touches to his plans. With a final flourish, he set out candles along the pathway. He was pleased with the effect they made.

Just before six o'clock, Alba passed the sign for the *rifugio*, which told her she had five more minutes to walk. She was hot, sticky and hungry, and looked forward to pulling off her boots and thick socks. Rounding the final corner of the track before the hut, she came across a line of flickering tea lights and she smiled. *Typical Alfi, always thoughtful.*

'*Benvenuta*, Alba,' he called. 'Welcome to Ristorante Alfiero!' He picked up a bottle of Prosecco from the table at the side of the hut and popped the cork as she approached, and she clapped her hands in delight.

'Wow, that's some welcome. Thanks!' she said, sinking down onto the bench after removing her backpack. 'You've been busy!'

'Actually, I fell asleep for a couple of hours and have had a mad rush to get this ready.'

'Book not very good?'

'Not that – I was tired.'

She clinked her plastic glass against his. 'It's so wonderful up here. I didn't pass a single person on the way. Bliss!'

The Prosecco was cool and sweetly sharp, hitting the right spot. When he produced a paper plate with tiny appetisers – cubes of *parmigiano* and little peppers stuffed with cream cheese – she laughed. 'This is getting better and better by the minute. You're such a smoothie, Alfie.'

'Something to soak up the alcohol, because we are going for a dip next,' he said.

'The pool!' she said. 'Glad you have the fire lit, though, it will be *freezing* in there. Are we sure?'

He nodded his head once, decisively. 'Yep, we are sure.'

The pool was known locally as the Mirror of the Moon, and was set in a shaded hollow two hundred metres below the *rifugio*. It was a steep hike down, but the place was idyllic, with natural steps leading to a plunge pool fringed with ferns and willow. Hardly anybody ventured there as it was a long, arduous way from anywhere and, shaded as it was, no good for sun worshippers. You had to be slightly mad to dip into its icy depths, but Alba adored it. She'd found crayfish in the crystal-clear waters. It was a time-stopped-still location, and she was touched that Alfi had remembered how much she loved the place.

Leaving the fire to smoulder, and trusting nobody would turn up at the *rifugio* at this time of the evening, they left their possessions and clambered down to the pool. It took them thirty minutes. On the way they startled a porcupine emerging from its hole for its night hunting, and they stood stock-still until it shuffled off into the undergrowth. These animals shot quills when under pressure, and they were painful if they hit their target.

The setting for the pool was ethereal in the fading light dappling through the leaves. Shadows danced patterns on the surface of the water, the shapes of stones round the edge like huddled figures, their language the murmur of water as it gushed over the natural steps. Alba had always felt the river possessed its own life. Her stepmother said it washed away worries.

'Last one in is a chicken,' Alba shouted, stripping off her top and shorts down to her underwear. 'I would have brought my bikini if I'd known this was on the agenda, but, hey ho…' She screamed as she hit the icy water. Once, years ago, they'd tried to jump in and touch the bottom, but neither of them had managed to fathom its depths.

Alfiero was wearing his trunks beneath his shorts and he jumped in after her. It was freezing and he was relieved, because catching a glimpse of Alba in her skimpy panties had stirred him. He stayed in the water longer, using the icy cold to help calm his erection, willing himself to think of anything else but her.

'I don't know how you can stay in so long,' Alba squealed as she hauled herself out of the pool to perch on a rock, watching him in the water.

You are so beautiful, Alfiero thought, treading water as he stared at her. *I could never imagine Beatrice ever doing anything like this.*

How cool is this guy, Alba thought, watching him in the water. *How lucky am I to have him as a friend!*

Unable to stand the chill any longer, Alfiero climbed out of the pool, thankful he was wearing baggy trunks. He sat down next to Alba and pulled a weed from her hair. She gasped when she saw the large scar beneath his shoulder blade, the skin puckered and purple. She touched it lightly.

He flinched at the touch of her fingers.

'Does that hurt? My God, Alfi, how did you get that?' The scar was triangular, and she looked at it more closely. It resembled the shape of the base of an iron. She touched him again, lower down on his back, and gazed in horror at the mark.

Don't touch me like that, Alba. Don't you know what you're doing to me?

He slipped back into the water and, turning to look up at her, he said, 'It was Beatrice.' The fact that he was finally able to admit what his girlfriend had done to him was a milestone. He'd kept so much hidden for so long, believing her behaviour was his fault, his inability to please her or understand her explosive nature. He had so much to thank Lodovica for and… Alba, too. It had been her idea to take him to see the hermit. It was more than that, though. Alba was straightforward and refreshing. And she was lovely. He realised he'd never really stopped thinking how lovely she was.

'How on earth did she do that?' Alba asked, mesmerised by the sight of the ugly scar as he climbed out of the pool again.

'She did it when I was asleep. I'd annoyed her, apparently, by not complimenting her on a new dress she'd been wearing that evening. So, she punished me with a hot iron.' He sat beside her. 'It looks worse than it is. But when it was healing, it irritated like hell.'

'She needs help, that girl. My God, Alfi. Why did you stay with her for so long?'

He shrugged. 'It's hard to explain. Rationally, I don't understand it myself. But I wasn't in a good place for a long while. I was very lonely after my parents were killed. But…' He fetched his towel to wrap around Alba's shoulders. 'It's over now.'

She was shivering and it was getting dark. He pulled her up. 'Let's get back to that fire,' he said. 'I'm hungry.'

When they arrived back at the *rifugio*, the candles were still spluttering along the path, matching the twinkling stars above.

This is so romantic, Alba thought. *What a shame lovely Alfi is just a friend.* She went into the hut to change into her jeans and fleece. The air had cooled down.

While she was changing, Alfiero hunkered down by the fire and cooked half a dozen wild boar sausages, a favourite of Alba's back in the day. He hoped her tastes hadn't changed. Beatrice had never touched anything remotely fatty, and existed on a diet fit for a rabbit: lettuce leaves, grated carrot, the occasional egg and maybe fish. He'd always felt guilty when they ate out and he was tucking into his pasta and meat.

Alba sat on the bench watching him, the firelight bringing out coppery-chestnut shades in his hair. The water had washed away the gel he used to straighten it, and she preferred his natural curls. He looked relaxed. He was wearing glasses again, and she commented, 'You look more like the Alfi I remember in those.'

'Contact lenses irritate me after a while.' He smiled up at her. 'Guess why I wore them in the first place?'

She poured them both the remaining Prosecco from the bottle. 'The things we do for other people, eh?' she said. 'Or, in my case, the things I stopped doing. James preferred to stay in bed at the weekend when I wanted to walk and explore London.'

Alfiero didn't want to think about Alba in bed with anybody. 'Beatrice would hate camping out at night and cooking over an open fire like this. It would ruin her nails.'

'Right!' she said. 'Let's exorcise ourselves of the pair of them and concentrate on the present,' she said, knocking back her Prosecco. She felt light-headed and needed food to soak up the alcohol. 'How are those sausages coming on? They smell good enough to eat.'

'Instead of slavering over them, do something useful. There's salad in that yellow container and a bag of crisps to open.'

'What? No twice-fried chips cooked in extra-virgin olive oil? Not good enough, Alfi!'

He threw a pine cone at her. *I want this evening to go on and on*, he thought, busying himself with turning the sausages one final time.

This is such fun. I could almost fancy this boy. She smiled at the thought. *It must be the romantic setting putting ideas into my silly head. It's the person that matters, not the place.*

As they were finishing the last of the meal, mopping bread into the juices from the sausages and oils from the vegetables, a huge clap of thunder followed swiftly by a downpour made them run for shelter in the *rifugio*. As they fled, they salvaged what they could from the table.

The hut was small, with two narrow wooden platforms secured to each side wall, useful for sitting at the pull-down table fastened with hinges to the end wall. The platforms were wide enough for one person to sleep on. A wooden flap acted as a window, but they closed that to stop the rain entering.

Alfiero lit the last tea light and placed it in the centre of the table. With a flourish he pulled a small flask from his rucksack.

She laughed. 'Your bag is like a magician's hat! What else are you going to produce?'

'A white rabbit?' he said, pouring strong espresso into two plastic cups and handing her one.

'Wait. My turn now. Some of Ma's fruit cake to finish off this brilliant meal,' she said, unwrapping the foil. 'This has been such a great evening. Thanks, Alfi.'

Her smile made his heart skip a beat. *It's not over yet*, he thought.

'This reminds me of the last time we were here together. Remember?' she said.

How could I forget?

'When you made a pass at me?' she continued. She laughed and his heart sank. It was obvious her feelings were still the same as back then. He remembered how he'd clumsily tried to kiss her, and she'd pushed him away, telling him it was tantamount to kissing a brother.

'What was I thinking of?' he said, trying to make it sound as if it had been a ridiculous idea. 'Typical randy seventeen-year-old, eh?'

If only she knew, he thought.

'Do you think you'll stay in Tuscany now?' he asked, changing the subject, but genuinely curious.

'I hope so. But I'm hoping to go to college and finish what I never started.'

'Meaning?'

'I'd like to enrol on an art course at the academy in Florence,' she said. 'I feel ready now. There's so much more to learn. I'd be a mature student.' She sniggered. 'I don't feel mature.'

'You and me both. I've messed up, certainly.'

'I don't think we should look at it like that, Alfi. We haven't messed up, just been dealt wrong paths for a while. But it's never too late to change route.'

He smiled. 'Nicely put.' He held up the flask. 'More coffee?'

She shook her head. 'Keeps me awake.'

I don't mind staying awake, he thought. *I could stay awake the whole night with you.*

'Spending all this time with Massimo, hearing about his time away from Italy as a POW, and then the amazing story of what went on here with Lucia and the partisans… It's been a revelation,' Alba said. 'I reckon we go on learning about ourselves throughout the whole of our lives. It's all good.'

The tea light spluttered and they were plunged into complete darkness.

'And on that deep note, I'll bid you good night,' she said. 'And thank you for a brilliant evening. The best I've had in a long while. You've chased away all the ghosts,' she added, thinking how James and her Seccaroni spirit, or whatever it was, had been dispelled. She hadn't even felt the need to relay to Alfiero the creepy conversation she'd had earlier with Lodovica. Alba made a kissing sound with her mouth.

'*Sogni d'oro,*' he said, feeling for his sleeping bag in the dark, listening to Alba as she settled down, wondering if his dreams would be golden too and filled with images of her. He was so disappointed that this beautiful girl didn't reciprocate his feelings.

Just as Alba was drifting off to the soothing sounds of raindrops pattering against the hut, Alfiero flicked on his torch, filling the *rifugio* with light.

'What is it?' she asked, sitting up.

There was a pause and then he spoke, his voice full of emotion. 'This evening has been bonkers, Alba. I've decided I need to be more bonkers. Fact is, I'd like to continue to be bonkers and spoil you for the rest of your life.'

'Alfi… are you drunk?'

'I'm completely sober. I can't keep quiet about this any longer. I love you, Alba. I think I always have, from way back…'

She tried to speak, but he held up his hand. 'Hear me out. I won't say Beatrice was a mistake, because she was probably meant to happen. Talking to Lodovica and Massimo has made me understand that. But she never made me feel… whole, complete, like I do when I'm with you.'

He moved over to sit next to her, taking her hand and looking deep into her eyes, but she shook her head and placed her fingers on his mouth to stop his words.

'I began to suspect, dear, sweet Alfi. But—'

He removed her hand and interrupted her. 'There have always been buts with you.'

'Shh! Let me speak now.' She searched for the right words, but it was hard to know how to stop herself from hurting her dearest friend, because that was the only way she could describe him. By now, they should be kissing passionately, carried away with the magic moment on the mountain. He had been so thoughtful; he was kind, good-looking, but she felt no chemistry. She struggled to explain.

'I'm not ready, Alfi…'

'Does that mean you might be ready one day? I'm prepared to wait.'

She felt whatever she said would be wrong. 'Alfi, I've no time for a relationship. And… I can't love you how you want me to.'

His shoulders slumped as she continued. 'You say you can wait, but that's not fair on you. I might never be ready.'

'I love *you*, I can wait as long as it takes,' he said.

Part of her wanted to take him in her arms, kiss him until dawn and make him happy, but it would be wrong.

'Alfi, you're a special part of my life, but… love is selfless, and I need to do my own thing right now. If I were in love with you, then you'd be the first thing I think about each morning. But I wake up and I think about all the things I long to learn at the academy, how I'm going to start or finish a painting or tweak a sculpture. I… I can't think long-term, Alfi. I love you, but as a friend.'

He switched off his torch. It was a relief for Alba not to see the expression in his eyes. The evening that had started so brilliantly had now disintegrated into embarrassment, made worse by the fact that it was pitch-black outside, they were on top of a mountain and there was nowhere for either of them to escape.

Neither Alfi nor Alba slept a wink that night, and the walk down the hill next morning was passed mainly in awkward silence.

CHAPTER TWENTY-SEVEN

Tuscany, 1944

It had been a little over one week since Lucia and Florian had made love in the cave. She ached to see him, but they were both involved now in different ways with the resistance and meetings had been impossible to arrange, with Lucia living with her parents in Tramarecchia and Florian now permanently on the move with the *partigiani*.

Rossa and Lucia were getting ready in the back room of the butcher's shop that belonged to Rossa's uncle and was frequently used for *resistenza* meetings in town. Rossa had whispered that Florian would be on tonight's mission. The girls had opened up to each other in the short time they'd been working together, and now Lucia was counting the minutes until she saw him. They were dressed in low-cut blouses and tight-fitting skirts that came to their knees. Rossa had helped Lucia apply a slather of red lipstick and comb her hair high on her head, pulling a few tendrils down to soften the look. Standing back to examine her handiwork, Rossa laughed. 'Dressed to kill,' she said.

'I hope not.' Lucia peered into the cracked mirror on the washstand and pulled a face. 'I look like a *puttana*,' she said, privately wondering what Florian would think of her disguise.

'Good. All the better to charm the trousers off fat Petrelli down at the Boccarini estate this evening.'

Lucia's eyes widened and Rossa laughed. 'Stop worrying, little one. The others will be there to step in when things heat up. Got everything?'

Lucia checked in her handbag for the umpteenth time, to make sure the brown twist of paper containing strong sleeping powder was still there. 'Don't lose that Veronal, *cara*,' Rossa said. 'It wasn't easy to get hold of.'

They let themselves out of the door leading to the cobbled alleyway, shoes in their hands to tread quietly. At this hour the streets were deserted, families inside eating their supper. A cart was waiting at the edge of the village, parked under a beech tree. Stancko held the reins, and he pulled the girls up to sit beside him, grinning as they struggled in their tight skirts. With a click of his mouth, he urged the old horse on and the group was on its way.

They took a mule track that was seldom used and every now and then, when the cart bumped over a stone, swearing issued from under the tarpaulin, covered by a layer of potatoes, under which Quinto, Florian and three other *partigiani* were concealed. They were stopped at a checkpoint halfway by a lone *carabiniere* and Stancko handed down three bottles of grappa, followed by a promise that he'd receive more where that came from. The leader had done his homework and knew where weaknesses lay. On their return, the man would be in his cups.

As they pulled away, Rossa whispered to Lucia, 'He won't remember a thing in the morning. That grappa is laced with some of the Veronal.'

The Boccarini estate, down the road towards Sansepolcro, had been in the group's sights for a while. The owner, Petrelli, was a self-made, greedy man who had turned his back on his humble beginnings. His vineyards extended across the lower slopes of the Apennines, and it was known that his principles swayed whichever way favoured him. He had removed the portrait of Mussolini from his wine labels soon after the summer of 1943, when he realised *Il Duce*'s powers were no longer what they were.

But it was generally known where his sympathies still lay. Tonight, Stancko had his eyes on whatever he could acquire for his band. They were running out of food; local people had no more to give, and cooler nights warned that autumn was approaching. They needed to stock up with supplies. Nobody could fight well on an empty stomach.

He pulled the cart to a halt outside the high walls of the estate and the girls jumped down. Rossa pinched her cheeks and encouraged Lucia to do the same as she undid another button on her blouse. Then she hugged her new friend and whispered, '*Coraggio*, Lucia. We can do this. *Andiamo!*'

They knocked twice before the vast oak door was opened by an old man. 'It's late, what do you two want?' he grumbled, his gaze sliding down Rossa's generous bosom.

She moved closer. 'We've smuggled potatoes down from Monteviale. Would your boss be interested?' She smiled at the old man and held up her basket. 'Perhaps you would like some, too?'

Monteviale potatoes were greatly prized, but the *Tedeschi* had soon discovered how tasty they were, and nobody local had been able to get their hands on them for a long time.

'Who's there at this hour?' a man's voice called. Petrelli waddled to the door, his belly straining at a white shirt flecked with sauce. He gazed at the girls and then said, 'Come in, come in, signorine.'

They followed Petrelli, the elderly manservant taking up the rear, along a hallway, its walls lined with oil paintings. Lucia had never been inside such an opulent place before, and she had to force herself to concentrate on the mission in hand and tear her eyes from the highly polished furniture groaning with silverware and huge painted plates. Her feet sank into the deep rug as Petrelli led them into a dining room. A long table laid for one took up most of the spacious room. A roast chicken sat on a serving dish, and selections of cheeses and cured meats that both girls had only imagined in their dreams.

'I heard you say Monteviale potatoes,' Petrelli said. 'They would have made a nice side dish with my chicken.'

Lucia's mouth watered as she gazed on the food and plush furnishings, thinking how many families could live in this huge room.

'Let's talk business,' he said, sitting down at the table and tucking his serviette into the top of his shirt. As the old servant moved to pour him more wine, he said, 'That will be all for this evening, Domenico. I shall see you in the morning.'

'Are you alone?' Rossa asked after the servant left, closing the door behind him. She sat down beside Petrelli and topped up his wine. Lucia moved to sit on his other side, and he looked from one girl to the other, a greedy smile on his face.

'I sent my family to Switzerland,' Petrelli said. 'It's not safe here with cut-throat brigands in the area. My wife and daughters would be in danger with rapists about.'

'You must feel very lonely,' Lucia said, her head in her hand, gazing at the loathsome man with a look she hoped was flirtatious.

Rossa placed her hand over his and moved closer. 'Such long, long nights with no company.'

Petrelli gulped as Rossa moved to sit on his lap. 'We'll look after you. We can talk business afterwards. We have all night.'

Rossa pressed Petrelli to her bosom and while his view was blocked, Lucia fumbled with the stiff clasp of her handbag. She hoped the sedative would work quickly; Rossa was performing far better than she ever could, and the thought of having to canoodle with this man was turning her already bubbling stomach. Her hand shook as she poured the double dose into Petrelli's glass and stirred it quickly, hoping he would not notice the cloudiness of his wine.

Rossa finished nibbling at the man's ear and stood up, straightening her blouse from where his hands had wandered. 'Let's go somewhere more comfortable, *caro*,' she said.

Petrelli, meek, mild and by now completely compliant, swallowed his drink, stood up and walked only a few steps before he swayed and started to stagger. '*Che in diavolo succede?* What the devil is going on?' he asked, his words slurring before he collapsed face down onto the Persian rug.

Rossa bent to check if he was still conscious, slapping his face, calling to him to wake up. But there was no response. 'Help me turn the fat oaf over,' she urged Lucia. 'As much as I'd love him to choke on his own vomit, it's not in our brief. *Dio mio, che schifo*, I need to get the disgusting taste of him from my mouth,' she said, swigging wine straight from the bottle.

The two girls pulled Petrelli onto his side and then Lucia opened the shutters and gave the signal to the others by switching the lights on and off three times.

'There's an old manservant somewhere in the house,' Rossa warned Stancko as she let the men in. Lucia gasped as she recognised her cousin Moreno, and they exchanged smiles. The group spread out to perform their allotted tasks. In the kitchen, the girls filled sacks with as much as they could carry. Anything that was not perishable went in: salami, cheeses, jars of preserves, jams, bottles of brandy, dried beans. Upstairs, they pulled blankets, towels and sheeting from an antique linen cupboard and stuffed them into more sacks. Candles, matches, medicines – anything remotely useful and portable was taken.

Within minutes, they had gathered downstairs in the dining room. Stancko had found the servant hiding in an attic room and tied him to a chair.

'Where are your *padrone*'s guns?' he asked the old man.

'The key's in his desk drawer. Don't shoot,' he pleaded.

'You'll be fine as long as you do as we ask,' Stancko replied, sending Quinto and one of the other *partigiani* off to find the guns. 'Anything else you can think of, old man? Pistols?'

The servant shook his head. 'Only the one he carries on him.'

'I've seen this man before,' Florian said as he bent to search Petrelli's pockets. 'In Badia headquarters more than once. He reported a group of youngsters to us who were hiding in the woods.'

'*Porca boia. Bastardo,*' swore Stancko. 'They were shot – all of them – and hung in the piazza.' He spat on Petrelli's body and then pulled out his automatic, aimed at the unconscious man and shot him between the eyes. His body twitched and his brains splattered onto the wool carpet.

Lucia jumped and watched, horrified as blood and gore mixed with the exotic patterns of birds and fruit. Seeing her distress, Florian moved to take her hand as Quinto limped into the room with a stocky young man carrying half a dozen rifles. 'If that one can't stand the sight of blood, then she's no good to us,' Quinto said, gesturing at Lucia in Florian's arms. He pointed to the young man holding a haul of rifles. 'This is Mattia. He's been most helpful. He's told me there are more guns in Petrelli's cupboards upstairs. The old bastard carries the key on him somewhere.'

'Take me with you,' Mattia said, his hands raised after he had deposited the rifles next to Stancko. 'I'm strong. I can turn my hand to anything, and I'm an excellent huntsman.' He looked over to Petrelli's body. 'And I hated that dirty *bastardo*.'

'If you hate his type so much, why haven't you come to find us before?' Stancko asked.

The old manservant intervened. 'He's my grandson, from Arezzo – he's only been here a couple of weeks, since the rest of his family were killed in the air raids. He's a good lad.'

After a short hesitation, Stancko said to the boy, 'You stick by my side and I'll see how we get on. Lead me to the rest of the firearms. Florian, you come too. And then we must leave.' Turning to the old man, he said, 'If you want to live longer, my friend, then you will keep quiet about this.'

'Take me with you,' he pleaded. 'I'm old, but I can cook. I could be of use. Petrelli held meetings here with the militia. I overheard them talk.'

'He's too old. Shoot him as well,' Quinto said.

'Go and load up the rest of the guns,' Stancko told Quinto, ignoring his suggestion, 'and be quick.'

'We'll set you free,' Stancko said, turning back to the servant. 'But we know who you are, we have your grandson and we will find you if you don't keep your mouth shut.' The terrified old man nodded.

Three of the partisans, together with Mattia, made their own return journeys on foot as the cart was now laden with spoils. Rossa, armed with a hunting gun, and Florian, his pistol in his hand, sat beside Stancko at the reins while Lucia and Quinto huddled in the back under the tarpaulin.

'Not the most romantic place for a cuddle,' Quinto muttered.

'In your dreams,' Lucia retorted, trying to move away.

'If I was your big *Tedesco*, I'm sure we would be at it already. I've seen the way you paw at each other. How could you stoop to fornicate with the enemy?'

'You have a foul mouth. You always did have,' Lucia said, pulling at something sticking into her back and producing a silver teapot. 'What use is this to a band of *partigiani*?' she said.

'That's mine. Hands off,' Quinto said, snatching it and lunging at her.

'Get off me,' she screamed.

Stancko stopped the cart and jumped down to rip the tarpaulin off. 'What the fuck is going on? This is not a frigging school outing.'

Quinto was unable to hide the silverware in time and Stancko leant over the side of the cart to yank it from him. 'What is this?' He pulled at a sack that Quinto was clutching. It jangled with a metallic sound as he lifted it.

'More spoils of war,' Quinto said.

Looking inside the sack, Stancko swore. 'Why take this? The family silver is no use to us. It was not in my orders to loot this.'

'I can sell it.'

'Who to? It has the fucking Boccarini estate crest stamped all over it,' Stancko said, holding up a jug and an oval platter. 'You obey my orders, or else you'll be the next one to get a bullet.'

He strode to the edge of the track and threw the sack into the forest. 'There are posters all over the place branding *partigiani* as brigands and thieves, and this doesn't help. You're a fucking waste of space, Quinto. Get up here beside me where I can keep an eye on you. Florian, you climb into the back instead.'

The rest of the journey was spent in silence. It was not the most comfortable place for a cuddle, but Florian and Lucia lay close as the cart bumped down the track.

The *carabiniere* was fast asleep at his post. A few hundred metres further on, Stancko steered the cart where the path forked to the left, and at the sound of his approach the doors to an old barn were opened by two men. He parked at the back and they pulled two false doors across to conceal it. They spent the next half hour piling up firewood to hide the false doors and left in different directions before first light, each carrying a sack on their backs of what they could immediately take from the cart's load. Stancko led the horse loaded with the guns back up the track.

Quinto swore under his breath as he saw Lucia reach up on tiptoe to kiss Florian goodbye. Nothing had gone right for him tonight, but he would salvage what he could. The girl might be off limits, but the silverware wasn't.

The following night, Quinto slipped away from Seccaroni. He had memorised the spot where Stancko had stopped the cart and flung the sack of silver into the woods. It was close to a rock known as the Madonna of the Beeches. A group of local girls had claimed to have seen an apparition there in the last century and it had become a place of pilgrimage in the area. It didn't take Quinto long to find the sack and most of the silverware scattered across the forest floor. The moon was full, and light glinted off one of the platters like a mirror. He jumped at his own reflection staring back at him as he bent to retrieve the plate. When his heart had stopped hammering, he collected three of the items. To smuggle them all back in one go would make it difficult to hide his prize. The remainder he concealed under a pile of dead branches for collection the next time he could get away.

One hour later, he walked back into camp, the silverware hidden under his cloak.

'Been for a crap,' he told the partisan on guard. 'Don't know what they threw into that fucking stew last night. It's given me a dose of gut-rot.' Back in the stone hut, he tiptoed past the sleeping *partigiani* and, lifting the lid of his box that contained his few ragged items of clothing, he gently placed the platter and two goblets inside.

On the following night, he waited until the house rang with the snores of his sleeping comrades and crept out to bury his box in the rubbish hole used for kitchen and human waste. He grimaced as his hand touched a warm mound of excrement, but he told himself nobody would ever think to plunge their hands here. His treasure was safe. At the end of the war, he would have a little nest egg to show for the years of misery he had suffered.

But it was not to be.

*

Quinto's screams echoed around the cellar where he was being tortured. He had been caught on his final trip to the forest. Extra guards were patrolling the area around the Boccarini estate that night, focused on reprisals, and he was caught red-handed by the militia, who arrested him and took him back to their headquarters at Le Balze. It was unfortunate that he ended up in the brutal hands of the IVth Battalion of *nazifascisti*, under the command of Oberleutnant Lehmann.

One by one his teeth were extracted until he confessed. Bending nearer to hear his agonised murmurings, the torturer, a short Sicilian called Salvatore Puglisi, more used to mixing with *mafiosi* than police, threw his hands up in exasperation.

'Stancko, Stancko,' lisped Quinto.

'Yes, I am growing *stanco*, too,' the Sicilian said, brandishing the pliers in Quinto's face. '*Stanchissimo*. Fucking tired of you not telling us anything useful about the murder. *Figlio d'un cane*. Names. We need names. Who killed Petrelli?'

The two words sounded identical: Stancko, the name of Quinto's leader, and *stanco*, the Italian word for tired. Quinto's meaning was completely lost on Puglisi.

Quinto howled as another tooth was wrenched from his bloody mouth, and he gripped hold of the perpetrator's arm. 'Florian,' he gasped, his mouth distorted, the words indistinct as he tried desperately to work his tongue around the letters. 'Florian the *Tedesco*,' he said, over and over, until Puglisi finally understood.

Quinto's suffering ceased for a couple of minutes while the German's name was registered. But when the interrogation continued and boiling oil was poured onto Quinto's withered leg, the pain was so intense he passed out. He never came round, his heart too weak to survive the ordeal.

'Take him out and throw him in the cesspit,' Puglisi said, frustrated that no more information would be forthcoming. 'Leave his body to rot.'

There was no priest to pray over Quinto's dead body; nobody to record his passing. Up at the camp, Stancko assumed that Quinto had done a runner. He was not missed; he'd been more trouble than he was worth.

Within hours of Quinto's confession, posters displaying a photograph of Florian were displayed in all the villages of the area.

ACHTUNG! BANDITEN! PARTISANIN!

Have you seen this man? His name is Florian Hofstetter. He is a dangerous criminal. Do not approach him but report his whereabouts to the German headquarters in Badia Tedalda. A generous reward is on offer for the person who hands him in.

Giacinta and Agata, Lucia's neighbours, read the poster on the board outside the office of the *carabinieri*. They looked at each other and moved fast. Inside, they told the young militia behind the desk where Lucia lived and how she had been seen fraternising with Hofstetter.

'When will we get the money?' Giacinta asked.

'As soon as we have caught this man.'

The hunt was on.

CHAPTER TWENTY-EIGHT

Tuscany, 1946

Massimo set himself several projects over the next few days to stop himself from climbing up to the cave. He wanted so badly to get through to his childhood friend. She must have endured so much, but he knew that he had to tread carefully.

He travelled down on the bus to Sansepolcro to visit his parents. While he was there, he quizzed his mother on how to cure pork. Another of his plans was to buy a piglet, once he had saved enough money from the odd jobs he was doing for the sheep farmer up the road. Pork would make a pleasant change to his diet of eggs, and fish from the river, and it would mean he didn't have to spend money on sausage and cured ham from the little grocer's shop. His mother had always hung hams and home-made salami in the storeroom to season, when he was growing up. His parents were in good health, but they still couldn't understand his need to stay alone in Tramarecchia, and he found it hard to explain his reasons. He left after a couple of hours, pleased to escape the dusty, busy city.

He constructed a large run for Lupino. It seemed cruel to chain him to the kennel when he was on trips to town and the market. As the cub grew, it was becoming more and more obvious he wasn't an Alsatian dog. Massimo also patched up an outbuilding, mending the roof with tiles scattered about the ruins of Lucia's old house, making it weathertight for the arrival of his pig. While he was in the ruined house, he sorted out good timbers from the useless, leaning what could be salvaged against the only remaining sound wall, its stones blackened from fire. The rest he chopped for firewood, piling it neatly and protecting it with a length of tarpaulin from the back of his own storeroom. Maybe one day Lucia would return to live in Tramarecchia and he could help her rebuild her family home.

Robertino wandered over to see what he was up to. 'This place is like a morgue,' he grumbled. 'Everybody's gone. Dino to America, Fausto dead, his parents down in Sansepolcro where there's more work. The place is full of ghosts and sadness. What is the point of repairing this hovel?'

For some reason, Massimo didn't want to tell him that he'd found Lucia, so he mumbled something about the building being an eyesore whenever he opened his door.

'Nature will take care of that for you,' Robertino said. 'There'll be creepers covering your eyesore before long.' He poked at a fallen piece of masonry with a stick. 'We're leaving too, next week. My signora is always nagging at me to go to her mother's house in Badia, and I've had it up to here anyway with this place. I'll be in my grave too soon if I stay. Got myself a job as a labourer for the *comune* as a street-sweeper, and I get a house with running water and electricity.' He turned to go. 'You'll have this dump all to yourself, Massimo.'

'I wish you good luck,' Massimo said, thinking to himself that he wouldn't miss the surly family. It was true that it was hard to scrape a living from the stony meadows aslant the mountainside. He had to fetch water from the fountain and burn paraffin lamps and candles at night. But Massimo relished his childhood home, and the freedom.

When the day came, he helped Robertino pack his belongings high on his cart. The sight of rolled-up mattresses, pots and pans reminded him of the times when families in the villages left each September for the Maremma coast. Down there they worked picking artichokes, or helped with shepherds and herdsmen who'd left with their animals on the annual *transumanza*. It had always been a way of scratching a living in the winter months, but even this custom was waning; another result of the war interfering with lives and traditions.

A couple of days after Robertino had gone, a thick mist enveloped Tramarecchia, something which often happened high up in the mountains. There would be no outside work for a while, so Massimo sat in the kitchen, sharpening tools, repairing a handle on a hoe and patching a pair of his father's rubber boots. He hated days like these when he couldn't be out in the open. There was too much time to think, his mind wandering back to the wretched days of fighting in Libya. He remembered how he and the other prisoners were forced to sit outside their tents in the searing heat during the day so that the Australian sentries could keep an eye on them. His thoughts turned to different scenes, and he wondered if Molly missed Suffolk and what she was doing far away in America with her GI husband. Denis would probably be walking now and keeping her busy. He couldn't imagine her living in a place like Tramarecchia.

Late that afternoon, there was a knock at his door. Massimo had been dozing in a chair and he woke with a start. Stumbling across the kitchen, he opened it slightly to find Lucia shivering on the step. He hadn't seen her for over two weeks, and she looked thinner than ever. Her hair was plastered to her scalp and she was soaked through from the mist. He opened the door wide and she went straight over to the hearth and extended her hands to the lazy flame. Throwing on more kindling, he coaxed life from the embers before placing a pan of milk on the heat. From upstairs he pulled a blanket from the single bed and brought it down to drape over her shoulders. He rustled up a frittata, adding porcini mushrooms that he'd collected the previous day, slicing them thinly into the bubbling eggs.

Slowly, some colour returned to her hollow cheeks.

'Can I stay with you until this fog is gone?' she asked. 'I shan't bother you.'

'You can stay as long as you wish.'

'When the mist descends, I feel unsafe. I can't see if anybody is coming to get me.'

'Who would be coming to get you? The war is over now, Lucia.'

'There are still people who hate me.'

'You're safe here. Everybody has left.'

'I saw Robertino and his bitches leave on the cart. I was watching from the pass.'

Her face was tense, worry lines furrowing her brow, and he wanted to smooth them away. He wondered how long she had been living on her nerves.

'My mother left some of her things here,' he said. 'Let's sort out some dry clothes for you.'

He went upstairs again to the trunk at the end of the double bed and pulled out a blue and white overall dress, a cotton blouse and a darned shawl. Downstairs, he placed them on a chair, and she picked up the pinafore, holding it against her.

'Trousers are easiest. Do you have a spare pair?'

'Only my best ones.' They were trousers Molly had given him to take to Italy. He was loath to part with them.

'These will do for while I'm here,' she said, picking up his mother's clothes and going to the storeroom to change.

When she returned, he looked at her in dismay. The dress hung off her even though she'd wound the ties around her waist twice to fit. She looked like a scarecrow with her bony arms and tatty hair. As a girl she'd been stocky and sturdy, her long plaits streaming behind her as she overtook the boys, even barefoot. He cursed inside at whoever had done this to her, but not wishing to upset her, he tossed out a compliment. 'Better than your old rags,' he said, and she did a twirl.

'I look ridiculous, Massimo, and you know it. But these will do for now.'

She perched on a stool near the fire, and he let her settle, waiting for her to talk.

'Even when I have the fire burning all the time, it's never warm in that cave,' she said, stretching her hands to the flames. 'At first, I couldn't bear to light one. The flames reminded me too much of…' She bit her lip and then continued. 'But I couldn't get warm, so I forced myself to collect wood. The matches we'd stowed away were still there and I was proud of myself when I conquered my fear. But there's never anybody to share moments with. I talk to myself a lot these days…'

She turned to look at him where he was sitting behind her at the table. 'Do you remember those times, Massimino? When we used to play there?'

He took a sharp breath at the affectionate use of his name.

'Of course I remember,' he said. 'Even though it seems a long time ago.'

'Another life,' she said.

He made no attempt to fill the silence, somehow understanding it was she who had to talk. He got up to prepare them both a hot, sweet cup of chicory coffee. She took it from him, folding her hands around his mother's cup. 'The pots we took up there are all broken now. I use an old tin for drinks. Mostly I drink infusions from mint I gather near the stream.' She drained the cup. 'But this is good.' She held it out for more and he obliged.

'I'm being lazy today, Massimino. Give me time and I'll work hard for you, I promise. I can cook and clean. I'll look after you.'

'I don't need looking after,' he told her. 'But there's plenty of room for both of us. Until you're ready to move back and I can patch up your old house.'

'Never. I shall *never* live in that house again.' She spat out her words. 'I'd prefer to remain forever in my cave than return to those four walls.'

She grew agitated, pacing about the room, clenching and unclenching her hands until he told her gently, 'Sit by the fire again, Lucia. I'll prepare us a bite to eat for later. Do you like minestrone? I can throw in some pasta, too.' It was like having to distract a child or an old person; the way he'd listened to his mother soothing his grandmother when she went funny in the head.

Eventually she stopped moving about and he went to the door and called to Lupino, letting him off his chain and encouraging him into the kitchen. The young wolf went straight over to Lucia by the fire and pushed up against her, nuzzling his head into her lap as she stroked the fur on his head and talked softly to the animal. Massimo had remembered how she had calmed down when she'd greeted Lupino by the river.

'If he's to stay indoors,' Massimo said, 'we need to treat him for fleas.'

'Rue, fennel, wormwood and rosemary,' she said immediately. 'My mother's remedy. I know where they all grow, and you have a rosemary bush by your door.'

As she stroked the cub, she started to sing the song he'd heard before.

'What language is that?' he asked after a while.

'It's German,' she said. 'Florian taught me the words.'

Without lifting her head, she said, 'If we are going to be spending time together, then we need to tell each other our stories. Tell me about your time in *Inghilterra*. Was it hard, Massimino?'

While the mist swirled around the house and the day's shadows lengthened, he opened up to his childhood friend, telling her about his time in Libya, not sparing any details to this girl. It was obvious to him that she understood about suffering. He described his journey to England, the camp in Suffolk and his time on the Spinks' farm. When he came to tell her about Molly, he was open about how he'd slept with her. He talked about the English girl with fondness and finished off by telling Lucia that he had never been in love with her. 'We were two lonely people who needed each other at that time. I do think of her occasionally, and wonder how she is getting on. I might write her another letter soon.'

He added fresh wood to the fire when he had finished, and fetched ingredients for minestrone soup for their supper. Side by side they chopped celery, carrots, tomatoes and onions and he added a jar of borlotti beans from his mother's store of bottled produce.

'Wait,' Lucia said, and she popped outside with a knife, returning with a handful of parsley and basil from Massimo's vegetable garden.

'How did you know where to find those?' he asked.

'I've been watching your house for a while. I wasn't sure it was you at first. You've changed. You're a man now.'

'The years of war have changed us all,' he said.

While the soup simmered in a large pan over the fire, he fetched a bottle of wine and two glasses.

'The wine you left me was the first I'd drunk in over two years,' she told him. 'It went straight to my head and helped me sleep.'

He poured her a half measure and she pushed her glass against the bottle for him to fill it. 'If I'm going to tell you what happened to me,' she said, 'I'll need more than half a glass.'

CHAPTER TWENTY-NINE

Tuscany, 1944

Lucia dozed on and off in the meadow in the shade of the pines, while the sheep fed on the grass, their bells tinkling rhythmically. She'd not slept for the past two days because of worry for Florian. She'd seen the posters. He was a wanted man.

Claps of thunder woke her and Primo started to bark. The thunder rumbled on and on until she realised it was artillery fire, broken up with the rattling of bullets from machine guns. There had never been such a long, sustained attack before. An occasional shot from a sniper would ring out over the mountains, or a machine gun might be aimed rather pointlessly at a passing aeroplane, the bullets never reaching their target, but she had never heard such an extended exchange. It was too close for comfort. She called for Primo and ran for the shelter of the woods, curling herself up by the dog's side, wondering how long the battle would last. The sounds were coming from the top of the valley, above the Sansepolcro road. As the shadows lengthened, the firing stopped. She slipped out of the woods and called Primo to gather the sheep and, keeping to the tracks, they hurried home.

Her mother was pacing the kitchen and when Lucia entered, she screamed and pulled her into her arms. '*Dio mio*, thank God you're safe. I can't find your father anywhere. He told me he was going to Badia to buy twine. I fear he's been caught up in the fighting.'

'Mamma, don't worry. He's probably in the *osteria*, keeping his head down with his friends while all this goes on. Don't worry! Let's make ourselves a cup of coffee and pour in some grappa. Calm down, Mamma. He'll be back soon, you'll see.'

But as the evening progressed, Lucia became increasingly concerned, and she ran out of things to say to placate her mother. 'Help me prepare polenta for when he returns,' she said, wondering if he ever would.

It was past eleven o'clock when the door was pushed open by Lucia's father, carrying the limp body of her cousin Moreno. He laid the young man down near the fireside and called to the women to tend to the large wound in Moreno's side.

'He's not the only one,' he said, knocking back a large tumbler of wine. 'Plenty dead on both sides.' He turned to Lucia. 'Leave your mother to tend to your cousin and come with me. There are some with worse injuries. Bring clean rags and medicine.'

Lucia scooped the cotton bag of worn sheets and towels they used for cleaning, as well as two jars of ointment and salves from the top kitchen shelf and hurried after her father, who pulled her up behind him onto his mule.

A full moon lit their way up to the little chapel of Rofelle, and Lucia clung to her father as he spurred the mule to a trot up the stony path.

'Signor Florian's information that he provided on his first meeting with us was correct,' he told her, above the clip-clop of the mule's hooves. 'Extra *Tedeschi* reinforcements had indeed been called in and we ambushed them along the road near Colcellalto. But there were more of them than us. The raid on the munitions store must have riled the *bastardi*. We lost eight, and there are as many injured.'

There were other women in the chapel when they arrived. Among them were Robertino's wife and his two daughters, Agata and Giacinta, busy cleaning wounds and applying bandages to a couple of young men lying on the stone floor. They glared at her and told her to tend to another lad who was slumped against the altar, blood pouring from his head. The wound was not as bad as it first looked, and she was pleased to be able to help, dabbing the gash and winding a strip of sheeting around his head. 'You'll live,' she said. She recognised him as one of the baker's sons. Once upon a time they'd attended the same primary school. He smiled shyly and she squeezed his hand. 'I'll let your mother know you're safe,' she muttered.

The lad next to him had lost an arm and would need more help than she could offer. They would have to get him to hospital quickly if he were to live through the night. She called her father over and asked for help in holding the boy down and applied a tourniquet with more of her sheeting, the ripping of the material as she tore it into strips doing nothing to drown out his agonised cries. She doubted he would live. She watched as her father pulled a bottle of grappa from his pocket and fed some to the boy, who coughed and spluttered as the fiery liquid hit the back of his throat. 'Hopefully that will deaden the pain,' he said, and then he told his daughter to go into the vestry where there was another wounded man to tend to.

She passed the body of a woman, half covered by an altar cloth. One arm was flung out, the fingers missing on her hand and blood dripping steadily onto the floor. Lucia bent down to mop it up and, horrified, she put her hand to her mouth when she saw the red scarf – the symbol that Rossa had once told her was her sign of protest against the *fascisti*. She fell to her knees, automatically making the sign of the cross over her friend's body. Then she gently removed the bloodstained headscarf and tied it around her own hair, whispering, '*Addio*, Chiara.' *That's her real name*, Lucia thought. And all the disguises in the world cooked up for resistance should not have to extinguish a person's real identity at the end. 'You were so brave. *Addio*.'

Tears blinding her, she groped her way into the vestry, where Padre Agostino was praying over a man on the floor. He looked up as Lucia entered and shook his head. 'This one has dreadful injuries,' he muttered. 'You're better off looking after the others.' The man wore a pale khaki jacket, like Florian's. She didn't think anything of it at first; she knew most *partigiani* wore a hodgepodge of garments, whatever they could lay their hands on. Maybe this partisan had been mistaken for a German in the crossfire. She turned to go, and then she heard her name whispered and she rushed to the man's side. Florian opened his eyes and she pulled his hand to her mouth, covering it with kisses. Her eyes travelled down his torso and she steeled herself, not wanting her dismay to show.

'You're going to be fine, *amore mio*,' she lied, knowing that nobody could possibly survive such injuries.

'*Meine Liebe*,' he whispered. She bent nearer, trying to catch his words, but he didn't say anything more; his eyes stared up at her from somewhere she couldn't reach.

The priest pulled her away. 'He's gone,' he said, closing Florian's eyes and covering his face with a cloth. 'He must have thought you were somebody else. You gave him what comfort you could, now go and tend to our own.'

Lucia's howls echoed round the vestry as she shook Florian and shouted, 'Stay with me, stay with me.' She pulled away the cloth and cradled his face in her hands, saying his name over and over, his lifeblood soaking into her clothes. Her father came to her and dragged her away as the other women crowded round the door to the little room, their faces filled with disgust.

'It's the shock,' Doriano told them, trying to find an excuse for Lucia's reaction, 'it's the injuries… she's not used to such carnage,' he stammered. 'My fault… I wasn't thinking when I asked her to help. I thought she could cope.' He was sure he hadn't convinced them.

'Wait here for me,' he whispered to Lucia, wrapping his jacket around his daughter, who was shaking with shock. 'Don't open your mouth again. If I'd realised it was him, I'd never have sent you to nurse him.'

Back at home, fit for nothing in her grief, Lucia remained in shock for the next few hours, trembling and shivering, never-ending tears coursing down her cheeks. her mother took the sheep up to the meadow the next day for her, and her father disappeared, saying he needed to sort something out. Moreno had died in the night and his body lay on the stable floor, waiting for his family to collect him for burial.

Alone, Lucia sat on the stone bench outside the door, her back against the wall, warm from the mild autumn, although she was cold through and through. That was when the three women came for her.

They dragged her into the centre of the little square in Tramarecchia and ripped off her clothes. Despite her struggling, three were no match for one. Primo, tied up in his kennel, strained at his chain and barked and howled while Agata pulled the red headscarf from Lucia's head and, with a pair of sheep shears, cut off her plait, laughing at her as she snipped at her scalp, telling her no man would ever look at her again once she had finished. Giacinta, encouraged by her mother, slopped a bucket of cow manure over Lucia's naked body. 'I expect your German gentleman gave you perfume and chocolates. Have some of this instead,' she jeered. Their mother tied a rope around her waist and pulled her like a beast around the square, shouting at everybody to come and look at the German's whore.

'He was a good man,' shouted Lucia. 'He helped the *partigiani*. Ask my father.'

The women slapped and kicked her as she said this. 'Because of you, they killed Moreno and many others. Because of you, there will be more reprisals. Shut up, you cow! We should rip out your tongue.'

They tied her to a chair in the middle of the square and left her naked, spitting at her as they walked past her on their way to fetch water from the fountain. She raised her head in defiance and spat back, but she wished she had died with Florian on the cold vestry floor.

As dusk fell, her father returned. Lucia hung her head and sobbed, helpless to cover her nakedness from him. She strained at the ropes tying back her arms, half-dead from cold and sorrow. With a roar, he strode over, pulling the knife from his belt, cutting the knots to release her, and once again he removed his jacket to cover her body. 'Who did this?' he shouted, but nobody came out to respond. He thumped on his neighbour's door, one arm around his daughter. 'Who did this to you?' he repeated.

From behind closed shutters, her attackers watched, but nobody came out to face him.

'Babbo, leave it,' Lucia said. 'Take me indoors.'

The tinkle of the ram's bell leading his flock announced the return of her mother, and Doriano went to warn her about what had happened. Taking one look at her daughter, her mother hurried inside and added water to the pot on the fire and pulled down the zinc bath from its hook.

She washed Lucia, gently rubbing rosemary oil into her scalp. 'Tomorrow, I'll even up your hair. You'll see – it will soon grow again, *figlia mia*. In the meantime, you can cover it with one of my scarves.'

To her husband she said, 'Why did they do this to our child?'

'Because of the German,' he said. 'They don't understand. They will never understand. Lucia was right. He was a good man, and his information helped us.'

'But there will be reprisals. You'll see. This is just the start.'

'Hush, woman. I will explain tomorrow to our neighbours. Tonight, we look after Lucia.'

Her mother rubbed some of her precious Marsiglia soap into Lucia's sore skin and treated her like a baby that night, putting her to bed, singing to her as if she was a newborn, but Lucia was numb to it all.

*

Lucia waltzed in the arms of Florian. The ballroom was vast; mirrors reflected candlelight from the silver holders on polished tables, and she caught sight of her long floating dress of spun cream silk. It clung to her body as she danced with her handsome German husband. A single red rose was pinned in her hair. Florian had bowed and handed it to her before the wedding dance, and he wore a matching corsage in the lapel of his black smoking jacket. They were alone, save for a group of three violinists in the far corner who played a haunting version of the lullaby he had taught her, and as they moved together, he sang the words softly in her ear.

As she danced to the dreamy music, her mind switched to a different scene. It was the Christmas vigil, and she was seated by the hearth, watching flames lick the festive yule log. She started to cough as smoke filled her lungs. She woke to hear her mother scream: 'Lucia, Lucia, get out! There's a fire. Get out!'

Instinct took over. Her father had run them through their escape plan so often in case the *Tedeschi* came on one of their raids. Her own route was through the bedroom window, and a leap from there onto the roof of the pigsty below. She shoved her feet into the stout boots waiting under the chair, pulled on her brother's old coat from the hook behind the door and within a minute she was outside. Huge flames were eating already at the roof timbers and, through gaps in the swirling smoke, she made out half a dozen German soldiers, reflections from the fire glinting on their helmets. Her neighbours cowered behind the trees. She heard Robertino shout frantically for her parents to get out and saw the look of horror on his daughters' faces before they turned to flee for the safety of their house. And then there was a loud cracking noise, followed by a volley of gunfire and Lucia bent low, running, running, running and zigzagging for her life through the trees along the path that led up the mountain.

It took half an hour to reach the cave: the place where they had gone as children to play, the place where she had made love for the first time with her beloved Florian, where she had lain in his arms and planned a future. Lucia dropped to the ground, heaving to catch her breath, sobbing in terror. She doubted her parents had escaped the burning house; she wished now that she had perished with them, cursed herself for following the instinct that had made her run. What was the point of anything now that she had lost all the people whom she loved best in the world? Her heart was broken.

She sobbed herself to sleep, waking at dawn to the distant sound of a cock crowing in the village she had abandoned. She was cold and her eyes stung. She was thirsty and hungry, but she remained on the dirt floor of the cave, wondering how long it would take to starve to death. Death could not come soon enough.

When darkness fell, she made her way down to a spot where she could spy on Tramarecchia. The ruins of her home smouldered, little pockets of flame lapping at the wooden beams that had crashed down in the heat. The village was ghostly quiet. She watched for half an hour without seeing anybody. No smoke seeped from the chimneys of her neighbours' houses. The only signs of life were a strutting cockerel and a couple of hens scratching in the dust. She crept nearer to peer through Robertino's kitchen window. No fire burned in his hearth.

She came across the scorched body of her faithful Maremmano, Primo, half-eaten by flames. And when she moved closer to the place she had once called home, her mouth opened in a scream, no sound issuing from her mouth. In the little piazza in front of her house, the bodies of her parents lay on top of each other, as if in a last embrace. At first, she thought they were asleep – she willed them to be asleep – but as she stumbled towards them, she saw the blood that had soaked their clothes from the bullet holes in their heads and she knew that they could not possibly be alive.

Lucia ran up the mountain path back to the cave, brambles tearing at her face, snagging at her clothes, her head filled with the horror of what she had seen. She threw herself to the ground and her whole body shook. She couldn't cry; her emotions were frozen. All night she lay there. Not even sleep came to rescue her from the nightmare.

Sometime after dawn, she felt a flutter in her stomach. It wasn't hunger; the sensation was like nothing she'd ever felt. It was like a beating of tiny wings. She placed both hands against her stomach, so flat until recently. She hardly dared breathe while she waited for the butterfly within to whisper to her again. And when it did, she understood that there was life after all. A new life that she and Florian had made together.

She sat up and scrabbled around in the half-light to find matches to light a fire from the kindling that her lover had stacked so neatly. With tears now streaming down her smoke-streaked cheeks, she made a silent promise to him that she would keep going. With her bare hands she dug in the dirt at the back of the cave and pulled out his last gift. She stayed very still for a few minutes, cradling the plaque to her body, rocking back and forth. A blackbird sang from a nearby tree and the cockerel crowed again, as she thought of the tiny being growing in her womb.

CHAPTER THIRTY

Tuscany, 1946

Late one afternoon, Massimo's father walked down the track to Tramarecchia and knocked on the door of the red house.

Lucia escaped from the back as soon as she saw him arrive and Massimo was left alone to talk to his father, who stood there, twisting his felt hat nervously round and round in his hands.

'Come in, come in, *padre mio*,' Massimo said. 'Shall I make us coffee?'

'Isn't that woman's work? Where is she?'

'If you mean Lucia, she's up on the meadow with our cow,' Massimo lied. 'Did you know I'd managed to save enough to buy one? And we have six goats for milk now, as well as the pig we're going to slaughter in the new year. Come and see the *orto*. I have planted it with fennel, broccoli and cabbage for the winter.'

'I haven't come here to talk about your farming, son. Your mother has sent me.'

'Ah,' said Massimo, feeling sorry for his henpecked father, 'then we shall need something stronger than coffee.' He ushered him into the kitchen and pulled a bottle of grappa from the corner cupboard.

'Your mother is upset that you are living in sin. People are talking.'

'We are not living in sin, *padre mio*. She is living in this house because otherwise she would live in a cave, banished there by people in this hamlet who did nothing to prevent what happened to her and her family.' He paused, staring angrily at his father. 'What were you and my mother doing that evening to stop it?' He poured a glass of grappa for his father, slopping some onto the table in his fury. 'And I hope you understand that I don't care what people think or say.'

'A man and a woman living in a house together. People put two and two together, you know.'

'They do not know how to count. Lucia and I do not even share the same bed.'

'Nevertheless,' his father said, 'you are living in the family house and we are not happy.'

'If you want me to leave, I shall.'

Massimo's father put his hand on his son's arm. 'We thought we had lost you once. I do not want to lose you twice. Would you not think about marrying the girl?'

'It takes two to decide such a thing,' Massimo said, getting up and showing his father to the door. 'Tell my mother she should not concern herself with the tittle-tattle of stupid people.'

He watched his father's stooped figure as he made his way out of the hamlet. He was irritated with the small-mindedness of his own parents, but he would laugh about it with Lucia when she reappeared.

'Well, I think it's a good idea,' Lucia said as they ate polenta and sausage that evening.

He looked at her in amazement.

'Don't look at me like that,' she said, shovelling in another forkful. 'It would have happened anyway if the war hadn't come along.'

'But—' he said, and she interrupted before he could finish his sentence.

'I think we're fond of each other, aren't we? We're getting along fine as we are. Having a ring on my finger won't change much, as long as we don't make a song and dance about it. We'll say what we have to say in front of God, and then people will shut up and leave us alone.'

He continued to stare at her, dumbfounded.

'You'd better close that mouth of yours, Massimo Conti, before a hornet flies in.' She rose from the table and fetched the pan of polenta from the side of the fire, ladling more onto his plate. 'And if you want me in your bed, that's fine. And if you don't, that's fine too.'

'So, you're proposing to me, are you?' he said, pushing his plate away.

'Well, I'd probably have to wait until we're old and past it for you to ask *me*.'

'And shall I kiss you now, or go down on one knee?'

'I shouldn't have to tell you what to do.'

He picked up his coat from the back of the door and left the house. It felt wrong to him, and he needed to think.

He took Lupino down to the river. At the weir he leant against the side of the dam wall and the wolf stretched alongside him as he stroked the fur on the back of the animal's neck. 'What am I to do with her?' he asked. Massimo lit up and dragged nicotine deep into his lungs. The water rushed past on its unwavering course, flowing down to the sea, knowing exactly where it was bound. He couldn't bear the thought of abandoning Lucia, but at the same time her proposal was the last thing he had expected. They had both experienced the innocence of a first love: he with Molly and she with her German soldier. But to marry without passion was wrong, in his mind. And passion couldn't be conjured from thin air. He lit another cigarette with the butt of his first and the wolf stood and stretched first his front, then his hind legs, opening his big mouth to yawn before wandering away along the riverbed to scent the undergrowth. He let the animal do as it wanted, and he decided that he would treat Lucia in much the same way. Eventually, Lupino returned to his side and they set off together up the hill to Tramarecchia.

She was sitting at the table when he returned, but she'd washed and tidied the pots and pans away and combed her hair back from her face. It was almost reaching her shoulders now, and she would soon be able to tie it back.

He sat down opposite her at the table and took both of her hands. 'This is my proposal to you, Lucia. When I have found a ring, we will go to the church up in Montebotolino and we will make our vows. There's a new young friar arrived in that parish. I think he will oblige. And then we will continue in the same way as we have done so far. What do you say?'

She squeezed his hands slightly with her own and whispered, '*Grazie.*'

Massimo had an old brass bullet case that he'd kept as a souvenir from his war, and he took it to his blacksmith friend, Giorgio, and asked him to fashion a ring. Next, he visited the Franciscan who had moved into the vacant house at the side of the church high up in Montebotolino, and briefly explained both their histories. 'My wife-to-be and I want no fuss, and we aren't churchgoers. Will that matter?'

Fra Amos smiled, tucking his hands into the sleeves of his brown habit. 'A fancy wedding does not necessarily lead to a good marriage. God sees into your hearts anyway. Come next Saturday at seven in the morning.'

Massimo did not linger to talk. If God knew what was in their hearts, then He must indeed be clever, because Massimo was at a loss to fathom his feelings for Lucia. He thanked Fra Amos and hurried back to Tramarecchia.

She wasn't at the house, and neither was Lupino. He busied himself hoeing weeds in the *orto*, cutting back extra leaves from the last of the tomatoes and pulling up withered courgette plants to throw on the compost heap. Lucia often disappeared for hours on end; he was used to it. He understood her need for space, and he let her roam wild, like he would have done if he'd been able to afford a horse to ride up and down the mountain tracks. He thought no person or beast should be tethered all the time.

The first time she'd gone off he'd been concerned, and he'd followed her as she walked down to the river. She'd rolled up her trouser legs and waded along the bed, climbing over sun-bleached boulders where the river gushed foam into little pools. She and Lupino had reached a spot where wild flowers grew, splashes of deep pink vibrant against the white-grey riverbed. He watched as she gathered an armful of the long-stemmed rosebay willowherb. Then, suddenly, she'd turned in his direction and shouted, 'I know you're there, Massimo. I swear I'll go crazy if you keep following me.'

He thought she must be a little crazy already, and her words echoed back to him from the walls of the narrow gorge they were crossing: *crazy-azy-azyyyy*.

He turned to leave her.

Just before dark, she'd slipped back into the red house and taken herself to bed. He wondered if he should ask her where she'd been; if she was all right. But he'd said nothing and not long afterwards, he climbed the stairs to his own bed, and nothing was ever said. Since that time, she'd disappeared frequently without explanation. They lived around each other in the same house, without really connecting. Like two moths hovering over a candle flame but never drawing near enough to burn.

*

Fra Amos was waiting for them at church the following Saturday. He had picked flowers to fill two enamel jugs, one at each side of the altar: the blue from cornflowers and chicory, together with yellow buttercups and hypericum, bright against the plain plaster walls of the musty church.

Lucia had dithered over what to wear that morning and as a result they were slightly late. First, she'd put on the cotton dress from Molly's parcel. It fitted her perfectly, its tiny waist making her look womanly after her everyday patched trousers and shirt. She'd woven a coronet of rosemary and thyme for her hair and studded it with dog daisies. Massimo thought she looked enchanting. But then, at the last minute, she'd undone the mother-of-pearl buttons, and in her haste, she'd ripped a couple from their threads. They rolled away across the kitchen floor. 'I can't wear this,' she'd said. 'It doesn't suit… I'll make curtains for the windows with the material instead.'

She'd reappeared, dressed in one of his mother's old wrap-around pinafores, a plain white blouse underneath – the country uniform of the middle-aged woman. She looked at him defiantly, her green eyes flashing a warning at him not to say anything. 'I'll wear this today to remember my own mother,' she'd said. And Massimo had no arguments against such sentimentality. He kept quiet, thinking how drab she looked. But then, what did it matter? This wedding ceremony was only a formality. It was never going to be the best day of their lives.

When the friar gave his short homily, Massimo was pleased with the words. They were true to the simplicity and humility of the Franciscan way, and the friar didn't preach or spout an unintelligible, irrelevant lecture. He seemed to have taken on board everything he'd been told about the newlyweds.

'I adopted the name Amos for very good reasons when I joined the Franciscans,' the young friar said, speaking to them where they sat together in the front pew. 'I love his way of thinking, and the passages from his book in the Bible. This world is governed by the wealthy and there is too much oppression of the poor. I fought in the last war too, and saw many bad things. So I decided to devote my life to praying they would never happen again, like Amos.' He paused and then quoted from a battered Bible, bound in an old leather cover. 'I understand what you have both been through. I pray that "justice will flow like a stream, and righteousness like a river that never goes dry".' He placed his hands on both their heads and gave them a blessing. 'Now, go away and learn to love each other.'

For their wedding breakfast, Massimo had prepared a simple picnic and wrapped it in a cotton kerchief. 'We should at least mark this day, Lucia,' he said. 'Let's go to the river. Today is warm enough.'

She accepted, walking side by side with him when the path was wide enough and, like a gentleman, he ushered her forward when the way narrowed. They didn't speak as they descended. But at the foot of the path, the sound of the river crashed into the silence and Lucia started to run, flinging off her clothes as she hurried to the water. She jumped in and splashed him, calling to him to join her. He thought later that if ever there had been a moment to consummate this wedding arrangement, this might have been it. But he felt no arousal at the sight of her cavorting in the shallows, her small breasts and slim hips glistening with water in the late-summer sunlight.

'I liked the friar's words,' she called to him, over the sound of the water gushing into the pool by the weir. 'He talked of streams and rivers.' She laughed. 'What would he think of this, our wedding dance in the water?'

'I think he would approve,' Massimo replied. And then he climbed in and splashed her back, like he had done hundreds of times when they were children in this very spot, and she squealed and dived beneath the surface to avoid him ducking her under the waterfall.

Afterwards they dried themselves off with their clothes and dressed again. They sat in the sunshine to eat. He'd packed a bottle of wine and he poured it into two enamel beakers, and she toasted him: 'To Massimino, my saviour. Thank you for today.'

'To signora Lucia Conti,' he said, holding up his enamel cup to hers, at a loss for anything further to add, thinking how odd it felt for this girl to be his wife.

For the rest of his wedding day Massimo worked hard, patching up Lucia's ruined house. She had agreed they could use the shell to create the boundaries of an orchard which would be protected in winter. He planned to plant peach and apricot trees, which were not usually hardy up here in the mountains. He kept himself busy all afternoon, clearing the ground of stones, slowly adding animal manure to enrich the poor earth.

He hoped that Lucia was at work inside, preparing a special wedding supper, but when he pushed open the door she wasn't there, and neither was there anything cooking over the fire. Lupino was missing from his kennel, too. He waited for them to return until well after dark, not bothering to light candles or lamps, sitting by the fire as it slowly went out, staring into the embers and wondering if anybody else had ever spent their wedding night in such a way. Finally, he stood up. It was past midnight and too late to be out, even if she had the wolf to protect her. He began to panic that she might have slipped on a river rock, twisted her ankle, or worse. Maybe Lupino had been attacked by other wolves and the pack had attacked her too. He grabbed a paraffin lamp, water, ropes and, at the last minute, a half-bottle of grappa, and went to search.

Instinct guided him towards the cave where she'd originally sheltered. It was pitch-black as he made his way up the mountain, and the air was chilly. The light from his paraffin lamp swung back and forth, the trees beside the path ghostly shapes as he felt his way, occasionally stumbling over a rock. Leaves skittered as they dropped on stones and a night animal rustled in the undergrowth. The sound of hooves on the path ahead caused him to stop. If it was a boar, then he had to be careful. His free hand felt for the knife on his belt, but as he held up the lantern, he made out the rump of a deer galloping back into the forest and his breathing returned to normal.

Turning the final bend before the entrance to the cave, he saw she had lit a fire. She was sitting, knees hunched to her chest, her arms clasped around her legs, staring into the flames. She looked up as he murmured her name.

'You took your time,' she said. Lupino lay by her side and she patted the ground for Massimo to sit on her free side. 'Come and keep us company.'

He sat down, although he wanted to shake her. 'Lucia, I thought you were lying injured somewhere. You can't keep doing this to me.'

'I will try not to, Massimo. You've been very patient.' She looked up. 'Too patient,' she said, throwing another stick of wood on the fire. 'It's time to tell you the rest of my story.'

Massimo had thought she'd revealed the worst to him, and he wasn't prepared for what was to come.

'I wanted to kill myself when Florian died,' Lucia said. 'My parents were gone, my brother killed in the war. I thought I was completely alone. But I was wrong.' She touched her stomach and then Massimo understood.

'You were pregnant,' he said.

She nodded. 'I couldn't have Florian, but we had made a child. Part of him remained. I never got a chance to tell him.' She bit her lip and he waited for her to continue.

'It was a little boy. I lost him, here, Massimo. Alone, in this place.'

She began to cry with great shuddering sobs. Lupino nuzzled her and whined and at the same time, Massimo moved to take her in his arms. She sank against him and he stroked her hair, not saying anything, waiting until she had stopped weeping.

'I buried him,' she said.

She stood up. 'Come,' she said, and he followed her with his lamp a few metres up a narrow animal track to a small glade on the peak. She pointed to a circle of white stones and a crude wooden cross entwined with dried daisies. A bunch of rosebay willowherb wilted in a jam jar and she pulled the stems out. 'This needs refreshing,' she said. She knelt and picked up the cross and turned to Massimo. 'This was given to Florian by a local family. He told me he rescued their baby.'

They stood in silence for a few seconds and then Massimo said, 'We will ask Fra Amos to bury him properly.'

'No, no.' She shook her head. 'It's best he remains here on the mountain. It's where he was made, and where his life ended before it could begin.' She wiped her tears on her sleeve and looked up at him. 'I'm only telling you because you married me, because you need to understand why I am the way I am.'

He waited for her to speak again but she was quiet. They walked back to the cave and sat by the remains of the fire. She settled into his arms, and after a while he realised that she had fallen asleep. Very gently, he laid her on the ground, covering her with his coat, and he stretched out beside her, sharing the warmth of his own body, watching the glow from the ashes until the fire died, listening to her breathing until he too fell asleep.

He woke next morning to find her already awake, watching him with her huge, river-green eyes. She smiled. 'You're a good man, Massimo,' she said. 'I have been blessed in my life with two good men.' She pulled his hand to her heart and said, 'You are here with Florian and the baby.' Then she traced her fingers round his eyes, down his nose and to his mouth, where she kissed him. Her touch was like the petals of a dry flower on his lips.

He couldn't respond, and he cupped her face with his hands. 'Lucia, stop! We have plenty of time. You don't have to make love to me. We can wait.'

Her brow puckered and she moved away. 'I have coffee up here, and apples I've picked from the wild. Will that do you for breakfast?'

'That will do perfectly, and then we'll go home.'

CHAPTER THIRTY-ONE

There was a slight change between them now that Lucia wore his ring. They were no longer like buzzards circling each other high in the clouds. Occasionally their wings would touch.

'I'll get you a new one when I've saved up,' he said, opposite her at the kitchen table. He reached out to touch the ring on her finger. It was beginning to turn green and tarnished, leaving a dark mark on her skin.

'I don't need a fancy ring, Massimo. I like this.'

He started to bring her little gifts he found around the countryside: a handful of wild strawberries and raspberries wrapped in a basket of ferns, a piece of driftwood shaped like a star. She placed it on the ledge above the fireplace and added the colourful stones he picked up for her along the riverbed. He dug up a root of evening primrose to start off her flower garden, and he enjoyed listening to her beautiful voice as she sang while she weeded. Often, she sang lines he didn't understand, and one day, leaning on his hoe, he asked her what they meant.

'Florian taught me, but he used to smile at the way I sang the words.' She closed her eyes to concentrate and then she sang again. The tune was gentle, lilting. He thought he might have recognised it from the wireless in the bar.

'Guten Abend, guten Nacht,
Mit Rosen bedacht,
Mit näglen besteckt,
Schlupf unter die Deck…'

And then she stopped. 'I don't know any more, but he told me it was a lullaby and I would sing it when we had our babies.' She stole a glance at Massimo but, as usual, he gave nothing away. 'There are words in the song that mean roses and carnations,' she continued. 'He was serious about me, Massimo, you know. I was called a whore by the people in this village, but he asked me to marry him when the war finished. We loved each other.'

'I believe you.'

He found a deeply scented rose growing beside an abandoned house and he climbed to the top of the ridge to search for wild pink dianthus and handed them shyly to Lucia. 'For your garden,' he said. 'These are flowers from your song.'

'*Grazie*, Massimo,' she said, and she kissed him on the cheek. When she walked away to find a vase, he rubbed the spot where her lips had touched.

*

'I *won't* come down to see them,' Lucia said one night some weeks later, when Massimo suggested they should announce their marriage to his parents. 'And you needn't ask me again. They did nothing to stop those girls and their mother that night. I don't care if I never see them again. I know they're your parents, Massimo, but that is the way I feel.' She pointed to the windows frosted with snow. 'And anyway, how could we travel in this?'

It was cosy in the kitchen with the fire blazing, the flames licking at river driftwood that hissed and spat in the hearth. But it was cold upstairs in the two bedrooms. After the first snowfall, Massimo had been woken by Lucia, who'd slipped into his bed and snuggled up to him. '*Porca Madosca*, Massimo. I think it's time you moved into my bigger bed, don't you? Yours is too narrow… and I'm bloody freezing.'

So he'd lifted her in his arms and carried her back into his parents' room. She'd kissed him long and deep until they both felt warm. From then on, they'd slept together every night. After several weeks of eating properly, Lucia had filled out, her breasts and hips no longer lean like a boy's. She surprised him with her fierce lovemaking. She often took the initiative, reaching for him sometimes even before it was time to light the candles and climb the ladder to their bed. On Christmas Eve, they'd eaten *baccalà* – the traditional dish of salted cod. She'd drunk her fair share of a bottle of rich red Chianti and, draining her glass, she'd climbed onto his lap, kissed him passionately and then slowly unbuttoned his shirt. They made love on the hearthrug and afterwards lay naked together for the rest of the night wrapped in a blanket, watching the flames dance before falling asleep.

'You gave me the best Christmas present,' Massimo said sleepily, nuzzling her neck, when they woke next morning. That was when she told him she wanted a baby.

When she discovered she was pregnant, in February, Massimo made her rest. He took over the cooking and cleaning of the little house. Over one metre of snow blanketed the houses, the landscape harshly beautiful. Icicles hung from the roof and words misted in the still air. Massimo had to clear a pathway to the stable to feed the cow, pig and goats. Lupino's coat had grown thicker for the winter and Lucia added extra straw to his kennel. He refused to come inside to the warm and started howling at night.

Lucia lost their baby at eight weeks, her blood soaking into the double mattress. Massimo carried the mattress from the single bed for her to lie on, making up temporary bedding for his side until he could go down to market to buy a new one. In the huge trunk at the end of the bed, he found his grandparents' old mattress case woven from thick cotton, and stuffed it with straw from the stable, instead of the dried corn leaves that were traditionally used. For the remainder of the time they were marooned by the snow, they lived in their own world, reverting to methods handed down by their ancestors. They ate bottled produce they'd set aside, and Lucia made flat *schiaccia* bread on a trivet in the hearth. Massimo was infinitely patient with his wife, almost fatherly in his tenderness.

In summer, it happened again. This time, Lucia was almost four months into her pregnancy. With this loss, she didn't cry but stayed for hours in a chair staring out of the window. Massimo tried to cheer her with gifts again: a bunch of helleborines, tips of old man's beard to add to her favourite frittata, but nothing would bring back her smile, and he had to coax her to eat and carry out everyday tasks. She went missing again. Massimo found her sitting on a rock by her first baby's grave near the cave. At over one thousand metres it was chilly, with a fresh bite to the wind, and she'd left the house without a shawl or coat. He removed his and fed her arms into the sleeves.

'I let Lupino go,' she said, her teeth chattering, her body shaking, and she held up the empty rope she'd used as a lead. 'He was howling again, and the wolves called back.' She pointed to the peak opposite, blue-green and mysterious in the sunshine. 'It was time to let him leave. Nothing lasts forever.'

'Come home, Lucia,' Massimo said, pulling her to her feet. 'Come home.'

CHAPTER THIRTY-TWO

Tuscany, present day

'For a while, Lucia and I went back to how we were before. Existing in the same house is how I would describe it,' Massimo said to Alba. 'But with time, something of the old Lucia returned, something of her sparkle. Some days when she woke up, she would turn to me in bed. "Let's forget our chores and have today to ourselves, Massi." And we would pack a simple picnic and escape to somewhere in the mountains where we had never been before. She loved to walk. That is how I prefer to remember her, Alba. Free and easy on the Mountain of the Moon. She was as loving as I think she could be.'

Massimo stopped for a moment, his eyes directed to the mountains bathed in sunshine. 'Nowadays there would be help for a couple like us, but there were so many people damaged by the war. We had to get on with life in the only way we knew how: day by day. Our love deepened into friendship, and over the years we grew to understand each other better... and accept. We had both suffered in different ways, although what she had been through was infinitely worse.'

'It *is* very sad, but you were amazing with her.' Alba was sketching his face as he talked, pinning his likeness to the paper, trying to interpret his character in a deeper way than a photograph ever could.

'I loved her, you see. Love comes in many forms. I was sad for her, and I wanted to care for her. She was part of my life, she became my life. I remember when she was born, even though I was only tiny, and I remember the joy of her family and all the others in our little hamlet that another baby girl had arrived to swell our numbers. In fact, in the end she agreed to meet my parents. It was awkward at first. I know they found her odd. But there was an eagerness after the war to forgive and forget. Lucia was a brave woman. I don't think I have ever met anyone braver in the way she battled her sorrows.'

Alba was silent. She didn't know how to tell Massimo what a wonderful man he was; how, without him, Lucia's battle would probably have been lost. If Alba had attempted to tell him this, her words would have turned to tears.

'What I am trying to tell you with this story of my life, Alba, is to take care to not miss the life you have or let it pass you by. Be honest with your feelings and take action.' He paused again and Alba waited.

'*Poverina*. My poor Lucia… I still think of her every day after all this time,' Massimo said.

Alba stopped sketching.

'Tell me, Massimo, did you ever come across the *predella*? Do you think it could possibly be the one missing from the altar panel in the little chapel up in Montebotolino?'

He shrugged his shoulders. 'I don't know, Alba. I never tried to find it. That cave became a very sad place for us both.'

'I might go and look for the cave myself. Maybe it's still buried there.'

'It will be impossible to find, *cara mia*. It was covered by a landslide more than thirty years ago. Don't waste your energy.'

'I struggle to understand how any of you could get over the war,' Alba said, resuming her drawing.

'There's no simple answer to that, *cara mia*. As for Lucia, I wonder if I treated her too gently or protected her too much. I should have remembered the feisty girl she had been before the war, and left her to find her own way. But I wrapped her up in my care like a delicate egg, fearing her shell would crack at any minute. I watched her when she slept, her eyelashes fanned on her cheeks like a drawing, her hands fluttering in her dreams, her straggly urchin hair like a street boy's. She'd been through so much, I was frightened of breaking her.'

'You loved her so much, Massimo.'

'I think I was even frightened of loving her, of being too romantic – God knows, I loved her so much. Maybe I should have let things take their own course. If you tie the vine the way it wants to climb, then it flourishes. I was always in a quandary over the best way to behave with her.' Massimo turned to Alba and sighed. 'There is silence with grief,' he said, 'and I think I was too silent. That is why I urged you when we first met to talk about your James, *cara mia*.'

'Perhaps that's simply the way we are. We bottle things up, believing that is how to stay strong,' Alba said, reaching to touch his arm. 'It's hard to change.'

'But I haven't been strong and silent with you, have I? I'm so glad we've shared with each other, Alba. If I could turn back the clock with Lucia, I would be different. I wasn't man enough. I was terrified half the time of damaging her.'

'She was already damaged. It's not a case of needing to be a strong man, Massimo.'

'You modern girls, with your feminist ideas. You say you don't want a strong man, but I think, deep down, a woman does.'

She shook her head to disagree. 'We need a soulmate, somebody to share our lives with. Nobody can be strong all the time.' She tried to capture his eyes; the mixture of mischief and torment. 'I'm sure you were happy together, weren't you?' she said, looking up from the paper.

'Oh yes, we were happy enough, but ours was not always a passionate love. Maybe... I should have done more.'

'Oh, Massimo, I think Lucia was a very lucky woman.'

While Massimo had been talking, the sun had descended, casting patterns across the grass, the view of the river valley turning golden in the evening light. The ball of fiery sun was caught for a few moments in the curve of a tree near to where they were sitting, and she pulled out her phone to capture the striking image with the silhouette of Massimo in the foreground.

'Shall we go inside?' the old man asked. 'I'm a little tired. And there is something I need to talk to you about.'

In his kitchen, they shared his favourite meal of spaghetti *alla carbonara* and drank a glass of wine.

'What did you want to say to me?' she asked, when they had finished their simple supper.

'When I die, I would like to pass on this house to you. Lucia and I couldn't have children of our own, but...' He caught hold of her hand, the age spots and blue veins pronounced in his paper-thin skin. 'I know I've found my family now.'

Alba brought his hand to her mouth and kissed it. 'Massimo, it's such an honour, but I hate to think about that happening. I hope it's a long time away. I don't know what to say,' she said.

'Then say nothing. Just smile and that will be a thank you.'

She obeyed, and he grinned at her and clasped his hands together in delight. 'Then tomorrow we will go to the lawyer's office in Badia and start the ball rolling. But first, there is something I want to ask you in return.'

'Ask away.'

'I want to hold a little party here very soon to thank everybody for their kindness to me. I will leave the invitations up to you. And I also want you to promise me that when I die, you will scatter my ashes in Tramarecchia.'

'I'm always up for a party, and I know who I'm going to invite, but I've already said I don't want to think of you dying.'

He laughed. 'Alba, I'm an old man. And I've led a very full life. Scatter me without a fuss. I can't bear the thought of being cooped up in that horrible cemetery.'

She sighed. 'I promise, Massimo.'

'That's sorted, then. Now, it's time for my bed. It's late and I need my sleep if I'm going to be partying.' He chuckled and she shook her head at him.

Before she settled down for the night, Alba changed the screensaver on her phone from the image of her and James to her favourite photo of Massimo sitting outside his house. By the side of the red door, a rosemary bush was in flower and old man's beard, or *Clematis vitalba*, scrabbled up the drainpipe. Babbo had told her that rosemary was planted in remembrance, and that vitalba was also known as traveller's joy. She decided both plants were significant and would remain, as long as they were kept under control. James was gone. She would never forget him, but she had moved on.

*

Lodovica was a fast walker; Alba found it hard to keep up at times as they climbed together towards the Mountain of the Moon. Halfway, they stopped to drink water from a spring in the woods that Lodovica knew about.

'I'm truly grateful for your help with Alfiero, Lodovica. He's such a special friend.'

'You're welcome. I warmed to him, too. At first, he was uncomfortable in my presence, but after a couple of days, he relaxed. How is he now?'

Alba told her a little about the night in the mountain refuge. 'Hopefully we'll be less awkward with each other in the future. I respect him, but…'

'You can't force feelings that aren't there, Alba. No need to explain.'

They continued their ascent in easy silence until just before they reached Seccaroni. Alba stopped. 'Thank you for coming up here with me. A while ago, I told you about my ghost in the ruins.' She laughed self-consciously. 'Now I believe it was simply my imagination, that my mind was in a state after losing James.'

Lodovica gazed around. 'I've never been up here before. The view is wonderful.' She walked into the ruins and touched the walls. 'It is very strange to think that my uncle was probably up here with other partisans during the war.'

Alba wandered over to the edge of the ridge and pointed out the gap in the rocks where she and her brother had found the silver goblets and plate. 'As you can see, it would be impossible for anybody to walk down there.'

Lodovica joined her and stared down.

'If what you believed you saw was imagination – due to psychological causes, your grieving for James – then so be it. But you're not the only person this restless spirit has tried to tap into. You and I have a connection, don't we, Alba, with this silverware?'

'Coincidence?'

'You know what I think of coincidences. We talked about that when we first met.'

Alba pulled a face. 'It's all too weird for me now. I really believe that what I thought I saw can be put down to my being in a bad place. I mean' – she swept out her arms – 'up here, on this beautiful afternoon, all is right with the world.'

'Nevertheless, it wouldn't do any harm to say a prayer up here for my uncle. From what you told me, nobody mourned his death. Everybody deserves a decent farewell.' Lodovica knelt on the floor of the forest, her head bowed. While Alba waited for some sign like in the movies: a clap of thunder, a darkening sky, or a raven to fall dead from a branch, she had to stifle a sudden giggle of embarrassment, and she wondered what words Lodovica was silently mouthing.

After a while, Lodovica stood up and patted the earth away from her long skirts. 'We can go now,' she said, her voice subdued. 'But I believe we need to return the silverware to where it came from.'

'How did you arrive at that conclusion?' Alba asked as they began their walk downhill.

'I believe it could only be Zio Basilio's wish. You told me about his horrible death and his betrayal of fellow partisans. He was a jealous and greedy man, and he caused the demise of many of his compatriots. I believe he regretted his actions. Returning the stolen goods would be atonement.'

'Weird as it sounds, it all seems to make sense,' Alba said. 'And I think I know what to do with your uncle's stuff.' She suggested taking it down to the boutique hotel along the Sansepolcro road. 'The new proprietors might like to recount the origin of these ornaments to their guests, and add a bit of history to their menu.'

Lodovica smiled. 'I'm tired now, Alba. I'm looking forward to doing nothing but sitting by my fire tonight.'

The two women walked down at a slower pace. Once or twice, Alba had to help Lodovica when she stumbled. It was as if her thoughts and prayers on the mountain had sapped her energy. Alba wasn't sure what she made of it all.

*

Tramarecchia came alive again on the day of Massimo's party. Alfiero had taken time off work. It was difficult for them at first, but Anna and Francesco were there to cushion the encounter and took charge, issuing instructions to cover any awkward moments. Alfiero helped Alba festoon the walnut tree with solar lights and arrange the long kitchen table in the piazza with a colourful cloth. The way to Massimo's house down the track was lined with Alfiero's trademark candles, and the butcher had lent them his large barbecue to roast the suckling pig that Massimo had so been looking forward to. Babbo had provided a five-litre demijohn of Montalcino wine and Anna had made a tiramisu as well as salads of aubergines, courgettes, tomatoes and rice. Massimo's eyes lit up when he saw the dish of *panzanella* on the table.

'*Cucina povera*,' he said, helping himself to another portion of the simple, traditional Tuscan country salad made from dry bread, cucumbers, capers, tomatoes, onions and fresh basil. On top of a home-made chocolate sponge cake, Anna had placed two figures standing outside a little house that she had sculpted herself from marzipan: one of Alba and the other, Massimo. She had also decorated a large pecorino cheese bought from the farm up the road, studding the round with fresh figs, grapes and walnuts. Alba took plenty of photos to use as inspiration for watercolours.

Alba introduced Massimo to Lodovica, who had walked along the track by the river to the party, and she watched as the pair chatted earnestly. At one stage, she saw the nun take Massimo's hands in her own and he nodded his head in agreement with whatever she was saying. Alba had guessed the pair would get on well.

'How are you doing?' she asked Alfiero when he topped up her glass with wine. 'Is Beatrice leaving you in peace?'

He smiled. 'I was warned it wouldn't be easy, that there was no smooth road to recovery, but I have to say that changing the locks and threatening to report her to the *carabinieri* the next time she stalked me worked wonders. I don't miss her at all. What about you?'

'I actually applied to the Accademia di Belle Arti in Florence to start soon, and I got a place on their foundation course because somebody dropped out. How's that for serendipity?'

He kissed her on each cheek, congratulating her. '*Bravissima*, Alba! But I'm sure they accepted you for your talent and not just because there was a space. That's amazing news. And not too far for me to visit you occasionally. I love Florence. Not that I need that as an excuse,' he added quietly.

'You're always welcome. You know that, Alfi.' She meant it, grateful for his generous spirit. Meeting again could have been a hundred times more awkward.

Their conversation was interrupted by Massimo knocking a knife against his glass, asking for silence.

'Thank you for coming today, my new friends.' He gestured to Alba to approach, and he took hold of her hand as she arrived at his side. 'This special girl has delighted me by becoming a daughter I never had. And I couldn't have chosen better.' He kissed her hand. 'I know she will care for my little house when I am gone.

'Over the last months, Alba has listened patiently to the stories of an old man as he reminisced. The circumstances of war led me to the other side of the world, and I took a few diversions, but I ended up back here in my beloved home village. I like to think I didn't take any wrong turnings, only ones I hadn't known I was going to walk. And on my journey, I came across love of different kinds…' He squeezed Alba's hand and she smiled back. 'And I found friendship. Many of my friends have gone from this world. Knowing them was a blessing. Raise your glasses to friendship and love, and remember – whatever is in your hearts, you must do it! *Cin cin, amici*. Remember, you cannot stop time.'

On the morning after the party, Alba woke to the sound of Freddie whining. She groped her way downstairs to let him out, her head a little worse for wear after the festivities, but the old dog refused to move from her side. He continued to whimper while she made a pot of strong espresso and then followed her as she climbed the stairs with a cup for Massimo. His face was pale, and she knew even before she touched his cold hands that he was gone. Freddie lay down on the carpet by the side of his bed, his head on his paws. 'Oh, Freddie,' Alba said, stroking his head, thinking to herself that perhaps her parents could look after him instead of returning him to the dog pound. 'I'm so sorry.'

She sat for a while, remembering the stories Massimo had shared. After whispering, '*Grazie, caro amico mio*,' she gently kissed his forehead and phoned her parents, tears coursing down her face.

CHAPTER THIRTY-THREE

In the weeks after Massimo's funeral, Alba threw herself into her work, determined to make her contribution to the tourist office exhibition a homage to her elderly friend before she left for Florence. She missed him greatly, and often went for walks to Tramarecchia in her free hours to paint. It was where she felt his presence. The trees were slowly losing their foliage, and when a leaf somersaulted across the stones, she looked up from her drawing, half expecting to see Massimo approach. The vine on the house at the edge of Tramarecchia was heavy with grapes, and she painted the pattern of tendrils curling round verdigris-coated copper guttering.

A stray kitten scampered into view, winding between her legs as she sketched, and she bent to fondle its black and white fur. It scampered off and she watched it enter the open door of her little house.

'Oh no, you don't,' she said, jumping up to follow. She didn't want the creature to hide and then get locked in. She found the kitten upstairs in the bathroom, sharpening its tiny claws against the ugly pine panelling lining the bottom half of the walls.

'Scratch away on that to your heart's content,' she said, bending down to stroke the kitten's matted fur. 'It's pretty grue-some.' She pulled away at one of the boards that had worked loose and opened the window to throw it out, deciding this would be the first room to tackle on her renovation project. Removing the panelling was dusty work, and she uncovered years of spiders' nests in the process. She worked for almost an hour, her arms beginning to ache, her body covered in grime. As she wrenched the last board away, she was about to give up for the day.

Removing the last piece had revealed a niche in the old stone wall, and resting on it was a piece of sacking tied with string. She reached in gingerly, having already been spooked by a scuttling scorpion, its tail upright, ready to sting. The sacking contained something heavy and she carefully carried the package downstairs into the fresh air. Cutting the string away, inside she found an envelope, a black notebook and an oilcloth covering a rectangular object.

'Oh – my – good – God,' she exclaimed, as she exposed a glazed terracotta plaque decorated in the characteristic colours of blue, white, yellow and green. A Madonna and baby, lilies decorating the borders, stared back at her. She ran her fingers over the raised features of the baby, biting back the tears, remembering how Massimo had told her he thought it buried forever in a landslide. Lucia must have removed Florian's gift from the cave and hidden it here for safekeeping.

She knew this was a priceless object. A *predella* from the base of a larger work, possibly a genuine *Robbiana* altarpiece like the two she had seen in the little church up in Montebotolino. They had been discovered two years previously on an antiques stall at the annual fair in Pennabilli, but the third had never been found. Could this be the missing one? She was sure Alfiero would know.

She turned her attention to the little notebook, bound in a thinner strip of sacking and stained with mildew. The handwriting inside was neat and, turning the pages carefully, she saw that it contained a series of intriguing maps with sketches of trees, insects, butterflies, fossils, a river, a cave and a mountaintop with handwritten notes at the bottom in a foreign language. They reminded her of treasure maps in a child's storybook. She put it carefully to one side. She presumed that Lucia had hidden these things because they must be important. But why hadn't she told Massimo about them? Or had he known all along?

Poking from beneath the *predella* was an envelope, yellow with age. She opened it and pulled out a thin piece of paper. The writing was barely legible, so she had to move closer to the window to read it. It was written in poor Italian, with a scattering of German words that she remembered from her school lessons.

> Lucia, *mein Schatz*,
>
> Your name rolls off my tongue like a word from a poem. I bless the day I met you – my very own treasure in this storm of war – my beautiful, funny, spirited Tuscan girl with whom I want to live out the rest of my days.
>
> This keepsake should be put in a special place. It can belong to us for a while. While we are apart, look often at the little baby and remind yourself of all the angels we will make together. One day we will return it.
>
> In the meantime, you have my heart.
>
> *Ich liebe dich.*
>
> *Ti amo.*
>
> Your Florian

She digested the words in silence, her hand to her mouth, her emotions ready to spill over. Maybe Lucia had concealed these items even from Massimo, because she wanted to keep a part of Florian secret. In that way, something of him would still remain alive for her.

Alba knew she must inform the authorities about her find as soon as possible, and make sure everybody was aware that Massimo had always searched for it. It was important that nobody should think he was involved in anything underhand. This discovery was part of the history of the war. The Germans

had purloined so many pieces of art, many of which had never
been traced, and this find represented one tiny missing piece of
a much larger jigsaw. With care, she wrapped the *predella* again
in the sacking, together with the notebook, but she placed the
letter in her rucksack. It was too personal to share with the
world. She felt as if she was holding a piece of Lucia, a girl she
had never met but who she felt very close to. She wondered what
Massimo would have made of the discovery, and how he would
have reacted. She would never know for sure, but she reckoned
he would have been pleased – as if a line had been drawn under
Lucia and Florian's story.

With that thought in her head, she reached up to the ledge
over the hearth for the urn containing Massimo's ashes. It was
time.

Alba made her way down the steep path to the river and
stopped on the weir. This was the right place. The river was alive;
it always would be. Massimo had told her so much about this
spot. It was a favourite place for Lucia, too – his Tuscan girl. She
paused and then started to unscrew the lid.

She tested the direction of the wind and then gently released
the contents.

'*Addio*, Massimo,' she whispered.

Some of the ashes dropped onto the surface of the water and
fish darted up from the depths to investigate. The rest were lifted
by a gentle breeze that sprang up unexpectedly and were dispersed
in the current that flowed by the stony banks, thick with willows
and ash saplings.

She walked slowly up the path with the empty urn to the
house she had named Ca' Massimo. Her heart full, she pulled out
her paints to capture the scene in front of her, selecting shades
of purple and blue for the mountains in the background, adding
dabs of cadmium red for the window frames and the rose climb-

ing up the stonework. Yellow ochre and sap green went into the dying grass, burnt sienna and raw umber for the old sandstone of the ruins. She sketched in the small figure of Massimo sitting at the door, capturing him forever on paper.

After locking up the house, closing the shutters and making sure she had left no foodstuffs lying about for vermin, she started on her walk back to her parents, wondering when she would next be able to return to the red house.

As she wandered along the old mule track, the evening birdsong a background to her thoughts as the shadows lengthened, she didn't feel alone. It was as if Massimo was walking beside her, encouraging her forward. A younger Massimo, a jaunty spring in his step, Lupino coming to his side between scampering back and forth to the edges of the beech woods. At one point, when a pine marten scurried over some rocks and up a tree, she almost turned to her imaginary companion to comment. But somehow, she knew she didn't have to. He was there, somewhere.

A Letter from Angela

I want to say *mille grazie* – huge thanks – for choosing to read *The Tuscan Girl*. If you enjoyed it and want to keep up to date with all my latest releases, just sign up at the following link. Your email address will never be shared, and you can unsubscribe at any time.

www.bookouture.com/angela-petch

This is another Tuscan story written from the heart and I loved writing it. If you enjoyed reading *The Tuscan Girl*, I would be very grateful if you could write a review. I'd love to hear what you think, and it makes such a difference helping new readers to discover one of my books.

I love hearing from my readers. You can get in touch on my Facebook page, through Twitter, Goodreads or my website.

Thanks,
Angela Petch

AngelaJaneClarePetch

@Angela_Petch

angelapetchsblogsite.wordpress.com

Angela Petch Author Page

Acknowledgements

How was I inspired to write this story set in Italy against a brutal but significant Second World War campaign, one which is often overlooked? There are many reasons. My father worked in Rome for the Commonwealth War Graves Commission when I was seven years old. We lived there for six years during the 1960s, and he took us to visit many of the beautiful war cemeteries. I remember feeling awestruck even at that tender age, and now that I understand more, I feel both humbled and horrified by the sacrifices made by so many – and not only by the armed forces. We should not forget the roles ordinary people played.

Rupert Brooke was one of my mother's favourite poets. Admittedly, 'The Old Vicarage, Grantchester' was written before the First World War, but the lines, heavy with homesickness, remind me of young men and women on all sides, who must have pined for normality during their terror-filled days away from their home countries.

> Say, is there Beauty yet to find?
> And Certainty? and Quiet kind?
> Deep meadows yet, for to forget
> The lies, and truths, and pain?… oh! yet
> Stands the Church clock at ten to three?
> And is there honey still for tea?

Ten years ago, I met an elderly gentleman on one of my walks in the Tuscan countryside where I live. While he pruned

an apple tree, we passed the time of day. Halfway through our friendly conversation in Italian, to my utter surprise Bruno began to talk in English. He told me he had been a prisoner of war in Nottingham, and had stayed in England for almost four unforgettable years. He was barely twenty then, and had never been away from this country village.

Fifty years ago, I stayed with my German penfriend in Wesel. Marianne's father was the Burgemeister (mayor), and proudly showed me around. He constantly mentioned the Second World War during my visit, and I was embarrassed, eventually asking him to change the subject. I told him, naively, 'It's not my fault that you are German and I am English. The war finished a long time ago.' He was upset, and later his wife explained that as a young man he had been a conscientious objector and his parents had been imprisoned and shot because of this. The war was never going to be over for him. I have never forgotten him.

So, over time, impressions from my formative years and more recent encounters lingered in my thoughts until I tweaked them into *The Tuscan Girl*. My parents belonged to this generation, but they seldom talked about their war. Soon there will be nobody left of these children of the 1920s, and their memories and secrets will disappear. I felt inspired to remember these individual struggles through fiction. Some of the characters and place names in *The Tuscan Girl* have been changed, but most of the events are, sadly, true.

Once again, my lovely Italian mother-in-law, Giuseppina, supplied many details, as did Alvaro Tacchini and Doriano Pela, local historians and writers. There are many other people to thank. Bruno Vergni was one hundred years old on 13 January, 2020 and he inspired the character of Massimo – although I have greatly tweaked him in my imagination. The real Florian, who likes to stay at Il Mulino, helped me with German expressions, as

did the author Sonja Price. Anne Marie Lomax checked my art techniques for Alba. Fulvio Pieghai at Badia Tedalda tourist office is always there for me with snippets and gems. *Grazie!* My friends on Facebook, Twitter and Chindi Authors are so supportive and generous. Thank you, one and all. My husband is very patient when I disappear for hours to tap away, and Ellen Gleeson and the team at Bookouture deserve a pocketful of gold stars for their quiet professional guidance. Last, but definitely not least, a heartfelt thanks to all my readers for your encouraging reviews.

Lightning Source UK Ltd.
Milton Keynes UK
UKHW040432110820
368039UK00001B/306